PRAISE FOR NANCY HERNDON'S ELENA JARVIS SERIES

"Nancy Herndon's characters, descriptions, and situations are both intellectual and laugh-out-loud funny." —*Mostly Murder*

"Nancy Herndon's mysteries are notable for some of the most varied, inventive and bizarre murders in the realm of crime fiction." —*El Paso Inc.*

"Refreshingly different . . . Herndon's characterizations are wonderful." —*The Mystery Review*

. . . and don't miss the other Elena Jarvis Mysteries:

ACID BATH

WIDOWS' WATCH

LETHAL STATUES

HUNTING GAME

TIME BOMBS

MORE MYSTERIES FROM THE BERKLEY PUBLISHING GROUP . . .

CAT CALIBAN MYSTERIES: She was married for thirty-eight years. Raised three kids. Compared to that, tracking down killers is easy . . .

by D. B. Borton

ONE FOR THE MONEY
TWO POINTS FOR MURDER
THREE IS A CROWD
FOUR ELEMENTS OF MURDER
FIVE ALARM FIRE
SIX FEET UNDER

ELENA JARVIS MYSTERIES: There are some pretty bizarre crimes deep in the heart of Texas—and a pretty gutsy police detective who rounds up the unusual suspects . . .

by Nancy Herndon

ACID BATH
WIDOWS' WATCH
LETHAL STATUES
HUNTING GAME
TIME BOMBS
C.O.P. OUT

FREDDIE O'NEAL, P.I., MYSTERIES: You can bet that this appealing Reno private investigator will get her man . . . "A winner." —Linda Grant

by Catherine Dain

LAY IT ON THE LINE
SING A SONG OF DEATH
WALK A CROOKED MILE
LAMENT FOR A DEAD COWBOY
BET AGAINST THE HOUSE
THE LUCK OF THE DRAW
DEAD MAN'S HAND

BENNI HARPER MYSTERIES: Meet Benni Harper—a quilter and folk-art expert with an eye for murderous designs . . .

by Earlene Fowler

FOOL'S PUZZLE
IRISH CHAIN
KANSAS TROUBLES
GOOSE IN THE POND
DOVE IN THE WINDOW

HANNAH BARLOW MYSTERIES: For ex-cop and law student Hannah Barlow, justice isn't just a word in a textbook. Sometimes, it's a matter of life and death . . .

by Carroll Lachnit

MURDER IN BRIEF
A BLESSED DEATH

PEACHES DANN MYSTERIES: Peaches has never had a very good memory. But she's learned to cope with it over the years . . . Fortunately, though, when it comes to murder, this absentminded amateur sleuth doesn't forgive and forget!

by Elizabeth Daniels Squire

WHO KILLED WHAT'S-HER-NAME?
REMEMBER THE ALIBI
MEMORY CAN BE MURDER
WHOSE DEATH IS IT ANYWAY?
IS THERE A DEAD MAN IN THE HOUSE?

C.O.P. OUT

NANCY HERNDON

BERKLEY PRIME CRIME, NEW YORK

C.O.P. OUT

A Berkley Prime Crime Book / published by arrangement with the author

PRINTING HISTORY
Berkley Prime Crime edition / April 1998

For information address: The Berkley Publishing Group, a member of Penguin Putnam Inc., 200 Madison Avenue, New York, NY 10016.

The Penguin Putnam Inc. World Wide Web site address is http://www.penguinputnam.com

ISBN: 0-425-16293-1

Berkley Prime Crime Books are published by The Berkley Publishing Group, a member of Penguin Putnam Inc., 200 Madison Avenue, New York, NY 10016.

PRINTED IN THE UNITED STATES OF AMERICA

10 9 8 7 6 5 4 3 2 1

For the officers of the downtown foot patrol in El Paso, Texas, and my fellow COPS volunteers, who walk the beats with them. Unlike fictional Los Santos, the El Paso COPS program has never lost a volunteer.

Acknowledgments

Special thanks to the El Paso, Texas, Police Department, and particularly to Sergeant Robert Pratt, coordinator of the Citizens on Patrol program, and to Officers Guadalupe Diaz, John Lanahan, Robert Torres, Steve Crank, Ana Soto, and Joe Lucero, with whom I patrolled the downtown streets and from whom I learned so many fascinating lessons on community policing. Ms. Niki Leach, special projects administrator at the district attorney's office, provided invaluable information on charges that could result from a drive-by shooting, and I also wish to thank dear friends Joan Coleman and Jean Miculka whose input on all my writing is much appreciated.

N.R.H.

1

Tuesday, October 22, 10:10 A.M.

On the day the road to the future collapsed under her, Monica Ibarra was twenty-three years old, eight months out of the Los Santos Police Academy, and still relishing her new assignment. Monica had spent her first half year of probationary duty in a patrol car with the Westside Regional Command, answering calls from strangers. Then she'd been transferred to the foot patrol at Central Command.

Walking a beat in the downtown area made her feel more invigorated, more a part of the community. She'd come to know the business owners—Koreans and Vietnamese, Mexican-Americans and Anglos—who ran stores that catered to shoppers from Mexico. She recognized secretaries and men in suits who worked in the high-rises. She knew the nicknames of transients who culled the Dumpsters behind restaurants and the names and arrest records of prostitutes, drug addicts, and small-time dealers.

As she walked the streets and alleys and talked with her partner or with someone from the Citizens on Patrol program, she admired the ornate facades of the older Deco buildings, watched the reflections of clouds in the green glass walls of the courthouse, inspected the second-story balconies on adobes in the barrios—a poor man's New Orleans, she thought. She waved to the Border Jumper trolley drivers in their green-and-red vehicles, directed tourists, chatted with waitresses and owners in the places where she ate lunch—burritos, pizza, tacos, pitas—the offerings of downtown Los Santos affordable to a cop.

She listened and spoke in Spanish and English, savored the swing of her own stride as she covered her beat, the uniform that made young men do a double take as she passed, the weight of her belt with gun, radio, and cuffs. She called out *"Qué pasa?"* to the men on Bike Patrol and considered the possibility of applying to the unit herself. Good for the thighs and hips, she figured. Monica liked to keep fit. A couple of times a week she visited the weight room at Central Command when her shift was up, shrugging off the teasing of fellow officers who liked to say, "Watching Ibarra work out's as good as a wet-T-shirt contest."

By next spring Monica hoped to have her degree in criminal justice from UT Los Santos. Before she was thirty, she'd have a husband and one baby, maybe a sergeant's stripes, if she was lucky and stayed on track. She wanted to be a lieutenant someday, just as her *novio,* Eddie Diaz, a deputy with the county, wanted to run for sheriff someday. They were saving for a wedding at San Ysidro del Valle, a big reception in the church basement, and a down payment on a house in the Lower Valley, somewhere near where their parents lived, a place with some land around it.

These things she had confided to Mrs. Hope Masterson Quarles, a very nice lady from the C.O.P. program who was accompanying her on a two-hour morning stint. In turn Mrs. Quarles confided that her husband, Wayne, had talked her into applying for the program because, as he said, citizens should support the police. A builder and developer, Wayne Quarles was running for mayor and too busy to patrol with the police himself. "That's why he volunteered me," said his wife, laughing. "Not that I wasn't glad to do it, but I don't know what possible good I can do you, Monica."

"Four eyes are better than two," Monica replied diplomatically. That's what the program leaders said, that and the importance of public relations and citizen support for the department. "If you see something suspicious, just tell me," she said, then added hastily, "but then, of course, you back off."

"They told us that at orientation," Hope Quarles agreed, "along with the request that we not bring a weapon or wear provocative clothing or T-shirts with lewd messages. As if I had any of those." She laughed again. "But doesn't my being with you put you at risk? You've got me instead of a real partner."

"Bert—my partner—he's in the same area," Monica replied. "All I have to do is radio."

"Is there much crime this time of day?"

"There's usually something going down," Monica answered. In truth, she was a little nervous about patrolling with Mrs. Quarles, but only because everyone in town knew her husband, the candidate. Still, nothing was going to happen. She could take care of them both. No problema.

Pointing to a *cambio* where people changed dollars for pesos and vice versa, she entertained Mrs. Quarles with the story of a burglar who had gotten stuck in Mr. Rafael "Peso" Fajardo's air-conditioning ducts during an attempted heist. She told tales about illegals stealing Nike knockoffs in border stores. "Hey, Mr. Chang," she called at one point, ducking her head into the open door of Ropa Frontera with its yellow-and-red sign and sale announcements in Spanish. "How's business?"

"Velly bad," Mr. Chang answered from behind his cash register. He wore dark glasses and a glum expression, as always, but he saw a prospect in Mrs. Quarles and asked if she wanted a special deal on a genuine Laura Ashley bedspread he had in the back room. "Thirty-nine dorrars onry." Mrs. Quarles refused his offer graciously but with a puzzled expression. Very likely she hadn't been able to translate "Raura Ashrey." They passed the flea market on Paisano, where, Monica explained, shoplifters from JCPenney downtown and stores like Mr. Chang's stashed their loot, where drug dealers sold to hypes.

Monica stopped a drunk and confiscated his bottle of cheap wine, reminding him that he couldn't drink on the streets. "The jail's full," she told Mrs. Quarles. "They're not taking Class C's unless they have over a thousand dollars in warrants." She called "*Hola,* Señora Benes," to a woman in an all-enveloping apron who was tugging a small girl down the street. The child hugged a bald-headed doll that was almost as large as she was. They had entered El Segundo Barrio, the Second Ward, so Monica told Mrs. Quarles about the after-dark battles with rocks and bottles that were waged by rival gangs in the area. Mrs. Quarles glanced around as if she expected to see tattooed youths erupting from alleys with weapons in hand. "The gang members challenge each other by tagging traffic signs." Monica pointed to a stop sign embellished with the initials of the Southside Locos, a gang that was evidently trying to start something with a rival, Los Reyes Diablos.

"Then what happens?" Mrs. Quarles asked.

"The best-case scenario is that we take off the graffiti before things heat up. Worst-case, someone gets hurt in a drive-by; then someone retaliates, and so forth." She spotted a guy heading north from the border and put him up against the wall, feet spread, while she patted him down and called in on her shoulder mike for outstanding warrants, not forgetting to check the paper bag he'd dropped into the gutter when they spotted each other. Monica knew him for a guy who smuggled *roche,* the date-rape drug, across the border. The bag contained only a candy-bar wrapper—this time. Since she had him on nothing but littering, he walked.

They headed back to Paisano past Sagrado Corazón, the church of the Sacred Heart. "We get calls from the priests to come and clear out the drug dealers and junkies," she told Mrs. Quarles, who looked shocked. They checked out an alley and found nothing but a slashed, discarded sofa and rows of utility meters sprouting from the brick walls.

"Illegal kids from Mexico used to come over and sleep on the fire escapes here," Monica said to her companion. "You had to pick your way through the syringes."

They checked out a bar where at least twelve disheveled people were drinking, many of whom greeted Monica by name. "We know their names; they know ours," said Monica. "Everyone trades information."

At Chihuahua and Oregon she stopped a prostitute and called in for warrants, asking the girl while they waited how she'd lost her front teeth. "Fell down," the girl answered.

Once the prostitute moved off, Monica said, "A john probably knocked them out. She's a heroin addict. Got three kids across the border and hepatitis."

Hope Quarles shook her head and frowned. "I never imagined how terrible things were here in Los Santos."

Monica reflected that this was a lady who didn't know the score and needed to wise up. Maybe she'd tell her husband, the candidate, how things were, and he'd do something about it—get the department more money, get the poor more jobs. . . . Monica's brother had just been laid off.

"What's that man doing?" Hope Quarles asked curiously. She was looking to her right down the alley beside Felipe's House of Fajitas.

Monica glanced past the Dumpster and spotted a guy in T-shirt and baggy pants held up by a rope. He had a shaved head and tattoos—gangbanger, she judged from the outfit—and he was drilling out the lock of a metallic tan '84 Mercury. "Car thief," Monica whispered happily. "You stay here, ma'am."

"Oh, my goodness," Hope Quarles murmured.

"Move behind the Dumpster if he shows a weapon." Eyes on the thief, hoping to get to him before he could run, Monica's last glimpse, peripheral, of Hope Masterson Quarles was of a middle-aged lady with curly blond hair, wearing her C.O.P. T-shirt under a silk jogging jacket. Her mouth with its pale lipstick formed a perfect O of surprise.

Monica drew her semiautomatic, called in her position

and the crime in progress, and asked her partner for backup. Then she padded silently down the alley, wishing Mrs. Quarles would be a little quieter. She heard the scrape of shoes on the cement, the rustle of paper. Mrs. Quarles had evidently taken shelter behind Felipe's Dumpster.

There was a low whistle, someone out on the street maybe, and before Monica could say, "Police. Put your hands up," the punk turned from the lock he was drilling and dropped sideways to the dusty, cracked surface of the alley. At the same moment Monica felt a terrible burning pain in her back. "Run, Mrs. Qua—" she gasped, and, falling, got off one shot as excruciating pain, then blessed unconsciousness closed over her. She never felt the hard landing.

2

Tuesday, October 22, 10:50 A.M.

The case was assigned to Crimes Against Persons detectives Elena Jarvis and Leo Weizell, but the alley entrances were crowded by their superiors—Lieutenant Beltran, head of Crimes Against Persons; Captain Stollinger, head of Criminal Investigations; Boyd Talley, Ibarra's sergeant; and Chief Gaitan himself. Mostly the brass was trying to explain to TV and print reporters and cameramen how the wife of a candidate for mayor had ended up dead in an alley with an officer of the downtown foot patrol shot in the back ten feet from her.

Monica Ibarra, the wounded officer, had been rolled away on a stretcher by EMS toward the ambulance on the street, blood seeping out from under her back and staining her lips, IVs running into her arms, her young face gray, while the medics hovered over her and gave each other orders, as if they were cast members on a TV hospital show. Cameras flashed as her body passed through the press mob. Blood suckers, Elena thought with unusual asperity. On a good day she got along with the press, even had a friend on the *Times*.

Ibarra's weapon was photographed by I.D. & R., then bagged and given an identification tag by Elena. Crime-scene techs swarmed in the alley with their cameras, video recorders, and fingerprint powder, their Baggies and latex gloves and tweezers.

Elena now stood beside the peeling adobe wall of Felipe's Fajitas. She could smell the pungent wood smoke that flavored the strips of skirt steak as they grilled over open fires, the rich aroma of the marinade, mixed with the reek of the Dumpster and the odor rising from Mrs. Quarles's body—blood and fecal release, the ugly stench of violent death. The woman's eyes were open, blue, and shocked, her face terrified in death, her C.O.P. shirt soggy with blood where the bullet had caught her—probably in the heart—and mushroomed instead of exiting, which triggered the disturbing thought that it might be a police bullet.

Los Santos cops used ammo that did its damage inside the target—stopped the criminal but didn't exit the body and hit innocent citizens or other cops. Only Mrs. Quarles was no criminal, and if she'd died with a nine-millimeter slug from Ibarra's gun in her chest, the shit was about to hit the fan.

"Notice her mouth," Elena said to Leo. The lipstick was slightly smeared on the lower lip, a smudge of it just above the gently rounded chin on the left side. On the upper lip the lipstick was gone, except at the corners of the woman's mouth. "Calderon," Elena said to the medical examiner, who was kneeling beside the corpse, "look at her mouth. Ask the coroner about it."

Onofre Calderon studied the body. "She's got smudges on the jacket, too." He pointed. "Upper left arm, lower right."

Elena eyed the marks thoughtfully and made a note on her case pad. Had Mrs. Quarles huddled against the wall or the Dumpster and gotten dirty while Ibarra was dealing with the car thief? Walking the alley slowly, looking at everything, keeping out of the techs' way, Elena tried to figure out what had gone down. The shooting had been called in by a customer who was heading toward Felipe's when he saw the two bodies in the alley. The man had rushed into the restaurant to call 911, then gone into incoherent shock. He was still in there babbling while Felipe's wife tried to tempt him into coherence with coffee, tostados, fajitas.

Monica Ibarra's partner, walking the same beat, had been first on the scene, having heard the radio call for backup on the arrest of a car thief. When Bert Krausling arrived, there was no one in the alley except the two victims, although a few people clustered at either end, peering in curiosity, titillation, or horror. No one admitted to seeing the escape of the criminal. Or criminals. In fact, Krausling said at least four people had beat it as soon as he showed up.

Shortly thereafter officers from the Bike Patrol, police cars, a fire engine, and two ambulances arrived along with Sergeant Talley and three others from Central Command, and Leo and Elena from Crimes Against Persons.

As word of the disaster spread, the press and the brass homed in like vultures. Patrolmen were now combing the streets looking for the four chickenhearted witnesses, people who obviously "didn't want to get involved." Krausling stood at the end of the alley wringing his hands, blond razor cut separating into points as agonized sweat soaked his head.

"No question someone tried to break into the Mercury," Elena said to Leo, her partner, after circling the car.

Leo squatted, studied the marks on the driver's door lock, and agreed. "If a car thief did this, he's probably back in Mexico by now."

"And we don't even have a description to give them at the bridges."

"The Mercury belongs to a Felipe Cazares," said an officer who had called in the plates. "Address is—"

"He owns the restaurant," said Elena. "Best fajitas in town." Threading their way through the crowd of press and brass at the alley entrance, ignoring shouted questions from people with microphones and notebooks, Leo and Elena made their way into Felipe's to ask about the car and anything the owners or customers might have seen or heard.

The 911 caller, mouth stuffed with fajitas, tears dripping

from his eyes, hadn't seen anything but the bodies, "a gringa and a *policía chicana,*" no one in the alley, not even anyone on the street that he'd noticed. It was early for the lunch crowd, he explained, late for the breakfast regulars, and the shoppers from Mexico had stopped coming—who'd know that better than he, whose *zapatería* near the border was going under for lack of business. "Pretty soon you'll be closing, too, Felipe," he called out.

The store owner went to pieces again when he realized that one of the two women in the alley was Officer Monica, whom he considered "*muy bonita.*" She had arrested several shoppers who, without paying, tried to walk out of his store, leaving their old shoes in his boxes and wearing his shoes on their smelly feet—as if he wouldn't notice what footwear walked out of his store.

Although the restaurant was becoming crowded, there had been only two other customers when Jose had come in to announce his grisly discovery. The two had seen nothing before they entered, nor heard anything while inside. Neither had the proprietors.

Ismaela Cazares, while plying the detectives with food, asked about Officer Ibarra, "such a nice girl." How was she? Badly injured, the detectives replied.

Felipe said, yes, it was his car, a good dependable vehicle, with a security alarm that he kept turned off because the drunks staggered against his car and set off the siren. If only he hadn't turned off the alarm, the *hijo de puta* who shot "little Monica"—who liked her fajitas with double salsa, guacamole, but no onions—would have triggered the alarm when he drilled the lock. Then Felipe, hearing, could have grabbed his gun from under the counter and rushed out to save the women.

Women were better off cooking food than carrying guns; that was Felipe's opinion. Look what had happened. Look at Ismaela—sixty years old— "You're sixty, not me," Ismaela interjected. Thirty years she'd been cooking here at

Casa de las Fajitas, Felipe continued, and no one ever shot at her.

Elena and Leo paid for their lunch over the protests of the owners, and Elena slipped off to make a call. She was missing an appointment with her psychologist, Sam Parsley. She provided Sam a take-out meal and permission to write an article about post-traumatic stress in cops, and Sam, while stuffing himself—the man had an incredible metabolism—provided therapy. He'd done wonders for her, her big, kindly bear of a psychologist, a professor at Herbert Hobart University.

"So we'll make it dinner," Sam said cheerfully. "I'm in the mood for pizza."

"Right," said Elena. "Three large. Half for me, two and a half for you. Six-thirty O.K.?"

When she hung up, Leo was waving her into a hall that led to the rest rooms. Congregated there, for a private conference presumably, were the chief and their superiors from headquarters. "This is going to be a very touchy case," warned Captain Stollinger, peering at them over the rims of his round, steel-framed glasses. He had to bend his head at an awkward angle to look at Elena because he was tall and she was short, comparatively. Tall, skinny Leo could pretty much look Stollinger in the eye.

"Politically sensitive," said Chief Gaitan. "I presume you know who she is—the dead C.O.P. volunteer."

"Wife of a mayoral candidate," said Elena.

"There's a potential lawsuit here," said Lieutenant Beltran. He'd just cost the city a bundle because Elena's housemate, Dr. Sarah Tolland, had sued him, the department, and the city for false arrest. And won.

"I thought the C.O.P. program made them sign a release," said Leo.

"Don't be naive," snapped Stollinger. "She's dead. He'll sue. Unless he wins, in which case we'll have a mayor with a grudge against the department."

"We've got an officer seriously injured here, too," said

Elena, thinking of Monica Ibarra—the crimson froth on her lips, her gray skin.

"No one's forgetting Officer Ibarra, Detective," said Chief Gaitan. "If she dies, we've got capital murder here, and we need an arrest. Fast. What's your preliminary take on the shootings?"

"It looks like a car theft gone wrong," said Elena.

"In that case, it's capital murder even if Ibarra survives," said Stollinger.

"There must have been two men," Elena continued, "one stealing the car, one on lookout at the end of the alley. Ibarra was shot in the back, so the lookout must have got her when she tried to arrest his partner. Then one or the other shot Mrs. Quarles in the chest to take out the only witness. That the way you see it, Leo?"

"At this point it's the only thing that makes sense," he replied, "which means they're probably in Mexico by now, in which case our chances of—"

"I don't want to hear that you can't close this case," said Stollinger.

"This is one we have to solve," Gaitan agreed.

"It's the middle of town," Beltran said grimly. "There have to be witnesses."

"Krausling, her partner, says there were people gaping at the ends of the alley when he arrived; two stayed but told Central patrol officers they hadn't seen anyone but the victims. We've got their names. Four at the other end disappeared by the time he'd checked the bodies and called in." Leo looked gloomy, partly, Elena was sure, because he wasn't getting much sleep, not with five-month-old quintuplets at home.

"We'll have to find those witnesses," snapped Beltran.

"Although they may have been witnesses after the fact," Elena reminded him.

"Would you *excuse* me," said a woman in lavender slacks. She was trying get through to the door marked DAMAS.

Stollinger glared at her, as if she were one of the

witnesses who had fled. Gaitan gave her a stunning white smile and cleared a path for her.

Always the ladies' man, Elena thought cynically. He'd been very taken with Elena's mother, Harmony, when she came to town a year ago. Harmony was, admittedly, a knockout, but she was married, a mother of five, and a grandmother. Elena thought the chief should confine his flirting to single ladies.

"Give the detectives all the help they need, Lieutenant," Stollinger instructed Beltran. "This has to be closed. Pronto. Officer shot, politico's wife killed. Looks bad. Very bad."

"It could ruin the C.O.P. program," said Gaitan, who had instituted it as part of the community policing philosophy that was sweeping not only Los Santos, Texas, but the whole country.

Elena wondered whether Officer Monica Ibarra was still alive. She might be their only witness to the killing. Somebody should have forced these men to look at the two victims. Then maybe they'd be thinking about something other than the bad publicity, the effect on departmental programs, and the possibility of lawsuits.

3

Tuesday, October 22, 6:45 P.M.

Elena had bought fajitas before heading for Sam Parsley's office on campus. "You'll like them better than pizza," she assured the disappointed psychologist. And he did. Sam had wrapped his second tortilla around a pile of meat and eaten it before she got through to Thomason General to inquire about Monica Ibarra, who was in surgery, the bullet having grazed her spinal cord before doing extensive damage to one lung. Elena tried to imagine a trajectory that would explain those injuries. Where had the bullet come from? She shook her head, knowing she didn't have enough information to speculate. As she hung up, Sam handed her a rolled tortilla with fajita shreds, salsa, guacamole, and grilled green onions bulging out the ends.

Nice man, Sam. He was always hungry, starving really, yet he'd taken the trouble to fix something for her. She remembered the first time she'd met him—a party at Sarah's university apartment. The dinner featured a minimalist menu, Elena's fault; she'd invited an extra guest to the catered dinner. And Sam—rumpled, bearded, with a wild head of curly, graying hair—looked like a big, hungry, friendly bear who couldn't find enough berries before winter set in.

"I've got a real touchy case," she told him, wiping her

mouth with a paper napkin. "The dead wife of a candidate for mayor and a severely wounded—"

"I read the evening paper." He was adding grilled onions to the meat in his fourth flour tortilla.

Elena popped a shred of skirt steak into her mouth. "We're going to be under the gun on this one. The chief—"

"Let's talk about the mountain lion," said Sam.

"You know, Sam," Elena responded earnestly, "I think I'm cured."

"Really?" He took a big bite and chewed.

"Really," she assured him. "You've done a terrific job. There was a time when I thought I'd never get over—"

"No more nightmares?" he interrupted.

"Nope," said Elena, swinging her legs up onto his couch and studying an intricate Escher print on the opposite wall.

"No flashbacks?"

"Not in a month at least."

"And you've moved back into your own house?"

"Well . . ." She shivered, remembering the terrifying snarl that had greeted her when she opened her own door, the evil gleam of cat's eyes under her dining-room table, and, in her bedroom, the one hazel eye of the corpse staring at her from a gnawed, bloody face. She'd thought it was Michael. At that time she'd thought she loved him.

"So you're still at Sarah's?" Sam prodded.

"Yes, but—"

"What's the first thing you noticed when you opened the door that night?"

Elena sighed. She'd told him the story a million times since May, described the traumatizing experience over and over in such detail that what Sam predicted had happened. She'd become desensitized to the horror of her own memories. So why couldn't she face returning to her house?

Sighing again, she laced her fingers together tightly and stared hard at the Escher print—an intricate fish design. "The first thing I noticed was the smell," she began. "The smell of shit and blood. I smelled it again today in the alley, but it wasn't the same, not so feral. A big cat stinks. Especially if it's been in your house all day. God, you wouldn't believe how . . ."

As she drove home from Sam's office, Elena listened on the radio to an interview with Wayne Quarles, the victim's husband. "She was everything to me," he said, voice breaking. "We were married for twenty-four years."

Poor guy, Elena thought. Mrs. Quarles had looked like a nice lady, even in death. She'd had a kind face, its lines softened by the passing years, but still pretty, a face with character and the impression of gentleness. No wonder the man sounded as if he was on the verge of tears.

"Will you continue your campaign?" asked the host.

There was a silence. Then Wayne Quarles said, "Yes. Yes, Hope would want me to. She urged me to run in the first place. We both felt that I could do something for the city that has done so much for us."

"Have the police given you any indication that they're closing in on the person or persons who shot your wife?"

"No. No, they haven't, but I have every confidence that they will find the perpetrator. We have a fine department. Working under difficult circumstances."

He had that right. The department was underfunded and understaffed, not to mention underpaid and overworked, and still Crimes Against Persons cleared most of the murders. Did better than most city PDs. But Mr. Quarles's confidence was going to be hard to fulfill this time. How could she and Leo catch a couple of murderous car thieves if they'd made it across one of the bridges to Mexico? Fingerprints maybe. Pray God I.D. & R. found identifiable fingerprints, and the Juarez cops cooperated, if it came to that.

"Do you have any word on the officer who was injured this morning, sir?" asked the interviewer.

"I called the hospital not a half hour ago," Quarles replied.

That was decent of him, Elena thought. A lot of men would be blaming Ibarra and wouldn't give a shit how she was faring.

"I'm sorry to say Officer Ibarra is in very serious condition," Quarles continued somberly. "The hospital doesn't seem to think she'll make it through the night."

That was news to Elena, although she wasn't surprised. She'd seen Ibarra in the alley. If she hadn't been bleeding, Elena would have thought she was already dead.

"I hope all of our citizens will pray for this young woman, as I plan to, and for all the brave officers who put their lives on the line every day. I'm sure Officer Ibarra did her best. Perhaps our prayers will pull her through."

Well, that would go over well with the police union, Elena thought. And cops voted; so did their friends and relatives. Every candidate wanted the endorsement of the police and fire unions. Then she reminded herself that Quarles was taking this a lot better than the brass had expected. So far, anyway.

"For the sake of my—my beloved Hope and for my children, who are devastated by their mother's death, I plan to demand that the federal government do something about these criminals who come across the border from Mexico. We all know that crime statistics fell during the Border Patrol's Hold the Line program."

The LSPD had something to do with that, thought Elena. Didn't he know about the programs targeting career criminals and—

"Now that the crime rate is again climbing, we need more agents on the border, more and stronger fences, more—"

"Is it known that your wife was killed by a Mexican national?" the interviewer broke in eagerly.

"It stands to reason," said Quarles.

Elena left the campus of Herbert Hobart University with its fifteen-mile-an-hour speed limit and turned her pickup onto a street that climbed higher up the mountain. Here, multilevel houses perched on cliff edges overlooking the lights of the Upper Valley and another mountain range to the west.

"I should never have encouraged Hope to volunteer for the Citizens on Patrol program," Quarles was saying. "Had I known that she would be exposed to lethal situations with only the two hours' training they gave her—" His voice caught in his throat. "She was unarmed, unprepared for whatever happened. I shall certainly, if elected, see that money for more extensive training is provided for these programs. For the police academy as well."

What was that all about? Did he mean Ibarra was poorly trained? If so, he was wrong; she had a top record at the academy and as a probationer. Elena had checked. And the academy was a top-rated training institution. The Border Patrol and the other federal agencies snapped up LSPD graduates at an alarming rate. Like the city didn't need its own people. Like there were plenty of cops on the street. Well, at least Quarles seemed to be aware of the problems and planned to address them.

"Remember Hope in your prayers," said Quarles. "And Officer Ibarra."

Elena turned off the radio. Even grief-stricken, Quarles had done himself a lot of good politically during that interview. How would his ratings look tomorrow?

And how was the incumbent mayor, Nellie Medrano-Caldicott, taking this? It was going to be hard to bad-mouth an opponent whose wife had been shot down on the streets.

4

Tuesday, October 22, 9:50 P.M.

Sarah's new house, bought with the settlement money from the city, was white stucco with a red tile roof and massive double doors whose fanlight extended into the second story. Banks of windows in back overlooked a narrow yard and a spreading vista of river valley, desert, and mountains. From one of those windows Elena could lie in bed and stare out at far horizons or, in winter, at banks of smog girdling the mountain and snaking down the Rio Grande.

As she pulled the pickup into Sarah's circular drive, she noted that every light in the house was on. Were Sarah and her wild-haired painter/lover, Paul Zifkovitz, searching for the perfect wall on which to hang another of his geometric masterpieces? Elena let herself into the foyer and was met by an apparently distraught Sarah, whose short blond-gray hair, usually so carefully styled, was standing up in tufts, as if she'd been pulling it. The circles of red on her cheekbones didn't look like a careless overapplication of blush, and Sarah had actually removed her suit jacket and unbuttoned the collar of her blouse. The remains of the bow were trailing raffishly down her chest.

"Where have you *been* today?" she cried.

"Working," Elena answered. "I left a message on your answering machine at the office."

"I was here."

"You didn't go to work?" Elena would have guessed that whatever the state of her health, short of imminent hospitalization, Sarah, chairman of electrical engineering at H.H.U., would go to work.

"I came back from the university because my house was burglarized. They took—" She looked on the verge of tears, which in themselves would have been an unusual occurrence. "They took my computer equipment—everything—drives, monitors, keyboards, tape backups, scanners—"

"I get the picture. Didn't you call the police?"

"Of course. Much good they did. They said I wasn't likely to see any of it again. And then—" Elena had walked from the foyer into the two-story living room and collapsed on Sarah's beige sofa, Sarah trailing her indignantly. "And then—you won't believe this!—the insurance company said they wouldn't pay."

"Why not?" That did surprise Elena; the theft of electronic equipment didn't. Local burglars, from either side of the border, would steal anything—your underwear, if they couldn't find something more valuable—but they loved electronic equipment. It was so fencible.

"They claim, since I'm an electrical engineer and computer scientist, that it's business equipment, but I didn't insure it as such."

"Bastards," Elena said sympathetically. "How did the thieves get in?"

"They forced the sliding glass doors in back. Then they came out the front door and loaded my possessions into an unmarked van. If the woman next door hadn't been on her way to a symphony board meeting and called the police from her cellular phone, I wouldn't have known until I got home."

"It happens," said Elena.

"Not to me!" Sarah retorted indignantly. "I can't believe it. They carried everything out in broad daylight."

"Come on, Sarah, you've still got the furniture."

"I'd rather they took that. It *is* insured."

"Computer stuff gets outdated every six months anyway."

"That's not the point," Sarah retorted. She flopped dispiritedly into a tobacco-brown silk chair. "The same thing could happen all over again. Every burglar in town probably knows by now that I'm a good electronics target. They're probably standing around in bars deciding who'll break into my house next."

Elena was amazed. Imaginative scenarios weren't Sarah's usual method of reasoning.

"And there's *nothing* I can do! Is there?" The question was a challenge, as if the burglary situation was Elena's fault.

"Certainly there are things you can do," Elena replied.

"What?"

"Well—you could get a dog. A big, mean—"

"I don't like large dogs."

"Then get a little, noisy one," Elena suggested.

"That seems like a rather simplistic solution," said Sarah, "and who would take care of it?"

"O.K.—you can get a silent alarm and hook into the Westside Regional Command. Then if someone breaks in, the police will be on your doorstep within five minutes. The Yellow Pages are full of companies that can set you up. I'll ask someone in Burglary who they recommend."

"Good."

"Then"—Elena grinned at her next suggestion—"you could organize a Neighborhood Crime Watch. Get everyone on the block involved so you're all watching each other's houses, looking for suspicious strangers, even patrolling. You could be block captain." Elena was careful not to laugh, although the idea of Sarah patrolling the neighborhood was so unlikely as to be hilarious.

To Elena's astonishment, Sarah whipped a notepad from

her handbag on the teak coffee table and wrote the suggestions down. "Anything else?"

"There are security companies. They install and maintain the system, monitor it through their offices, and call the police. You send fewer false alarms to the department if you go through a security company."

"Why would I have false alarms?"

Elena chuckled. "I'm told it happens all the time."

"Only to the electronically challenged I'd imagine," Sarah replied, looking contemptuous of those who hadn't kept up with modern technology. "I rather imagine I could set up a system myself, if I had the time. What about a gun?"

Stranger and stranger! "I thought you were a gun-control advocate."

"I am also a woman who has no desire to be a victim. If I'm robbed again I shall shoot the robber."

"Burglar," Elena corrected, "and you weren't here when the house was burglarized."

"The security system will take care of thieves in my absence, not to mention my alert neighbors, once I've organized the watch program. I shall recommend that they all get guns. Who do I call about organizing a program?"

"Headquarters, but Sarah, you don't know how to shoot."

"I'll take a class. Perhaps there's one on the Internet."

"Learning to handle a gun requires actually shooting it, and you can't do that in your backyard. It's illegal."

"You can help me choose the proper weapon for my purposes."

"What purposes? Blasting anyone who looks like a burglar in the dark? Like me? Or Zif?"

"I wonder if I should apply for a concealed-weapon permit?" Sarah mused.

Elena threw up her hands. Her friend was going absolutely berserk over the uninsured loss of her computer, but Sarah would calm down, probably forget about the whole thing once she had new equipment up and running. And in the meantime it never hurt to have an alarm system. Elena wondered whether anything had been taken from *her* room. Probably not. Her possessions weren't worth anything on the hot-property market.

5

Wednesday, October 23, 8:00 A.M.

Leo was already in his cubicle on the telephone when Elena arrived and dropped into her gray-blue tweed chair across the aisle on Homicide Row, the far end of the Crimes Against Persons enclave.

"Have a good session with your shrink last night?" Leo asked.

"Same old, same old," she replied. "We ate fajitas, and I told him about the mountain lion."

Leo found it hard to believe that nothing went on during those sessions but the endless retelling of Elena shooting the cat and discovering the bloody body of her lover's twin brother. "Parsley must have the hots for you," said Leo. "Otherwise, he'd be charging more than food."

"He likes to eat. And he's an academic. He gets a paper out of it, maybe tenure when he comes up next year."

"Say, did you see the paper last night?"

"No. There was a big crisis when I got home. I suppose our case made headlines."

"You bet your booties. And the chief said he'd assigned his best detectives. That's you and me, babe."

Elena shrugged. "What's he going to say? He assigned two dumbheads?" She booted up her computer, asking,

"How are Concepcion and the babies? How's my cute little goddaughter, Elena, Junior?"

Leo sighed. "When I got home yesterday, Concepcion was in tears and every damn one of them was howling. They were wet or had gas or wanted a bottle or—"

"You two need to hire a baby-sitter and get out of that house," Elena advised sympathetically.

"Yeah, like you could find a baby-sitter who'd take on five five-month-old babies. Even Concepcion's mother and sisters know better than to get roped in unless they come together, and they're never free at the same time."

"Well, I'll do it," said Elena. "Friday night. There's a big LULAC dance you can go to. How's that sound?"

"A dance?" Leo's eyes lit up. His great love was tap dancing, but, like his father, who toured the country entering ballroom-dancing competitions with the lady next door, Leo liked to dance with women, too, especially his wife. "You'd do that?"

"I'll bring Sarah to help," said Elena, thinking that the prospect of such an unlikely activity would take Sarah's mind off the theft of her computer equipment.

"Does she know anything about kids?" Leo asked.

"She saw more of yours born than you did. This will be an added educational experience for her."

"You mad at her or something?"

Before Elena could answer, they were called to collect forensic evidence and headed downstairs to I.D. & R., where the latent-fingerprint expert informed them that there were no prints on the car other than those of the owner and his wife, none on Ibarra's gun but Ibarra's, and no identifiable latents on the Dumpster but those of the victim, Mrs. Quarles, and a homeless man named Homer Contreras, who had been arrested in Los Santos for vagrancy, petty theft, and public intoxication. The detectives wrote his name down, but without much hope that he was the car thief/murderer.

Two shots had been fired from Officer Ibarra's gun, according to a member of the crime-scene team. One slug they thought they had found in the tire of the Cazareses' Mercury, the other in the body of Hope Quarles. Elena felt anxiety tightening her stomach muscles. "The DPS lab is doing the ballistics right now," the tech added.

"The autopsy—" Leo began.

"Last night. No one's wasting any time on this one."

And if it was Ibarra's bullet that killed Hope Quarles, how had that happened? Elena wondered. Had Ibarra heard something, a cry from the victim perhaps, and turned around, shooting wild and hitting Quarles instead of a lookout posted at the end of the alley. Had the car thief then shot Ibarra? But would Ibarra turn her back on him? Elena shook her head. "It can't be Ibarra's slug in the victim," she murmured to Leo.

"Let's hope not," he replied, face grim.

"Page us when you get the ballistics back," she told Harry Baylor of I.D. & R.

As they left, she suggested to Leo that they talk to the coroner, and he agreed. They picked up a car and drove to Thomason General, where they could check on Monica Ibarra, after which they'd visit an adjacent building where autopsies were performed.

A resident told them that Ibarra was still unconscious and had been since surgery the night before.

"Is she going to make it?" Elena asked.

He shrugged.

"We need to talk to her," said Leo.

"Maybe this afternoon, if she lives that long."

The ICU waiting room was crowded with the family—mother, father, siblings—not to mention Monica's fiancé Eddie Diaz, who came over to introduce himself. He was wearing a brown deputy sheriff's uniform.

"How did it happen?" he asked. "Monica's good at her job. She wouldn't have fucked up like the newspaper said."

"What did the paper say?" Elena asked.

"Oh, a bunch of stuff about maybe the police should stop asking citizens to volunteer if they can't protect them, and what was Monica doing while Mrs. Quarles was getting shot?"

Elena sighed. "We won't know for sure until we talk to her." She kept back the possibility that Monica's gun had killed her C.O.P. partner, Hope Quarles.

Diaz looked haggard. "Well, whatever happened, it wasn't Monica's fault. She's a crack shot. She musta been gunned down before she could protect the woman."

A crack shot? Elena wasn't happy to hear that. She and Leo edged away from the frightened deputy and hurried to the morgue, the coroner's domain, where Dr. Wilkerson told them he'd just heard from DPS. The bullet he'd taken from Hope Quarles's body the night before had come from Monica Ibarra's nine-millimeter Glock, the kind of weapon carried by most LSPD officers below the age of forty. Elena groaned. "Did you discover anything in the autopsy?" she asked hopefully. "Anything that might call in question Ibarra's—"

"The Quarles woman died of a gunshot wound to the chest. If you weren't going for a head shot, it was perfectly placed. Destroyed the heart."

Elena knew what he was saying. A solid head shot meant the person you hit wasn't going to shoot back. A chest shot—well, you could be killed by someone with a fatal chest wound. But Hope Quarles had been unarmed; she wouldn't have been shooting back. And Monica Ibarra shouldn't have been aiming at that particular heart.

"The only thing I can tell you that might help—I.D. & R. says Ibarra's body was ten feet from Quarles. My guess is that the shooter was closer than that, but I can't be sure. Any good lawyer would call me on that opinion, so it won't help in court," said Wilkerson.

"Is toxicology being done on both women?" Elena asked.

"Sure, but it takes time. Talk to DPS, not me. I'm surprised to get the ballistics back so fast. I was surprised to hear I had to get the autopsy done ASAP. 'What's the big hurry?' I said."

"Don't you read the papers, Wilkerson?" Leo muttered.

"No," said the coroner.

"She's—she was the wife of a candidate for mayor."

"So." Wilkerson gave them a grisly smile. "Now he can go for the sympathy vote."

"We've got to talk to Ibarra," Elena said as they left.

"If she ever comes to," Leo agreed. "Central Command is looking for the disappearing witnesses. Wanna chase down the drunk whose fingerprints were on the Dumpster?"

After checking several of Contreras's known haunts, they found him dozing in the shelter of a highway overpass. Ibarra's partner, who knew many of the homeless in the downtown area, told them where to look. "But I never saw him yesterday," said Bert Krausling. "I figured he was hitting the Eastside rib places this week."

Such was the case. Homer "Tabs" Contreras had an alibi. Fifteen minutes and five miles from the shooting, the proprietress of Sukie's Alabama Barbecue had been running him off the premises. "Found the ol' bastard pissin' on the wall when I went out back," Sukie told them. She knew exactly what time that had been because her favorite soap opera was coming on and she missed a segment while calling the police. Tabs, so called because he collected beer-can tabs under the impression that they were worth money, had been picked up by a unit patrolling Interstate 10, driven farther east, and let out. The officers didn't want to take him downtown, although he would have been amenable to a real bed and a hot meal at the jail had the jail not been full.

So much for that lead. It hadn't looked very promising when they decided to pursue it. "Just goes to show how little we've got," Leo commented.

"Let's call the hospital again," Elena suggested.

With no news there—Ibarra was still alive and still unconscious—they doubled back to Sukie's and tried her barbecued pork ribs and coleslaw.

6

Wednesday, October 23, 3:07 P.M.

When Monica Ibarra recovered consciousness in the ICU, she wasn't an easy interview, not with the needles and tubes attached to her and her inability to talk or even stay awake for extended periods.

"Just a few minutes," the doctor warned them.

Elena asked the young woman to respond to questions by raising one finger for yes, two for no. The paralysis from which she suffered—the doctors were hoping it wasn't permanent but made no guarantees—didn't extend to her hands.

"Did you go after the car thief?" they asked. One finger went up for yes. "Did you get a good look at him?" Again, yes. "Did he shoot you?" Monica lay still, then raised three fingers. "You don't know?" Elena guessed. One finger. "Did you shoot anyone?" Three fingers. "You don't know?" One finger. "Did you fire your weapon?" Yes. "How many shots?" One finger. "You only fired once?" One finger. Leo and Elena exchanged glances.

"Did the car thief have a partner?" Ibarra lifted one finger, paused, two fingers, then one again. "You're not sure, but you think he had a partner?" Elena guessed. One finger. "The car thief was a *man*?" Yes. "Did you see Mrs. Quarles again after you entered the alley?" The hand lay still on the sheet.

"She's drifted off," Leo said as the doctor came in and asked them to leave. Nurses took Ibarra's vital signs while the detectives were hustled around the drawn ring of hospital-green curtains and out of the ICU.

"She seemed pretty sure she only fired one shot," said Leo. "And she must think—or want us to think—it was the one that went into the tire of the Mercury."

"How was she?" demanded Eddie Diaz, his once crisp deputy's uniform now rumpled. "You didn't tire her out?"

"I think she goes back to sleep before that happens," Elena said reassuringly.

"She looked awful when I was in there," said the deputy. "She's a beautiful girl, and she looks like death—I mean, she looks—"

"Better than she did in the alley," Elena assured him. "And her mind seems O.K. She answered questions."

"How?" demanded the fiancé. "She couldn't talk to me."

"She raises one finger for yes, two for no," said Leo. "An' I got a feeling she's gonna make it. She's got guts."

"You're right," said Diaz, embracing the reassurance. "She does. If that's what it takes, she'll be O.K." But he sounded like a drowning man grasping at a slippery rope.

Elena was afraid that guts wouldn't help if Monica had shot a civilian. She might recover only to find herself embroiled in a legal and professional nightmare.

"Are you through with the interrogation?" asked the doctor, emerging from the ICU and confronting the detectives.

"No," said Leo. "We need a description, and she's the only witness to one death and her own injury."

"Well, I don't see how—" the doctor began.

"Could she write, do you think?" Elena asked. "She can move her fingers. Maybe if we put a pen in her hand and paper on the bed, she could give us a description that way."

"I don't want her life endangered," said the fiancé. "For God's sake, she almost died."

"She still may," said the doctor.

"Oh God!" Diaz turned away to hide his tears.

"Can we try the writing?" Elena asked. "Without doing her any harm?"

The doctor frowned, thought about it. "Only a few minutes at a time," he warned. "And you stop if I say so."

"Right," Leo agreed.

"It could take you hours," the doctor warned. "You saw how she fell asleep. I'm surprised she managed to stay conscious as long as she did."

"She's a cop," said Elena. "She wants the guy who shot her caught, and she's the only one that can tell us who to look for."

It took them six hours, spelling each other outside and inside the ICU. One word at a time, in staggering letters that Ibarra couldn't see and they could hardly read, Leo and Elena got a description of the car thief—shaved head, baggy white pants held up by a rope, black T-shirt, Los Reyes Diablos tattoo on the left forearm. Ibarra had drawn it—a devil's head with a horned crown. The guy was a gangbanger, they said to each other as they left the hospital. Well, they had a lead.

Which was more than Central Command had turned up. Sergeant Talley, Monica's superior, insisted that her partner be hypnotized in the hope of causing him to recall the faces of the four people at the head of the alley, the ones who had disappeared. It worked. Krausling was able to produce computer pictures of the four people, and the Foot and Bike Patrols had hit the streets by afternoon with the pictures.

They located three of the four witnesses. The first was an addict who swallowed a balloon containing black-tar heroin when the police stopped him. Once they completed the Heimlich maneuver and confiscated his stash, they arrested him. He hadn't seen anything but the two bodies. The second witness was a clerk, late for a job at an electronics store that was blasting a sexy rock song onto the sidewalk during the interview. She said she couldn't afford to be any later than she already was that morning; she'd had to drive her sick kid to her mother's house because the day care wouldn't take him, but she hadn't seen anything anyway.

The third witness was a barmaid on the eleven-to-seven shift at the Quick Coyote, and she hadn't been willing to miss out on any tips when she hadn't seen anyone kill those people. She remembered the fourth witness, an old man who kept saying in Spanish, "What's in there? I can't see." The old man had walked out into the street two blocks away and been run down by a low-rider who left the scene. Central Command found the old man at Thomason. The low-rider was still missing. This information Elena got from Sergeant Talley by phone. She, in turn, passed on Monica's description of the gangbanger.

7

Wednesday, October 23, 10:20 P.M.

Elena plodded toward Sarah's door, where she inserted her key and entered the foyer, dropping her purse on the burnished walnut-and-copper console after removing her gun. She'd lock it up later in her room. She was running a hand beneath her French braid when an alarm went off. A very loud alarm. An alarm that could probably be heard across the river in Mexico, up the interstate in Las Cruces, across the desert in Columbus, New Mexico, in heaven itself. She clapped her hands over her ears and looked for a turnoff switch. There was a keypad, newly installed, on the wall beside the door, but Elena didn't know the code.

Paul Zifkovitz, wearing a paint-smeared, unironed shirt, baggy pants, and huaraches and swinging the collapsible wooden easel on which he had been painting upstairs, came rushing down—no doubt planning to defend Sarah's possessions from thieves. Spotting the gun before he recognized Elena in the shadows of the entry, he stopped short on the stairs and cried, "Don't shoot. You're welcome to whatever you can find."

At that moment Sarah rushed in from outside with a long wooden tree stake in her hands, charging like an unhorsed knight. Elena dodged. Having recognized her at the last minute, Sarah stopped and looked up at her lover. "Paul, did

I understand you to tell the thieves they were welcome to whatever they wanted in my house?" she demanded.

"They had a gun."

"*I* had a gun," said Elena, hearing the sound of a siren and knowing what was about to happen. It did. Two officers, weapons drawn, raced in to disarm Elena and protect the householders, whom they also asked to drop their weapons, the easel and the tree stake, respectively.

"Officers Page and Lezarda," said Page brusquely.

"Detective Elena Jarvis from Crimes Against Persons," said Elena. She reached for her ID.

"Hands over your head," growled the young patrolman. He stuck her gun in his belt but kept his weapon trained on Elena while his partner watched Sarah and Zif suspiciously, in case they were bizarrely armed criminals instead of the householders they claimed to be.

"I live here," said Elena. "Look in my bag. My ID's there." She moved away from the console so he could approach the handbag without getting close to her.

"Keep her covered, Virgie," said Officer Page. He pulled out Elena's billfold and snapped, "Says here you live on Sierra Negra."

"That's my house. I've lived with Dr. Tolland since March." The female officer gave her a curious look, then glanced at Zif and Sarah, no doubt trying to figure out which was Elena's lover. "Will you look at my ID?" said Elena impatiently. "I've been on duty since this morning, and I want to lower my hands, take my shoes off, and sit down." The male officer was rooting through her purse.

"You didn't waste any time getting an alarm put in," Elena said to Sarah.

Officer Page had found the ID. "Say!" he exclaimed, looking impressed. "You're on the Quarles case, right?"

"Yeah, lucky me."

"I had it done immediately," Sarah said huffily. "Why did you set it off? As a police person, you're supposed to know about these things."

"I didn't know the security code," Elena replied dryly.

"How's Monica?" asked Virgie Lezarda. "I went to the academy with her."

"In bad shape," Elena replied.

"I want to commend you officers for your prompt response," said Sarah. "It's very heartening to know that the system does what it is supposed to do."

Officer Page scowled. "It's not supposed to be tripped unless there's an intruder in the house, ma'am. Detective Jarvis here says she's a resident. That being the case—"

"I shall provide her with the security code and the operations manual. If she'd come home or called—"

"For God's sake, Sarah, I'm working a high-profile case. I've been in and out of the ICU all evening. All I had to eat was barfbag hospital food."

"Barfbag?" Sarah flushed with displeasure. "What a disgusting—"

"You've got that right. I had a tuna-salad sandwich that was worse than disgusting."

"What you need to top it off is a large brandy," said Zif, coming the rest of the way down the stairs. "I think we all need one." He ran a large, paint-smeared hand through his hair, leaving a trail of barely discernible viridian green behind like phosphorescence on a night pond. "You officers want to join us in a brandy?"

"Is that a bribe?" Page demanded.

"I'd consider it a threat," said Elena. "Have you ever *tasted* brandy?"

"Oh, come *on,* Page," said his partner. "The guy was being hospitable."

Page grunted. "The police department doesn't like false alarms, ma'am, sir," he said. "There are fines—"

"I trust it will never happen again," snapped Sarah.

The patrol officers departed, the householders retired to the living room, and Sarah launched into an enthusiastic account of her activities that day: applications for a concealed-weapon permit and for a permit to buy a weapon; acquisition of materials on the Neighborhood Crime Watch program; and visits to five neighbors, all of whom were enthusiastic about joining once they heard about the theft at Sarah's house.

Elena told about her partner Leo finding his babies all howling and his wife in tears.

"Poor woman," Sarah said absently. She was making notes in a loose-leaf notebook that was to be devoted exclusively to the Neighborhood Watch venture.

"I knew you'd feel that way," said Elena. "That's why I volunteered the two of us to baby-sit on Friday."

"What!" Sarah looked horrified.

"So poor Concepcion can get out of the house."

"But I—I—" Sarah was sputtering. "I don't know one end of a baby from the other," she protested.

"You can tell by looking," said Zif. "We'll all go."

Elena gave him a dubious look.

"Hey, I've got younger brothers and sisters," he said.

Sarah studied him with narrow-eyed suspicion. "What's this sudden interest in babies, Paul? You not getting any ideas, are you?"

"Only artistic ideas, love," Zifkovitz replied.

Elena covered her grin with a discreet hand. Last spring Sarah's ex, Gus McGlenlevie, inspired by the birth of Leo's quintuplets, had suddenly decided that he wanted to be a daddy. To that end he suggested that he and Sarah remarry and procreate. Sarah had been so upset by his courtship that she moved off campus to get away from him.

"We're due at their house at seven," said Elena.

"Why do I let you get me into these unlikely situations?" Sarah groaned.

But Elena wasn't to be dissuaded. She had a plan. Before the birth of the five children, she'd told Sarah about Leo's impending financial problems, and Sarah had arranged for the university to support the quintuplets in return for the right to study their upbringing. Elena's newest idea was that one night of baby-sitting and a few subtle hints might induce Sarah to suggest that the university provide the harassed parents with baby-sitting services. It couldn't hurt to try.

8

Thursday, October 24, 8:00 A.M.

Campaign Manager Demands Investigation

> Fermin Gil, campaign manager for mayoral candidate Wayne Quarles, complained yesterday that police are giving the family no information on the investigation into the death of the candidate's wife. Gil suggested that police authorities are guilty of a cover-up in order to protect Officer Monica Ibarra. He demanded an investigation into her conduct at the scene of the crime.
>
> When Candidate Quarles was asked to comment, he said, "I'm sure Officer Ibarra did her best. My family and I hope for her speedy recovery and an answer to the questions that plague us about the tragic death of my wife."
>
> Los Santos *Times*, Thursday, October 24

As an indication of the department's anxiety about the case, especially after the article in the morning paper, Leo and Elena weren't doing any footwork. Other officers hit the streets to round up known car thieves and members of Los Reyes Diablos and bring them in for questioning. Other detectives were assigned to help with the interrogations.

In fact, C.A.P.'s interview rooms and visitor's chairs were

crowded with suspects. Out in the lobby they sat around grousing under the watchful eye of Carmen, the C.A.P. receptionist, who was interested in their hairstyles and prone to give advice to people whose coiffures didn't meet her exacting standards. At one point when Elena entered the small reception area, she found Carmen doing a hair makeover on a fifteen-year-old girl, a member of the gang's female auxiliary. Her boyfriend sat scowling, evidently under the impression that his true love, who wore a nose ring and a crowned-devil tattoo, was defecting to the enemy.

To break up fights and see that no juvenile rights were violated in the adult environs of headquarters at Five Points, juvenile officers lounged in C.A.P. and in the front reception area, keeping an eye on the teenagers they and the Gang Task Force had brought in. No one was taking any chances. One of these suspects might have killed Hope Quarles—providing he or she had gotten hold of Ibarra's gun.

Elena hoped it had gone down that way, although Ibarra's prints on the weapon did nothing to bolster the theory. As yet, no one outside the department knew about the prints or the ballistics, so Quarles's campaign manager had it right in part when he complained—maybe not a cover-up, but certainly the department was withholding information. Leo and Elena had been told to let the official spokesman take care of the press and family.

Soon lawyers as well as detainees began to show up. Those suspects who had verifiable alibis were turned loose. Those who didn't were sent on to Elena and Leo. A typical car thief told them, "Nobody wants an 'eighty-four Mercury. I'd be embarrassed to steal one." The detectives took such statements with a grain of salt. Older cars did, in fact, get stolen. They ended up in the chop shops, providing parts for other old cars, which abounded on both sides of the border.

The gang members all protested their innocence—but did it as unpleasantly as possible so as not to violate their own sense of *machismo*. During one such interview Elena received a telephone call, labeled an emergency by the operator, the only type of call that was supposed to be put through. Afraid the hospital might be notifying her that Ibarra had died, Elena answered with trepidation.

It was Sarah, who said she had wonderful news. How had she gotten through? Elena wondered. Good news wasn't usually considered an emergency. "Your mother's coming to visit!" Sarah cried, breaking into her thoughts. "She couldn't get hold of you, so she called me."

"When?"

"This morning."

"No, when's she coming?"

"Oh, in a few days. She has to finish a coat she's making." Elena's mother, a weaver in Chimayo, New Mexico, had turned traditional weaving skills, taught to her by her Hispanic in-laws, into a thriving couture business that targeted rich tourists in Santa Fe.

"Hey, you done with me?" demanded the kid in the visitor's chair. He wore a black leather baseball cap turned backward, baggy jeans, unlaced high-tops, a crucifix, and a black T-shirt that displayed a male with a machine gun mowing down other males. "I got stuff to do, you know."

"Like what?" Elena snapped back. "Sniff spray paint?"

"I beg your pardon," Sarah exclaimed.

"Bitch," muttered the kid.

"Watch your mouth, peanut brain," Leo admonished from across the aisle. His interrogatee, a career car thief, looked surprised. Elena's gangbanger sneered.

Elena said, "Not you, Sarah."

"I should hope not. I invited her to stay with us."

"Gee, thanks." Elena loved her mother, but not the reason why her mother planned to visit. Harmony thought it was time Elena moved back into her own house and, to that end, would cook up some weird cleansing rite with some spooky local witch to rid the place of its terrifying memories. Still, Sam Parsley wasn't ever going to accept that Elena was cured unless she could face life in her own house.

". . . have to get back to my canvassing. I've taken the afternoon off to recruit more neighbors," said Sarah.

"Listen, I don't have to sit here all day while you—"

"Shut up!" Elena snapped at the kid with the crucifix.

"What?"

"Not you, Sarah. Thanks for calling." She hung up and got back to her interview.

After that kid came an older gangbanger with a picture of the Virgin of Guadalupe stenciled on his T-shirt. Only a glimpse of the Holy Mother showed under his gang jacket. His head was shaved, but not his chin. Could he be the one? she wondered, remembering Monica's painfully elicited description. Bald . . . shaved head, she had written in straggling letters. But this man had deep acne scars pitting his cheeks and forehead. Surely, Monica would have listed his disfigurement—unless she'd fallen asleep while meaning to write down "scars," then forgotten when she next awoke.

"Seein' you got so many of my compadres in here, I guess you think one of us did it."

"Did what?"

"Shot the cop an' killed that gringa with her. That's what this is about, right? But it ain't me," said "Chuco" Palenque, who was reputedly the Diablos' gang leader. "We don' shoot at no cops. An' why would we shoot the big-shot gringa? Nothin' in it for us."

"You got caught stealing a car, had to kill the cop before she shot or arrested you, then had to kill the witness because you were facing a capital-murder charge?"

"The cop wasn' dead."

"How could you tell?"

"I heard it on the radio."

"Where were you when—"

"At home tryin' to sleep. Ask my ol' lady."

"Mother? Girlfriend? Wife?"

"Girlfriend."

"Who'd lie if she knows what's good for her. Right?"

He gave Elena a sly sneer. "Then ask the city inspector who come to see if our place meets city code. Big surprise. He says it does. Never even noticed the rat turds or the broken pipes or the exposed wirin'." He handed Elena the form that contained the inspector's signature, Chuco's, and the time. Eleven-fifteen. "He says we cut down the weeds or the city will do it an' charge us. I say tell it to the landlord, an' how come he don' care about the inside, where he prob'ly won' let his worst enemy live? He says don' give him no crap. I say *chinga tu madre*."

"Really? Did he speak Spanish?"

"Not to me, but he knows what I'm sayin'."

At the end of the afternoon Elena pointed out to Leo that none of the Devil Kings or even the car thieves were wearing white pants—baggy pants yes, but not white.

"Maybe the word went out that the shooter was wearing white, so no one wants to be busted on a clothing ID."

"Or Los Reyes Diablos never wear white because it's not gang colors," Elena suggested. The Gang Task Force verified that but said the color of pants didn't count. Jackets, hats, tattoos, jewelry—those were the important things. After that conversation Elena said dryly, "Maybe they just know it isn't chic to wear white this late in the season."

"What's that mean?" Leo asked.

"Something Sarah told me once," she replied. "Let's go back to the hospital. I called, and the ICU nurse said Ibarra can talk a little."

"Lemme call Concepcion." Leo reached for his phone.

"I'll go get the mug shots I.D. & R.'s been collecting all day," Elena offered. "Maybe Ibarra can ID someone."

"By the way, Concepcion says you're an angel for volunteering to baby-sit and thanks a million," Leo called after her as she strode down Homicide Row.

"De nada," she replied. She wasn't going to tell the Weizells what she hoped to accomplish by dragging along the reluctant Sarah to feed babies, change diapers, and get spit up on. Time enough for that if the plan worked.

9

Thursday, October 24, 5:15 P.M.

At the hospital they found Monica out of the ICU, her bed cranked to a half-reclining position. The tubes and machines had been removed, but she was flushed and feverish. She looked more alert, but very anxious.

"She's dead," Monica whispered, her voice weak and sibilant. Elena had to lean forward to hear her. "Why didn't you tell—"

"We didn't want to upset you." Elena broke in hastily on Ibarra's torturously produced words.

"Ballistics?" Monica asked. "Same gun—that—got me?"

Neither detective wanted to answer, but they did have to ask questions. Ibarra, unfortunately, seemed so fragile, as if the wrong word could tear loose her hold on consciousness—even life. "Are you strong enough to talk?" Elena asked.

Monica looked from one to the other, and the anxiety level in her eyes rose. "Hope—so nice—" She blinked back tears. "Told her to stay—behind Dumpster. How could—"

"After you went into the alley, when did you see her next?" Leo asked.

"Didn't. Someone—shot me. Think I tried to—warn—" She stopped, breathing shallowly, pain on her flushed face.

"What kind of gun did the car thief have?" Elena asked.

"Didn't see—he dropped—I had gun out. Think I—pulled trigger. Just—" She stopped again, evidently having come to the end of her recollection.

He dropped? What did Ibarra mean? Elena wondered. That the thief had dropped his gun before she could identify it? Or that he had dropped down? Could Mrs. Quarles have rushed to Monica's defense and been killed by a stray bullet from the gun of a policewoman already losing consciousness? No. Hope Quarles's body had been at the end of the alley. There would have been blood and drag marks.

"Did you fire a second shot?" Leo asked.

Breathing with difficulty, Ibarra laid a hand on the bandages that covered her chest. Her ability to move her arm seemed hopeful to Elena. The doctor hadn't mentioned the paralysis before they came in, just the fever. Maybe the damage to her spine wasn't permanent. Elena glanced at her legs. They hadn't moved.

"Only remember—one. Not sure—"

"Not sure that you fired a second time?" Leo prodded.

"First time." Again she looked from one to the other. "What bullet—in me?"

"Twenty-two," said Elena.

"Gangs carry—small-caliber. He—gang. But Hope—"

"You described him to us: white pants, black T-shirt, shaved head, Los Reyes Diablos tattoo, over twenty. Do you remember anything else? What about his face?"

"Nose," said Ibarra.

"Crooked? Flattened?" Elena waited to take notes, but Monica had closed her eyes, perhaps drifted into sleep.

"You see anyone with a memorable nose during the interviews?" Elena murmured to Leo.

He shook his head. "You?"

She pictured the people she'd questioned but couldn't remember any standout noses either.

Ibarra's eyes flickered open. "Left."

"What?"

"Left side," she whispered, eyes closing.

When, after waiting for her to wake up, they asked again about the thief's nose, Ibarra didn't remember. Sighing, Elena suggested that she look at mug shots, and Leo lifted a briefcase from the floor beside his chair. Just at that moment, however, the doctor pushed back the curtains in the double room. A nurse followed, took Ibarra's pulse and blood pressure, and inserted a thermometer in her ear, something Elena found very strange. It might be faster than the thermometer-under-the-tongue routine, but what if it punctured the patient's eardrum? Shaking his head, the doctor motioned them out. In the waiting room, they encountered Ibarra's mother and father, visibly upset.

"You didn't tell her what the papers are saying, did you?" Asencio Ibarra demanded.

"What *are* they saying?" Leo asked.

"That maybe Monica killed that woman. It's not true. And my daughter's in no condition to hear—"

"We didn't say anything like that to her," said Leo.

Had the ballistics information gotten out? Elena wondered.

"Saying she should be tried for manslaughter!" cried Mrs. Ibarra. "Whatever happened, she was doing her job."

"Who said that, ma'am?" Elena asked. "About Monica being tried for—"

"A politico. The husband's campaign manager."

Gil—who was coming off like a junkyard dog, Elena thought. Of course, for all they knew, Monica *had* killed Mrs. Quarles. Forensics looked that way, but no one outside the department knew that. If Quarles was so supportive of the department and Ibarra, why didn't he shut Fermin Gil up? "If it's shown that Monica actually shot Mrs. Quarles," Elena said cautiously, "and we don't know that, it would have been an accident. She'll have to go before a grand jury—"

"A grand jury?" Mrs. Ibarra wailed. "Like some criminal?"

"No, ma'am. It's standard procedure. The D.A., when an

officer shoots someone, takes it to the grand jury for investigation—to avoid the appearance of impropriety."

"And I voted for him," Mrs. Ibarra said despairingly, as if her vote had brought her daughter to this pass.

"You can go in again," said the doctor. Elena picked up the case of mug shots. She heard Mrs. Ibarra's soft tears behind her, Leo's footsteps, Mr. Ibarra's rumbling words of consolation to his wife.

Off and on for an hour they showed Monica mug shots. She recognized some of the pictures, but not as the car thief. None of them had a nose that rang any bells.

At the end of the viewing session Monica said, "Mrs. Quarles. What kind of—bullet?"

While Elena was debating what to say and Leo was looking to her to respond, Monica drifted into sleep, her face more flushed than it had been when they arrived. They tiptoed away, having avoided the young woman's question, relieved to see an empty waiting room. The relatives were probably downstairs eating toxic treats from a machine.

Leo cornered the floor nurse and asked if Ibarra was going to make it. "She looks like her temp's about one-oh-five," he said.

The hatchet-faced nurse scowled. "Do you consider yourself a fever-at-a-glance expert?"

"We just want to know how she's doing," Elena interrupted. What a meanmouthed woman!

"Better," said the nurse, "but she's not out of the woods, and if she lives, we don't know what the long-term effects will be." She stared at the detectives, her mouth set in a grim line. "But I've told a police representative that already. Maybe you should communicate with each other and spend less time questioning her. She needs her rest."

"She wants to help us find who did this," retorted Elena, bristling. Once in the car, she said, "How'd you like to have that 'angel of mercy' taking care of you?"

"I had her the time you got me shot in the leg," he replied.

"Just give her a little pinch on the bottom and she cheers right up."

Laughing, Elena started the car. "You're a real sexual predator, Leo." The thought of her partner pinching that skinny-assed termagant struck her as hilarious, although she usually took that kind of male chauvinist banter amiss.

10

Thursday, October 24, 8:15 P.M.

Elena arrived home with a bag of tamales and the expectation of settling down in the breakfast nook to eat, drink a beer, and enjoy the lights of the valley. Instead Sarah reproached her for arriving late when they had an appointment to visit a gun store on Doniphan Drive. "They're only open until nine," said Sarah, handing Elena a Coke. "You can eat your tamales in the car, but you can't drink beer there." So Elena found herself sitting on an upholstery-protecting plastic sheet, unfolding and peeling back greasy corn husks, and munching tamales while Sarah drove the Mercedes, too fast, down the mountain.

"My application has been approved. All we have to do is choose a weapon," said Sarah, speeding through a yellow light that turned red before they cleared the intersection. Elena inhaled a piece of tamale and started to cough.

"You should take smaller bites," Sarah told her.

"You should stop running red lights," Elena gasped. They arrived at Gunsmith, Inc., before eight-thirty and were greeted by an obsequious proprietor with a winking gold tooth. Having called ahead, Sarah was greeted like a long-lost sister. Elena, hungrily ingesting her third tamale as the man pulled out weapons for display, supposed Sarah had said something like, "Price is no object."

"Now, here is a beautiful model, madam. A steal at only nine hundred dollars."

"You say *stolen*?" Elena asked, stuffing corn husks into the bag from which her meal had come. The napkins provided with her order had become essential. She wiped her greasy fingers while the proprietor, whose name was actually Herb Gunsmith, eyed her with distaste.

"Stolen? Certainly not," he said. "And we here at Gunsmith's discourage eating and drinking on the premises."

"If you want to sell Dr. Tolland a gun, you'll have to let me finish dinner. Otherwise, I'll take her to Casa Firepower on Alameda."

"A low-class establishment," Herb said disdainfully.

"But cheaper," added Elena, fishing for another tamale.

"I'm sure madam would not wish to purchase an inferior weapon." He made a little bow in Sarah's direction.

"I'm sure madam doesn't need that much firepower," Elena retorted. "Show her something sensible." Had his family name influenced his choice of profession? Or had the family been gunsmiths for the last five hundred years? She'd have to tell Sam about Herb Gunsmith.

"Are you a firearms expert, miss?" Herb asked snidely.

How come he called Sarah "madam" and herself "miss"? Elena wondered. "Cop," she said, flashing her badge.

Herb beamed at her, the lights under his tasteful glass counter ricocheting off his eye-catching gold tooth. Obviously, he knew that Los Santos police officers had to purchase their own weapons. "Always happy to serve our men in blue—and women," he added hastily. "I have a marvelous weapon to show you, Detective."

"I've got one," said Elena, fishing among the corn husks for another tamale.

"Many officers like to have a spare," said Herb.

"Not me. She's the one who wants the gun."

Sarah had been trying out the .44 Magnum. "I think Elena

is right. This would not fit comfortably into a handbag. Perhaps you have something less . . . weighty."

"Would madam care to look at one of the new plastic models?"

"Plastic?" Sarah exclaimed. "I want something to fend off criminals, not—"

Elena's pager beeped, and she asked to use the telephone, again worrying that the call would be about Monica Ibarra, who perhaps wanted to make a dying statement, or was dead and would never speak again, leaving them with a case on which they had, unfortunately, no useful leads. She didn't recognize the number, but called and said, "Jarvis."

"Sergeant Vincent de la Rosa," responded the caller.

"Vince?" Elena was surprised. He was an officer at the Westside Regional Command and had nothing to do with her case. They'd gone to the academy together, then traveled in different directions on the force, Vincent more rapidly than she, but then his uncle was a captain. Not that she wouldn't rather be in C.A.P. than fooling around on the Westside with some boring assignment like community relations or barking-dog control.

"My men just brought in a guy named Paul Zifkovitz. They caught him climbing through the window of a house on Westmoreland in the Sussex Hills development."

Elena glared at Sarah, reached over the counter, and said to Herb, "She'll take that one."

"Why?" asked Sarah, who never did anything unadvisedly.

"Because it's what you need. Not that you need a gun."

"We have fifteen minutes until the store closes," Sarah protested.

"And I would be happy to stay late if madam wants to—"

"Zif got arrested for breaking into your house," said Elena. Gunsmith just wanted to keep Sarah around until he could entice her into buying something more expensive.

"Why would he break into my house? He has a key."

"Guess we'll find out if we get to the Westside Command before they haul him downtown for booking."

"I'll take that one, Mr. Gunsmith," said Sarah, pointing to Elena's choice. "And a bullet."

"We don't sell them singly, madam. You'll have to buy a box," said Herb.

"Jarvis," De la Rosa's voice roared in Elena's ear.

"Yeah, Vince. Don't arrest him. He and the owner are—ah—close personal friends. The new security system must have screwed up again. But we're on our way to vouch for him. Unless, of course, he broke a window or something. Do you want him arrested, Sarah, if he broke anything?"

Sarah was not amused.

Putting the two boxes, one containing her new gun, the other ammunition, in the glove compartment, Sarah followed Elena's directions to the Westside station, all the while regaling her with the Neighborhood Crime Watch effort. "I've enrolled everyone on the block except this dreadful couple across the street."

"You got any Kleenex?" Elena had finished the tamales but run out of napkins.

"Backseat," Sarah replied. "He had black hair just dripping with some odoriferous hair preparation, a big black mustache, very dark skin, a heavy Hispanic accent—"

"Do I detect a little bigotry here?" Elena asked dryly.

"You do not. He answered the door in his *undershirt*! And he made no effort to put on more suitable attire when he invited me in, which he obviously didn't want to do. And his wife! A young woman with multicolored eye makeup, a ridiculous head of long, curly hair, and a dress that barely covered her nipples. She was wearing high heels, no stockings, and diamond earrings at four in the afternoon."

"Maybe if you invite them over for dinner, you'll get to like them," Elena suggested. She loved to tease Sarah.

"Hardly," said Sarah.

"Turn right here."

Sarah wheeled around the corner and pulled into the parking lot. "He *laughed* when I told him about the Neighborhood Watch. Loudly! He said no man was going to join, especially if a woman was the organizer."

"Sounds like a real prick," Elena agreed, sliding out of the car.

"And their furniture is unbelievably tasteless," Sarah continued as she followed Elena into the reception area. "Perhaps I should have investigated the neighbors before I bought the house."

"Right. I told you not to let Gus stampede you."

"Gus McGlenlevie never in his life made me do anything I didn't want to do," Sarah said stiffly.

"We're here to spring a man named Zifkovitz," Elena said to the desk officer. She showed her badge. Officer Prado made a phone call, and Vincent de la Rosa came out to meet them.

"I do not want to press charges," Sarah explained earnestly. "This was a misunderstanding precipitated by the fact that my security system is newly installed—"

"Our records show that this is the second false alarm, ma'am," said the sergeant. "We take a dim view of false alarms. They use up patrol time that could be devoted to more serious matters."

At that moment Zifkovitz arrived in the custody of Officer Virgie Lezarda. "Neat place," he said to Elena. "I've never been in jail before."

"You still haven't," she replied. "What happened?"

"Well, I used my key—"

"This man has a key to your house, Professor?" De la Rosa broke in.

"That's right," Sarah told him. "Do you have a problem with that?"

"Cool it, Sarah," Elena murmured. She could tell that Sarah was about to give De la Rosa the lady-of-the-manor treatment for daring to allude to her personal life.

"And I forgot to do the keypad thing," Zifkovitz continued. "Then I remembered I hadn't brought the turpentine in."

The eyes of three Westside officers narrowed. "What was the turpentine for?" asked the sergeant.

"To clean my brushes."

"You're painting her house?"

"No, man. Canvas. I'm an artist. And Sarah has great light on the landing of the stairs. So when I went back out for the turpentine, the alarm went off and the door blew shut with my key on the hall table, so I figured I better get in and shut off the alarm before—"

"Before we came and arrested you." De la Rosa sighed and said to Sarah, "Don't let it happen again." He then turned to Elena. "Hear you got the Quarles case."

She nodded.

"Bad luck."

Elena thought so, too. No one in the department was going to thank her if her investigation didn't clear Monica Ibarra and find some scumbag to arrest.

11

Friday, October 25, 10:00 A.M.

As they often did, the detectives attended the victim's funeral, hoping to learn something germane to their case. Every important person in town attended as well—the chief, the D.A., Mayor Eleanora "Nellie" Medrano-Caldicott, who was running against the bereaved husband, state representatives and senators, the local congressman, and even one U.S. senator. A lot of politicians had given up a half day of campaigning, but then the victim's father had been a big political contributor, a power behind the scenes.

Wayne Quarles evidently wielded power in his own right; he'd gotten into the runoffs his first time out. Now, he'd moved up in the polls to within a few points of the incumbent mayor. Local pundits were saying that Quarles had the momentum. The Los Santos *Herald-Post* had predicted last night that Quarles would win and use the mayoral spot as a springboard to higher office. The editorial writer felt Los Santos needed someone to represent the city at the state and national level, which Mayor Nellie didn't, being interested primarily in local issues. Elena wondered whether the writer meant Los Santos needed someone who wasn't female or Hispanic, someone who had money and would, therefore, cut a greater swath in the big, wide, white, good-old-boy world.

Leo had complained that they were wasting their time, that no Diablo Kings or car thieves were going to be at the funeral, but Elena wanted to eavesdrop on the mourners between the service and the burial and afterward at the cemetery when people had a chance to chat. That way she'd get a feel for the family and their circle, in case Hope Quarles's puzzling death wasn't a street crime, an idea that her partner pronounced "nuts." "We've got the car with the thief's marks on it, Ibarra's call for backup, and her description of the gangbanger," said Leo, but Elena didn't want to miss anything through tunnel vision.

The funeral provided several surprises. First, the service was conducted in H.H.U.'s Art Deco chapel by the university's president, Dr. Sunnydale, who claimed Hope Quarles had been a valued supporter of the Hobart Foundation, always generous with her time and money, a loyal friend of the late beloved founder. Elena grimaced. Any connection between the deceased and the university, its TV-evangelist president, and its video-game-king founder added the promise of major nuttiness.

Then President Sunnydale pointed out that the Quarles family, in loyalty to the university, had sent their only son, Wayne Quarles, Jr., to H.H.U. Yeah, right! Elena thought. With their money, they could afford a good school. Sending him to H.H.U. meant that he was dumb or a screwup.

She studied Junior, who had his mother's blond looks but without the sweetness Elena remembered in Hope Quarles's face. He was sitting with the family, slouched on his tailbone in his beautifully tailored black suit, with one ankle resting on his knee, a red sock casually displayed. He looked half-asleep until Sunnydale mentioned a bequest to the university from the "dearly departed."

Heads snapped along the row—the candidate's, the son's, and the Pickentides' of Houston—the latter being Hope's daughter, son-in-law, and two-year-old granddaughter. Elena identified the family from the obit. The child was untying the bows on her shoes and showed no alarm over the mentioned bequest, but her mother, who also resembled Hope Quarles, looked surprised, and Willis Pickentide raised one eyebrow and glanced with a sneer at Junior. Or was he looking at the candidate? Elena made a note: *Check will. Check Junior.*

If H.H.U. was a beneficiary, had someone from the university done Hope in, or hired it done, in order to fill the university's coffers? Vice President for Academic Affairs Harley Stanley had already proved himself willing to overlook an instance of computer fraud when that tolerance was profitable to the institution. But would he initiate a crime, a murder? *Check H.H.U.*, she wrote.

"It was the father of our dearly departed Hope who began construction on our campus, and his company, which became Hope's company, although the dear woman always left business to men and concerned herself with womanly pursuits—the raising of her children, volunteer work—dear Hope was often a chaperon at our university dances. . . ."

Elena swallowed her feminist outrage at the "womanly pursuits" comment and shortly thereafter stifled a yawn. Sunnydale had obviously lost track of whatever it was he planned to say. He was nattering on about the Christmas dance last year, which Elena had attended, although she hadn't noticed any Quarleses there.

". . . a wonderful role model for our young women at H.H.U.," Dr. Sunnydale intoned enthusiastically.

In that case the "dearly departed"—why did he keep calling her that; he sounded like a mortician—must have been very well dressed, for fashion seemed to be the main preoccupation of H.H.U. coeds.

". . . gladden our hearts and the hearts of her grief-stricken family to realize that the dear, departed lady is even now in heaven, perhaps playing a favorite video game with our late beloved founder, Herbert Hobart, whose contribution to the video-game industry is unparalleled in the annals of technology."

Elena had never heard that video games were a feature of

life in the hereafter, but then Sunnydale had once comforted a pair of bereaved parents by suggesting that their daughter was in heaven working away on God's computer.

Strange man, Sunnydale. His California ministry must have been completely off the wall before the IRS closed it down. She had pulled her attention back to the service when Wayne Quarles, red-eyed, handkerchief in hand, got up to eulogize his wife. In Elena's experience the spouses usually kept their mouths shut at services, but with all this big money and big political clout in attendance, maybe he couldn't resist. Elena could see Mayor Nellie, in a nifty black suit and big black hat with veil, champing at the bit. If they'd let her, she'd probably have been glad to deliver the eulogy and cut into the sympathy vote that was heading in Quarles's direction.

". . . I blame myself," Quarles was saying. "My admiration for my dear wife's dedication to the public good prevented me from dissuading her from this dangerous mission, a mission that resulted in her untimely and tragic death."

Whoa, thought Elena. Last time he'd said it was his idea that Hope volunteer. Now he was making out like it was hers. Not that it made much difference, Elena supposed. And what dangerous mission? Citizens on Patrol had been going for a couple of years, and no one else had been killed. *Whose idea was Hope in C.O.P.*? she wrote.

"I trust the Los Santos Police Department will have *some* word for us in the near future as to who—who could have done this dastardly . . ."

Elena scowled. The department was pulling people off other assignments to scare up leads, and what did they have? A gangbanger/car thief with a nose. They didn't even have a description of the nose. What kind of game was being played here? Quarles absolving the department initially, later hinting that the cops weren't doing everything they could, his campaign manager, Fermin Gil, calling for an investigation of the department.

". . . our children, Wayne, Junior, and Wendy Quarles Pickentide; our dear son-in-law, Willis Pickentide, who loved Hope as if she were his true mother; our granddaughter, Willa, fondly called Willie by all of us—" Willie, having finally managed to untie both shoes, had been swinging her legs, which motion sent the objects in question flying just as the candidate introduced her.

One shoe skimmed the coffin, taking a few pink roses with it; the other caught Mayor Nellie in the hat. The mayor got even after the service by holding a press conference during which she showered her opponent with sympathy, then suggested that grief for such a fine woman, Nellie's dear friend Hope, might make it impossible for poor Wayne to continue the campaign. If so, the voters and his many friends would understand if he withdrew.

"We're going to bury her on election day," Fermin Gil announced when he was asked later for a comment on Mayor Nellie's interview. Elena thought this an unfortunate choice of words under the circumstances. "The latest poll figures show we're ahead," said Gil.

"Which poll is that?" asked a TV reporter.

"Our poll," retorted Gil, climbing into a limousine.

Elena wrote *Fermin Gil* in her notebook. It couldn't hurt to check him out.

"You want to attend graveside, too?" Leo asked.

"No, but we're going to," Elena replied.

Chief Gaitan, striding by just then, murmured, "Meeting in my office immediately after the burial."

"Here's where they want to know why we haven't solved the case," Leo muttered.

Elena nodded, hoping the chief never got wind of the fact that her mother was coming to Los Santos.

12

Friday, October 25, 1:30 P.M.

As they waited for the chief, Leo complained, "I never get a real dinner anymore unless I cook it myself."

"So go out to dinner before the dance," Elena responded. "Sarah and I can come at six-thirty."

"Great. Concepcion will love it," Leo agreed enthusiastically. "Say, did you notice at the funeral that the son didn't look like he gave a shit about his mother?"

"Except when Sunnydale said something about H.H.U. being included in her will."

"Right. *Then* he looked upset," Leo agreed. "I saw you write his name down. You thinking we should check him out? Not likely he has connections with the Diablo Kings."

"Still . . ." She shrugged. "Can't hurt to ask around."

"Discreetly," Leo added. "So far the husband hasn't been nearly as nasty about her death as he could be."

Elena had been absently smoothing the end of her French braid while she sipped coffee provided by the chief's secretary. "Quarles is hard to figure," she began, but the conversation went no further because at that moment Gaitan returned, trailed by Captain Stollinger and Lieutenant Beltran.

"Well," said Chief Gaitan, striding into his wood-paneled office, "did anyone else find Wayne Quarles's remarks a little less friendly than they were initially?" Leo and Elena followed their superiors in.

"No question," said Stollinger. He sat down and pushed his steel-rimmed spectacles into place. "First, he wants the public to pray for Ibarra. Now he only hopes she'll get better so he can find out what happened. Sounded like it occurred to him she might be the shooter. And the campaign manager . . . Gil is out for our blood."

"It *was* Ibarra's bullet," Beltran said gloomily. The lieutenant was a stocky, graying Hispanic who reminded Elena of her father, Ruben Portillo, sheriff of Rio Arriba County. "How much longer can we keep that quiet?"

"Until we find out what happened," said Gaitan, tall and handsome in a very Latin way. "I want absolutely no leaks. Is that understood?" He turned to Elena and Leo. "So what *do* we have? What does Ibarra say? And why haven't I seen a report?" He slapped a square hand down on his desk. "Right here. I want a report right—"

"Ibarra says she fired only one shot," Elena broke in before he could work himself up. "And it went wild because she was losing consciousness. That would be the bullet we retrieved from the tire. She says she couldn't have shot Mrs. Quarles because the woman was behind her."

"Do we believe Officer Ibarra?" Stollinger asked.

"She's half-dead, Captain. She'd have a hard time either acting or lying," said Elena, "and she was upset when she found out Mrs. Quarles was dead. She wanted to know why we hadn't told her right away."

"I believe her," said Leo. "Problem is we don't know how it happened. She's described a gangbanger/car thief, but when we showed her mug shots of every Diablo King we had on file, she couldn't ID anyone."

"Could the gang have been using someone new, say some young guy being initiated?" Stollinger suggested.

"She thought he was over twenty," Elena replied.

"How good a look did she get?" Beltran asked. "If she took a hit right away—"

"Someone other than the car thief must have shot Ibarra," said Elena. "I've looked at those crime-scene photos. It had to be someone behind her. Mrs. Quarles could have been shot by the car thief, I guess."

"With Ibarra's weapon?" Gaitan demanded.

"She doesn't remember seeing a gun on him."

"And the prints?"

"Maybe he wiped the gun and put it back in her hand."

"And what was Hope Quarles doing while all this was going on? Why didn't she run?" Stollinger demanded.

"Someone at the head of the alley cutting her off?" Leo suggested. "Hell, we don't know what happened. It's crazy, shooting a cop and a citizen over an 'eighty-four Mercury."

"Well, if you two don't think Ibarra shot Quarles, then you've got to find out who did," said Stollinger. "Pronto."

"We've got three things happening here," said Gaitan, "all worrisome. Fermin Gil is attacking us, Quarles is starting to blame us for his wife's death, and his numbers are going up in the polls."

"Maybe they're playing good politico/bad politico," Elena suggested.

"Meaning?" Gaitan asked, frowning.

Nervously, Elena replied, "Quarles is cozying up to the police union; Gil is going for the I-hate-cops crowd; and both of them are looking for law-and-order and sympathy votes." Did she sound too cynical? Was Gaitan a Quarles supporter? She should have kept her mouth shut.

"It's a possibility, but don't let anyone hear you saying that," said Gaitan. "Whatever's going on, we could end up with a mayor who hates our guts and cuts our budget."

And dumps our chief, Elena thought. Even if Gaitan did lust after Elena's mother, she didn't want to see him demoted. He was a good chief.

"You have the full resources of the department behind you," Stollinger concluded grimly, his buzz cut bristling like a nest of aluminum spikes. "Find the killer."

• • •

When they got back to Crimes Against Persons, Milton Freer of Texas Life & Casualty was waiting for them in the reception area. A short, neat man with colorless eyes and eyebrows, he sat motionless, his hands folded patiently in his lap.

"That's them," Carmen said as Elena entered. Then to Elena: "Mr. Freer, an insurance guy."

Milton Freer rose and produced a business card, which announced that he was, in fact, chief of investigations. "I'm looking into the Quarles policy. My company would appreciate any information you could give us on the death of Mrs. Hope Masterson Quarles."

"How much was she insured for?" Leo asked.

"Three million dollars," Freer replied.

Leo whistled. "Come on back."

They all sat down in one of the small interrogation rooms. "Taken out recently?" Elena asked.

"Two years ago," said Milton Freer.

"Beneficiary?" Leo asked. Both he and Elena had produced their case notebooks.

"Wayne Bartholomew Quarles, the husband."

Elena and Leo exchanged glances.

"I don't want to give the wrong impression," Freer continued. "There is a three-million-dollar policy on Mr. Quarles as well, with his wife as beneficiary. Still, the company always looks into these things. Especially in a case of unnatural death."

"We don't have much to tell you at this point," said Elena. The information he had just given them was more important than any they had dug up on their own. "However, we will let you know if—"

"You have no suspects?" asked Freer, looking more disappointed than ever. "None?"

"A car thief maybe," said Leo.

"I suppose Mrs. Quarles signed a waiver when she became a member of the citizen policing program?"

"I suppose she did," Elena agreed, thinking that the waiver wasn't good for much if Monica Ibarra had actually shot Hope Quarles. The city could be sued by both the Quarles family and the insurance company.

Freer rose. "My company will be looking into the death as well, although we certainly won't get in your way, and any information we garner from our investigation we will turn over to the proper authorities."

"That's us," said Leo.

"The FBI—"

"Nope."

Freer sighed again. "Ah, well. If there is anything we can do to forward your efforts, please call upon us. And we would appreciate any information you could give us—relative to this claim."

"Have you reason to think Mrs. Quarles might have died because of the insurance?" Elena asked bluntly.

"None. But it's always a possibility. Three million. A lot of money."

"They're already rich," Leo pointed out.

"The rich are often more acquisitive than those less fortunate," Freer replied. "Also, those who appear to be rich are not always what they seem. Good day, detectives."

"Was he trying to tell us something?" Elena wondered aloud once the door had closed behind him.

"Or just indulging in wishful thinking?" Leo grinned. "After all, his company stands to take a big hit here. Shit. Three mil. I can't even imagine it."

"I guess we'll have to investigate Wayne Quarles."

"Very discreetly," Leo agreed.

"Yeah. Because of the mayoral race." Elena stood up, then sat down again. "Still, you wouldn't think a man running for mayor would hire a hit on his wife. Especially during the campaign. That sort of thing, if it got out, would be pretty hard to put a positive spin on."

13

Friday, October 25, 6:15 P.M.

"Did you notice the men going into that house across the street?" Sarah whispered. She and Elena were loading Sarah's Mercedes for the trip to baby-sit at the Weizells'. Having missed dinner at home, Elena carried a foil-wrapped meal from Casa Jurado and two cold cans of beer.

Sarah, who had dined on her usual TV dinner, was loaded down with a briefcase containing two books of poetry and a number of classical-music tapes and compact discs—to entertain the little ones, she had explained—not to mention several engineering and computer-science journals, her laptop computer, and the page proofs of an article to be published in January. All of which proved to Elena that her friend had no idea what kind of evening they faced.

In response to Sarah's question, Elena glanced at the three men exiting a metallic-gray car across the street. Then hearing the beep as Sarah thumbed her car security control, Elena opened the door on the passenger side, dropping both beer cans in the process. "Damn," she muttered, juggling the number-three combination dinner.

The beer cans rolled down the driveway into the street. Sarah cried, "Don't put that paper plate on my upholstery," and Elena, scowling, was forced to deposit her dinner on the car roof so she could chase the beer cans to the opposite curb. The three men were laughing.

Scumbags, Elena thought, and scooped up her cans of Tecate. One of the snickerers was ugly, too, she noticed as she took a second look. She was tramping across the street when Zifkovitz exited the front door with sketch pads, pencils, and charcoal. Elena could tell right then who would be doing the baby tending—her—and who would be following their own pursuits during this venture—Sarah and Zif.

"Did you set the security system?" Sarah called.

"You bet," Zifkovitz replied, and dumped his art supplies in the backseat. "No one will set foot in your house without bringing the police down on their unsuspecting heads." He plucked Elena's dinner off the roof and handed it to her once she had climbed into the car.

"Wow, look at this!" Zifkovitz exclaimed, while reading the evening paper and giving a bottle to Leo, Jr. "Didn't you say you were working the Quarles case, Elena? The husband's got a half-page ad in the A section. 'Eliminate Crime on the Streets. Elect Wayne Quarles, the candidate who understands the toll that crime takes on Los Santos families.' And get this. In the bottom corner it says, 'In loving memory of Hope Masterson Quarles.' Am I being cynical, or is that lacking in subtlety?"

"Well, he said his wife wanted him elected," Elena offered. "She seems to be campaigning from the grave." Elena had a bottle popped in the mouth of Angel Jose, who was sucking lustily and drumming his heels on her thigh. Admittedly, his kicks weren't powerful, but if she didn't get the baby back in his crib soon, she'd have a bruise nonetheless.

"I applied for my concealed-weapon permit today," said Sarah. "Stop that!" She was trying to feed baby Sarah, a finicky eater. "Why does she keep turning her head away?"

"Burp her," Elena advised.

"What?"

"Put her on your shoulder and pat her back." Sarah, it would seem, knew absolutely nothing about babies.

Sarah shifted the infant awkwardly. "I've also signed up for the qualifying classes."

"I'll tell you," said Elena, putting Angel Jose into a crib, then picking up baby Elena, plopping her into a baby seat, and fastening the belt. "You made Concepcion pretty nervous with all that talk about guns. She must have thought she was leaving her kids in the care of Bonnie."

"Bonnie who?" asked Sarah, who frequently missed the point of jokes.

"Bonnie and Clyde," said Zif. He propped Leo, Jr., in the corner of a crib, handed him a rattle, and started to sketch. The baby tried to stuff the rattle into his mouth.

"Who are Bonnie and—" Sarah began. "Oh, disgusting! Shame on you." Holding little Sarah away, adult Sarah craned her neck to look at the shoulder of her blouse. Sarah had dressed casually for the baby-sitting adventure—shantung slacks and a beige silk blouse, which now sported a blotch where the baby had spit up.

Elena compressed her lips to keep from laughing at the indignant expression on Sarah's face. "Put a diaper on your shoulder before you burp a baby," Elena advised.

"Now you tell me?" Baby Elena, who had just received a mouthful of puréed spinach, spat it out on her ruffled bib. "Did you see what *your* baby just did?" Sarah asked smugly.

"Sure." Elena scraped the spinach off the bib and spooned it back into her namesake's mouth. "Just because it's good for her doesn't mean she likes it."

"I don't know how Concepcion stands this." Having wiped off her blouse, Sarah was again trying to feed her little namesake. "I never realized how messy babies are."

Before Sarah could expand on her thesis, Elena grabbed the TV remote from the end table and turned the set on. Wayne Quarles's face appeared on the screen. ". . . rampant crime, and my opponent has done nothing to—" Elena quickly thumbed the off button. She didn't need any reminders of the candidate and the particular crime she and Leo were investigating. Without much success.

Sarah had finally managed to get her assigned baby to finish the bottle and, having put the child into a baby seat, was shuffling through her bag of tapes and CDs. "Ah, Mahler's Fourth," she exclaimed. "Let's try this."

"Sarah, why don't you give it up? They didn't like 'The Four Seasons,'" Elena pointed out.

"And they certainly won't like Mahler," said Zif.

Elena was changing the diaper of Angel Jose, who had just shot a stream of pee onto her cheek, as boy babies were wont to do. She wiped it off with a clean diaper.

"Did that child urinate on you?" Sarah demanded.

"They're especially not going to like the fourth symphony," said Zifkovitz. "Mahler was clinically depressed when he wrote it. He never manages to finish any theme."

"As if five-month-old babies would recognize a theme," Sarah said scathingly. She inserted a CD into the appropriate drawer, punched a button, and nothing happened. "I think the university should buy the Weizells some equipment that actually works," she muttered, and returned to reading the instruction booklet. She had played the Vivaldi on a tape player that functioned without incident, although with poor sound quality, according to Sarah.

Zifkovitz now had Leo, Jr., propped up and naked, in the living-room playpen. There were baby containers—cribs, playpens, seats—in every room, much to Sarah's dismay; her first comment upon looking over the house was that every child should have its own room. Elena hadn't argued. Maybe Sarah could get the university to kick in on a bigger house, although Elena thought the Weizells might consider regular baby-sitting more urgent than a house or a new stereo.

"Hold still, kid," Zif said to the baby, who promptly began to cry.

Elena looked over and noticed the puddle surrounding Leo, Jr. "You took his diaper off? For Pete's sake, Zif."

The artist grinned. "People have been painting naked babies for centuries."

"Fine. That means you get to mop up the puddle," Elena retorted. "Preferably before it leaks onto the carpet."

"Sure, as soon as I finish the sketch," said the artist, who had Gabriella drooling on his shoulder and staring, wide-eyed, at his earring while Zif worked on a charcoal of her older brother.

Mahler's Fourth boomed into the room, and baby Sarah woke up and shrieked from her infant seat. "I told you they wouldn't like Mahler," said Zif.

"Well, I'm not picking her up again." Sarah looked down at the red-faced baby. "She ruined my blouse."

"Just remember the diaper on the shoulder next time," Elena reiterated. "And Zif, if you let Gabriella swallow that earring"—the child was now grabbing for it—"you'll have to perform the Heimlich maneuver, because I'm not running the risk of breaking any ribs on Leo's kids." She finished fastening the sticky tabs on Angel Jose's diaper, then checked Elena, Jr., and found that she was wet, too.

"Turn off the Mahler, Sarah," she said, switching Elena and Joey on the changing table. Angel Jose was called Joey because his father insisted that no kid should be stuck with a name like Angel. Leo didn't, however, say that in front of his father-in-law, the first Angel. "Babies like TV and lullabies, not classical music," said Elena.

An indignant Sarah removed the Mahler CD from the machine, covered herself with two clean diapers, and reached down for baby Sarah. "Hush," she said. The baby continued to howl. Sarah picked her up, baby seat and all, and carried her to Leo's recliner. "You can just forget about TV," she said to the baby. "I won't be a party to causing a child your age to become addicted to a mindless form of entertainment." Baby Sarah stopped crying and shoved her fist into her mouth. "See, she agrees with me," Sarah said to Elena.

"No, she's just forgotten what the Mahler sounded like. Turn it on again, and—"

"Gabriella's wet, Elena." Zif added several smudges to his abstract portrait of Leo, Jr., as he spoke.

"How come I have to change all the diapers?" Elena muttered. She carried Angel Jose, then Elena, Jr., to cribs in other rooms, after which she took Gabriella off Zif's shoulder for a diaper change, having thumbed the remote control to catch the beginning of *Homicide, Life on the Streets.* A lot of cops didn't like cop shows. Elena did.

In the recliner, with baby Sarah in the infant carrier beside her, Sarah was reading a Robert Frost poem aloud. The baby had gotten hold of the full sleeve of her silk blouse and was, unbeknownst to Sarah, blissfully gumming it.

When Elena looked up from her diapering, another political ad for Wayne Quarles was running. "If I'm elected mayor," he said, "I promise you, your family won't have to go through the tragic loss that has just occurred in my family. I'll see that well-trained, well-equipped police officers are out there protecting you."

Did he mean they'd get usable computers in the patrol cars? she wondered. A lab so they wouldn't have to wait months on the Texas Department of Public Safety for forensics? If he could swing all this, she'd vote for him. Well, maybe not. Elena had no beef with Mayor Nellie. In fact, the mayor had gotten them a raise.

Taking Gabriella to the sofa, Elena lay down with the baby in the crook of her arm and settled in to watch the Baltimore police, as depicted by TV actors, doing their thing. By the time Sarah had complained for the tenth time about the "intellectual vacuum" on the tube and the ten-o'clock news began, Elena had seen yet another Quarles ad. Two in one hour seemed excessive to her. Or had she just been too busy to notice how often politicians customarily intruded on public recreation?

Elena's pager went off just when Sarah cried, "Look what

you've done to my sleeve!" Having finished another Frost poem, she had discovered the wet spot on her elbow.

Elena called the number on the pager screen. "Detective Elena Jarvis. I was paged."

"Hold for Sergeant Vincent de la Rosa," said the answering officer.

Oh Lord, what now? Elena wondered. "Hi, Vince."

"My men responded to an alarm and caught a woman breaking into the Tolland house. She claims she's your mother."

Elena could hear Harmony's voice in the background saying, "Let *me* speak to her."

Unbelievable, Elena thought. False alarm number three. If Sarah had gone for the dog option, life would be much simpler.

14

••

Friday, October 25, 10:35 P.M.

Sarah refused to let Elena take her car. Since the alleged break-in had been at Sarah's house, Sarah thought she should be the person to vouch for Harmony. However, Elena knew that the sergeant was going to deliver an unpleasant lecture about false alarms to whoever visited the Westside Command to retrieve Harmony. Given Sarah's frustrating evening of child care and her general resentment of the Los Santos Police, who had unjustly jailed her and accused her of murder, not to mention offering her no hope for the retrieval of her computer, Elena decided that a meeting between an angry Sergeant de la Rosa and an angry and sharp-tongued Sarah was a prescription for trouble.

With misgivings, she made the trip by cab, only to discover that Harmony had wasted no time in charming the Westside contingent. Vince, three patrolmen, and the desk officer surrounded her, laughing at her stories of the sixties at Berkeley.

"Will you look at my daughter's aura?" Harmony cried when Elena arrived. "Vincent, do you see auras?"

De la Rosa, looking rattled, admitted that he didn't.

"Stare at her with unfocused eyes," Harmony told him. "If you can learn to see auras, you'd find it very helpful in your work. Aggression, for instance. It stands out like a goat in church. If you see it surrounding a criminal, you can—"

"Shoot him," De la Rosa suggested dryly.

"Well, maybe not shoot him," said Harmony. "You could just disable him. Nonviolently. I'm always telling Ruben—that's my husband, the sheriff—"

"Mom," said Elena, "Vincent doesn't—"

"I've told him a hundred times. The ability to see auras would be invaluable to law-enforcement officers."

"They do that up in New Mexico, ma'am? The cops?" asked a young patrolman, who had been eyeing Harmony's long black hair and trim figure as if she were Miss America.

"I'm working on it, dear," she said with a warm smile.

He blushed. Elena said, "Can I take her home? As Dr. Tolland told you on the phone, my mother's an invited guest. I don't know how she set off the alarm."

"I opened the door," said Harmony, tossing the end of a hand-woven shawl over her shoulder. "No one answered, and it was unlocked. I was astonished when the siren went off, and as I told Vincent, I tried a few combinations on the keypad, but it really didn't help since I don't know the—"

"The door was unlocked?" Elena asked, remembering Zif saying he'd secured the house.

"Your friend Dr. Tolland has a lot of nerve," De la Rosa snarled, "giving our detectives a hard time about that burglary when she can't be bothered to lock her doors. This is the third false alarm. She'll be fined if—"

"I'll have a serious talk with her, Vince," Elena assured him.

"Calm down, Sergeant," Harmony soothed. "Your aura is suffering, and anger is bad for the health and the spirit."

"I'm not angry," De la Rosa snapped, then made an effort to smile. "Ma'am." To his astonishment, Harmony went up on tiptoe and kissed his cheek.

"Mom," cried Elena. The other officers looked envious.

De la Rosa cleared his throat. "You can take your mother home, Detective."

"Thanks," Elena said, and hustled Harmony toward the

door, but before they'd cleared the building, Harmony was exclaiming, "What an absolutely darling young man. Is he married?"

"Mom!"

"Oh, don't be so square, Elena. I think you and the sergeant would make a very handsome couple."

Elena groaned, climbing into the waiting cab, wondering if her former academy classmate had heard Harmony's remarks.

As they entered the house and Elena tapped the security code on the keypad, Harmony was explaining her plans to rid Elena's house of its ghosts and evil memories. "I have an herbal recipe I got from a *curandera* in Truchas," said Harmony. "It's been in her family for centuries, although she says that she herself hasn't the personal power to use it successfully. However, she assures me that your local—"

"Mom, that stuff only works if you believe in it."

"My dear daughter, it will work no matter how you feel about it. Where will I be sleeping?"

"A guest room upstairs."

"Oh, too bad. I was hoping to share your room. Then I'd be able to observe you while you're sleeping. That would tell me whether or not this psychologist has healed your spirit. If you don't want to move back into your house, even after I've had it cleansed for you, it seems to me that you're not—oh, my goodness. No wonder you don't want to move. Look at that view!" They'd reached the window on the stair landing where Zif liked to paint.

"It's not the view, Mom. I just—"

"Well, if it's not the view, we'll fix your house. I'll just drop my bag off upstairs. We need to take the herbs from my truck. If it rains tonight, they could be ruined."

Resigned, Elena followed her mother as Harmony chatted on. "What we'll do, the *curandera* and I, is burn the herbs in a special stone basin. I've brought it with me." Elena checked to see that she had her key before they left the house. Under no circumstances did she want another false alarm reaching the Westside station from Sarah's system.

"If you'll just help me drag this bundle from the truck," said Harmony.

Elena stared at a huge square something wrapped in burlap. "Is that the basin?"

"No dear, the herbs."

"For God's sake, Mom, you'll burn my house down."

"Don't be ridiculous, Elena. We feed the fire for several hours while chanting the proper incantations. Do I have to climb up into the truck bed myself?"

"No, ma'am." Elena sighed and scrambled up to drag the bundle toward the tailgate. That's when she saw the stone basin. "We'll never get this bowl out by ourselves."

"I know, dear. I thought your Lieutenant Beltran could bring his winch over. He was so sweet about moving my loom the last time I was here."

"I'll get Zif to do it," Elena muttered. She didn't want her lieutenant, much as he had liked her mother, to get wind of this weird cleansing ceremony. As she wrestled the burlap bundle of herbs across the truck bed, she said, "At least you can leave the basin in the truck. I don't think anyone would have much luck stealing it."

"Not likely," Harmony agreed. "It's magical. They'd bring terrible ill fortune on themselves if they—well, my goodness, Elena, you almost knocked me over with the herbs."

"Sorry," said Elena, the unwieldy bale of herbs having gotten away from her. Together they lugged the bundle into the house and stored it in the laundry room. The herbs emitted a fairly pungent odor, but Sarah sent her laundry out; she'd never notice the stink in the unused room.

"Well, Mom, I'll bet you're all worn out after your drive and being arrested and everything. You'll want to go to bed." Elena was thinking that she'd better get back to the Weizells' to rescue Sarah and Zif from the babies.

"Nonsense," said Harmony. She was eyeing Sarah's

living room. “Sarah doesn’t seem to have any color sense.”

“Sure she does. She just likes beige and brown.”

Harmony turned to Elena and studied her. “You’re very loyal to your friend, aren’t you, dear? I think I’ll stay up so that I can say hello to her.”

Elena stifled a groan. What was her mother up to now?

15

Friday, October 25, 11:30 P.M.

As it turned out, Elena didn't have to drive back to the Weizells'. Sarah, sounding rather snippy, informed her by telephone that the anxious parents were on their way home. "I simply asked Concepcion why little Sarah wouldn't stop crying. After all, I'd read the child seven poems by Emily Dickinson and sung her several arias from *Martha*. I know you think of classical music as a failed strategy, but *Martha* is very light opera. She should have loved it."

"Did you check her diaper?" Elena interrupted.

"Yes, and it was disgusting. Fortunately, Concepcion called just about then, and since she insisted on coming home, I thought the diaper could wait."

Twenty minutes later Sarah arrived, looking grim, and went straight to the telephone after greeting Harmony.

At that point Elena didn't care what was bothering her housemate; she just wanted to get some sleep, but her mother insisted on fixing Sarah a snack. "She looks positively disheveled," Harmony whispered.

Sarah now had two stains on her blouse and one on her trousers. Her makeup was completely gone, and her hair sported a patch of what was probably puréed spinach. Why had Sarah been trying to feed a baby spinach that late?

"Dr. Millard Fillmore Fong," said Sarah into the telephone, tapping a well-manicured fingernail against the phone base. "Well, wake him up." Again she waited, still tapping. "Millard, I'm disappointed in you." Dr. Fong evidently interrupted her. Elena had lost interest in sleep and was listening eagerly.

"No, it cannot wait until tomorrow morning, Millard. If you were doing your job, you'd have realized that the Weizells need a larger house and a nursemaid."

Elena congratulated herself on being a very crafty woman. Her plan was working.

"Much you know. No woman should be expected to take care of five babies."

Millard Fillmore Fong didn't have a chance—not with Dr. Sarah Tolland on the warpath.

"I know that's the focus of your study," Sarah said impatiently, "but it's inhumane to expect Mrs. Weizell to do it all. Three people would be too few to handle the problems presented by so many infants."

As Sarah had found out by being one of three people trying to care for five babies. Elena tilted her head and smiled at her mother, who smiled back.

"Nonsense. A larger house and hired help are not going to contaminate your results. You just factor in the new coordinates. Don't you know anything about mathematics?"

Harmony nodded to Elena. "Very forceful, isn't she?"

"Marvelously so," Elena replied, happily picturing all the blessings that were about to shower down on Leo and family.

"I do not have a prejudice against Asian-Americans. I have a prejudice against insensitive men."

Humming to herself, Elena went to the kitchen to bring in tea and cookies.

"Believe me, Millard, two hours every Tuesday afternoon does not make you an expert on child care."

Elena placed the tray on the coffee table, murmuring to Harmony, "You can always count on Sarah to get things done."

"I'm sure, dear. I can understand why you admire her."

"Fine, don't take my word for it. In anticipation of that attitude, I've volunteered you and your wife to baby-sit for the Weizells tomorrow evening. You should be there at seven-thirty so they can make the eight-o'clock movie. And Millard, I'm sure you'll find it an eye-opening experience." She wore an expression of malicious glee as Dr. Fong apparently attempted some further protest.

"Then cancel your engagement," Sarah ordered. "You wouldn't want your chairman to think you're more interested in social activities than your research, would you? Not when you're coming up for tenure." Sarah listened smugly for a minute, then said, "I thought you'd want to snap up this opportunity, Millard. They'll be expecting you.

"There." Sarah put the telephone into its cradle with satisfaction. "That should convince Dr. Fong that he needs to improve the Weizells' living conditions."

Since the strategy had worked when she pulled it on Sarah, Elena imagined it would work on Fong as well.

"My dear Sarah," said Harmony, "you're an admirably dynamic woman. And you must be exhausted. Do sit down and have a nice cup of herbal tea and some cookies."

Sarah sighed. "That sounds wonderful, Mrs. Portillo." She followed Harmony into the living room and accepted a cup of tea and a made-in-Chimayo cookie.

"Sit down, girls," said Harmony. "Sit down."

Sarah and Elena, each wanting to protest being called a "girl" but too polite to do so, sat on the sofa while Harmony took one of the tobacco silk chairs and beamed at them over her teacup. "You must both think me very dense."

Sarah looked blank and selected another cookie. "What's the unusual flavor in these?" she asked.

"It's an herb I pick in our meadow. It has powers of spiritual healing. Naturally, I thought that since Elena was still living here, she must still be distressed by that terrible experience with the mountain lion. Silly me."

"My spirit's O.K., Mom," said Elena. "These herbs aren't going to make Sarah sick, are they?"

Sarah paused, a cookie halfway to her mouth. Having been exposed in the past to Chimayo folk medicine, she looked alarmed.

"Of course not, Elena. I wouldn't dream of hurting your . . . friend." Again Harmony gave them a besotted smile. "You could have told me, you know."

"Told you what?" Elena was beginning to feel uneasy.

"About your—ah—relationship. I suppose I should have guessed, but it never occurred to me that you'd changed your . . . orientation."

"What are you talking about, Mom?"

"Your love for, Sarah, dear. And hers for you."

Being a reserved person, Sarah looked uncomfortable. "Elena and I are good friends," she said, "but—"

"My dear, these are modern times," Harmony interrupted. "Lesbian relationships—"

"What?" Sarah gasped.

Elena started to laugh. Trust Harmony to jump to crack-brained conclusions from perfectly innocuous data.

"And I'd be delighted to give you a beautiful wedding."

"Mrs. Portillo!" Sarah protested.

"Oh, goodness, dear, don't stand on ceremony. Call me Mom. You know, I missed being the mother of the bride when Elena eloped with Frank—no wonder their marriage didn't work out—so let's do have the ceremony in Chimayo. I doubt that our priest will let us use the Santuario, but—"

"Mrs. Portillo," said Sarah earnestly, "I don't know why you'd think—"

"That you'd want a church wedding? Of course. I imagine you're an agnostic, aren't you, Sarah? Well, why not a nontraditional exchange of vows in the meadow? I attended many ceremonies of that sort—"

"In your commune days?" Elena suggested. "Before Dad made you stop growing pot by the river?"

"There's no need to bring that up, Elena," Harmony said primly. "No one will be smoking pot at your wedding."

"I hate to disappoint you, Mom, but there's not going to be a wedding." She glanced at Sarah, who looked shell-shocked. "Sarah and I aren't lesbians. In fact, I may be languishing in wallflower country, but Sarah's got a hot affair going with an artist named Paul Zifkovitz."

"I think I'll retire now," said Sarah.

16

••

Saturday, October 26, 9:45 A.M.

Elena sat in her truck as Harmony and Sarah pulled away in Sarah's Mercedes, their mission: to buy a rifle. Sarah had talked of nothing but guns and security at breakfast, and Harmony, never one to sound the voice of common sense, had suggested a rifle or shotgun, for which Sarah wouldn't need a permit. Harmony reasoned that a burglar confronted by a woman with a handgun would naturally assume that if she fired at all, she would miss, whereas a burglar confronted with a rifle would assume the woman was a hunter and a crack shot and give up rather than risk injury.

"Just picture yourself, Sarah," Harmony had urged, "on the stairs, pointing a rifle at the intruder. With that weapon in your hands, your aura alone would terrify the burglar."

"Unless he doesn't see auras," Elena had muttered.

Sarah didn't seem to put much faith in the aura aspect of the argument, but evidently she could picture herself with the rifle and liked what she saw. Elena had visions of the new house becoming an arsenal if Sarah didn't come to terms soon with the loss of her computer. In the meantime Sarah might well shoot herself or an innocent bystander.

Sighing, Elena turned the key in the ignition, her intention to begin a discreet investigation of Wayne Quarles. Leo wouldn't be accompaning her because he was baby-sitting while Concepcion did the weekly grocery shopping. The university had provided her with a secondhand station wagon that would carry all the babies to doctor's appointments or all the formula, baby powder, puréed glop, disposable diapers, baby oil, ad infinitum, that Concepcion charged each week at a store that sent her bills directly to H.H.U.

Elena's first stop was Thomason General, where she dropped in on Monica Ibarra. She or Leo or both visited the officer every day, hoping for more information. Monica was still suffering the effects of having only a lung and a half, partial paralysis, fever from an infection the doctors hadn't yet overcome, and now an allergic reaction to the antibiotics.

When Elena sat down beside her, the young woman's eyes were closed. Sweat beaded along her hairline, and her breathing was shallow and labored. Then her eyes opened, and recognizing Elena, she whispered, "Did you find him?"

Feeling guilty about her daily interrogations of someone so little able to answer, Elena shook her head. "Have you remembered anything else about him?"

"What did I—tell you—before?" Monica's face was strained. "It's so hard—to think."

Elena repeated the elements of the description obtained with so much time and difficulty. When she finished, she added, "Once you said something about his nose, but you never told us what you'd noticed about it."

Monica's eyes closed. "I can't even picture him—anymore. Worries me."

"Maybe it's the painkillers they're giving you."

"Should I tell them—to stop?"

"Not if you hurt." The man was probably across the border anyway.

Monica's mouth trembled into a grateful smile. "When it wears—off—I do—hurt."

"If you're too tired, I can go."

"No. Wanna—help. Funny. Hope saw him—first."

"The car thief?"

"Said—what's he doing? I—happy. Thought—big bust."

Elena wished Mrs. Quarles had been looking the other way. Better Felipe had lost his car than what happened. "Can you remember anything else Mrs. Quarles told you?" Since she was planning to ask around about the family, the husband particularly, she'd start here. "Anything about why she joined C.O.P., or about her husband and kids."

Monica frowned, thinking. "She joined for—him."

"How come?"

"Show—support."

"Support for us? For the cops? Or for him."

"For him. To help campaign."

And Quarles at the funeral had said he should have dissuaded his wife from joining, which was tantamount to denying that he had talked her into it.

"She said—" Monica resumed, "little enough—to do. Couldn't give—money."

"To him?"

"To—campaign."

"Why not?"

When Monica fell silent, Elena wondered if this conversation was fading from her mind as well, washed out by painkillers and pain. "Will," Monica answered at last.

"Will who?"

"Father's."

Elena puzzled over that answer. "*Will* as in money someone leaves you?"

"Yes."

"Her father's will?" Elena searched her memory. "Robert Masterson's will?"

"Don't know—name."

"Time," said the nurse.

Elena laid her hand on Monica's. "Catch you later."

"Later," agreed the young officer hoarsely. The sweat at her hairline was now inching down the sides of her face, and Elena felt guilty and anxious.

• • •

Knowing that Quarles was scheduled to give a luncheon address to a civic group, Elena timed her arrival at his headquarters to miss him and his campaign manager. As she drove, she saw two new billboards promoting his candidacy. Mrs. Quarles couldn't contribute to Wayne's campaign because of her father's will? Now suddenly, when she was dead, paid ads for Quarles were everywhere. Elena heard one on the radio even as she was puzzling over the sequence of events.

Last night there'd been all those ads on TV. If Quarles had the money for this kind of media blitz, wouldn't he have started it earlier in order to catch the absentee voters? In Texas, anyone who wanted to was allowed to vote early at special polling places.

Elena had to park two blocks away and walk to Quarles headquarters, which consisted of a huge front room crowded with desks and telephones, walls papered with Wayne's picture on posters, and a room-length banner hung above three doors. The doors evidently led to private offices. Amigo Man, the city tourism symbol, beamed across the message LOS SANTOS LOVES QUARLES toward a smiling silk-screen image of the candidate at the other end.

An eager young woman wearing a fringed leather vest, divided skirt, western hat, and boots hopped up to greet Elena. On her chest two buttons were pinned. One said, HI, I'M CINDY MALLOW. The second, a large campaign button, announced, QUARLES FOR MAYOR, A REAL WEST TEXAN.

What did they think Mayor Nellie, a native, was? Elena wondered. Or maybe women couldn't be "real West Texans." Cindy handed over a leaflet and asked if Elena would like to volunteer or perhaps ask questions about Mr. Quarles's positions on the issues.

Elena was tempted to ask what his position was on funding free mammograms for poor women at Planned Parenthood. The city council, over the mayor's objections, had canceled the funds appropriated for this purpose.

Instead Elena flashed her identification and asked to speak to the candidate. She was told that he wouldn't be back for at least an hour. Elena said she didn't mind waiting, since the department was determined to discover who was responsible for the tragic death of his wife. As one of two primary investigating officers, she hoped the candidate might have thought of something since they last talked, something that might help in the investigation.

"Oh, wasn't it shocking?" Cindy cried as she provided Elena with a cup of coffee, a campaign button, and a seat by her desk. "Poor Mr. Quarles is just devastated. And so brave to forge on with the campaign." She blinked back tears at the thought of the candidate's fortitude in the face of grief.

Elena nodded sympathetically. "You must miss Mrs. Quarles's help here."

"Here?" Cindy looked confused. "Well, she made appearances at some of the functions and speeches, but she didn't actually come here much."

"Did she make speeches herself?"

"Ah . . . no."

"Help raise campaign funds?"

"She didn't even contribute," Cindy said indignantly. "And she had pots of money."

"Really? Did they ever argue about that?"

"Of course not. They adored each other."

"Well, I don't suppose it matters. I've seen his advertising everywhere. The campaign coffers must be full."

"Yes, isn't it wonderful? At first we had to pinch pennies. Now we're getting our message out everywhere."

"New contributors?"

"I think it's Mr. Gil's doing. He's a real go-getter."

Elena wondered what he'd done so recently to turn campaign financing around. She wandered through the room talking to other workers, drinking coffee, reading campaign leaflets, listening to the volunteers spreading Wayne Quarles's law-and-order message by phone. Had that been the focus of his campaign before Hope's murder?

When she asked that question of a middle-aged male in a cardigan sweater, he said, "Wouldn't you get interested in law and order if your spouse died while volunteering with the police?"

The take on the Quarleses was pretty much the same from everyone with whom Elena fell into conversation: the couple had been devoted; Mrs. Quarles wasn't a particularly active campaigner, but then she was a very private person; she didn't even participate actively in the business her father had left her; it was run by men he had chosen before his death; her interests lay in the arts and education; she was a member of the symphony board, the arts council, the mayor's advisory committee on the public schools, the Hobart Foundation board, things like that.

Elena asked if Mrs. Quarles had been a friend of the current mayor and was told they were friendly acquaintances, although Hope Quarles had fully supported her husband's bid to unseat the mayor, agreeing that it was time for a change, time to make Los Santos a safer place to live. The one other piece of information Elena garnered was the name of a cousin to whom Mrs. Quarles had been close. Then her investigation was interrupted by the arrival of the candidate and his campaign manager.

Wayne Quarles looked surprised to see Elena but not hostile. Fermin Gil, on the other hand, bristled, especially when he realized that Elena had been on their premises for an hour. "We've got a campaign to run here. Why aren't you looking for the car thief who shot Hope instead of wasting the time of Wayne's campaign workers?"

Laughing easily, Quarles said, "Ease up, Fermin." Then, to Elena: "My campaign manager thinks every second taken away from the campaign is a vote lost. What can I do for you, Detective?"

"Just a few questions, sir." Elena was itching to ask why Hope Quarles hadn't contributed to his campaign and how he felt about it, but she didn't want to give notice that she considered him a suspect, even if an unlikely one. Anyway, she could probably pick up that information elsewhere. "We wondered whether your wife had any enemies."

"You can't be serious!" he exclaimed. "Hope didn't have an enemy in the world."

"I see what you're up to," snapped Gil, face red with outrage. "Because she was killed in a street crime, which your officer failed to prevent—"

"How is poor Officer Ibarra?" Quarles interrupted.

"Still alive," Elena answered. She didn't like Gil at all.

"—and you can't find the killer," Gil continued, "you're postulating some conspiracy? Is that it?"

"For heaven's sake, Fermin," said Quarles, "you're the one who's being paranoid." He seemed somewhat irritated with his campaign manager.

Gil, however, wasn't about to be shut up. He gave Elena a contemptuous look. "It won't wash, officer. You'll have to do better than that."

"Detective," Elena corrected coldly, then turned back to Quarles. "Your wife was a rich woman. Wealthy people are resented no matter how little they deserve to be."

"Hope was generous to a fault, and kind. She wasn't killed over money," said Quarles. "Take my word for it."

She may have been generous and kind, Elena thought, but she didn't contribute to the campaign. Elena knew she'd have to get hold of Robert Masterson's will. And Hope Quarles's will. And find out the origin of the new campaign money. Not that she actually thought Quarles had had his wife killed; he seemed genuinely grief-stricken. Fermin Gil, on the other hand—well, Elena had to wonder what he stood to gain if Quarles were elected.

17

Saturday, October 26, 2:05 P.M.

As she was driving to the home of Liz Burke, Hope Quarles's cousin, Elena decided that she should talk to the officers of Masterson Construction as well as finding out about the wills of both the victim and her father, but those interviews would have to wait for Monday when Leo would be with her. He always livened up the dull parts of an investigation. Then another idea occurred to her. Maybe she should talk to Mayor Nellie, reputedly a friend of the deceased. The mayor might provide a different perspective. Elena stopped at a pay phone, called Medrano-Caldicott headquarters, and made a late-afternoon appointment.

Elizabeth Masterson Burke was a widow with a sprawling ranch house northeast of town. Desert trees and cactus in tastefully landscaped groups surrounded the house. Beyond the yard were a stable and a meadow where two horses grazed on nurtured grass, but the land surrounding the watered area was dry and brushy. Mrs. Burke, too, looked dry, thin, and sunbaked, her eyes a faded blue, her hair a brittle gray. She told Elena that her husband had been a cardiologist who dropped dead at fifty-two.

"Massive myocardial infarction. Doctor heal thyself," she said ironically. "My father was an obstetrician. Had a killer stroke at sixty-one. Moral—don't marry an MD."

Liz Burke and Hope Quarles had grown up together, their fathers being brothers. "We've been close all our lives," said Mrs. Burke. She and Elena were sitting in living-room chairs made of distressed oak with plaid cushions. The pegged-plank floors were dotted with handwoven rugs, and a fire burned in a massive native-stone fireplace.

"Hope came out here to ride at least once a week, and I went into town to meet her for lunch and whatever committee meeting we had to attend." Mrs. Burke rubbed her hand on the thigh of her jeans and propped one booted foot against a wagon-wheel coffee table. "I can't believe she's dead. It's like losing half of myself."

"I'm so sorry," Elena replied sincerely.

"I expect I'll grieve longer for Hope than I did for Josh—that's my late husband. He was never home, so it didn't make such a big hole in my life when he died. And it was no big surprise. The man had chest pains and said it was indigestion, told me not to nag him. Can you imagine a cardiologist being that blind?"

"Mr. Quarles seems to be taking his wife's death pretty hard." Elena wanted to steer the conversation into clue-yielding channels.

"Why wouldn't he? Hope adored him; that does wonders for a man's ego. And she aged well. I don't suppose you knew her, but she was still a pretty woman."

"I—ah—saw her."

"Dead? In that alley?" Mrs. Burke shuddered and stared bleakly through a great picture window that looked out on miles and miles of desert. "She didn't suffer, did she?"

"Died instantly," Elena assured her. "Were you implying that—ah—your cousin loved her husband more than he did her?"

Liz Burke returned her attention to Elena. "I suppose so, but that's not to say Wayne didn't love her. For a man who was always focused on himself and his latest deal, he cared as much as he could."

"I was told at campaign headquarters that she didn't

contribute to his campaign or even take a very active role."

Mrs. Burke shrugged. "Hope was shy with strangers. With people she knew she was very warm. To strangers she seemed reserved, I suppose. As for the money—I'm sure she'd have given him anything he wanted if she could, but Uncle Rob's will didn't allow her to underwrite Wayne's projects. She tried to tell the lawyers a campaign wasn't a business venture, which was what her father had meant by 'projects,' but they didn't buy it, so Wayne had to raise his own money." Mrs. Burke smiled wryly. "I'm sure he had no problem. Women all over town are standing in line to kick into the Quarles for Mayor campaign. If Nellie won on the women's vote last time, she's out of luck this year."

"You're saying Mr. Quarles is a ladies' man?"

"Not in the tomcat sense, but women do like him, and he likes them. He's one of those rare men who act like they're listening to what a woman has to say."

"But he isn't?"

"He's just being charming and roping in another female fan. He collects them."

"Did Mrs. Quarles resent that?"

"Heavens, no. She used to tease him about being a flirt, and he claimed his mama told him a gentleman should be attentive to the ladies. Wayne's a southern boy at heart, from East Texas. He and Hope met at UT Austin."

East Texas? What liars politicians were. His campaign buttons labeled him a "real West Texan." Well, back to the case. "What did her father have against him?" Elena asked.

"Business stuff." Liz Burke shrugged. "He didn't like Wayne's style—too impulsive, too freewheeling, too willing to bet the farm. You know what I mean?"

"I suppose," said Elena.

"Hope was the apple of her dad's eye. He wanted her to marry Bud Holmes. Bud wanted that, too, I reckon. If she had, the will would have been different, I can tell you. As it is, Hope is—was—the owner, but with no say in the running of the company, and Bud's the CEO. Wayne's the competition. For all Uncle Rob didn't think much of him as a businessman, Wayne's done real well since he went on his own."

"So I've heard, but didn't he resent the will?"

"Why should he? His own company gets big contracts. I suppose he wouldn't have minded having Masterson's, or the running of it, but I never heard him complain."

Elena didn't see that she was getting anywhere with this line of questioning, so she asked about Hope's will.

"No idea," said Liz Burke. "Since we weren't expecting to die anytime soon, we didn't talk about it."

"What do you know about Fermin Gil?"

"He's a lawyer; corporate, I guess. He's Wayne's lawyer—sort of the rabid-skunk type. Always foaming at the mouth and looking to bite someone."

Elena suppressed a smile. She hadn't liked Gil either.

"I don't really know him very well. I always avoided him at Hope's parties, but someone said he started out—this would have been years ago—as a criminal attorney, defending murderers and drug dealers. Wouldn't surprise me at all."

Elena decided this was worth following up, although, if Gil's connection with the criminal world was really old news, it probably wasn't significant. Besides which, being a criminal lawyer didn't make you a criminal—most of the time. "What about the children?"

"Spoiled rotten," Liz Burke answered, "but Hope loved them. Maternity fries your brains, I guess." She grinned. "I wouldn't know. My husband, the doctor, shot blanks. Probably gave his equipment too many X rays when he was in med school and wanted to diddle the nurses without having to marry one. Did you know med students did that—X-rayed their cocks? Or maybe it's their balls."

Elena tried not to look astonished.

"Doctors' wives know all kinds of medical trivia," Mrs. Burke continued. "Anyway, you asked about Hope's kids. The girl's not too bad. Married rich. Young Pickentide—

hell of a name, isn't it?—his daddy has big Houston bucks, so Wendy can camp out at the Galleria spending the family fortune without throwing any tantrums because she's not getting everything she ever wanted."

"And Wayne, Junior?" Elena asked. The sullen H.H.U. student had showed little grief or even interest at the funeral, except at the mention of a big bequest to H.H.U.

"Currently a worthless pimple on the buttocks of higher education," was Mrs. Burke's assessment. "They had to send him to six different high schools, one a military-academy-cum-reform-school. Then his grades and his disciplinary record were so awful that H.H.U. was his only option."

"Is he dumb?" Elena asked.

"I doubt it. He figures on lots of money coming his way, so why put himself out? He said that to Wayne once, and his father threatened to cut him off. The kid said his mother wouldn't, which was probably true. Hope always claimed that Wayne, Junior, was going to be a fine man once he matured. I figured the chances of his maturing past age thirteen were about zero, but I didn't say that to Hope. I wouldn't have hurt her for the world. She really was a lovely person."

The cousin looked so devastated that Elena wished she would cry and get it over with. She had that air of pioneer stoicism, though, so she'd probably tough it out sans tears, as, Elena remembered, she had at the funeral.

Impulsively Elena laid a hand over Elizabeth Burke's and said again, "I'm so sorry for your loss."

The words were trite, but the sentiment was heartfelt, and Liz Burke responded, "You're a good girl, Detective. I know you'll find out who killed her. If you have the chance, put a bullet in him for me."

Although she wasn't crazy about being called "girl," Elena took it as a compliment in this case.

• • •

On her way back, Elena heard four ads for Quarles and one for Mayor Nellie, but Medrano-Caldicott headquarters was humming when she arrived, and the mayor shook hands vigorously and said, "I hope you're hot on the trail of whoever killed Hope. There was a fine woman."

"You knew her well?" Elena asked.

Mayor Nellie, whose black hair was shot through with bold streaks of silver and permed into short curls from the ears up, shrugged. "A mayor knows the movers and shakers in her community."

"Hope Quarles was a mover and shaker?"

"In her quiet way, she got things done. She was intelligent and sensible, and she had a strong grasp of what was doable, a quality I admire. A lot of things aren't doable in politics or any public arena. Wayne needs to learn that." Then, looking wry, she added, "Let's hope he doesn't get the chance. If he screws up his own business, that's O.K. If he screws up city government, that's a disaster."

"He's certainly doing a lot of advertising," Elena observed pointedly.

"Tell me about it. Must have been saving his pennies for a big push at the end. Hell, I'm the incumbent, but I don't have the kind of money it takes to put my name and face before the public every fifteen minutes." The mayor took a seat behind a desk and waved Elena to a chair. "Not that I expect to lose. There's always a big absentee vote—people who don't want to wait in long lines on election day—and I figure I'll be strong among the foresighted. Then, if we can get the Lower Valley to the polls on November fifth, I'll be O.K. no matter how much he spends. Maybe my margin won't be as big as last time, but I'm not looking for a mandate. I just want to keep the city on track." She gave Elena a wide smile. "Hope you're voting for me, Detective. Don't forget I got the cops a raise."

"I remember." Elena smiled. She did like Eleanora Medrano-Caldicott. "Who's doing the big contributing to the Quarles campaign, would you think?"

"The man's rolling in money; he can provide his own funds," said the mayor. "Unlike me. Being a public prosecutor doesn't net you any big bucks." The mayor had made a name for herself as the first assistant D.A. and then as D.A. when her boss retired and she ran for his office. "It burns me that Quarles is blaming me for crime on the streets. Like I got Hope killed. What a crock! This town has more budget problems than a college kid with a credit card. Still, I think I've put as much as humanly possible into law enforcement. What do you think, Detective?"

"Well, ma'am, there are things we could use—like a forensics lab. . . ." No use missing a chance to get in a budgetary hint. "But I think we do a pretty good job."

"That you do, no matter what Quarles says."

"Actually, when I heard you were friendly with Hope Quarles, I decided I'd ask if you knew of any enemies she might have had."

The mayor looked perplexed. "I thought it was a car thief, a gangbanger."

"Officer Ibarra couldn't ID any of the gang photos we brought in, and believe me, the Gang Task Force keeps close tabs on them."

"How about a wannabe?"

The wannabes, kids who hoped to join and needed to impress the gang with their willingness to commit violent acts, were sometimes the most dangerous of all. "The problem is, wannabes are younger than the man Monica Ibarra described."

Nellie Caldicott sighed. "That makes it hard. Well, enemies. I'd say no. I can't imagine anyone feeling enmity toward Hope Quarles, and I don't know of anyone who did. Much as I hate to admit it, since this is, in a manner of speaking, my town, it must have been a street crime."

"Which makes it hard to close," Elena concluded glumly.

"You thinking someone from across the border?"

"If it were just a car thief, yes, but why the Diablo Kings tattoo?"

18

••

Saturday, October 26, 5:30 P.M.

On her way upstairs, Elena made a detour into the kitchen to hug her mother, who was cooking dinner and describing to Zifkovitz the "charming rifle" she and Sarah had purchased that morning. Fending off a proposal that she give Sarah lessons in marksmanship, Elena hurried off to her telephone, a separate line so police business wouldn't interfere with university business or awaken Sarah in the middle of the night. Elena called Paul Resendez, a reporter at the Los Santos *Times*, to ask if he'd noticed the increase in Quarles's advertising since his wife died.

"Who hasn't?" Resendez replied.

"Is so much publicity usual?"

"Hell, no. People are even talking about it in the newsroom, like, 'If Advertising thinks we're giving him more coverage because of the money, they can think again.' 'Course, our ad guys are having financial orgasms, not only because of the volume, but he's paying up front. No problem with getting stiffed when the campaign is over."

Elena frowned. Ads must take time to prepare. So wouldn't this media blitz have been planned before Hope's death? But the gist of the stuff, the dangerous-streets, law-and-order pitch, seemed fortuitously timely. "Is he advertising more heavily than Mayor Nellie?" Elena asked, checking on the mayor's contention that she didn't have that kind of money.

"No question. Of course, he needs to; he's behind in the polls. You seeing something here? Case-wise?"

"I was noticing all the hype and wondered," Elena replied vaguely. "Do you know much about Quarles? His business? His relations with his late father-in-law?"

"Sure. Listen, if there's a story here, I want it."

"Paul, I'm feeling my way at this point."

"So when you hit on something good, you'll tell me, right? In return for which I'll buy you breakfast tomorrow and tell you all about Candidate Quarles."

The department didn't approve of making deals with reporters, but Elena had done it before—with Resendez. He'd been a good source of information for her since she was promoted to C.A.P. "O.K." she agreed.

Dinner was late, but Elena, Zif, and Harmony sat around drinking beer and eating chili con queso and tostados in Sarah's living room while the chili verde simmered. Sarah drank white wine, nibbled Blue Castillo cheese on French bread, and regaled the other three with her recruiting success. She'd convinced four more families to join her Crime Watch program; that was everyone but the couple across the street, who didn't seem to be home.

"I actually walked around to the backyard to see if they were in their pool, although I'd have considered the weather a bit nippy for swimming," Sarah recounted. "They have a driveway that leads to their garage but also circles the house to a large paved area in back. And two really dreadful dogs. If they hadn't been chained, I truly think they'd have killed me. They must be Dobermans or—or—pit bulls. One of the vicious types."

"Those two don't look much alike," Zif said dryly.

"Well, I don't know anything about dogs." She turned to Elena. "How could you suggest that I get a dog? I'd have a nervous breakdown with a creature like that around."

Elena grinned and poured more beer into her stein. "I didn't necessarily mean for you to get an attack dog, Sarah. You could buy a poodle. Anything that barks would do."

"Poodles are frivolous," said Sarah. "Anyway, I've recruited the whole block except for the people with the wolf pack. We're having our first meeting here tomorrow afternoon with an officer from the Neighborhood Watch program. I'm having the refreshments catered."

"I have a meeting with the *curandera* tomorrow," Harmony interjected. "But I'll certainly be home by afternoon."

Elena groaned at the thought of the *curandera*. "I have a meeting with the press. I don't know when—"

"Elena, I told the recruits you'd be here," Sarah protested. "They're quite excited about meeting the detective on the Quarles case, so I do hope you won't disappoint me."

Since Sarah was housing her, rent-free, Elena didn't suppose she could refuse. With that, they all went in to dinner, Sarah taking one of the new medicines that had come out in nonprescription form and were guaranteed to prevent gastric distress no matter what you subsequently ate, even Harmony Waite Portillo's tongue-dissolving chili verde.

As they were carrying the dirty dishes into the kitchen after dinner, Sarah's doorbell rang. The Fongs, Drs. Mai Liu and Millard Fillmore, burst in, looking bedraggled. Sarah offered brandy, which they accepted with alacrity. Then she asked how the baby-sitting had gone.

Millard Fong scowled at her.

Mai Liu Fong said, "I cannot understand how Millard failed to notice the impossibility of their situation."

"Their situation," said M. F. Fong, looking sulky, "is what I am to investigate. If it changes, I will be studying something different, and not what I have been studying for the past five months. It would not be scientific to—"

"It would not be humane to let unfortunate Mrs. Weizell continue to deal with many babies," said his wife. "It was not humane to drag me, your wife, over there."

"That was Dr. Sarah Tolland's idea," snapped M. F. Fong.

"I spent an evening with the babies." Sarah's smile was ingenuous. "Most instructive. I was sure you'd want to experience the same thing, as you're both psychologists."

"I, for one, do not wish to repeat such an experience," said Mai Liu. "I shall not again sit babies. Anyone's babies. Millard . . ." She turned to her husband, mouth set in a steely line. "Millard wishes to tell you that he will petition university to find Detective and Mrs. Weizell a more roomful house."

"Of course I cannot promise—" Dr. Fong began.

"And Millard has decided to add laboratory requirement to his family-dynamics course."

"Only if the vice-president for academic affairs agrees," Dr. Fong added.

"Each member of class will volunteer four hours of week to study of Weizell household, will they not, Millard?"

"Possibly," said Millard. "If it can be arranged." He pushed his little round glasses up on his nose.

"Students will take notes, assist in care of infants, entertain with suitable educational activities consistent with ethnic heritage." Mrs. Fong nodded smartly, her blunt-cut black hair bobbing. "I will volunteer to design ethnic activities since I am ethnic psychologist."

Whatever that was, Elena thought, wondering what activities a naturalized Chinese woman would consider appropriate for babies whose combined heritage was Mexican-American and Anglo tap dancer. And how would Concepcion react to having a bunch of students visiting her house, messing with her precious babies? Well, she'd probably appreciate a larger house, if Fong could arrange that.

"But we will not sit infants again," Mai Liu Fong concluded.

Millard Fillmore Fong agreed. "I do not think it will be necessary to the project, my peach blossom."

"Do not peach-blossom me, Millard Fillmore Fong," she

snapped. "One of infants spit up purée of green beans on my article for *Ethnology and Inner-city Dynamics.*"

Elena was glad cops never had to read stuff like that.

"It sounds like a very exciting scholarly adventure to me," said Sarah. "Will anyone have more brandy?"

"Do you have much interaction with *curanderas,* Dr. Fong?" Harmony asked. "They're very ethnic."

19

••

Sunday, October 27, 10:45 A.M.

Elena slept late, awakened to a fall wind blowing the fronds of a weeping willow across her window, and rose to dress for her brunch at Jaxon's with Paul Resendez. If he'd chosen to meet her someplace in the Lower Valley, she might have managed to return home too late for Sarah's Crime Watch meeting. But Jaxon's was on North Mesa, close to home.

She parked the truck in front of the red-brown adobe structure with its purple-and-teal trim—Jaxon's latest adventure in outdoor color schemes—and hurried up the steps to the veranda, fifteen minutes late and very hungry. Resendez, a smoker, awaited her in the bar. He'd ordered Bloody Marys and eggs Benedict. Usually Elena resented having her meal ordered for her, but he wasn't a date, he was paying, for a wonder, and she liked his choice, so she let it go. The smoky haze made her feel right at home; she might have been at her desk in C.A.P., with three-quarters of the detectives puffing on cigarettes. How many years before the secondhand smoke killed her? she wondered.

"So Wayne Quarles," Resendez began when they were midway through their drinks. "Nate Camarino, our business editor, says Quarles is the loose-cannon, go-for-broke, entrepreneur type."

Elena nodded and began to take notes.

"Started out by marrying Hope Masterson, then went to work for her dad, which the old man wasn't very enthusiastic about." Resendez lit a second cigarette from the butt of the first. "But then other sources say Masterson wouldn't have thought the president of the United States was good enough for her. And he might have been right. She was a very classy lady."

Their waiter served the eggs Benedict and asked if they'd care for a second round of drinks. "Sure," said Resendez. "Never let your glass run dry; that's my motto."

Elena nodded. She wasn't on duty, and two drinks might mellow her out enough to get her through the Neighborhood Watch party that afternoon.

Resendez cut himself a dripping, delicious piece of his entrée, chewed it, took a drag from his cigarette, and resumed. "So Quarles worked for the old man, ten years maybe, and he wasn't real popular there. Masterson and Bud Holmes—he's the CEO now—weren't the type to take chances. Solid bids, reliable construction—that was the way they operated. Wayne, on the other hand, was always suggesting something that would make a mint if it worked and generate red ink if it didn't."

"Like what?" Elena asked, cutting through her muffin.

"According to Nate, Quarles wanted to build a mall on the Westside. That finally got done, and it's doing great, or at least breaking even—the economic problems in Mexico have hurt retail business all over town. But back then there wasn't the population west of the mountain to make a mall profitable, and Masterson Construction didn't have the capital or the experience to build it. The old man said no. Quarles was pissed, but that didn't stop him from coming up with more flamboyant ideas."

"Which her father vetoed?"

"Every one." Resendez grinned, flashing nicotine-stained teeth. "Otherwise, Rob Masterson treated old Wayne pretty good, once it was obvious Hope wasn't going to change husbands. Masterson paid him good money and gave her a big allowance and a house and car. As I heard it, Wayne took his salary and went into the market."

"How did he do?"

"Don't know. The market was on a long roll, but as I said, he's given to betting against the odds."

"No gossip about his finances?"

"That's the odd thing," said Resendez, stubbing out another cigarette. "He's a high-profile guy in every way except info about his net worth." Resendez stared at her plate. "Aren't you going to finish that?"

Elena shook her head. They'd given her three eggs and all the trimmings. It was a little much.

"Give it to me, then. Unless you've got some horrible, infectious cop disease."

She laughed and pushed her plate across the table while Resendez continued his story. "Then the old man died, and he left it all to her, and all tied up. The company was to continue being run by Holmes and the board, on which Wayne didn't have a seat; Hope did. The profits went into trust. She could spend the money any way she wanted except on any project of Wayne's. If she made a big expenditure, it had to be O.K.ed by the bank and the lawyers."

Elena whistled. "How did Wayne take that?"

"He went out on his own. Got financing—God knows where—and started his own company. Maybe he'd just stayed at Masterson's to please her; I don't know. She couldn't complain about his leaving the company after her father did him that way."

"Well, I've heard he's made a fortune, so maybe her father was wrong."

Resendez pushed Elena's plate away and waved to the waiter. "Now for cheesecake."

"Oh, Paul, I don't—"

"Sunday's not complete without cheesecake." The waiter was sent off to bring dessert, and Resendez continued. "Like

I said, no one knows for sure what he's worth. He's launched some projects that must have made him big bucks, depending on what kind of deal he had on financing. He got in on the low interest rates, so the market for housing was great, and there's been money in town in the nineties—all the Anglo NAFTA and *maquila* execs who don't want to live across the border in Mexico where they work. Take Sussex Hills—"

"Sarah lives there," Elena interrupted, surprised. "In fact, I'm staying in her house. Did he build that subdivision?"

"Yes, ma'am, he did. And I guarantee you, he made a bundle off it. I know for a fact he got the land cheap. Bought it before H.H.U. went in, built on it afterward."

"So why don't you know if he's rich?" Elena tipped her head to the side to avoid a plume of smoke.

"He's had projects that look to Nate like losers. The Trujillo Sports Complex, for instance. Quarles bid low and got it, and he should have made money, but he had bad luck—bad weather, labor trouble, vandalism. He couldn't bring it in on time, and there was a penalty clause in his contract. Every day he went over deadline, it cost him, and he went two months over. That one had to be red ink."

And Mayor Nellie had said Quarles was so rich that he could finance that heavy campaign advertising out of his own pocket. Maybe she was wrong.

"And then there was his Juarez venture," said Resendez.

"I didn't know Los Santos builders had projects in Juarez." Mesmerized, she watched a spark drift onto Paul's plaid shirt and create a small, black-edged hole. He didn't even notice.

"He used Mexican labor, but the contract was his—a country club and a bunch of fancy houses. He figured to sell to rich Mexicans and retired U.S. citizens. Unfortunately for him, the peso dropped like a hawk on a chicken, and the rich Mexicans didn't buy in." The reporter waved his hand, dribbling ashes.

"Then the rebellion in the south and the Salinas scandal—

well, the Americans didn't buy in either. So it's only partially sold, and God knows what kind of shape he's in. No one's even sure where he got the dough to finance it—his own or maybe Mexican money."

"Isn't that kind of thing a matter of public record?" Elena asked. She was doing more note taking than eating.

"He didn't get his loans from banks here, and Quarles Construction isn't a public company. But I'll tell you, if his investors are Mexican, they're hurting. Maybe he's not if he didn't have much of his own money in that project. Anyway, that's what I know about Wayne Quarles. For a wheeler-dealer, which he is, he keeps his finances private."

"What about his marriage? His family?"

"Well, he and Hope were married over twenty years, and I never heard that either of them was getting any on the side. They seemed to be pretty happy together."

Resendez picked up his cigarette and inhaled, which made Elena happy. She hated the smell of smoke from cigarettes burning in ashtrays.

"As for the kids, the daughter's a lightweight, but there's no scandal about her, and I never heard she didn't like her mother. What's not to like? Hope Quarles adored her kids and gave them everything they wanted. The boy—well, he's a screwup. He got a town girl pregnant a couple of years back; he was home for the holidays from whatever prep school or military prison hadn't kicked him out yet, and impressing the hell out of the little high-school girls. His father had to buy her off. Paper wouldn't print it, even though I had two sources. I think the publisher was a friend of Hope's, and no one told her what Junior had done. She'd probably have made him marry the girl."

"Anything else on the son?"

"All kinds of rumors, none that I could substantiate."

"Like what?"

"Fights, drugs, rape, but that's rumor. The pregnant kid is fact. If you're looking for a murderer in the family, I'd choose him, but I thought it was a street crime."

Elena sighed. “I have to cover all the bases.”

“A hit, disguised as a car theft gone bad?”

“Sounds dumb, doesn’t it?”

“Sounds like wishful thinking. Your perp is probably drowning his sorrows on Juarez Avenue and wondering why he went after an old Mercury in the first place.”

“I suppose. You ever heard that Los Reyes Diablos have a branch in Mexico?”

“Nope. If you’re not going to finish the cheesecake . . .”

Elena pushed the plate across the table. How did he stay so skinny when he ate like that? she wondered. Maybe smoking while you ate kept the calories from sticking to your bones.

“So . . . you ever going to date me?”

Resendez brought the subject of dating up about three times a year, and Elena might have considered it, except that the idea of dating a guy who went through life in a cloud of smoke didn’t appeal to her. “Nah, Paul,” she replied. “You’re too cute. You’d break my heart.”

“Story of my life,” he said philosophically, and dug into her cheesecake, fork in one hand, cigarette in the other.

20

Sunday, October 27, 3:55 P.M.

The Neighborhood Watch meeting was in full swing, affluent couples scarfing down hors d'oeuvres and swigging white wine as they told each other that, by God, they weren't letting their neighborhood be taken over by the criminal element. Sarah had bullied every householder within two blocks into attending, except for the socially unacceptable couple across the street, who, according to the general consensus, wouldn't have fit in anyway. Elena reflected that these people acted as if they were organizing a country club instead of a citizen protection group.

The presentation had been made by Officer Bert Krausling, who had been so traumatized by his partner's injury that the brass transferred him to the Watch program. Whoever had been responsible for the death of Hope Quarles and the wounding of Monica Ibarra had a lot to answer for, Elena thought angrily. Poor Krausling, who hated his new assignment, had made an inept presentation at best.

Several women murmured that he was a handsome young man, but surely the LSPD could have found someone more articulate. Didn't the department care about impressions? Couldn't they have sent someone more important, a captain perhaps? This was, after all, a neighborhood that contributed a lot in taxes. It wouldn't have been inappropriate if that charming Chief Gaitan had appeared himself.

Sarah, on the other hand, had given a rousing pep talk and been elected block captain, a post which she accepted graciously. Elena wondered how long Sarah would appreciate being stuck with that nonacademic responsibility. Sarah also displayed her handgun and rifle, advising others to arm themselves as well. Ladies who demurred were given pamphlets on personal protective devices—Mace, pepper spray, stun guns. Although the neighbors seemed intrigued with their new venture into armed self-defense, Elena was appalled. She envisioned them shooting each other. Night and early-morning joggers would be at risk. Offspring coming home from college and teenagers sneaking in after hours would get shot. Husbands would gun down insomniac wives and vice versa.

Harmony then offered to teach householders how to protect themselves in case of physical attack—she didn't mention that her expertise was in protecting oneself from police attack during riots. Elena gave her mother credit for realizing that this crowd, although many were baby boomers, had spent their college years going to frat parties instead of protesting the Vietnam War. However, when Harmony suggested that the guests might be interested in learning to see auras in order to identify the potentially dangerous, Sarah thanked her quickly and hustled her off to serve canapes, while newly recruited neighbors were whispering among themselves, "What did she say? . . . Auras?" Not only was the crowd unsixties; it was not into New Age.

Elena herself came in for a lot of interest. Under Sarah's eagle eye, she fielded queries about firearms with answers that ranged from noncommittal to discouraging. She emphasized the time and trouble it took to learn how to shoot, how badly disarranged one's hair could become when wearing the ear protectors, how politically correct gun-control advocacy was these days. The latter argument didn't carry much weight with NRA members, and there were several, men and women. To them, she couldn't resist expressing spurious sympathy over the organization's growing financial problems.

Many neighbors asked her about the Quarles case and why she hadn't yet solved it. She heard a lot of weird theories as to why Mrs. Quarles had been killed, the weirdest of which was that the killing was a political plot by Hispanics to see that Wayne Quarles, an Anglo, lost the mayoral race to Mayor Nellie, an Hispanic. Elena responded wryly that since the crime had been committed, Wayne Quarles had not dropped out but rather increased his advertising and improved his ratings.

"Well, of course," snapped a portly lawyer. "He's not going to let them get away with it. Bad enough to lose a wife without losing the election, too."

Now, there was a sensitive attitude, Elena thought. She did ask each person who mentioned the Quarles case whether they had known the deceased or her family. The answers varied from "My daughter Jane was a symphony debutante with her daughter Wendy" to "Quarles built all our houses, you know. Deliberately put up a two-story across the street that obstructed my view, the bastard."

The most interesting reply was, "I know the family very well. Hope and I were on the symphony board together."

Elena abruptly abandoned her series of polite nods and uh-huhs to say, "Tell me about them."

The symphony supporter, Norma Grolinger, replied, "Hope was a fine person. She'll be sorely missed by the community and her friends."

"Did she have any enemies?" Elena asked.

"None," Mrs. Grolinger answered without hesitation. "I don't think Hope Quarles ever said an unkind word to or about anyone, and when people were at each other's throats, she could step in and calm everyone down."

"What about her family?" Elena asked.

Mrs. Grolinger rolled her eyes. "Her father was a tyrant and a chauvinist, but there wasn't anything he wouldn't do for Hope, even accepting Wayne, whom he never liked. On the other hand, Robert Masterson never let Hope have any responsibility, even though he planned to leave her that company. She sat on the board, but like Rob Masterson, they treated her as if she were a child. I don't know how she put up with it."

"Do you think the board members or company officers resented the fact that she inherited the whole thing?"

Norma looked surprised. "Why should they? They still have the power."

"And the immediate family?"

"Well, if it weren't that I know better, I'd have taken Wayne for a philanderer, but the truth is, I've never heard even a whisper that he was unfaithful to her, and if he had been, she'd never have believed it."

"The children?"

"As I said, she never said a harsh word to anyone, even Wayne, Junior, although she should have taken a belt to that boy. He was in trouble from the time he was old enough to walk. I remember when he was three. The child stole ten dollars from Hope's purse, gave it to the maid, and had her buy him a mountain of candy. Hope found out about it when he threw up on an absolutely gorgeous sofa she'd bought at Charlotte's. It was brand-new and had to be reupholstered. Then, instead of spanking him, she sat him down and gave him a very serious lecture on the evils of thievery and betraying the trust of one's family.

"Much good that did. The boy's amoral. He's always done exactly what he wanted without the slightest consideration for anyone. And Hope was probably still trying to turn him around with gentle persuasion to the day she died, not to mention talking his father into helping him toward decency by bailing him out of whatever trouble he'd gotten into."

"Could you tell me more specifically what—"

"I certainly could not. I shouldn't be gossiping at all. Especially to a detective."

"But, Mrs. Grolinger, I'm investigating—"

"I don't know what I was thinking of. Hope's probably turning over in her grave." The lady turned, dragged her husband away from a discussion about guns with Sarah, and left.

Elena made a mental note: Follow up on Wayne, Jr., family scumbag.

21

Monday, October 28, 6:53 A.M.

"I don't think I can eat chilis so early in the day," Sarah confessed, staring at Harmony's huevos rancheros.

"Nonsense." Harmony sat down to her own breakfast.

From the window of the dining nook, Elena was staring across the valley to the mountains, where sunlight, having crept over the Franklins to the east, cast a rosy mist into the western darkness.

"Once I get the cleansing set up with the *curandera,* do you girls want to attend?" Harmony asked.

"No." Elena had dragged her attention from the window.

"Thank you, Harmony," Sarah replied less abruptly, "but my experience with *curanderas* hasn't been—"

"One little mishap?" Harmony laughed. "Believe me, our local healer will never again give that purgative to an Anglo visitor."

"Sarah, do you know a student named Wayne Quarles, Junior?" Elena couldn't get her mind off the case.

Sarah shook her head and rose to answer the telephone.

"Do you need my help, dear?" Harmony asked. "You seem to be obsessed with this Quarles case."

"Oh gosh, Mom, the whole department's working it. I don't think you need to pitch in." The last time her mother got involved in one of her cases, there had been a near riot at headquarters, orchestrated by Harmony. If the chief hadn't fallen for her mother, Elena would probably have been on his shit list for the rest of her life. And then Harmony almost managed to get herself killed by the suspect, so no, Elena didn't want the help of her beautiful, if eccentric, mother. "But I appreciate the offer, Mom."

"Excellent," Sarah said to the caller. Then she returned to her breakfast, chuckling. "Dr. Fong called the vice-president for academic affairs yesterday about a larger house for the Weizells," she informed Elena. "The administration is talking six bedrooms." Taking a sip of orange juice, she added smugly, "I do believe I handled that perfectly, sending the Fongs over there to baby-sit Saturday."

And I handled you just right, Elena thought, grinning. Sarah's Friday night with the Weizell quintuplets had been the yeast that made the whole plan rise.

As soon as she got to work, Elena told Leo he was about to acquire a bigger house.

"Like I could afford one," was Leo's response.

"Well, H.H.U. can," Elena retorted. "And at the suggestion of your guardian angel, Dr. Sarah, Millard Fillmore Fong has talked the university into paying for a Weizell family, multibedroom extravaganza." Leo looked thunderstruck and wanted more information, but Elena had a call in to a detective in Fraud and Forgery, requesting a check on Wayne Quarles's campaign finances. Everyone in the department had been told to lend a hand on the Quarles case if asked. "He was running a moderately expensive campaign before his wife died. Now he's spending money like crazy. We want to know where it's coming from, Brady."

"I'll get back to you," Brady Fister promised.

Leo called Darrell Mindenhoff, Hope Quarles's lawyer, about her will. Elena thought it interesting that Fermin Gil, Wayne's lawyer, was not Hope's as well. "He says they're reading the will this afternoon at his office and we should come on over," Leo told Elena.

"Good. If there are surprises, we'll see how the heirs react." She tapped her teeth with a pencil, thinking. "Let's visit Bud Holmes, the CEO at Masterson Construction. Since Hope's father didn't like Wayne and once wanted her to marry Holmes, maybe we can find out how much she was making from the company and how her father's will read."

Masterson Construction was housed in a three-story glass rectangle on Lomaland with a cement extension that looked like an airplane hangar. Not much of an advertisement for their product, Elena thought, even if they did do business all over the Southwest. Maybe they'd rather keep costs down than make a fancy impression. Not a bad idea, when you thought about it. She'd just read that the average Los Santos house cost around seventy thousand, but most local citizens couldn't afford to buy one.

They were shown into a functional office—major floor space, industrial carpet, metal furniture—and greeted by a burly man with a bald head and square, tinted bifocals. "I can spare you fifteen minutes," he announced. "Then I gotta be at a zoning commission meeting."

"Don't you have flunkies for that sort of thing?" Elena asked.

"Rob Masterson was a hands-on kind of president. I'm doing my best to run the company the way he did. That what you're interested in? The way I run Masterson's?"

"No, sir," said Elena. "We're interested in the death of the owner."

Holmes's face darkened. "No better woman ever lived than Hope Quarles. If it would help, we can put up a reward for information leading to an arrest and conviction."

"Rewards bring out all the crazies," said Leo. "Then we spend our time running down false leads."

"You got any leads?" Holmes watched Leo shrug. "You're not at liberty to say, right? Well, no one here killed her. Hope was like everyone's daughter. Knew everyone's name.

Great lady." He looked wistful, as much as a man with a square, jowly, weather-roughened face could.

"What was the problem between her husband and father?" Elena inquired.

"Why do you ask that? Because Rob left all the money to Hope? She was his kin, not Wayne."

"I understand that he left it so she couldn't spend any on Wayne," said Elena.

"It was Rob's money. He could leave it any way he wanted, and he wanted her to have it. Every penny."

"Sounds like he didn't trust Wayne," said Leo.

"He didn't," Holmes admitted. "Man's all flash and no substance. A gambler. Not on the horses or anything like that. In the construction business."

"But he seems to have done very well."

"Maybe." Holmes's face closed.

"What can you tell us about his company?" Leo asked.

"Can't. Doubt anyone can except Wayne and his accountant. If I had to guess, I'd say he's in debt, but I don't know that. Precious few people do. Maybe Hope, but I wouldn't even bet on that. Why are you asking about Wayne? I thought a criminal shot her."

"Did her father's will indicate what would happen to his money after her death?" Leo asked.

"My God!" Holmes exclaimed, his blocky face flushed. "You think Wayne killed her for the money?"

"We didn't say that," Elena hastened to assure him. "We have to cover every avenue, and you haven't answered—"

"The restrictions on how she could spend the money only applied to her lifetime. Don't reckon Rob figured Wayne to outlive her. Who would?"

"So she could leave it to anyone she wanted?"

"Jesus, if that self-centered bastard had her killed—"

"We have absolutely no evidence that points that way, sir," said Leo. "What was her income?"

"Most years about three hundred thousand from Masterson's. A lot of the profits go back into the business and into employee bonuses—her idea—and some goes to charity." Holmes looked at his watch. "I'm late." He strode toward his door, suit jacket straining across wide shoulders. "If you think Wayne had anything to do with her death, you tell me. Got that? Even if you can't arrest him, we'll run him out of the business." He flung open the door, leaving them in his office. "Drive him right into bankruptcy," he muttered. "No reason not to now that Hope's gone."

"Not one of Quarles's fans would be my guess," Leo murmured dryly as they followed the Masterson CEO out the door.

"Hope he keeps his mouth shut about this interview. We're supposed to conduct this inquiry discreetly," Elena murmured back. Her beeper went off, and she borrowed a phone from the receptionist.

"Brady, you got something already?" she asked.

"Yep. What I got is this guy really wants to be mayor. God knows why. It don't pay that much. Anyway, he just put a hundred and seventy-five thousand into his election fund."

"From where?" Elena asked.

"He borrowed it from Border National."

"On what collateral?"

"This is probably what you were looking for. He borrowed on a short-term note against the insurance policy on her life—the late Mrs. Quarles."

Elena whistled thoughtfully and told Leo once they were back in the car.

"Still doesn't mean he killed her," said Leo. "Just that he had a motive, although why you'd kill your wife to get elected is beyond me, and like you said, it doesn't seem like a very smart thing to do in the middle of a campaign when Nellie's people are watching your every move."

"Well, it's something." Elena frowned, thinking. "Now we know for sure that he didn't have the money for this big publicity push until Hope died. So if we can tie him to a gangbanger stealing a car . . ." She sighed at the difficulty of that.

"Or to Monica Ibarra."

"Come on, Leo," Elena said uneasily. "Don't say that."

"Well, if we're figuring a mayoral candidate and rich-guy contractor for hiring a hit, it's no bigger stretch of the imagination to figure a cop for the hit man."

"Woman. And I never heard of a hit woman."

Leo grinned at her. "You're always telling me that women can do anything men can. Anyway, I saw a movie about two hit guys, man and woman. They fell in love."

Elena grinned back. "Only in the movies." She headed onto Lomaland toward the interstate. "Let's go see what we can find out about Wayne, Junior. If you think people don't like the father, you should hear what they say about the son." She repeated some of Norma Grolinger's remarks.

"Sounds like a typical H.H.U. student to me," Leo quipped.

"Sarah didn't know anything about Junior. Think I'll ask Bunky Fossbinder," Elena mused. She had amusing memories of Bunky from several of her H.H.U. cases.

"What kind of name is that?" Leo demanded. "We put him on the stand in court, and the jury would fall off their seats laughing."

22

Monday, October 28, 1:05 P.M.

Bunky Fossbinder, who knew the victim's son, said Junior had a nose problem, a euphemism for heavy cocaine addiction. One of Bunky's fraternity brothers described Junior as someone you wouldn't let your sister date because he never took no for an answer.

The fraternity brother referred Leo and Elena to the president of the Feminist Coalition, Collie Reed, who said Junior Quarles had been blackballed by her group, which meant he couldn't get a date with any of the coalition's members or anyone else they warned off. Elena asked if Collie knew any girls who might be blackmailing Junior or threatening criminal charges or a civil suit. Collie Reed grinned and replied that they had ways of taking care of his kind without causing scandal. She did suggest that the detectives check the high-school girls Junior had been dating now that he couldn't get a date on campus. Unfortunately, she couldn't provide names.

Happy Hobart, the founder's nephew and president of the senior class, provided the most useful information. He said Junior was in hock to his eyeballs with his dealer, not a healthy situation. The dealer's name was Paco, but Happy thought that was an alias because the guy was Anglo. He didn't know how to get hold of Paco because Happy himself didn't do drugs, being of the opinion that drugs interfered with an entrepreneur's ability to turn a profit, not to mention wasting money that could have been put to profitable use.

"What's your latest scam, Happy?" Elena asked.

"No scam." Happy was indignant. "My safe-sex dating service is a huge success. Why, I could quit school right now and make more money than I'd know what to do with. I've got a national computer network, and I'm thinking of going public, selling stock, you know?"

"What the hell was he talking about?" Leo asked later.

"It's a computer dating service. Everyone on their list has been tested for sexually transmitted diseases, including AIDS. They're matched up by sexual preference, or maybe I should say sexual peculiarities. I gather it's a sort of pornographic fantasy land."

"Is that legal?" Leo asked, appalled.

By three that afternoon the detectives had stopped at headquarters to write reports on their computers, eaten at Pizza Hut, listened to four Quarles ads on the radio, seen three Quarles billboards, checked on Monica Ibarra, who was no better and hadn't remembered anything, and presented themselves at the offices of Mindenhoff & Ball, attorneys-at-law, whose environs included paneled walls, glass-fronted bookcases holding weighty legal tomes, carved mahogany furniture, maroon leather upholstery, gray-haired secretaries, and a general air of hushed solemnity.

Gathered in the conference room were Wayne Quarles, his two children, his son-in-law, Hope's cousin Elizabeth Burke, Drs. Sunnydale and Stanley of H.H.U., Fermin Gil, three lawyers from Mindenhoff & Ball, two middle-aged Hispanics, whom no one introduced, and Elena and Leo, whose presence was immediately questioned by Gil.

Darrell Mindenhoff, a tall, thin man between fifty and sixty with an amazingly large, round face fringed by thinning silver hair, clapped Gil on the shoulder and boomed, "Why, they called to ask about the will this morning, so I told them to come along."

"Outrageous," Gil snarled.

"Nonsense. The will has to be filed in probate court. It will be open to public scrutiny, so I can't see the least harm in cooperating with—"

"They're asking questions all over town about the family. Someone from the LSPD has been nosing into Wayne's finances; these two talked to Bud Holmes at Masterson's; they've asked questions about the boy at the university."

How did he know that? Elena wondered, shocked at the rapidity with which information got back to Gil. He was talking about interviews they'd conducted that morning, for Pete's sake.

"They've talked to Hope's friends and relatives. Isn't that right, Liz?" Gil turned an accusing look on Liz Burke.

"Are you spying on me, you little vermin?" snapped Mrs. Burke. "I'll bet you got called that a lot when you were a kid. Fermin the Vermin."

"What are you saying, Fermin?" Quarles demanded, looking shocked.

"I assure you, sir, if anything untoward happened at the university," Vice-President Harley Stanley began, "the administration had nothing to do with it. Young Wayne is one of our outstanding students. I'm sure nothing was said about him. . . ."

The vice-president obviously had no idea what Junior was outstanding for, Elena thought. She said, "Our inquiries are entirely routine."

"I don't understand why you'd be making any inquiries at all," said Wayne Quarles. "You know who shot my wife. Do you imagine that someone in the family would dress up as a gang member to—to—I'm appalled. Detective, I am truly appalled. And insulted. I—"

Darrell Mindenhoff cleared his throat. "We do have a will to read here. Perhaps, gentlemen—and ladies—you could discuss the investigation later."

"We certainly shall," said Quarles, his glance fastened on the detectives. Leo shoved his hands into his pockets and shifted his feet. Elena stared back as she sat down in one of the chairs placed against the wall. She chose her position so that she could see the faces of Quarles, Fermin Gil, and Junior when the will was read.

Darrell Mindenhoff sat at the head of the long conference table, towering over the group in skinny solemnity. "Before we begin, I would like to say that I, for one, have known and admired Hope all my life and feel her death deeply." He drew a handkerchief from his breast pocket and patted his lips. "Given the fact that we pride ourselves in being a Christian law firm, and considering the devotion that everyone in this room had for Hope," he resumed, "I think a prayer for the soul of our late, beloved friend Hope Quarles would be in order. My partner, Harold Ball, will—"

Before the partner could offer the requested prayer, President Sunnydale stood and boomed, "I shall be glad to oblige. Dear Lord, if it be Thy will, accept the soul of our dear, most gracious, and generous patroness . . ."

Another loud voice heard from, Elena thought. Sunnydale could go on for hours, if her past experience with his prayers was any indication. Wondering if other lawyers introduced will reading with a prayer, she closed her notebook and bowed her head. A Christian law firm? What did that mean? They tithed? They were all born-again?

". . . adored wife, cherished mother, a woman who devoted herself selflessly to the good of her family and community. Find for her in heaven, O Lord, a place close to the holy throne. Comfort us in our bereavement that she was torn so untimely and tragically from our bosoms."

Elena, studying the faces on the far side of the table, saw a tear slip down the husband's cheek. You had to be pretty grief-stricken to be moved by a prayer spoken by a TV evangelist, she decided. Maybe, in chasing information about Quarles, she was barking up the wrong tree.

But the son—the little bastard actually drummed his

fingers, although soundlessly, on the table. Was he hopped up on cocaine right now? And how much were the dealers into him for? The gangs dealt drugs. He might have used his dealer to arrange the death of his mother. He could have told his creditors that when he inherited, he could pay off his debts and be in nose candy for the next fifty years. Elena wondered how much he expected to get from the estate. Her eyes moved to Fermin Gil; the man was scowling at her.

"Amen," President Sunnydale finished. The others echoed him, and Darrell Mindenhoff opened his folder. Not some manila or clear plastic artifact: a folder at Mindenhoff & Ball was tooled leather with a partnership crest on the cover.

"Ahem." Mindenhoff's signal that the important stuff was about to commence. And then he began to read the will. The Hispanic couple, who had evidently been in the nature of family retainers for about forty years, received an annuity; the woman wept and murmured in Spanish to her husband that *"la señora"* was an angel. There were gifts to favorite charities. Hope Quarles had left the Los Santos Symphony and the arts council generous bequests. She willed her cousin Liz a number of cherished family mementos: jewelry, silver, art objects, quilts, and a mother-of-pearl inlaid table that had belonged to their mutual grandparents. H.H.U. was generously remembered.

Hope's grandchild and daughter came in for a big chunk of money. Wendy Quarles Pickentide turned to her husband and said two words: River Oaks. Elena supposed Miss Wendy wanted a house in that exclusive area of Houston, but why didn't they already have one if Willis Pickentide was so rich? The son-in-law scowled at his wife, but Wendy looked adamant and very pleased with herself.

" 'To my son, Wayne Quarles, Junior,' " read Mindenhoff, " 'a trust fund containing a quarter of my holdings in Masterson Construction, to be administered by the trustees Darrell Mindenhoff, Harold Ball, and my husband Wayne Quarles, one third of the profits to be dispersed yearly—' "

"One third!" cried Junior. "How come Wendy gets hers and mine's tied up? How much does that amount to a year?"

Mindenhoff stared at him disapprovingly over the top of narrow reading glasses, which he had put on before opening the leather folder. "Around sixteen thousand a year," he said. Junior turned pale. "Now, if I may continue." Mindenhoff cleared his throat again. "'. . . dispersed yearly beginning at the end of the year following my death.'"

"Next year? I've got to wait fourteen months until—"

"'Until my son reaches the age of thirty-five,'" Mindenhoff continued, "'at which time the trustees will consider running the trust for another ten years or relinquishing control to my son.'"

Well, Hope Quarles may have adored Junior, but she'd seen his faults, Elena realized.

"She must have been crazy! She must have hated me!"

To Elena he looked both panic-stricken and furious.

"She loved you, you ungrateful twerp," said Liz Burke.

"I want to contest the will."

"Do you have the money for futile legal suits?" Mindenhoff asked smugly. "I assure you, young man, that no one has succeeded in breaking a will that I drew up. Now, with your permission . . ." He looked toward the candidate, who nodded graciously.

Wayne, Jr., muttered, "Bitch," under his breath.

"Oh, you're disgusting," hissed his sister.

"Why? You got your money up front."

"Shut up, Junior," said his father.

The lawyer signaled again with a discreet throat clearing. "I might point out that the following are Hope's very words. 'To my beloved husband Wayne, whose success in the construction business has made me so proud and whose devotion has given me so much happiness, I leave the remainder of my estate—'"

Quarles smiled—the sort of fond, humoring smile that men gave women to whom they offered little responsibility but much approval for their womanly devotion. Elena felt like gnashing her teeth.

"'—for his enjoyment. I hope that, should he survive me, he will retire and use this money for all the frivolous and delightful pursuits he has forgone in the interest of building his business. Darling, you showed them all. Now reap the benefits of your hard work and my love. To this end, but for different reasons, I honor my father's original will in specifying that this money is to be spent for leisure pursuits and good living as opposed to business pursuits, which have caused you, my dear, so much stress over the years. You hid it well, but I, your devoted wife, know how many times you have been worried and overworked.'"

Elena was watching Wayne Quarles very closely as this extraordinary bequest was read. He showed absolutely no emotion. His face was as blank as a movie screen when the evening's entertainment was over. Of course, Wayne had the three mil from the insurance policy—or would have it soon. He'd already borrowed against it. But she couldn't see him retiring and sailing the seven seas on luxurious cruise ships. And what about Hope Quarles? What had she been thinking when she concocted that extraordinary will? Elena wondered if Mindenhoff had been privy to his client's feelings.

23

Monday, October 28, 6:00 P.M.

"After the sports, they're going to broadcast an interview with your victim's husband," Zifkovitz called from the living room. Sarah had her television tucked behind heavy teak doors in a giant, wall-hogging entertainment center. "He's making some big announcement."

Elena wondered if Quarles, having found that his inheritance money couldn't be spent on the campaign, was announcing his withdrawal. Dropping wearily onto the beige sofa, she stuffed a tobacco silk pillow behind her back and let Zif pour her a margarita from a crystal pitcher. If Quarles withdrew, Mayor Nellie Medrano-Caldicott would be happy. "Where's Sarah?" Elena asked.

"Setting up patrols." He grinned. "She's packing heat."

Elena groaned as the TV sportscaster blathered on about some Dallas Cowboys scandal.

"She took the rifle because she hasn't got her concealed-weapon permit. Rifle's too big to conceal."

"Unless she puts it in a golf cart." Elena took an appreciative sip from her cocktail glass. "I'm not too crazy about modern art—"

"Philistine," he interjected.

"—but you make a terrific margarita."

"I'm a Renaissance man," said Zif.

"Ladies and gentlemen," said Quarles on the TV, "I'll preface my remarks by pointing out that I have been extremely patient with and supportive of our police department, especially under the circumstances of my wife's tragic death."

Elena sat up, plunking her cocktail glass on a coaster—woe be unto the careless person who left a water ring on Sarah's furniture. Obviously, Quarles was about to say that he intended to be patient and supportive no longer.

"In return, I'm sorry to say that certain elements in the police department have been deceitful, secretive, and hostile." He shook his head. "I do not think that I or my family deserve such treatment in our time of grief."

The reporters hurled questions at the candidate, who was giving the interview at his headquarters, where his handsome face repeated itself endlessly on every wall, as if Quarles were being mirrored everywhere in varying emotional states—smiling, looking solemnly dignified, determined, pensive, even modestly amused.

"Let him speak!" Fermin Gil shouted.

"Important forensic evidence has been withheld from us. Evidence that changes the whole complexion of my wife's murder. The bullet that killed my Hope did not come from the gun of the car thief, as we have been led to believe."

He paused for dramatic effect, and Elena took a deep, nervous breath.

"It came from the gun of the police officer on the scene. Officer Monica Ibarra shot my beloved wife."

The question was, how had he gotten that information? The department had been keeping it absolutely under wraps until they had some idea of what really happened.

"For whatever reason, Officer Ibarra—"

What the hell did he mean by that? Was he insinuating that Monica had gunned Hope Quarles down on purpose?

"—killed my wife with a bullet through the heart, and we were not told. The Crimes Against Persons detectives and their superiors have been engaging in a cover-up of the worst kind, deceiving both the public and the bereaved family in an attempt to protect one of their own."

Bull! Elena thought angrily.

"Perhaps more appalling, in the attempt to protect the killer, the detectives in charge have targeted not the person whose bullet killed my wife, but us, Hope's family. It has come to my attention that my campaign finances and my business records are being scrutinized. Our friends, relatives, and business associates are being questioned. Students at the university are being asked unfriendly questions about my son at a time when he is too grief-stricken to defend himself. We are, in a word, *suspects*!"

His voice was charged with outrage. If he had nothing to do with his wife's death, and Junior was innocent as well, Elena could understand why he'd feel that way, but it appeared to her that his outrage was somewhat disingenuous: he was, in effect, making a campaign speech. By holding his press conference at campaign headquarters, he reminded voters that although he'd lost his wife and was being scrutinized by the police at the worst period of his life, he was still a candidate for mayor. And there were plenty of voters out there who had beefs with the department: everyone who'd ever had a traffic ticket, everyone whose house had been robbed and the burglars never caught, the belongings never retrieved. If Sarah were watching, she'd probably decide to vote for Quarles.

"We, the victims, are being made into suspects. Well, I, my fellow citizens, do not intend to take this deception quietly. I will not withdraw from this election under a cloud. Instead, I tell you here and now that I shall do everything I can, within the bounds of gentlemanly conduct, to win this election, to win for Hope, who supported my candidacy with all her heart—"

But not her money, Elena thought.

"I dedicate my campaign to Hope, God rest her soul, and to much-needed reform in the police department."

The other shoe had dropped. With a big, loud clunk. If Gaitan was listening, he'd probably just turned pale.

"I hope all who are listening will support us in this campaign for a more honest, more humane police department. The average officer on the street is, I have no doubt, a fine person and a dedicated public servant, but where corruption and double-dealing exist, it must be rooted out. I hope that you will go to the polls on Tuesday, November fifth, and vote your consciences."

Quarles thanked the audience—campaign workers cheering loudly, reporters shoving their mikes in his direction, shouting queries. He fielded no questions. A cordon of supporters cleared the way through the crowd so that he could leave. Fermin Gil, however, stayed and said something, in response to a reporter's question, that sent a shiver up Elena's spine. "Who do you think is behind the cover-up, Mr. Gil?" the TV reporter asked.

"Oh, I can tell you that. The lead detective on the case is a woman named Elena Jarvis."

What about Leo? He was on the case, too.

"Everyone knows she's a radical feminist."

I am? She blinked, never having thought of herself in those terms.

"And Monica Ibarra, the cop who shot Mrs. Quarles, is a woman. Jarvis is protecting another female cop. She ought to be suspended, and I promise you that I'll be on the line to Chief Gaitan about just that matter as soon as I can get my hands on a telephone. Keeping that a secret—the origin of the bullet that killed Hope Quarles—is inexcusable. Harassing the Quarles family is even worse. There's a political agenda here. You can bet Detective Jarvis is a supporter of Nellie Medrano-Caldicott, another woman. Well, the voters will see through this. They'll see that the woman who should have been protected was Hope Quarles, and the man who should be supported is her husband."

"Sounds like you're in deep shit, kiddo," Zifkovitz observed. "Did the cop really shoot her?"

"We don't have a clue," Elena replied moodily. "The point no one mentioned is that Ibarra was shot, too. Who shot her? Hope Quarles? The scenario that makes the most sense is that someone else shot them both."

A reporter at Mayor Nellie's campaign headquarters asked the incumbent for comment on the Quarles statement. "If the police are at fault, we'll look into it," said the mayor. "And I resent Fermin Gil's implication that I am somehow involved in a cover-up with political motivation. I'm upset about Hope Quarles's death myself."

Thanks, Nellie, Elena thought angrily. A little support would have been nice.

"If the Quarles campaign is blowing political smoke, we'll find out about that, too." The mayor looked grim.

The news anchor announced that Chief Armando Gaitan was unavailable for comment. "No one's asked me what I think," Elena seethed. But maybe that was a good thing. She wasn't in a mood for discreet responses. Then, while climbing the stairs, she got her anger under control and turned her attention to the fact that Quarles knew way too much about the police department. He had information he shouldn't have been privy to, which meant he had an inside source.

Elena sat down on her bed, the door closed, and drummed restless nails on her knee. Finally she made up her mind and called a number she rarely used, Lieutenant Beltran's home phone. Saying a quick prayer that he wouldn't be angry at this intrusion, she listened to the ringing, then to his gruff voice answering. Elena identified herself and asked if he'd heard the Quarles interview on the six-o'clock news. Beltran hadn't; he'd been eating his dinner and didn't appreciate being interrupted. Elena apologized and told him that Quarles knew from whose gun the bullet that killed his wife had come. There was an ominous silence. She broke it by telling him that Fermin Gil seemed to know about every interview they'd conducted involving the Quarles family.

"Why are you asking questions about them in the first place?" Beltran asked.

"For a number of reasons," she replied, "but the thing is, it looks like we've got a leak, and that's not good, no matter who's receiving the information."

"I'll get back to you," Beltran said, and hung up.

Sighing, Elena put her telephone into answering-machine mode. A lot of reporters left messages. So did the chief's secretary, telling Elena to be in his office the next morning. She assumed that was Beltran—getting back to her. As she prepared for bed, pulling on a long H.H.U. T-shirt that Michael Futrell had given her in the days when they were lovers, she thought that Gaitan better not throw her to the wolves. If he tried, she'd—she'd—sic Harmony on him.

Speaking of whom, where was her mother? Oh yes, she was having dinner with elderly friends from the Socorro Heights Senior Citizens Center, where she had given weaving lessons the last time she was in town. If Harmony heard Fermin Gil's comments on the radio while she was driving home, she just might be heading for Quarles headquarters. And Elena doubted that Fermin the Vermin was any match for Harmony Waite Portillo, who didn't suffer gladly attacks on her offspring.

24

Tuesday, October 29, 7:00 A.M.
Los Santos *Times*:

POLICE ACCUSED OF
POLITICAL BIAS

Fermin Gil, campaign manager for mayoral candidate Wayne Quarles, accused the Los Santos Police Department of attempting to scuttle the Quarles campaign by conducting an investigation of the candidate and members of his family while covering up the department's culpability in the death of Quarles's wife.

"They've assigned a femiNazi detective named Jarvis to the case, who's protecting Officer Monica Ibarra. According to forensics experts, Ibarra shot Mrs. Quarles," Gil asserted.

"Detective Jarvis was seen at Caldicott headquarters supporting the incumbent mayor.

"The woman should be excluded from the investigation. Voters don't want the LSPD trying to tell them how to vote. That's police-state tactics."

After seeing the *Times,* Elena dreaded the meeting in the chief's office. She was also worried about Monica. Given the precarious state of her health, hearing about this flap could kill her. Accordingly, Elena left the house early and headed for the hospital. Since Monica hadn't seen a newspaper or watched a TV newscast, Elena advised the doctor to keep the latest developments from her, and the doctor agreed wholeheartedly. "She's not doing well at all," he said.

Elena had noticed that. Monica was glad to see her and clung to her hand, but the young woman's skin was hot and dry, her breathing labored. The oxygen tubes were back in her nose, and although her color was high, it was an unhealthy shade. She managed to answer only one of Elena's questions.

Elena had said, "You're sure it was her husband's idea that she volunteer for C.O.P.? I know she was big on volunteering, but her usual stuff was the symphony board, the arts council, and educational interests."

"Husband," Monica croaked. "She said—he got her—do it. Volunteered—her. Looked good—campaign."

Elena nodded. Quarles's signals might have been mixed on that issue, but Monica seemed sure, which meant Hope had made it clear that that particular civic adventure wasn't her own idea. Satisfied, Elena drove to headquarters and the eight-o'clock meeting. The same people were gathered who had come the morning Hope Quarles died—Gaitan, Stollinger, Beltran, and Leo.

"We've got a big problem," Chief Gaitan announced as soon as everyone was seated. He turned to the detectives. "What have you turned up on the Quarles case?"

"We can't find the car thief," Leo reported. "In fact, we're beginning to wonder if he really had any connection with Los Reyes Diablos. The Gang Task Force has really rousted them, squeezed them, done everything short of putting their leader, Palenque, on the rack, and they got nothing."

"No one's going to confess to shooting a cop and killing a high-profile woman," said Stollinger. "What I want to know is how the ballistics info got out."

"Internal Affairs is looking into that," said Gaitan.

"And how they know who we're interviewing," Elena

added. "If Quarles is actually responsible for his wife's death, that would explain how he knew what gun she was shot with, but not how Fermin Gil knows who we're talking to—even people we interviewed just yesterday."

Gaitan nodded. "Beltran told me. I.A. will look into that, too."

Elena relaxed. Beltran had acted on her suggestion.

"But no matter who had a loose mouth, the cat's out of the bag. They know Ibarra's bullet killed Quarles."

"That doesn't mean it was Monica's finger on the trigger," Elena objected. "She swears she shot once, with Quarles behind her somewhere, and she was already going down herself. Hell, if the wound doesn't kill her, the stress of being accused will," Elena added bitterly. "I saw her this morning. She looks awful, worse every time I go in."

"Did you learn anything from her?" Beltran asked.

"She says that the husband was the one who talked Hope Quarles into joining C.O.P. It was a campaign strategy, and his idea, not hers."

"And that's why you've been asking questions about him?" the chief demanded. "He and Gil are making us look like unfeeling, ass-covering jerks."

"His having talked her into joining C.O.P. is only part of the story," Elena replied. "The man is going to get three million in insurance money from his wife's death, and he's already borrowing against it for his campaign."

"Is he?" Gaitan frowned.

"Also his finances may not be as solid as they look."

"I thought he was *muy rico,*" Beltran muttered.

"Maybe not. He's had some big projects go bad on him. And he couldn't get his hands on the money his wife inherited from her father because her father fixed that in his will. I have to admit Quarles didn't blink an eye when *her* will was read, and it did pretty much the same thing, left him half her estate but only for fun, no business. But still he didn't *have* to get upset; he's got that three mil coming from Texas Life and Casualty.

"And then there's the son." Elena felt as if she were fighting for her career, although no one in the room had threatened her. So far. "Hope's cousin says Junior's a loser. Same take on him at the university."

"How a loser?" asked Stollinger.

"Sexual predator, cocaine addict, rumored to be in hock to the pushers."

"Well, well. You *have* been busy, Jarvis." Gaitan tipped his head back and stared at the ceiling. "You just might be onto something."

Elena let her breath out in a sigh of relief.

"Which doesn't get us off the hook right now."

She stared at the chief helplessly. Surely, she wasn't going to be disciplined for doing a good job.

"All right, here's what we're going to do," Gaitan continued, a crafty smile lighting his eyes. "Weizell is going to lead the investigation of the car thief. Then I'll announce that you, Jarvis, will be suspended without pay and investigated by Internal Affairs."

"What!" she cried indignantly. "You just said—"

"Quiet!"

Elena shut up.

"We're sending you over to Vice. They'll fix you up so your own mother won't recognize you. By the way, I hear that Harmony's in town."

Elena glared at him.

"And you'll go right on investigating the Quarles family. Just because they're making a political issue out of this doesn't mean we're letting it go. Find out about the son, about the finances, about the relationship between Quarles and his wife. See if he's got a woman on the side."

"No evidence of that," Elena muttered sullenly.

"Well, look into it," Gaitan snapped.

"If I'm suspended, I don't have any authority—no badge, no right to carry a gun, no departmental car, no support services, no pay—how am I supposed to eat if—"

"You'll get all the support you ask for. We'll run it

through I.A. You'll report to them. I'll pay your salary from a discretionary fund, and your gas, and any legitimate expenses you run up."

"So Vice is going to doll me up like a prostitute, which is what they do with female officers, and people are going to answer my questions without asking who the hell I am? Chief, I don't think—" She stopped, then snapped her fingers as she had an intriguing thought. "Texas Life."

"What about them?" asked Stollinger.

"Their head investigator—what was his name?—Freer. Milton Freer. He said they'd do anything they could to help find the killer. Of course, it's Wayne Quarles they want to nail so they won't have to pay off on the policy. Maybe I'll ask Freer for a job."

"You're not telling them what we're doing. No one is telling anyone outside this room." Gaitan glared at them. "Not your wives, not your girlfriends—"

"We don't have girlfriends, Chief," said Leo. "We're all married, except Elena."

"So she won't tell her boyfriend," said the chief.

"I don't have one," she muttered. "I won't even tell Milton Freer, O.K.? I'll simply say that you dumped me just when I was drawing a bead on his beneficiary, and I'm willing to keep after Quarles if they put me on the payroll. Then if Quarles finds out I'm still asking questions, who's he going to complain to? The insurance company doesn't have a political agenda."

Gaitan smiled. "Very good, Jarvis. With you functioning outside the department, if we've got a leak, it's plugged for the Quarles-family part of the investigation."

Elena nodded.

"So you're suspended. Glen Patkin will be your I.A. contact." He thought for a moment. "And if you get the job with Texas Life, let Patkin know right away. Then we won't have to pay your salary."

25

••

Tuesday, October 29, 3:15 P.M.

First Elena phoned the vice sergeant, who couldn't fit her in for costuming until eight that evening when the female vice officers were outfitted as streetwalkers to lure horny citizens into their clutches. Then she drove downtown to the bank tower where Texas Life & Casualty was headquartered. Milton Freer was wary when she told him she had been suspended, excited when she told him what she had found out about the financial problems of the Quarleses, father and son.

"Well, it wouldn't be the first time a husband had his wife killed to collect on a big insurance policy," said Freer, rubbing his hands together in the expectation of saving his company three million dollars.

"It could have been the son," Elena warned. "He was the one who flipped when the will was read."

"But the father didn't need money from the will. He plans to get it from us." Freer bared his teeth. "Insurance fraud is a villainous crime. People say, 'Who cares about the insurance companies? They have lots of money.' But every time we take a big loss, a fraudulent loss, the rates go up. The moral tenor of the country goes down." His voice soared in evangelical fervor. Elena wouldn't have thought he had that kind of passion in him.

"So do you want to hire me?"

Freer calmed down and looked wary again.

"You did indicate that you had a stake in the investigation," Elena pointed out. "Well, I'm the only one interested in pursuing this angle. The rest of them are still looking for the lone car thief, or car thief and accomplice, which doesn't save you a penny unless Wayne Quarles hired the hit.

"Of course, I can drop it, take a vacation, then sue the department if they don't reinstate me and give me back pay, but frankly, I don't want Quarles to get away with it. So it's up to you, Mr. Freer." She stood, slinging her bag strap over her shoulder. "You want a few days to think it over? While the trail goes cold and the department decides that, politics or no politics, they can't afford to stick it to a female cop with a great record for solving crimes?"

"Five hundred dollars a day and expenses," said Freer, "and you keep working for us until the case is solved."

Five hundred? Elena blinked. For five hundred a day, she might consider hiring on forever, only they probably didn't pay that to their ordinary salaried investigators. "O.K.," she agreed. "I plan to use a disguise. Don't want him to know I'm still on the trail."

"A disguise?" Freer looked as if a disguise might be against company policy.

"I'll start tomorrow. Be interesting to see if you recognize me." Elena tucked her thumb against the strap of her bag, which no longer held her badge. She felt naked without it, and sad. Five hundred dollars a day was nice, but she was used to C.A.P., lousy pay and all. She'd miss Leo, and Manny Escobedo, her sergeant, and all the guys on Homicide Row. She hoped Wayne Quarles was guilty. The son of a bitch had gotten her into this undercover mess.

Sitting in her car with rush-hour traffic beginning to build up, her appointment with Vice three hours away, Elena thought about Monica Ibarra, whom she wouldn't be seeing for a while. One more visit, Elena decided. To remind the kid that someone believed in her—in case she heard about the accusations from the Quarles camp.

Elena drove her truck to Thomason General and parked. Couldn't use her police parking pass anymore to get into no-parking slots. What a bummer. She was directed to the ICU, where the doctor saw her and said, "Thank God. Monica's been asking for you, and we couldn't get hold of you."

"She must be worse if she's back in ICU," Elena said, alarmed.

"Yeah, worse. And upset. She woke up, and her stupid brother told her you'd been suspended."

Elena bit her lip.

"She's going into surgery again tomorrow morning."

"Why? What's—"

He sighed. "We've got to take out the rest of that lung—only way now to stop the infection."

"Does she know what you're going to do?"

"Of course she knows." The doctor looked insulted. "You think we'd do something that serious without telling the patient? But we don't like her going into surgery so upset. We're hoping you can—"

"I will," Elena promised, and entered the ICU without asking permission. The doctor didn't protest, didn't even follow her in. "Monica?" Elena sat down. She was tired to death, but she had more stuff to do before she could go home to bed, and this was probably the most important thing. "Monica?" She spoke softly and took the young woman's hand.

Monica Ibarra, dark hair in damp strings around her face, opened sad eyes and stared at her visitor. Then the tears began to slip unchecked over her cheeks. "We're both—going—down. Aren't—we?"

"No," said Elena.

"I—know. About you. About me. They all—think I—shot her."

"I don't think that."

"Didn't. Couldn't—have."

"Monica?" The young woman turned her head away, but Elena had to get through to her. "I know you didn't. Monica? I *know* that."

"Tomorrow—surgery—you know?"

"Yeah. The doctor told me."

"Doesn't—matter now."

"Yeah, it matters."

"Both of us—going down."

"No, Monica, we're not. Just because I'm suspended"—Elena wished she could tell the truth about this ruse, but she'd sworn to keep her mouth shut—"that doesn't mean I'm giving up. I'll go right on looking for the real killer."

"How?"

Elena grinned. "The insurance company."

"What—"

"Texas Life. They hold a big policy on Hope Quarles's life, and they know *you're* not the beneficiary. So they're paying me to find out why she was killed."

"Yes?" Monica looked hopeful.

"So you hang in there. Hear? You stay alive, and I'll stay on the job—even if it isn't with a badge."

The smallest smile tipped Monica's pale lips. "I—try," she said.

"And so will I." Elena squeezed her hand. "I can't come to visit you for a while."

"No?" Monica looked desolate.

"But I'm going to be out there. Looking out for both of us. And I'll call. O.K.?"

"No phones—here."

"To check up on you."

"Miss—seeing you."

"You'll see me when we're both back on the department. When your probation's up and your two years on patrol, maybe you'll go for detective, and we can work together."

"With—one lung?"

"Why not?" Elena smiled. "They'll owe us. Because they didn't stand up for us when we were the good guys."

Monica smiled, too. "Good guys," she agreed, her voice alarmingly weak.

"Chuckie, this is the worst looking wig I've ever seen. I don't think even a two-dollar whore would wear it."

"Get real, Jarvis. There are no two-dollar whores, and if there were, they sure as hell couldn't afford a classy wig like this. Look at all that hair."

"That's just what I mean. I'll feel like the Dolly Parton of Juarez Avenue."

"So do something with it," said Chuckie Dolan. "If you don't want to attract johns, put it in a bun or something. What do you want it for anyway?"

"I'm going undercover, but not as a hooker." She had been relieved that Dolan seemed unaware of her suspension. Even though the chief had sent her over here, Dolan might have questioned accommodating a suspended officer, and what could she have said without explaining a plan that wasn't supposed to go beyond the group in Gaitan's office and one I.A. officer? "A bun, huh?" She looked at herself in the mirror. "Can I stick bobby pins in it?"

"Hell, yes. You can pin it, curl it, even put it in your washing machine."

"Great. Wash-and-wear hair." When her new employers got a load of this wig, they'd fire her before she'd begun.

Unfortunately, nothing else was available, because Elena had stayed until Monica fell asleep, arriving at headquarters late for her appointment with Vice. So she took the wig, thanked Chuck Dolan, and left.

As she turned the corner, she heard another vice officer say, "Wasn't that Elena Jarvis? How come she's leaving with one of our wigs?"

"Why not?" Dolan asked.

"Because she's suspended."

"Oh, shit," said Dolan.

Elena quickened her step. Not only was she suspended, but now Dolan might accuse her of misappropriating a departmental hairpiece.

26

••

Tuesday, October 29, 9:15 P.M.
Los Santos *Herald-Post*:

DETECTIVE SUSPENDED
FOR POLITICAL BIAS

Accused of conducting a political vendetta against mayoral candidate Wayne Quarles, Crimes Against Persons Detective Elena Jarvis was suspended without pay by LSPD Chief Armando Gaitan. The following statement was issued by the chief's office:

"Detective Jarvis's conduct will be investigated by Internal Affairs. Until such time as she is cleared of all charges or appropriate disciplinary measures taken, Detective Jarvis will remain off duty. The police department does not and never has sought to influence elections in the city of Los Santos. Our role is strictly one of community service and protection."

When Elena arrived home, no one was in the living room, so she curled up on the sofa to read the evening paper, not a reassuring event. The chief's statement sounded as if he really meant it and she might never get her job back. But no, that was silly. She'd chase down all the information available on Quarles, and then they'd take her back.

"Armando, I am truly disappointed in you," came an indignant voice from the foyer.

Elena sat up abruptly. That was her mother on the telephone, and Armando was undoubtedly the chief.

"Political vendetta indeed! My daughter isn't interested in politics. I think it's shameful that you've knuckled under to some cheap, whining politician."

"Mom?" Elena sped into the foyer and poked her mother.

Harmony put a finger to her lips. "Unless you revoke that suspension, Armando, you're going to be very sorry."

"Mom!" Elena poked her mother harder.

"I certainly am threatening you. . . . Oh, you think it's funny? Do you remember the last demonstration I mounted against your department when you were harassing that gay poet? . . . Oh yes, you were, and you were ignoring the concerns of senior citizens, which doesn't surprise me at all when you're not even loyal to your own employees."

"Mom, please hang up," Elena begged. She didn't know how she was going to explain the fact that she didn't want her mother's support, but she had to get Harmony off that telephone.

"You poor dear," cried Sarah, rushing down the stairs just then. She actually gave Elena a hug. "The TV news covered your suspension and that disgusting Fermin Gil crowing about it."

"That's right, Armando, a big, ugly, embarrassing demonstration. Right under your turncoat nose."

"Now, you needn't worry about money, Elena," Sarah went on. "You're welcome to stay here indefinitely."

"And I'll write letters to the editor, Armando. And all my friends at the center will. And Sarah's neighbors. And the whole faculty and administration at H.H.U."

"I wouldn't count on the administration, not when they just got a bundle from the Quarles family," Elena muttered, having given up hope of stopping her mother. For one thing, Elena couldn't get away from her housemate, who was saying, "If they actually fire you, you can become chief at the university."

"What about Chief Clabb?" Elena asked.

"He should retire, poor fellow."

"You can attack us with billy clubs and tear gas, but we won't be intimidated," Harmony declared.

"I've already got a temporary job, Sarah," Elena assured her friend.

"No, I do not want to go to the symphony with you on Friday night," said Harmony, slamming the receiver down.

"What job?" Sarah asked, amazed.

"She works for the LSPD," said Harmony, "and she will continue to do so if I have anything to say about it."

"It's O.K., Mom," Elena said soothingly.

"It is *not* O.K. We won't take this lying down," Harmony promised. "We'll protest, stir up public opinion—"

"Solve the case," Elena interrupted, "and then they'll take me back and apologize. And while I'm solving it, I'll be making five hundred dollars a day. And expenses. Courtesy of Texas Life and Casualty."

"Good heavens." Sarah looked shocked. "Maybe you should forget the police department and stay with this job."

"She'll do no such thing!" exclaimed Harmony.

The telephone rang, and Elena picked it up to avoid the developing argument. "Elena Jarvis," she said, hoping it wasn't a reporter calling for a quote on her suspension.

"How are you holding up?"

"Sam?"

"Sarah, my daughter is a public servant," said Harmony. "She's not devoting her life to some insurance company."

"That's right, it's Sam, your trusty therapist. You want to come over and talk?"

"No, I'm O.K., Sam, but thanks."

"She's following in her father's footsteps as a law-enforcement officer and guardian of public decency."

"You sure?" Sam asked.

"And my daughter is not going to allow a brilliant career to be sidetracked by some pantywaist bureaucrat."

If Harmony meant the chief, he'd be horrified to hear himself called a pantywaist bureaucrat. "I'm fine, Sam."

"Goodness, Harmony, I wouldn't dream of trying to tell Elena what to do," said Sarah. "She's her own woman."

"Why don't you go to the symphony with me Friday night," Sam suggested.

"The symphony?" Elena's heart sank. She didn't like symphonies.

"Is that Armando?" Harmony demanded suspiciously. "I am *not* going to the symphony with him."

"It's Sam, Mom," said Elena. "He just invited me—"

"There's nothing like classical music to soothe a troubled soul," said Sam. "I'll pick you up at seven-twenty."

"Oh, I don't—"

"For heaven's sake, say yes, Elena," Harmony told her. "You haven't had a date in months."

"It's not a date, Mom. He's my therapist."

"Good, then he can help you deal with this terrible blow dealt by your thankless employers." Harmony grabbed the phone. "Sam? This is Elena's mother. She'd love to accompany you to the symphony. Were you planning on taking her to dinner before or after the performance?"

"Mom!" cried Elena, horrified.

27

••

Wednesday, October 30, 6:55 A.M.

"Where did you get this wig?" Harmony asked, holding up the mass of flowing blond hair with distaste.

"A friend in Vice," Elena replied. She was scanning the newspaper while her mother and Sarah dealt with the difficult problem of trying to make her look like an insurance-company employee when all they had to work with was Elena's casual wardrobe and the tacky departmental wig.

An offended Sarah remarked, "No one would wear this hair except a—a—"

"Whore?" Elena suggested. "Or a police officer trying to look like one."

"Why do you have to disguise yourself?" Harmony asked. "Quarles can't have you suspended from Texas Life and Casualty."

"But he can warn people not to answer my questions if he knows I'm still on the case."

"A chignon, I think," said Sarah. "And a hat to cover the top hair, which is entirely too—*puffy*—for a business person."

While Harmony bundled up Elena's own hair and tugged the offensive wig down over it, Sarah went upstairs to search for a hat. Elena read through the front page article headlined QUARLES DETECTIVE SUSPENDED. With no more comment coming from headquarters, the press and the Quarles camp were having a field day: Fermin Gil ranting about the coldheartedness and political bias of targeting for investigation a grieving family while letting violent gang murderers go free; Nellie Medrano-Caldicott denying any hand in the investigation; some jerk at the newspaper speculating that Detective Jarvis was such a renegade cop that the brass had jumped at the excuse to suspend her. Renegade cop? Where did they get that?

"Well, there's your chignon," said Harmony. "Take a look." She handed Elena a mirror.

"Harmony, I don't want to be critical, but that chignon is much too loose. We want her to look businesslike," said Sarah, bringing in a mannish brown felt hat with a wide brim and small feather. "Besides that, we'll never get the hat over it, and the hat may—though I can't guarantee it—keep the wig from being dislodged."

Now, that would be embarrassing, Elena thought, having your wig come off. How would she explain to some interviewee why she was wearing a tacky blond wig when she had perfectly good black hair of her own. She glanced at the hat in Sarah's hand, the hat that was to save her from the humiliation of wig displacement. Even with the feather, it was a very conservative hat. Good thing, too.

"You're welcome to try your hand with the wig, Sarah," Harmony offered. "It's heavily permed, or whatever they do to fake hair." She studied her daughter. "What are we going to do about her eyebrows? Those are not the eyebrows of a blonde."

"You're not dyeing them," said Elena.

"Of course not, dear. Sarah, don't you think an insurance investigator would wear makeup?"

"I've got mascara on," Elena protested.

"There's some makeup in my bathroom," said Sarah. "Since it's mine, it's appropriate for a blonde."

Harmony nodded. "I'll get it."

Elena groaned. She didn't want a bunch of glop on her face. Mascara and a little lipstick were enough for any woman. Sarah took over the hairdressing, and Elena glanced at the weather report in the newspaper to get her mind off the unpleasant transformation she was undergoing. Middle sixties and fair, no surprises there. Then she read the letters to the editor, where she found an intriguing communication.

> I am very disappointed in the small-minded attack of the Quarles campaign that led to the suspension of Detective Elena Jarvis. Anyone who reads mystery stories knows that the police have to look at the family as suspects in a murder. Detective Jarvis was simply doing her job, for which she should not be punished. It speaks ill of our police department that they would knuckle under to political pressure and ill of the candidate that he would allow his campaign manager to exert that kind of pressure. It seems to me that three women have become victims in the case—Mrs. Quarles, Officer Ibarra, and Detective Jarvis.
>
> Pamela Honnecker
> Former Quarles Campaign Worker

A lady after my own heart, thought Elena as her housemate stuck yet another bobby pin into the yellow hair. Harmony bustled in carrying a pair of glasses. "I bought these for outside wear in Los Santos," she said, "but you'd better borrow them, Elena. They'll cover up your eyebrows, and glasses do make people look different."

"I can't wear your glasses, Mom." Then Elena thought a moment. "When did you start wearing glasses?"

"Clear glass," said Harmony. "For protection during dust storms. I got them at your new Walgreen's. They even have a drive-through prescription window." Harmony laughed. "Chimayo doesn't even have a pharmacy. Sarah, that's a nice, prim bun, and low enough on the neck to accommodate the hat, but I can see Elena's hair around her forehead. You'll have to comb the bangs back down and loosen the sides."

"It won't look as respectable," Sarah grumbled. "Hadn't we better put the makeup on first?"

"Absolutely. We don't want to get foundation in the hair." Harmony drew up a kitchen stool and perched on it while she applied foundation and rouge to Elena's face.

"It itches," Elena complained.

"Nonsense," said her mother, and popped the glasses on. "Those take care of the eyebrows reasonably well."

Then Sarah stepped back to study the hair and shook her head. She went to work, combing front hair down over Elena's dark hairline. "There," she said, and placed the hat on Elena's head.

Elena pushed her mother's dust glasses up on her nose and looked at herself in the mirror, where she saw a stranger with blond hair, pink cheeks and lips, and heavy glasses. "You two are miracle workers," she admitted. "I hardly recognize myself. The suit even matches the hat."

"Of course," said Sarah, who had provided the suit.

"But a *skirt*?" Elena added unhappily. "It's hard to climb a fence in a skirt."

"Insurance executives don't climb fences," Harmony assured her.

"Well, I'm not wearing heels," Elena grumbled.

As she had predicted, Milton Freer did not recognize her. "Amazing," he said when she presented herself at his office. "Shall we plan our investigative strategy? I've had business cards made up for you."

Obviously, Milton was not one for chitchat. Elena accepted the box he pushed across the desk and inspected the sample card on the cover. It said, *Matilda Carr, Insurance Investigator*. "Matilda?" she asked. Even in this getup, she didn't see herself as a Matilda.

"One of our people on maternity leave." He buzzed for

his secretary, who came in with a camera, took Elena's picture, and, in fifteen minutes, returned with a Texas Life ID card and a company American Express card. "For expenses," said Freer. "Please don't use it for personal charges, Miss Carr."

"I'm surprised you didn't get me a doctored driver's license," she snapped.

"That would be illegal." He then produced a mobile phone and handed it to her. "Please keep in touch at all times. And be reminded that it's not for personal use. We pay for every call you make or receive." Freer folded his hands on his empty desk while Elena inspected her new phone. Cool! she thought. "Have you any suggestions for this investigation," Freer demanded impatiently, "or did you plan to follow my lead?"

Elena scowled and took her case notebook from her purse, which had felt all wrong on her shoulder without her gun. Well, now she'd have the cell phone. She couldn't shoot anyone with it, but the weight would be familiar and comforting. "I plan to see Hope Quarles's lawyer, Mindenhoff, and a disaffected campaign worker who wrote a letter to the editor in this morning's paper. Also, I want to locate someone named Paco, the son's pusher."

"Are you saying that Quarles, Junior, is a drug addict?"

"And possibly in debt to this Paco. Maybe he had his mother killed for the inheritance. Also he's a rather nasty womanizer; maybe someone's blackmailing him—"

"If he's behind her death, it will do Texas Life and Casualty no good. His father will have to be paid. I do not see why we should pay you to investigate the son."

"Well, let's not be cheap about this, Milton," Elena said, exasperated.

"Why are you interviewing Mrs. Quarles's lawyer?"

"Because I want to know whether the son and the husband knew that her will tied up the money she left them. If they knew, there'd be less motive to have her killed."

"Aha! For the husband it would still be profitable. Our company provides the profit."

"Exactly, but not for Junior."

"And the campaign worker?"

Elena sighed. Milton, it seemed, was a control freak, a man who had to know and direct everything. Thank God her sergeant wasn't like that. "I want to know about campaign finances. He's borrowing already against the insurance money."

"What bank?" Freer asked. "I shall warn them that—"

"Don't. Let him dig himself into a big financial hole. The more stressed he becomes, the more likely he is to make a mistake. Now, can I tell you what I want you to do?"

"As long as it's understood that I am directing this investigation."

"Right," Elena said dryly. "I figure you and your company are probably better equipped to handle this aspect."

"Does it relate to the beneficiary?"

"Yes, Milton, it does. According to my sources—"

"What sources?"

"They're confidential. If you want to use them, you'll have to trust me that they're reliable. If, on the other hand, you want to develop your own sources—"

"No need to get defensive, Miss Carr."

He sure did like to call her Miss Carr; the man was primmer than her hat.

"Quarles has mounted a couple of projects that were probably big money losers," she said, controlling her irritation. "The Trujillo Sports Complex and a country-club development in Mexico. We need to know how much he lost, who his investors were, and how big a hit they took."

"If you're thinking the investors murdered his wife, again I must point out—"

"Come on, Milton, you can't run an investigation by ignoring any angle that might turn up information you don't want to hear. Now, do I get an office, or do I share yours?"

The latter possibility evidently horrified Milton Freer. "You may have Mrs. Carr's office. In Personnel."

Elena grinned, betting to herself that Personnel was as far away from Investigation as possible. Old Milton obviously didn't like taking orders from a suspended female police detective who was half his age.

28

••

Wednesday, October 30, 10:05 A.M.

Elena called Glen Patkin, her contact in I.A., but not with much enthusiasm. No cop willingly interacted with I.A.

"Ma'am," he said, "this is Internal Affairs. Perhaps the operator connected you with the wrong extension."

"This is Jarvis," said Elena. "Matilda Carr's my alias, and you're supposed to be my contact."

"Oh, right." He laughed. "Well, we're faking an investigation. Of course, if we turn anything up on you—"

"Are we cooperating here, or do I call the chief?"

"No sense of humor," Patkin grumbled.

"I.A. isn't supposed to be humorous," said Elena.

"We're much maligned. What can I do for you, Ms. Carr?"

"There's a pusher named Paco dealing at H.H.U. One of his clients is Wayne Quarles, Junior. That's the information my partner and I got when I still had a partner instead of some insurance-company geek. Can you get Narcotics to check this guy out? What I want to know is: Is it true? If so, how much does Quarles, Junior, owe this Paco? Incidentally, the pusher's supposed to be an Anglo. Is Paco connected to the Diablo Kings? Would he arrange a hit so he'd get paid? *Did* he arrange a hit?" Elena checked off the last item on her list of questions. "That's it."

"O.K.," said Patkin. "Anything else?"

She gave him the number of her new mobile phone. "Oh, and tell the chief I'm sorry about my mother," she added.

"Your *mother*? What's that about?"

"You don't need to know. Just tell him."

"Hold on."

What for? Elena wondered. In seconds she had Chief Gaitan on the line and was stammering apologies. "I'll try to keep her from acting on those threats," Elena promised.

Gaitan laughed. "Your mother is a delight, Detec—ah, Ms. Carr. I'll never forget the bicycle racer/gay activist/ senior citizen protest she staged last year."

"Me either," Elena said gloomily.

"You needn't discourage her."

"But, Chief—"

"The more bad publicity there is about your suspension, the more pressure we put on Quarles. Serves him right for accusing us of playing politics."

"O*kay*." Elena didn't think the chief knew what he was getting into, but who was she to argue? He obviously had a vengeful streak when it came to people who tried to manipulate him. Now that she thought about it, he and Mayor Nellie had gone a few rounds with each other on occasion.

"I'd tell you to give Harmony my best, but she might smell a rat. And good luck—ah—Ms. Carr. We're counting on you to find whatever's out there."

"Yes, sir."

After hanging up with the chief, Elena made an appointment with Darrell Mindenhoff, wondering if her disguise would stand up to scrutiny from someone who had seen her in her other persona. Then she tracked down Pamela Honnecker by the simple expedient of calling the five Honneckers in the telephone book and asking for Pamela. On the third call an answering machine said, "Pamela and Rick aren't at home. Bunnie and Tim have their own number. Call them or leave us a message at the beep."

Imagine having a separate phone line for your kids, Elena marveled. Not everyone in Chimayo had even one phone. Of course, the Portillos did because Elena's father had always been in law enforcement.

Elena left her mobile-phone number on the answering machine. Last of all, she called the hospital and learned that Monica was still in surgery. Was that good or bad? Elena wondered. The young officer had been scheduled to go in at seven; it was now ten-thirty. And if she survived the operation, Monica would have only one lung, or at least less of the injured one than she'd had before. Would she have to take disability and leave the force? And what would happen if the grand jury found her culpable in Hope Quarles's death? Well, a trial. Manslaughter? Negligent homicide?

With these thoughts running through her brain, Elena rose and headed for the elevator and her appointment with Hope Quarles's lawyer.

"I really don't think that I can talk about the family, Ms. Carr," said Darrell Mindenhoff, who was ensconced in a large leather chair behind his desk. "Client-lawyer confidentiality, you know. Are you married?"

"What?" Could proper, middle-aged Counselor Mindenhoff be coming on to her? Was it the blond hair?

"Are you married? I myself am separated and looking for a relationship. Preferably with a younger professional woman of sound Christian principles. I find that meeting suitable ladies is not as simple as it was in my youth."

He'd be surprised if he knew exactly what her profession was. Fortunately, he hadn't shown a sign of recognizing her as the black-haired police detective who'd attended the reading of Hope's will. "I'm not married, but I am seeing someone," Elena replied. Talk about half-truths. She'd be seeing her therapist Friday, but that could hardly be called a date. In fact, Sam might well back out since Harmony had hinted—*insisted* was more like it—that he should provide dinner as well as a symphony.

Boy, she dreaded the symphony. The last time she'd been at the Civic Center—with Michael—she'd fallen asleep during an opera, then disturbed the whole orchestra section, Michael in particular, when her pager went off in the middle of an important aria. "Since your client is dead, I don't see that confidentiality applies," she said to Mindenhoff.

"A lawyer's responsibilities extend beyond the grave," he replied. "Perhaps you'd like to have lunch with me." He glanced at his watch. "It's about that time. Your significant other—I believe that's the modern catchword, or should I say phrase?—at any rate, he can be told it's a business lunch."

How much did he want to make time with her? Elena wondered. "Unless you have information that you would feel comfortable imparting," she said sweetly, remembering to speak in a higher voice, "I don't see how we could call it a business lunch."

"I might dredge up an item or two"—he twinkled back at her—"and I can certainly take the lunch off my taxes. So it has to be business, doesn't it?"

"I'm sure Mr. Quarles, even though you are not his attorney, will be most grateful. Texas Life and Casualty can't pay off until our questions are answered."

Lacking the clout of a police badge, Elena flirted shamelessly with Darrell Mindenhoff, who took her to the exclusive International Border Club and ordered a bottle of expensive wine, most of which he drank himself while Elena enjoyed her crab bisque, Caesar salad, pork tenderloin in prune sauce (which she ordered only because he insisted—prune sauce, for Pete's sake; actually, it wasn't bad), and chocolate decadence. Since Harmony had announced that she would not be home tonight to cook, this feast would save Elena from exposure to TV dinners at Sarah's. With her meal, Elena sipped a half glass of wine and watched Mindenhoff, who, having consumed his third glass, was waxing garrulous on the subject of the Quarles family.

"You should have seen the expression on the boy's face when he discovered that Hope had tied his money up for what, to Wayne, Junior, must seem forever."

"Really," Elena murmured as if she hadn't been there for the reading. Mindenhoff had already told her in detail about Hope's will. "No matter how it was left, he'll end up with a lot of money. Wasn't he pleased?"

Mindenhoff chortled. "Shocked would be a more apt description. I'm sure he thought Mama failed to see his faults. However, you can take my word for it, Hope Quarles had the sharpest mind in that family. The others just didn't realize it."

"The son had no foreknowledge of her will?"

"No one did, only Hope and I and Bud Holmes. Bud knew that if anything happened to Hope, Masterson's would continue without interference from any Quarles heir."

"Her husband didn't know—"

"No, indeed. Wayne has thought all these years that he couldn't get his hands on her money because of her father's will, but I think, no matter how Rob Masterson had framed his will, which I drew up, by the way"—Elena smiled and nodded admiringly— "Hope would have kept the money in her own hands. Which is not to say she didn't love Wayne. She did. No accounting for taste, is there?"

"Aside from the fact that our company will probably have to pay him a lot of money, Mr. Quarles seems charming and successful. I notice his results in the polls are improving."

"He can thank whoever killed Hope for that. Every voter who's been a crime victim will vote for him now. Which is a pity. I wouldn't tell this to just anyone, Ms. Carr—may I call you Matilda?—but Wayne Quarles will not make a good mayor. The man has no conservative instincts when it comes to money. If he's smart and he wins this election, he'll devote himself to politics and get out of business while he still can."

Someone else who thinks Wayne Quarles is in financial trouble, Elena noted.

"Now that he has the resources to live the good life, he can find himself some pretty young thing"—Mindenhoff beamed at Elena as if she were his personal choice in that particular line— "and live a life of luxury. All charm and no substance, that's Wayne. He's lucky he had a smart wife who fixed things so that he won't starve no matter what he does."

"I see," said Elena. "But wasn't he devoted to her?"

"Oh, certainly. I'm not saying Wayne would want to see her dead. After all, your company carried the same huge policy on his life. I remember his lawyer, the estimable Mr. Gil, saying Wayne was a fool to carry so much insurance when Hope had her own money."

"And the daughter? How did she react to the will?"

"She was pleased. Wendy is a shallow girl. God knows where her brains—or lack of them—came from, but she loved her parents. Every time young Pickentide annoys her, she comes running home. She'll miss Hope dreadfully, even after she's bought her house in River Oaks. That's what she plans to use her money for.

"The husband's not too happy; he's an urban type and likes living in a penthouse overlooking downtown Houston. The man said once—in mixed company, mind you—this was at a party at Hope's, and he'd had quite a bit to drink." Mindenhoff held up the wine bottle questioningly and, when Elena shook her head, poured the rest into his glass.

She figured the more he had to drink, the less likely he was to suddenly recognize her through her disguise.

"What was I saying?" he asked.

"Something about Wendy's husband and his penthouse."

"Oh, yes. He said the sight of the Houston skyline from his penthouse garden always gave him an erection."

"Goodness," Elena exclaimed primly. "I hope his mother-in-law didn't hear him."

"And I hope that I haven't offended you, Matilda." Belying his words, Mindenhoff was now leering at her.

Her pager chose that opportune moment to beep, and she

returned the call on the new cell phone, then wished she'd thought to leave the room. If Patkin was calling, she'd have to disguise the conversation. Her caller picked up immediately.

"Hey, Elena, it's Rafer Martin."

"Hi," she replied. Rafer was a physicist and the trombonist in the H.H.U. jazz group with which Elena sang.

"I called to say how sorry I am about your suspension. In fact, I just sent off a letter to the *Herald-Post*."

"Why, thanks," Elena told him. If the chief wanted controversy, her friends and family certainly seemed willing to provide it.

"How about having dinner with me? I'll try to cheer you up."

"What about Helen?" Elena asked. His wife had once made an embarrassing scene while under the mistaken impression that Rafer and Elena were having an affair.

"We're separated."

"I'm afraid separated isn't good enough, Rafer." With Mindenhoff listening to every word, she took the opportunity to send him a message. "I just don't date married men, even separated married men." Mindenhoff looked disappointed.

Rafer said, "Can't say I blame you, given my particular wife. O.K. if I call when the divorce is final?"

"Sure," said Elena.

Mindenhoff chose that moment to signal for the check.

"You've been very helpful," Elena said as he signed the bill, "and thank you for a lovely lunch."

"All comes off the taxes." He smiled with philosophic resignation. "Although I don't see what I've said that could help Texas Life and Casualty."

29

Wednesday, October 30, 2:30 P.M.

What had she gotten from Darrell Mindenhoff, aside from that expensive lunch? Elena asked herself as she drove toward the Quarles home with the idea of questioning their neighbors. One, Junior had expected ready cash from his mother's will and been disappointed. If he'd acted on his expectations and had her killed in order to pay his drug debts, he was a prime suspect in a murder-for-hire case. His pusher might have the gang contacts to set up a hit, although you had to figure killing a person who was in the company of a policewoman was a dumb move.

Number two, Wendy, the daughter, looked to her mother to provide a haven in times of disappointment. Will or no will, Wendy might have nagged that River Oaks mansion out of Willis and probably didn't have Diablo Kings contacts. Not a good suspect.

Three, Wayne Quarles. Everyone seemed to think he and Hope were a loving couple. He hadn't known the will was going to cut him off from business funding; no one knew for sure whether he even needed business funding. On the other hand, he had known he'd get a big chunk of money from the insurance company if she died, and he was borrowing against that money already. The questions were: Did he want to become mayor so much that he'd have his wife killed, did he really need to get money that way, and did he have any murder-for-hire contacts? So far the son seemed to be the best suspect among the family members, but the husband was still a possibility.

Was there anyone else? Elena asked herself. Maybe someone at Masterson Construction? Bud Holmes for instance? There was no mention of him in the will; he already had control of the company, not to mention a nifty stock-option plan provided for him in Rob Masterson's will. But what if Hope had been taking too big an interest in his empire? What if she'd found out that he was fiddling with the books or skimming profits or something? Elena considered pulling over to call Glen Patkin in I.A. again. She'd read the statistics on accidents involving people on cell phones, but she'd been working with a police radio since she graduated from the academy. Wasn't that the same thing? She called but didn't pull over.

"No word yet from the narcs on Paco," he said.

"This is something else. Ask Fraud and Forgery to check on Masterson Construction, see if there's any indication of financial irregularities there. The CEO is Bud Holmes. Have them look at him in particular."

"What are we looking *for* here?" Patkin said.

"Any reason that someone at Masterson's might want the major stockholder out of the way. According to her lawyer, she was a pretty smart lady. Maybe she found out something she wasn't supposed to know."

"O.K. I'll pass the word and get back to you."

Elena had no sooner hung up than her pager beeped. The screen number looked like C.A.P., and she wondered whether she should call. She was supposed to be out of contact—persona non grata. Curiosity got the better of her, however, and Harry Mosconi, a fellow detective, answered.

"Hey, Jarvis," he said. "I just wanted you to know I think you got shafted on this suspension business."

"Thanks, Harry."

"Wanna go out for a beer tonight?"

Harry was divorced and always on the lookout for a date during those periods when he wasn't dating his ex-wife. "I'd love to," Elena answered, "but what would Beltran say if he heard you were taking my side?" Harry was a good guy, but she didn't want to date him.

"He already knows it. The whole unit, sergeants included, signed a petition of protest this morning and shoved it under his door."

"Harry, that's the nicest thing anyone's said to me this week." The thought of their loyalty made her blink against tears. Getting soft, Jarvis, she thought. "I'll tell you what, Harry. I'll take that beer when I get reinstated. In fact, I'll buy, for all you guys."

"The sooner the better," Mosconi said gruffly.

She clicked off and took a road up the mountain toward the Quarleses' neighborhood, where she found, after several attempts, a lady who was delighted to engage in a good gossip.

Glenda Barrow told Matilda Carr that she had considered Wayne and Hope a puzzling couple. "At a party, if they were talking to the same people, they always had their arms around each other. If they were circulating and ran into each other, they'd kiss cheeks. But I sometimes wondered if they ever spent any time alone. He was *always* out—days, weekends, nights. And she was so *busy*! I swear Hope belonged to half the good-works groups in town—everything from Junior League to help for the homeless. And then she joined that C.O.P. program. Because Wayne thought it would be good for his campaign. Well, I guess he's sorry now that he pushed her into that. What a terrible thing! And the police don't seem to be doing *anything*! Do you think that policewoman really shot her? Why would she do that? Hope was never rude to anyone in her *life*."

Elena thought the marriage sounded strange, too. Where

was Wayne spending his time if he was never home? And how many people were holding Monica responsible for Hope's death? As soon as she left the Barrow house, Elena called the hospital to check on Monica. The doctor, who took his good old time about answering his page, said, "I thought you were suspended."

"That doesn't mean I'm not worried about her."

He sighed. "That makes two of us. She survived the surgery; we even saved a piece of the lung, but she hasn't regained consciousness."

"I guess that's bad?"

"I guess it is."

Elena tried two more houses on the street, which was in the same subdivision as Sarah's but farther up the mountain. The houses were bigger and seemed to cling even more precariously to the cliffs. She interviewed a Mr. Leavell, who said, "Quarles is the charlatan who built this house."

"Are you dissatisfied with it?" Elena asked. If a person liked ostentation, this house had it all.

"It's all right, but I discovered after I bought it that there were liens."

"Ah—that means—"

"I'd think an insurance-company employee would know what I'm talking about. What did you major in in college, fine arts?" he asked. "Liens—Quarles hadn't paid all the subcontractors. Of course, I bought title insurance, and they'd have paid off, but I shouldn't have had to be bothered with something like that. I called Quarles himself and told him I planned to sue him for the aggravation. He told me it was just an oversight and he'd take care of it."

"Did he?"

Leavell shrugged. "After a few months. That's no way to do business."

Maybe not, Elena thought, but it certainly was interesting. Sussex Hills was the project on which Resendez thought Quarles would have made a mint. Leavell's revelations provided the first concrete information she'd received that Quarles was in financial difficulties.

"How long ago was this?" she asked.

"Couple of years," Leavell replied, "but I haven't forgotten. No sir."

If Quarles was in trouble two years ago, things could easily have become worse since then. That three million from Texas Life might have been crucial to a wheeler-dealer whose deals were going sour.

The rest of her visits in the neighborhood were unproductive. When she ran out of places to stop, she called Texas Life. "Any news on his finances?" she asked Freer.

"Yes," Freer replied, "but I'm not sure what it means. He got a lot of private financing on the sports complex, but the money sources seem to be dummy corporations. Tracing them leads us nowhere. As for the country club across the river, we've got a list of investors, Mexican citizens. Many are legitimate business people, and they're living in the houses. Others are less easily accounted for, men and women who list themselves as proprietors, but of businesses we can't locate, and people we can't get any information on at all. Does this mean anything to you, Detec—Ms. Carr?"

"Maybe," Elena responded hesitantly. "Let me think about it. In the meantime it's five, and I'm going home."

"Well, you're a contract employee. Within reason, you set your own hours. Have you found out anything noteworthy?"

"Bits and pieces," said Elena, "some contradictory."

"That doesn't sound promising."

"You'd be surprised."

"I see. Conference in my office at nine. Do you want me to fax you the names of Quarles's investors?"

"I don't have a fax," Elena admitted.

"What? No fax?"

Was he going to take away her five hundred a day and tell her to get lost because she wasn't into modern technology?

She drove back to Sarah's, thinking about Freer's discoveries and what they meant. Two possibilities occurred to her.

Hope could have been evading the terms of her father's will through dummy corporations and shadowy Mexican businessmen in order to help her husband. The loss of that money would explain the terms of her own will. Even in death she refused to invest another dime in her husband's ill-fated deals.

The second possibility, money laundering, was more sinister. Elena didn't like the idea of a mayor who was tied to criminal interests, a mayor who'd have his wife killed and then blame it on the police.

Or—could they, the money launderers, have invested with Quarles, lost the bulk of their investment, and taken it upon themselves to provide him the wherewithal to repay them, the method: killing his wife—which meant an instant—more or less—three million, plus the inheritance. If he didn't know the inheritance money would be tied up, Juarez drug lords certainly wouldn't. And they—whoever they were—would have the contacts to hire a hit. They might even think it was funny to implicate a policewoman and give Quarles, whom they had in their clutches, a better chance at becoming mayor.

On both sides of the border the tentacles of the drug dealers reached everywhere. They had corrupted government in Mexico and suborned the occasional law officer in the U.S. Buying themselves a mayor and using violence to accomplish that goal would seem only good business practice to such men.

Or was her reasoning the result of that huge, rich lunch she'd eaten with the lecherous lawyer? She remembered Grandmother Portillo saying that gluttony was not only one of the seven deadly sins but also bad for the health—mental and physical. *Abuela* had illustrated her point by mentioning Hermisillo Fava, who had lost his memory and never recognized his children, grandchildren, or great-grandchildren again after eating half a roasted goat and an uncommonly large quantity of frijoles.

Of course, Hermisillo had, at the time of his memory loss,

been the oldest man in Chimayo, ninety-nine years old. Looking back on the story, Elena decided that he had probably developed Alzheimer's, poor man. He'd lived seven more years, but nobody ever said it was quality time.

30

••

Wednesday, October 30, 7:15 P.M.

Elena had a cup of sorbet for dinner. Ninety calories—to help balance out lunch. She also declined to walk neighborhood patrol. "That's all right," Sarah said magnanimously. "I'll be armed."

"With what? You don't have your concealed-weapon permit. You gonna walk around with a weapon in your hand?"

Sarah produced pepper spray and Mace. "I should be quite safe, even without an actual gun. I've been practicing a quick draw from my purse." She demonstrated by whipping the Mace from her handbag and aiming it at Elena, who ducked and muttered, "You've gone completely crazy."

Before an argument could develop, Elena's pager beeped, and she glanced at the screen. That was a narc number. Information on Paco? Eagerly she went to the foyer and returned the call.

"Elena? It's Frank."

Frank? Her ex had been put on the Paco investigation? Now that she thought about it, Narcotics wouldn't be calling her. As far as they knew, she was suspended. "What?" she asked suspiciously. Frank had stopped playing practical jokes after Harmony sicced a *curandera* on him, but Elena hadn't gotten over the need to be wary of Frank.

"I wanted to warn you, babe. Someone reported a pot party at our old house."

"What?"

"Now, don't panic. I know you're not livin' there, but it looks to me like someone's out to get you—what with this happenin' after the suspension an' all."

"A pot party?" Elena pictured the huge stone basin and those bales of herbs in her mother's pickup. "Mom's in town," she said with a groan.

"Harmony? I thought she gave up pot years ago. Well, anyway, I gotta get over there."

"Yeah, thanks for the warning, Frank."

"Did my mother say where she was going?" Elena asked Sarah, who was slipping her Mace into an expensive snakeskin handbag that matched her mid-heeled shoes. Anyone else would wear walking shoes or sneakers to go on patrol.

"Just that she wouldn't be home for dinner."

Elena sighed and prepared to rescue her mother from the narcotics unit.

When she arrived on Sierra Negra, police cars with lights revolving on their roofs and unmarked narc cars were nosed against the curb in front of her house. Smoke, strongly scented, wafted from windows and doors, cops of various descriptions crowded the yard, and in their midst were Gloria Ledesma, a cranky neighbor, and two women wearing indignant expressions, white robes with hoods, and neck chains dangling arcane symbols. In other yards up and down the block, Elena's elderly neighbors craned to watch the excitement.

Harmony, one of the white-robed priestesses, was demanding that her friend Lieutenant Beltran be called. He had, she said, lent two of his sons and a winch to aid in the transportation and placement of the magic stone basin, which should tell these policemen that, aside from how foolish they looked, they were making a big mistake by interfering with a religious ceremony in progress, one that was being carried out under the protection of a responsible police lieutenant.

Elena groaned. Beltran might be smitten enough with Harmony to lend sons and equipment, but Elena was sure he'd had no idea what Harmony was up to.

Marialita, the *curandera,* had backed Frank into a small thicket of palo verde trees and was lecturing him on religious freedom and her intention to sue the department for interfering a second time in her sacred practices. Frank looked terrified, having already had one disastrous brush with the lady, whom Harmony described as "a woman of power."

Before Elena could throw herself into the melee, the herb smoke sent her into a paroxysm of coughing. If she wanted to reoccupy her house, she'd never be able to do so now, not if she aired it out for three years. Harmony hurried to her side, trailing policemen like an antebellum southern belle with a horde of suitors. Frank dodged around the *curandera* and approached Elena.

Gloria Ledesma, arriving ahead of the other two, cried, "How was I supposed to know it was your mother? I thought some teenagers were using your house as an opium den."

Elena nodded, coughing. "Perfectly understandable," she gasped. Harmony pounded her on the back.

"You're the detective who got suspended, aren't you?" one of Frank's colleagues asked.

Elena nodded

"I don't care what anyone says, that doesn't smell like pot," said a third narc.

"They was in the livin' room feedin' dried stuff into a fire in a big stone bowl," reported one of the uniforms. "We figured they was inhalin' the stuff an' gettin' high."

"Estúpido," hissed the *curandera.* "We are driveeng out the evil speerits with the herbs of cleanseeng. Now we must start again. Hours lost."

"Mom, I'm allergic to that stuff." Elena sneezed.

"Nonsense, dear. You're allergic to the evil spirits, who are your own particular demons."

"Aquí," said the *curandera*, thrusting a wet cloth under Elena's nose. "Breathe een the protective meest of the good speerits."

Elena tried to dodge, but the *curandera* had flinty fingers. Willy-nilly, Elena inhaled a sweet, spicy scent, and her lungs cleared.

"This is your house?" the narc sergeant, Artie Potts, asked Elena.

She nodded.

"These two women have your permission to be here?"

She nodded again, feeling light-headed. "One's my mother. She came down from Chimayo to—to—" It sounded so kooky, she hated to explain.

"To reed the house of the speerits of the mountain lion, whose anger steel burns that he died at her hands." The *curandera* gestured toward Elena. "She deed not appease his soul at the time of death, so hees vengeance leengers een her house. Also the eentruder leengers, unfairly blameeng thees young woman for hees death. He, too, must be expelled."

Marialita turned to Elena with a sweeping gesture. "Now, daughter of the weaver, you must go away while we conteenue our ceremony. Now ees not safe, as you have seen, for you to be here. Later, when the rites are concluded and the speerits appeased and banished, you may return."

Elena looked at the house. Rites or no rites, smelly herbs and stone pots notwithstanding, the thought of reentering that door made her shiver.

"Look," said the sergeant, "we gotta know what you're burning in there. And the fire department, they're—"

"None of the herbs are proscribed substances," Harmony informed him angrily. She reached into a pocket of her robe and slapped a handful into the sergeant's hand.

"Yeow!" he cried. Evidently the herbs of cleansing were prickly.

"Go have them tested. If you find anything, you can come back," said Harmony. "And don't tell me about the fire department. We're burning the herbs a handful at a time."

"Hey, listen, lady, with that much smoke—"

"The windows are closed to keep the smoke in. You're the one who opened them." Harmony was becoming impatient. "If you don't go away before the last batch burns down, you'll ruin the ceremony."

"No wonder you're suspended," Sergeant Potts muttered to Elena. "Letting crazy, probably illegal stuff go on in your house."

"Hey," Frank interjected, "I don't know anyone in the department who thinks Elena should have been suspended. That was politics."

"You know her?" the sergeant asked him suspiciously.

"Thanks, Frank," said Elena.

"Yes, Frank," Harmony chimed in. "That was very supportive. Your aura-cleansing last year obviously did you a world of good."

Frank turned pale. His "aura cleansing" had involved a hallucinogen that nearly got *him* suspended.

"You need another?" asked the *curandera.*

"Lady, I wouldn't let you near me if my aura was rotting and turning black," Frank replied, backing away.

"What aura?" asked his sergeant, who had transferred into Narcotics too recently to know the story of Frank, strung-out on an aura-cleansing hallucination, kissing a drug dealer whom he took to be Elena, then attacking his lieutenant in her defense. Nor did the sergeant seem to have made the connection between the two detectives named Jarvis.

"I think I'll go home," Elena announced. "That is, if you guys are going to leave my mother alone. She may be a little weird, but she doesn't do pot—not in years."

"How lucky I am to have a police person for a daughter," Harmony observed dryly.

31

••

Thursday, October 31, 9:05 A.M.

Since she hadn't found any solid evidence of Wayne's guilt, Milton Freer did not seem particularly pleased with Elena's report. She, on the other hand, was delighted with the lists of dummy corporations that had invested in the Trujillo Sports Complex and the names of the Mexican investors who had lined up to pay for the Juarez country-club development. However, she was disappointed to find that he had no more information than he had gathered the day before. She resolved to call Glen Patkin in I.A. and ask him to put LSPD investigators to work. If Quarles was indeed laundering money, she could even get help from the FBI, maybe the DEA. Money laundering, at least in Los Santos, was an activity largely practiced by drug dealers.

She mentioned to Freer the matter of liens on at least one of the houses that Quarles had built in Sussex Hills, suggesting that Freer have his staff contact all other householders in the development to see if any had had a similar experience. Freer was shocked. He seemed to think that a man who would play his customers false and try to cheat his subcontractors would hardly balk at killing his wife. "This is good news indeed, Ms. Carr," he said enthusiastically. "I'm beginning to feel much more sanguine about the outcome of our investigation."

Having made her bow to the corporate chain of command, Elena retreated to her own office, where she opened a desk drawer, looking for a notepad, and found instead a half-knitted bootie, still on the needles, no doubt the work of the real, and pregnant, Matilda Carr. Had the woman whose name Elena was using already gone into labor, booties unfinished? Thinking of hospitals brought Monica to mind. A call to Thomason produced the depressing news that the young patrolwoman was still in a coma following her second operation. No one wanted to venture a prognosis, and the doctor to whom Elena had talked in the past was unavailable.

Her second call was to Glen Patkin at I.A. to report the dummy corporations and mysterious Mexican investors that provided Quarles's financing on his least successful projects. "Doesn't that setup, particularly the no-name corporations, suggest money laundering?" she asked Patkin.

"Maybe," he agreed. "Fax the names over, and I'll have someone check them out."

Fax? How was she going to fax the material when she didn't know how to use a fax machine? There might be one in this very office; she'd never have known by looking.

"Better yet, let's meet," said Patkin. "I've got a lot of information to pass on."

"You want me to come in to headquarters? Are you going to set up a fake grilling about my investigatory sins? Parade me past roomfuls of people who think I'm really under suspension, then send me home in tears?"

"I had something less dramatic in mind," Patkin replied dryly. "Like lunch somewhere cops don't gather."

"Great," said Elena. "We can go to a really expensive restaurant at the department's expense. For sure, we won't see any cops if anything on the menu costs more than five dollars." Then she remembered that she was talking to Internal Affairs and added hastily, "Just kidding. How about Casa Jurado on Cincinnati?"

They settled on one o'clock, and Elena went off to her

interview with Pamela Honnecker to find out what it was that made the volunteer quit the Quarles campaign.

Honnecker was a young-looking woman with white hair styled in a smooth, short pageboy. Elena wondered what her age had been when her hair went white and, for that matter, what her age was now. Her skin was smooth and tanned, with only faint smile lines around the eyes, her figure slim and athletic. In fact, she wore a jogging suit and arrived at her own door, running, as Elena drove up.

"Come in," she invited, barely winded. "Unless you're late, I just ran a ten-minute mile, which isn't bad, considering how steep the hills are."

She took Elena to her sunny kitchen, poured them both tall glasses of iced tea, put out a plate of cookies that tasted dauntingly healthy, and, leaning back in a maple kitchen chair with blue-sprigged cushions, said, "I can't imagine what an insurance company would want with me. My husband isn't taking out some huge policy on my life, is he? If so, he'll have to murder me to collect, because I am one healthy lady—low-fat diet, lots of exercise, and I don't associate with people who smoke."

Elena smiled. "You're in luck. I don't." She was thinking, disheartened, that maybe Honnecker had dumped Quarles because people smoked at his headquarters.

"You're the one who's in luck," Honnecker retorted. "This is a smoke-free house. I don't even allow cigarettes in my yard."

On the other hand, that my-husband-will-have-to-kill-me-to-collect remark hit awfully close to Elena's line of investigation. Could Mrs. Honnecker have been thinking along those lines when she quit the Quarles campaign?

"So what does Texas Life want with me?" Mrs. Honnecker asked. "You're not here to sell me insurance, are you?"

"I'm investigating the Quarles claim, because Hope Quarles was murdered. You'll have read—"

"About it in the papers. Of course. Why me?"

"Your letter to the newspaper. We wondered why you quit his campaign."

"Because I won't work for a hypocrite," snapped Mrs. Honnecker.

"Could you explain that?"

"And get sued for slander?"

"Anything you tell me will be confidential," Elena promised. "We just want to be sure that—ah—Mrs. Quarles's death was—"

"Natural? She was murdered. So you want to know whether he killed her? Evidently not, if you believe the newspapers. They're saying the policewoman's bullet killed Hope. Otherwise—well, never mind."

"The bullet may have come from the policewoman's gun," said Elena, "but Officer Ibarra was shot down herself. Which suggests that someone shot her, then used her gun to shoot Mrs. Quarles."

"I can't see Wayne Quarles shooting a policewoman." Pamela Honnecker shook her head.

"Or hiring it done?" Elena asked. "That possibility, bizarre as it may seem, makes us want to know why you disapprove of him."

"He's too much of a snob to know any gang members or car thieves or people like that," Pamela hedged.

"You don't have to be friends with a killer to hire him. You just need a contact."

"Oh." Mrs. Honnecker looked thoughtful. "Goodness knows, I wouldn't put any kind of association past Fermin Gil. He started out defending all sorts of scum. My husband used to say Fermin would have defended Hitler if the fee was right. Not that Fermin does criminal cases these days. Wayne and his corporate buddies provide Gil with income enough for three lawyers."

"And is that why you dislike Mr. Quarles? Because of his association with Fermin Gil?"

"Not really. As I said, I hate a hypocrite." She seemed to make up her mind. "Wayne Quarles, who was always bragging about his wonderful marriage, has a red-hot affair going with Madelaine Rocca. In fact, Madelaine had the nerve to tell me that he was going to divorce Hope for her. I told her she was a fool if she thought so."

An affair? Now, *that* was interesting. No one Elena had talked to thought Wayne Quarles was unfaithful.

"But now he doesn't have to get a divorce, does he?" Pamela Honnecker continued bitterly. "Hope, who thought Wayne was Mr. Perfect, is dead, and I'm sure Madelaine is all primed to step into her shoes as soon as decency and the campaign allow it."

"You think that will happen?"

"I wouldn't bet on it. Who knows what *he* wants? But then, maybe he did have Hope killed so he'd be free to marry Madelaine. Why not? He'd get Hope's money and Madelaine's political know-how." Pamela made circles with her glass on the table, studying the changing water rings. "She ran Nellie's first campaign. Did you know that? Then she jumped ship and came over to Wayne, maybe even suggested that he run. I think she had a falling-out with Nellie."

"In that case, why isn't Ms. Rocca his manager?"

Pamela laughed. "Fermin and Wayne are joined at the hip. Don't ask me why. I think Fermin's a rat. But if Wayne starts something, Fermin's second in command. Or maybe first in command, with Wayne as a figurehead. Who knows how it works?"

"About Madelaine Rocca . . ."

"Right. Well, it just infuriated me—them dragging Hope to rallies and exhibiting her like some trophy because everyone loves Hope—loved her—and here Wayne, with all his big talk about family values, is hanging out in motels with the woman who runs the campaign office."

"You're sure they—"

"Of course I'm sure. That's why I quit. And I told him so, too. He had the nerve to deny it. So I said, 'Then Madelaine's lying? I can hardly wait to tell her.' " Pamela

Honnecker's infectious laughter bubbled up. "You should have seen his face. I hope I caused a big fat fight between them."

"Was this before or after Hope Quarles was killed?"

Pamela's face turned dark. "After. It was actually all that public mourning that made me so mad. I'd probably have stayed with the campaign for Hope's sake, because she really wanted him to have it—the mayor's job. But I can tell you, Hope was hurt that he never encouraged her to be more than a showpiece wife—probably because he was afraid if Hope spent any time at headquarters, she'd discover what was going on with Madelaine."

Another version, thought Elena. Previously she'd been told that Hope wasn't particularly interested in politics or her husband's campaign, which was why she hadn't been more active.

"And don't think I haven't noticed that suddenly he's got twice as much paid exposure since Hope died. Maybe he had her killed to finance his rotten campaign. Maybe you ought to talk to the police about him."

"Maybe *you* should," Elena suggested soberly.

Pamela shrugged. "I don't have any facts."

None of us do so far, thought Elena, and sighed.

32

Thursday, October 31, 11:30 A.M.

Wearing Sarah's brown tweed suit and hat, the blond vice wig, and Harmony's glasses, Elena strode into Quarles headquarters and presented her Texas Life & Casualty card to Cindy Mallow, with whom she had talked on her first visit. Cindy didn't recognize her but directed her to a small private office, where Elena found Madelaine Rocca, wearing a dramatic red-and-black pants suit that matched her black hair and red lipstick. The lady announced in her first breath that she had no time for insurance agents.

Elena nodded sagely and replied that she quite understood: the campaign was more important than the three-million-dollar claim filed by the candidate against Texas Life & Casualty. "We can put off the investigation until Mr. Quarles's associates have time to talk to us. No problem at all, Ms. Rocca." Elena smiled pleasantly.

"You might have mentioned that you weren't trying to sell me a policy," Rocca snapped. "How can I help?"

"Were you aware of any marital troubles between Mr. and Mrs. Quarles before her murder?" Elena asked, sitting down and flipping open her notebook.

"I really couldn't comment," said Madelaine Rocca.

"Why not? As the second in command here, you must see a lot of the candidate, not to mention his wife."

"Hope Quarles took little interest in Wayne's candidacy," Madelaine said stiffly.

"And he never said anything about her?"

"If you mean anything unpleasant, no. Mr. Quarles is a gentleman. He—"

"Perhaps you can tell me who disliked Mrs. Quarles."

"Why would you ask that?" Madelaine demanded.

"Because she was murdered."

"By a car thief."

"I doubt it," said Elena. "And I'm sure the police do, too."

"This is just some ploy by the insurance company to deprive Mr. Quarles of money that should rightfully—"

"That's what I am trying to determine, Ms. Rocca. Whether Mr. Quarles has a right to three million dollars of Texas Life and Casualty's money. Until we know who killed Mrs. Quarles, we can't really tell, can we?" Elena pushed the ill-fitting glasses back onto the bridge of her nose. "Now, do you know of any enemies who—"

"No," Rocca said.

"What about you, Ms. Rocca? I believe you and Mr. Quarles have an ongoing—how shall I put it?—intimate relationship."

"What?" Ms. Rocca looked stunned.

"Oh, I'm sorry," said Elena. "Am I to understand that your liaison with Mr. Quarles was just a passing thing?"

"Our relationship is—is—"

"Sexual in nature?" Elena poised pen above notepad.

"—is none of your business."

"An insurance investigation leaves no sheet unturned. Where were you the morning Mrs. Quarles was killed?"

"Right here," cried Madelaine Rocca. "Your questions are insulting and ridiculous. You can't possibly suspect—"

"Where was Mr. Quarles?"

"I—I don't—"

"Not here?"

"I believe he was making a speech at—at—I'd have to check his schedule. You can't think—"

"You've claimed that Mr. Quarles planned to marry you."

"Who told you that?" Ms. Rocca turned pale.

"Since you don't deny it, it must be true. Of course, it may be untrue that he actually said that—"

"I don't have to listen to this."

"Of course not. I have no official status in the investigation, although my company is liaising with the police. I'll just tell them about the gossip I've gathered and your unwillingness to cooperate. They'll want to question Mr. Quarles—"

"Shut up!" Madelaine Rocca screamed at her. "You're trying to come between us."

"I'll just write that down," said Elena.

"Neither one of us had anything to do with her death."

"You can only speak for yourself, Ms. Rocca. You can't know what Mr. Quarles may have done—"

"The killer was bald and tattooed. Wayne—"

"—or paid someone to do," Elena concluded. "What can you tell me about Mr. Quarles's business affairs?"

"Nothing," Rocca sputtered. "I mean his business wouldn't be any of your business. And—and he didn't need her money, if that's what you're implying."

"How do you know?"

"I do know."

"You're involved in Quarles Construction?"

"No, just the campaign, but—"

"But he *told* you his business was doing well?"

"Everyone knows how successful he's been, in *spite* of his father-in-law and his wife."

"Indicating cause for resentment on Mr. Quarles's part?"

"I didn't say that."

"You implied it."

"You're twisting my words."

Elena sighed loudly. "You're very defensive, Ms. Rocca. I'm just searching for simple information—to substantiate awarding or denying a claim. It seems to me that you were kept in the dark about your lover's affairs—"

"Wayne told me everything!"

"—or he was telling you lies, at best hiding things from you."

"He was not!"

"Then the only conclusion I can reach is that *you* are telling me lies or hiding things from me."

Rocca leaped up from her desk, having spotted the candidate. "Wayne," she called. He came over and allowed himself to be introduced to Matilda Carr, whom he glad-handed as soon as he heard that she was from Texas Life & Casualty. A few words from Madelaine Rocca on the nature of the interview, however, wiped away his urbane smile.

"I'll tell you what I told the police," Wayne Quarles began. "I did not kill my wife nor conspire in her death, nor at this traumatic time in my life do I appreciate being held under suspicion by an incompetent police force or an insurance company that evidently wants to renege on its contractual obligations. You might keep in mind, young woman, that the last female who attacked my reputation, some upstart girl detective, is now suspended without pay."

Girl detective? Elena swallowed a snarl. "Indirect threats from beneficiary," she said aloud, and wrote it down.

"I shall certainly call your superior to tell him that you have been harassing my campaign workers and slandering my good name," Wayne Quarles announced.

"Direct threats," Elena said, and made another note.

Quarles turned away from her. "Madelaine, we have a strategy session in"—he consulted a weighty Rolex—"two minutes." Then to Elena, he added, "Good day, Ms. Carr." He looked rather pleased with himself, obviously of the opinion that he had cowed his opponent.

"Good day, sir," she replied. "I'm sorry that you've taken our necessary and routine investigation amiss." Elena took great pleasure in the knowledge that Wayne Quarles was crowing over a pseudo-victory, for Elena Jarvis was not suspended and Matilda Carr wouldn't be, while Madelaine Rocca had all but admitted an adulterous relationship with Quarles.

Elena glanced at her Timex and headed for the appointment at Casa Jurado with Internal Affairs. Now *she* was the one who'd have to watch her tongue. She hoped to be more discreet than Madelaine Rocca had been.

33

Thursday, October 31, 1:00 P.M.

Glen Patkin was a surprise—blond, ruggedly handsome, with an engaging smile and a sharply tailored gray suit. Elena would never have guessed by looking at him that he was an Internal Affairs snoop. He evidently found her a surprise, too. "Why haven't we met?" he asked when she slipped into a seat at his table, having given her false name to the owner and been directed to the other side of a dividing wall.

"Because I've never been suspended before. You found anything on me yet?"

"We're working together, remember?" Patkin protested. "This could be the one time since I transferred to I.A. that I can talk to a fellow cop without being treated like the enemy."

"I'll have a Corona," Elena told the waiter, "*salpicón* to start, then the number-two plate." Patkin frowned when she ordered beer. "You can have half the *salpicón*," she offered.

He ordered Coke and steak *tampiqueña*. "I take it Texas Life is paying for this," he said when the waiter had left.

"I don't see why not, and you can stop taking mental notes about an officer drinking on duty. I work for the insurance company now, and they couldn't care less."

"Right. Are you married?"

"Why do you want to know?"

"Because I like blondes."

"It's a wig. Got it from Vice. The suit and hat belong to my roommate. My real hair is black, and I usually wear a French braid, slacks, and a jacket."

"That's O.K. I still want to know if you're married."

"Divorced." He was cute. Still, her marriage to Frank the Narc hadn't been a success, too competitive. She tried to imagine being married to a guy from Internal Affairs. You'd be afraid to go to bed for fear you'd say something in your sleep that your husband considered incriminating. "So what information do you have for me?"

They both scraped *salpicón*—marinated, shredded beef decorated with bits of cheese, cilantro, and slices of avocado—onto flour tortillas and began to eat. "First," said Patkin, "there's the son. Someone beat him up yesterday and threw him over this fake waterfall at a fraternity house. His face looks like three rounds with Muhammad Ali, and he's got two broken ribs and a broken leg from the fall down the chute into the dry pool. He claims he doesn't know who attacked him."

"Have you checked out Paco, his pusher?" Elena filled her second tortilla with *salpicón*.

"Narcotics has been investigating him. Small-time dealer, customers mostly in high schools and colleges. Word is that he's supplied through Los Reyes Diablos."

"It fits," said Elena, excited. "Hope Quarles's killer had Diablo King tattoos. Maybe Paco got some gangbanger to pop her so the kid could pay his debts. Junior probably promised Paco his money plus a bonus to take care of Mom."

"Maybe. Narcotics busted Paco yesterday afternoon. Found a little coke on him. Eyewitnesses from H.H.U. identified him as the guy who attacked Quarles, Junior. The narcs got an assistant D.A. to offer Paco a plea on the assault and possession charges in return for info, but all they got was that Junior owed him thirty thou and wouldn't pay after he inherited from Mom. Evidently Paco didn't believe the money was tied up like Junior said. On the other hand, Paco says neither he nor Los Reyes Diablos had anything to do with her death. He says Junior never approached him about a hit, and he never approached the gang."

"Well, Paco would say that," Elena pointed out. "Getting pled down on assault and possession won't help him if he implicates himself in a murder-for-hire case."

The I.A. officer snapped his fingers and asked, "Say, is Frank Jarvis in Narcotics your ex?" Elena nodded. "Well, Frank and his partner must have had this Paco in interrogation for six hours this morning—got him up at five-thirty and grilled him till noon. Nothing. He won't change his story. Not that anyone takes his word for anything. Both the narcs and C.A.P. are looking into it. Paco's name, by the way, is Johnny Ray Zumbel."

"So Junior or Paco or both look good as guys who contracted out the murder of Hope Quarles," Elena summarized, making notes in her casebook. "Texas Life'll be pissed. Hell, they may even fire me. They want the killer to be Wayne, Senior, so they don't have to pay the three mil."

"Well, don't jump for the kid yet." Patkin was cutting pieces off his steak *tampiqueña* and chewing with gusto while Elena took bites of taco, chili relleño, and rolled enchilada. "Fraud and Forgery found out that Hope Quarles asked for an audit at the last Masterson stockholders' meeting. Nothing turned up against Bud Holmes, the CEO, but the purchasing agent, guy named Innolem, got canned."

"Why?"

"For soliciting and taking bribes from subcontractors and suppliers, skimming, that sort of thing."

"Did the company prosecute him?"

"Not so far."

Elena sipped her Corona thoughtfully. "Maybe Hope was pushing for prosecution, and he didn't want to go to jail."

"Could be." Patkin consulted his notes while Elena savored her chili relleño. "Fraud and Forgery is still trying to find out who's behind the dummy corporations that financed Quarles here in Los Santos, and they're querying the Mexican police about the investors in the country club. That stuff takes time, so they'll have to get back to us."

Elena nodded. "Better them than me. They're probably digging through computer files, and I hate that stuff."

"Just what I like," said Patkin, grinning, "a woman who's less technologically adept than me. Hurts a man's ego when his computer crashes and some woman comes along, presses a few keys, and says, 'There you are, dummy. How come you didn't know how to do that?'"

"So you're saying you don't like smart women?" Elena asked, ready to cross him off her list.

"I'm saying I don't like my older sister's nyah-nyah attitude about my computer problems."

His sister could show him up at a computer keyboard? It was sort of endearing that he'd admit it. And Elena herself hated to be twitted because she was technologically challenged, as they said these days when you looked like a retard in the world of bytes and rams. Even the language was designed to confuse everyone but nerds and kids in grade school. "Well, I'm accumulating lots of suspects," said Elena. "The father, the son, the father's mistress, the son's pusher, the purchasing agent, some violent scumbag off the street who likes to kill people for the heck of it—"

"The candidate has a mistress?"

"And she expects a wedding ring. Whether that's in his plans I couldn't say."

"Well, here's one more for you. You thought maybe Quarles might be laundering money. There's one guy in Narcotics who's heard a rumor that a Miguel Barrajas on Quarles's country-club investor list may be connected."

"Barrajas," she said, searching her memory. "Probably a million guys are named Miguel Barrajas."

"The narcs are going to ask around. Is the insurance company good for dessert?"

They both ordered flan.

"Once you get publicly reinstated, you want to go to a movie or something?" Patkin asked.

"Not till I'm cleared, huh?"

"Hey, I'm in Internal Affairs. I've got my reputation to think about."

"What about my reputation?" Elena asked, laughing. "No one wants to be mixed up with I.A."

"Story of my life," Patkin said glumly. "I've even had civilians refuse dates with me because I'm I.A. They think if they do something wrong, I'll tell their mothers."

"The Socorro Heights Senior Citizens Center has announced that it will be mounting a protest at police headquarters over the suspension of Detective Elena Jarvis," a radio announcer reported on the three-o'clock newsbreak.

Elena groaned. Clearly her mother was at work.

"Jarvis was suspended for concentrating her efforts in the Hope Quarles murder case on the victim's family rather than the LSPD officer whose gun fired the fatal bullet. That officer, Monica Ibarra, remains in a coma at Thomason General.

"Last year the same senior citizens' group, seated in lawn chairs, held up traffic to and from the police garage for several hours while protesting the arrest of a young homosexual poet suspected of killing his father."

Elena groaned again. No doubt her mother and all those sweet seventy- and eighty-year-old women were going to get arrested again, this time because they thought, wrongly, that Elena was being discriminated against. And she couldn't say a thing to disabuse them of that notion.

34

Thursday, October 31, 3:15 P.M.

Wayne Quarles, Jr., lay in a hospital bed at Sierra Medical Center, his cast suspended from the ceiling, his ribs taped, his face bruised and swollen. Johnny Ray Zumbel, alias Paco, had obviously been very unhappy about Junior's failure to pay the drug money he owed the dealer.

"Good afternoon, Mr. Quarles," said Elena, handing him her business card. "My sympathies on your loss."

"I'll recover," Junior mumbled, without looking at her card. "Who are you?"

"I was speaking of your mother's death, although Texas Life and Casualty extends its sympathies for your own—ah—accident. Fortunately, we don't cover you with health benefits." She chuckled. "Little insurance humor there."

"What's funny?" Junior snarled.

"Evidently nothing," Elena replied. "My company holds the policy on your mother's life."

His eyes lit up. "Am I the beneficiary?"

"Did you expect to be?"

"I didn't know there was a policy."

Elena raised her eyebrows. "But you did expect to be remembered more generously in her will?"

"Damn right," Junior affirmed. "I wouldn't be in this fix if she hadn't wanted me to wait fifteen years to get my money. I'm screwed. Although I don't know why you'd care."

"We're interested in determining who killed your mother."

"How would I know?"

"If you expected to benefit from her death—"

"You think I killed her?" Junior's good eye rounded. "Do I look like some punk Hispanic criminal?"

Elena studied him thoughtfully. "Actually, with the black eye, and then you have dark hair—"

"I do not. I'm sweating. 'Cause I'm in pain. Could you hold that water glass for me?"

"In a minute," said Elena. "I'm sure you're aware that Paco, your pusher—"

"I don't know what you're talking about."

"—gets his product through the Diablo Kings, who may have killed your mother."

"You think Paco had Mom killed?" Junior looked dumbfounded. "Like he thinks if he gets her killed, I'll inherit a lot of money and I'll pay him off? Maybe that's why he got so mad when I said I wouldn't get any money this year, and not much for the next fifteen. Hey, could you punch that button that calls the nurse?"

"In a minute," said Elena.

"You're a real mean woman, you know that? I need help here, and all you can say is, 'In a minute.' *Nurse!*" His bellow for help brought two nurses hurrying into the room. "Get the police," Junior commanded.

"Actually, there's a detective outside waiting to see you," said a young Hispanic RN, whose name tag read CARMEN MIRANDA. Her mother must have been a fan of old movies, Elena reasoned, wondering how the nurse liked being named after a dancer who cavorted through films with a basket of fruit on her head. Nurse Carmen ducked into the hall while the second nurse took Junior's pulse and said, "You shouldn't get excited." She turned to Elena. "You'll have to leave."

"Right," Junior agreed. "She can't do me any good. She's some insurance flunky."

Just then Leo, Elena's sometime partner, followed the returning Nurse Carmen into the room, saying, "You've *never* seen a Carmen Miranda movie? Great dancing."

"I don't want to hear about it," Carmen snapped.

"You from the police?" asked Junior.

"Crimes Against Persons," Leo answered. "You ready to tell us who attacked you?" He ignored Elena.

"I want you to arrest a guy named Paco. He probably killed my mother."

"There are at least a hundred Pacos in Los Santos," said Leo.

"This one has long brown hair with a bleached skunk strip, a gold cross hanging from his left ear, and a gold eyetooth. He hangs out at the Quick Coyote."

"And you think he killed your mother?"

"He must have. I owe him money."

"For what?"

"Ah . . . poker. I lost it playing poker."

"How much?"

"What difference does it make? Just find him."

"He's the one who beat you up?"

Junior started to answer, then thought better of it, belatedly mindful of having claimed that he couldn't identify his attacker. "I don't know, but he must have killed Mom."

"And you know that because you asked him to, right?"

"Get real. If I'd asked him to, he'd have wanted money, and that was the whole problem. I didn't have any. So you arrest him. Get him to confess. And don't let him out on bail. Killers don't get bail, right?"

Elena decided to slip out, thinking over the conversation as she did so. Junior had jumped at the idea that Paco might have killed Hope Quarles, seemingly because he saw Paco's incarceration as a way to get out of paying his own debt, as well as a way to escape any further persuasion of the sort he'd just suffered. It didn't seem to have occurred to him that anyone would think he himself had been behind the killing.

But then again, maybe he was smarter than he looked. In which case, he'd just put on quite a slick performance. Which was it? Elena didn't know. Surely, Junior wasn't so dumb as to trust Paco not to give him up if the pusher had, in fact, been hired to kill Hope by her son. Either way Elena had only speculation, little fact.

And in the meantime she had a date at Masterson Construction to talk to Bud Holmes about Hope Quarles's request for an audit of the company books.

Elena turned on her truck radio as she headed for Masterson Construction, anxious about the demonstration on her behalf that had been announced earlier. Maybe it had fallen through. A cold wind had blown in from the northeast that morning, driving dust across the interstate, making bits of paper dance along the concrete like giant dandruff flakes. It stood to reason that the elderly wouldn't want to demonstrate on such a day. Any temperature below fifty was considered a cold snap in Los Santos, where summer meant hundred-degree days, and winter could pass almost unnoticed.

". . . of Hispanic Women has gathered in front of police headquarters carrying signs that say, 'Reinstate Detective Elena Jarvis, Los Santos's only female Hispanic homicide detective.' "

Elena stared at the radio with dismay.

"Spokesperson Celestina Ortiz—"

Celestina Ortiz! The *colonia* dweller once suspected of planting bombs all over the city?

"—Chairperson of the Activist Subcommittee of the Council of Hispanic Women—"

Elena hoped activism didn't include explosives.

"—pointed out that the LSPD does not have a fifty-fifty ratio of men to women, much less a seventy-thirty ratio of Hispanic to Anglo, in accordance with the population of the city, and that Crimes Against Persons has only one female detective outside the Sex Crimes Squad. Ortiz said, 'It's just like in construction. No one wants a female bricklayer. We do a better job and show up them sloppy males. The head cop suspended Jarvis because she's good, an' them male detectives was prob'ly complainin', an' because them rich Anglos didn't wan' her nosin' into their business.' "

Words of wisdom from an unemployed bricklayer, Elena thought. She sighed and turned onto Lomaland. At least the news report hadn't mentioned her mother, although Harmony was surely involved. Elena doubted that her fellow officers in C.A.P. were going to appreciate this expression of support for her, not when Ortiz had claimed Elena was showing up her male counterparts. In all likelihood, by the time she was publicly reinstated, no one in the unit would be speaking to her.

35

••

Thursday, October 31, 4:10 P.M.

When Elena walked into Bud Holmes's office, he remarked brusquely that he had no policies with Texas Life & Casualty. Then, frowning, he asked, "Do I know you?"

Elena gave him the Matilda Carr ID and replied, "I don't think so." He was the only person so far to question her identity. Did that mean her wig had slipped? She poked the chignon surreptitiously.

Holmes shrugged and looked at the business card. "What can I do for you, Ms. Carr?"

"As perhaps you are aware, there was a large policy on Hope Quarles's life. Naturally, we're looking into her death."

"Her husband may have had one. We didn't."

"No sir, but she was murdered. We won't be paying off until we know who killed her and why."

"And you think someone here might have had a hand in Hope's death? I don't remember hearing any evidence that it was more than a street crime."

"Murders are always closely scrutinized," Elena replied vaguely. "I understand that Mrs. Quarles demanded an audit of the company's books at the last board meeting."

"True. She did." Holmes frowned. "But—"

"And problems were found in the purchasing department."

Holmes nodded. "I certainly felt like a fool when the reports came in. I'd pretty much ignored Hope when she said she thought something was going on."

"And the problem led to the firing of a Mr. Frederick Innolem."

"Yeah, we fired him as soon as the auditors reported their findings."

"Was any further action contemplated?"

"He had to sign an agreement to pay back the money he'd skimmed, and we reported the bribes we discovered to the IRS and stopped doing business with the companies that offered them."

"Didn't Mrs. Quarles want him prosecuted?"

"You think Fred hired someone to kill Hope?" Holmes looked completely astounded.

"Her actions pretty much ruined him, didn't they?"

"Innolem ruined himself."

"And he didn't resent her?"

"I suppose he did." Holmes now looked very upset. "But what good would killing her do him? He was caught already."

"How is it that you, who were in touch with the day-to-day operations of the company, had to be warned of Mr. Innolem's machinations by a—an outsider?"

"Hope pretty much owns the company," Holmes protested.

"But she was not involved in its operations."

He sighed. "No, and what a fool I was for discouraging that. Hope turned out to be sharper than any of us gave her credit for. As you say, she saw what I was too close to notice. I'd known Fred for years and trusted him. I was wrong." He stared at his hands, large, callused hands with blunt-cut nails. "What a pair we'd have been, Hope and I. If I'd encouraged her to take an active part in the company, she'd have been happier and the company more prosperous.

Every suggestion she ever made was a winner, but we all—those of us her father left in charge—took her at his evaluation, and Rob never saw Hope as anything but his pretty little girl." Holmes bowed his shining dome like a bald eagle ashamed of having neglected his nestlings. "And now it's too late," he murmured sadly. "She's gone."

Elena had rarely seen a man look more downcast.

"She was right to turn me down," Holmes muttered.

"I beg your pardon?"

"I wanted to marry her. That was a long time ago, and I was a young man in love, but Hope saw that I was in love with the girl her father wanted her to be. I suppose that's why she chose Wayne. I never thought much of him, but at least he had the sense to see that she was smarter than he was. While I . . ." He spread those blunt-nailed fingers helplessly. "I wanted to put her up on a pedestal. And I did, too. All these years I kept her out of the business because that's what her father thought should be done, and I loved Rob Masterson as much as I did Hope."

"You did?" Elena let herself look puzzled.

"Rob was the closest thing I had to a father after mine was killed," Holmes explained. "He and my dad fought together in World War Two, same platoon. Rob moved my mother to Los Santos when the war ended so that he could keep an eye on us, and when my mother killed herself, he took me in, into his home when I was sixteen, later into the business. He was pretty unhappy when Hope refused to marry me. He had it all planned out. The two of us would inherit the company and produce the next generation."

"What's your financial stake in the company?" Elena asked. Since he was talking so freely, she might as well push. The more you knew about the principals, the more likely you were to discover the who and why of a murder.

Holmes leaned back in his chair. "I make two hundred and fifty thousand a year, plus a bonus based on profits, and I own about five percent of the stock, through a stock-option deal that was set up in Rob's will. Hope's death doesn't change anything as far as I'm concerned. Except that I feel damned lonely. About the closest I had to a personal life was when Hope came in for board meetings or showed up at my office and took me out to lunch."

Holmes earned almost as much from the company as Hope had, maybe more. Elena was amazed. And had Wayne Quarles known his wife was having lunch with a former suitor? Had he cared? Maybe not. After all, Wayne had Madelaine.

"And you don't think Mr. Innolem would have hired someone to kill her?" Elena asked bluntly.

"I doubt it," Bud Holmes replied. "He turned over the deed to his house to make restitution. Then he moved to Phoenix to live with his son and daughter-in-law. Naturally, he lost his pension. I wouldn't think he'd have the money to hire a killer. He was skimming and taking bribes to pay gambling debts. Evidently he flew to Las Vegas every month and lost steadily for about ten years. Hope saw him there, saw him lose a bundle, looked over the books herself and asked some questions, then demanded the audit. But as I said, that was months ago."

"Did he have a drug problem?" Elena asked, trying to discover a connection to the Diablo Kings.

"Didn't even drink. I guess we each have our weaknesses. Alcohol would be mine if I let it." He glanced at a wall-mounted wooden clock that had been chiming the quarter hours as they talked. "You want a drink, Ms. Carr? This is the time of day when I have the first of two."

"Sure, why not?" said Elena. "Do you have any beer?" She regretted that choice instantly as being out of character with her insurance-company persona.

Holmes rose and opened a small refrigerator sitting on the floor behind his desk. From its depths he pulled out a bottle of Shiner Bach, opened it, and poured it into a glass, which he handed Elena. She took an appreciative sip. Being an insurance investigator certainly had its perks. If she drank on duty while not under suspension, she'd be suspended.

Holmes was pouring himself a straight Scotch, no ice. Blah, she thought. While he put the bottle away, she mused over what he'd told her. She could check Innolem out, but he didn't look promising as the murderer, nor did Holmes.

"What about her marriage to Wayne Quarles?" Elena asked when Bud Holmes resumed his seat, drink in hand.

"She was wasted on him," said Holmes. "Of course, maybe that's just sour grapes from a man who lost her and never found another woman he wanted."

"So you didn't like Quarles?"

"He'd have fit right in in the nineteenth century, when men expected to make and lose several fortunes in a lifetime. He's a gambler. No sense of financing. Always looking for the big killing that comes from luck instead of careful planning."

"Would you say he's been successful?"

"Don't know. Probably not in the overall. Fortunately, they didn't have to live on what he made. Rob made sure Hope would always have enough money and Wayne couldn't get his hands on it."

"And the marriage. What did she think of him?"

Holmes drained his glass and reached back for the bottle to pour another, then sipped thoughtfully, taking his time before he answered. "She loved him. But I wouldn't say she trusted him. Her will shows you that. She didn't have to tie the money up the way her father had, but she did—for both her husband and son. That's another reason I think she was smarter than any of us realized." He studied the remaining Scotch in his glass. "I'd say, on the whole, she was disappointed in her marriage, but I can't point to anything she ever said. Again, maybe it's just wishful thinking on my part. I should be embarrassed to admit that. You'd think, loving her as I always have, I'd want her to be happy, but here I'm saying her life was a disappointment. She was always affectionate to him in public. It's just—" He stopped abruptly. "*You* think Wayne had her killed?"

"That's never occurred to you?" She watched him closely,

remembering that Holmes had offered to drive Wayne into bankruptcy if he'd killed Hope.

"Well, two detectives from Homicide kind of suggested it, and I was really furious for a while, thinking he might have. But then I figured that kind of stuff only happens in books. In real life it's some junkie or mugger."

"So you don't think it's possible that Mr. Quarles could have—"

"Who's the beneficiary of the policy your company holds?" he interrupted. "But then why am I asking? Of course it's him. Unless it's the kids. Is it him?" He looked at her sharply.

Elena nodded.

"For how much?"

"A lot."

"That son of a bitch." Holmes's face flushed.

"Of course, there was the same policy on him with Hope as beneficiary," Elena remarked.

The CEO took a deep breath and clasped both hands around his highball glass. "I think he loved her," Holmes admitted.

Had he? Elena wondered. Quarles hadn't been faithful, but then there were plenty of unfaithful men who loved their wives. Frank, her ex, had claimed to love her, but it hadn't prevented him from fooling around. If Quarles had loved Hope, would he have had her killed anyway? For the money?

36

••

Thursday, October 31, 6:30 P.M.

Rather than return so late, Elena called her office for messages. The first was from Milton Freer. His people had traced two of the dummy corporations that had financed the Trujillo Sports Complex. The stockholders were Mexican nationals, Mexican nationals living legally in the U.S., and Mexican-Americans. Little else was known about them. Elena saw nothing there to negate her hypothesis that Quarles might be a party to money laundering.

The three other messages were from Wayne Quarles, all asking that she call him and apologizing for his unpleasantness that morning. In the last he said that he would be back at campaign headquarters by eight-thirty. Intrigued, Elena decided to respond in person. Then she called Glen Patkin to pass on the names, addresses, and nationalities from the two dummy corporations the insurance company had researched. She had to leave the information on his machine. These days people never talked to each other; they communicated with taped messages.

She turned off her cellular phone and glanced at her watch. With less than two hours before she could see Quarles, it didn't seem worthwhile going home. Accordingly, she stopped at a steak house and treated herself to a prime-rib dinner paid for with her corporate American

Express card. What a life! Luxury on the job. Except that eating alone in a restaurant demonstrated the pathetic state of her social life.

Elena sighed and poked a slice of apple pie with her fork. Actually, three men had recently shown an interest in dating her, but two were still married, and the other was I.A., which was tantamount to being asked out by a leper. And of course Sam, her therapist, was escorting her to the symphony, a consolation prize for being suspended, which seemed unfair, since Sam was unaware that the suspension was window dressing. She wondered what Wayne Quarles was so anxious to tell her, and whether he'd want to say it if he knew that she was the detective whose career he'd seemingly brought to a screeching halt.

Signing the credit-card slip with a flourish, Elena went out to her truck and pulled back onto Interstate 10, listening to the local news. A labor lawyer named Alope Randall, whom Elena had once half suspected of murder, was saying that she'd be glad to represent Detective Jarvis pro bono. Randall went on to make a speech about the rotten way Hispanic women were treated in the work place.

How had her mother roped Alope Randall into this? Alope usually represented garment workers who had been shafted by their employers or NAFTA. Maybe Randall, half Mescalero Apache, was friends with Harmony's *curandera*.

"Do Hispanic men support their women in the struggle for racial and sexual equality in the workplace?" Randall asked rhetorically. "They do not. Police Chief Armando Gaitan should have more pride in his ethnicity than to suspend a competent woman detective of Hispanic descent at the behest of a man who has, in the past, employed undocumented workers on his building projects."

Elena hadn't known that Quarles employed illegals. Had he done so in order to undercut Los Santos workmen? And then charged a fortune for houses he built with cheap labor? *Maquila* supervisors could afford his houses, NAFTA entrepreneurs could, but the average Los Santoan, who hardly made enough to live on, couldn't afford to buy any house at all. Her own home, which she and Frank had bought cheap on a VA loan, took a big chunk of her salary now that she was making the mortgage payments by herself, and she wasn't even living there.

Meanwhile another woman on the radio was advising, "If a patrolman stops you on a traffic violation, tear the ticket up and throw it in his face."

What was that? Elena stopped thinking about houses and concentrated on the radio.

"Practice civil disobedience, women of Los Santos! Until the suspension of Detective Jarvis is rescinded."

Oh Lord, who was that preaching civil disobedience? And had Harmony put her up to it?

"That was Myra Talamantes of the Council of Hispanic Women calling for what amounts to a women's strike against the Los Santos police. Word has just reached us that coeds at Herbert Hobart University and UT Los Santos have declared solidarity with the Council of Hispanic Women and the Gray Ladies Circle. No statement has yet been issued by the Los Santos Police Department, but fourteen women were arrested late this afternoon for blocking access to headquarters at Five Points. Stay tuned for the latest on the situation, and now back to our regular programming, *Rock and Roll After Dark* with Los Santos's favorite disk jockey, Pino Peña."

Elena turned the radio off and shuddered. Was her mother in jail? Pulling out her cell phone, she called home to see if Sarah had any news about Harmony.

She got the answering machine.

"I *don't* employ illegal aliens," Quarles protested. "And I don't know why I'm being targeted by Hispanic women. This is going to kill me at the polls if it doesn't stop."

"You didn't get that detective suspended?" Elena asked, tickled at the irony of the situation. Without recognizing her in her blond wig, Wayne Quarles was asking for sympathy from the very woman whose career he had attempted to jeopardize.

"I simply mentioned to Chief Gaitan—"

"And the media," Elena murmured.

"I may have said something to the press," Quarles admitted, "but only because I was shocked that while I was grieving for the death of my wife, which was, after all, a matter of negligence on the part of the police—"

"Didn't I hear that Officer Ibarra was shot as well?" Elena couldn't resist that verbal jab.

He gave her a flat stare. "As I was saying, that detective was taking the easy path and blaming a blameless husband rather than finding out who really killed Hope. After all, Officer Ibarra herself said a car thief was the culprit. And I didn't ask for anyone's suspension. I simply voiced my concerns to the chief of police. He is the one the Hispanic women's organization should be blaming."

"I believe they are," Elena murmured.

"He's not running for office," Quarles pointed out. "I was doing very well with Hispanics, who generally prefer a man to a woman in a position of power. How was I to know that detective was Hispanic? Her name is Jarvis, and she didn't *look* Hispanic. She's a radical feminist, you know. Most Hispanic women are more traditional than that. The voters should disapprove of her, not me."

The man was a deep well of ethnic stereotyping, Elena thought. "Was this why you wanted to see me?"

"No. Ah . . . sorry. I'm a little upset. I was booed tonight at a rally where I expected a lot of support. I think that detective's followers must have infiltrated the crowd."

"Really?" Was Harmony actually stirring things up politically? Or was Quarles just getting paranoid because his attempt to derail the investigation had backfired in a way he hadn't expected? That thought gave Elena a good deal of satisfaction.

"I wanted to talk about your investigation, Ms. Carr."

"Yes, I believe you suggested that you'd complain to my

superiors as you did to Detective Jarvis's. Did you get me over here to tell me—"

"I wanted to apologize for my attitude this morning, but particularly for the impression Ms. Rocca may have made."

Elena noticed that he was wearing a sport shirt instead of his usual suit. Trying to look like a man of the people? That silk shirt didn't quite do it.

"I wouldn't want you to think my wife's death is advantageous to me or in any way something I wanted. Good Lord, I adored Hope."

"Did you?" Elena allowed herself to look dubious in light of her knowledge of Quarles's affair with Madelaine Rocca.

"I know, I know. It looks as if—well, I'm going to have to make some embarrassing admissions here, but I do want you to understand. I was unfaithful. I—I'm not even sure why. I suppose because Madelaine is young and beautiful and a very successful woman in her own right—she owns her own public relations firm. And I was flattered—stunned really—at her interest in me."

Elena eyed him with suspicion. The man seemed to be too much the egotist to be stunned by any woman's interest.

"I came from a very ordinary middle-class family in Weatherford. My father was a pharmacist. All my married life I've felt that Hope was more than I deserved, and her father did his best to reinforce that feeling. The man never trusted me to make a single decision and made sure I wouldn't be in any position of responsibility in his company after he died. That's why I formed my own company. Trying to prove myself to Hope, I suppose."

"And didn't you? Surely you've been very successful?"

"I have. I'm not afraid to take chances, so I've increased my own share of the market much more than Masterson's, with their conservative outlook, has." His eyes shone with smug satisfaction. "But I never *felt* that I was measuring up. I hope you realize that this conversation is confidential, Ms. Carr," he added hastily.

"Of course," said Elena.

"You're a very understanding young woman." Quarles smiled and laid a hand on hers. He was sitting at a desk in his small campaign office, she in the visitor's chair. "It's a relief to talk about these things," he said. "God knows, I've kept this bottled up for years."

"It sounds like a very difficult situation. You must have resented Mrs. Quarles."

"*Resented?* Lord, no! Have I given that impression? All I've ever wanted was to prove myself worthy of Hope." He looked so forlorn that Elena found herself starting to believe him.

"And now—not only have I lost Hope, but I can never make up to her for having been unfaithful. Not that she knew it. I may not have been able to resist Madelaine, but my first priority was always to protect Hope."

He stared earnestly into Elena's eyes, and she felt as if she were the snake, he the snake charmer.

"I *loved* Hope. Madelaine was just an infatuation. A consequence of my own sense of inadequacy. She made me feel appreciated." He sighed miserably. "And now I can't bear to look at her. Isn't that ironic?"

"She seems to think you're going to marry her."

"Never!" he exclaimed, then murmured more calmly, "I'll never marry again. How could I? No woman could measure up to my Hope." Quarles glanced at his campaign poster on the wall to the left. "I just want to win the election. Because that's what Hope wanted for me. It was the one time that I felt she truly thought I was doing the right thing. She was so very civic-minded, you see, such a fine woman. Everything a woman should be." He turned his head away, but not before Elena saw tears in his eyes.

"I don't know how I'm going to be able to face the future without her." His voice choked. "And I—I just wanted you to know. How I felt. I didn't want you to have the wrong idea. Madelaine was a mistake, and one for which I'll never forgive myself."

Especially if it keeps you from cashing in on the

insurance policy, thought Elena. Still, there was real emotion in what he'd said. Maybe he hadn't been responsible for his wife's death. But if not Quarles, who? The son? The purchasing agent? Madelaine? A street criminal acting totally on his own? She had too many suspects and not enough evidence. But she'd tell Patkin to have Leo check out Rocca. If only Monica could ID the car thief, Elena thought. If we could talk to him, we'd find out what happened that morning. And why.

Elena refused Quarles's offer of coffee and thanked him for his frankness. As she drove home, she saw crowds of children in costume and realized that it was Halloween. When she'd lived in her own house on Sierra Negra, she kept a big bowl of Mexican candy to pass out to the trick-or-treaters. Had Sarah realized it was Halloween? Probably not. During most of her years in Los Santos she had lived in an apartment on the H.H.U. campus, which was walled and gated to keep out the riffraff. If Sarah was handing out anything, it was probably TV dinners. Elena laughed aloud at the thought and turned the truck up the mountain toward Sussex Hills. What a dumb name for a subdivision in Los Santos. It hardly sounded like a neighborhood on the U.S.–Mexico border in the middle of a desert.

When she reached Westmoreland, Sarah's street, she sighed with relief. She was so tired! The thought of going straight to bed seemed wonderful. Elena felt as if she could sleep for twenty-four hours. Unfortunately, tomorrow was a working day, and if she turned up any leads, Saturday and Sunday might be as well.

Madelaine Rocca. Would she have had Hope killed so that she could marry Wayne? Well, there was the money—Hope's fortune, Wayne's business profits. And the prestige—she'd be married to the mayor, or at least a rich guy. And Madelaine seemed to be taken with him as well. Elena decided that she'd definitely call Patkin tomorrow and have him put someone on Madelaine Rocca. Maybe *she* had killer connections.

37

•••

Friday, November 1, 12:35 A.M.

Sarah stood at her bedroom window staring across the street. She'd had a dreadful evening. Little children kept ringing her doorbell and demanding treats, and she'd had nothing suitable left once she'd handed out three boxes of Godiva chocolates, piece by piece. The latter had been given to her by her obnoxious ex-husband, Gus McGlen-levie, during his misdirected campaign to find a woman willing to bear him a child. Several youngsters were quite rude when she tried to distribute small bunches of grapes and banana halves, but not as rude as those she'd had to turn away empty-handed.

Finally, on the advice of her returning housemate, Elena, she had put out the lights, ignored the doorbell, and retreated to her bedroom, where she kept watch in case any children attempted to perpetrate on her the trick portion of trick-or-treat. And guard duty fell to her alone. Elena went straight to bed, and Harmony was still out. Sarah considered their lack of support a poor recompense for her hospitality.

Then her vigilance produced an unexpected reward. Two trucks pulled into the driveway of the house across the street and disappeared around the side, presumably to the cement parking area in back. Since there were no lights showing in the house and no cars in front or in the driveway, she assumed that her unpleasant neighbors were not at home. Obviously, they were being robbed.

She imagined thieves carrying out all the tasteless furniture and the couple's expensive electronic equipment, leaving an empty house. Which would certainly serve her neighbors right. Considering the man's contemptuous response to her explanation of the Neighborhood Watch program, she ought to let the burglary proceed. However, as a good citizen, she couldn't do this. Besides, her intervention would prove to the offensive Mr. Barrajas the worth of the program.

Therefore, Sarah dialed 911 and, explaining her position as watch captain on Westmoreland Drive, reported a crime in progress. It gave her great satisfaction to imagine herself explaining to her neighbor how she had saved his household possessions. In the meantime she'd just sit here and watch the police apprehend the thieves. No doubt the patrol car would be arriving any minute. As she waited for this occurrence, Harmony's pickup pulled into the drive. Sarah rushed downstairs to tell her the news.

"How long have they been back there?" Harmony asked, dropping her bright woven shawl onto a chair.

Sarah shrugged. "Ten minutes or so." Then she thought about what she had said. If the burglars escaped, the tardy police might accuse her of yet another false alarm. "Could they empty out a house that fast?" she asked Harmony.

"It would depend on how many men they have and how much they plan to steal," Harmony responded. "Everything in the house would take quite awhile, but only the expensive things, if they know where the good stuff is, wouldn't take long." Her eyes suddenly lit up, and she added, "Maybe we can stop them from leaving."

"They may be armed," Sarah warned. "And dangerous."

"You're right. You get the rifle, Sarah, and I'll park my truck so they can't get out of the driveway."

"Perhaps we should awaken Elena."

"Absolutely not," said Harmony. "Since the department

suspended her, they can hardly expect her to do their work for them. The situation will make for excellent publicity when the press arrives. We'll point out that we citizens had to apprehend dangerous criminals because Chief Gaitan suspended a competent officer who would have handled the problem herself had she been allowed to do so."

"Excellent point," said Sarah. "You think the press will cover this?"

"I'll call them."

"A media interview will give me a chance to extol the efficacy of the Neighborhood Crime Watch program."

"Be sure to bring bullets for the rifle," Harmony reminded her.

Sarah rushed off to the kitchen, where she had stored the rifle beside the broom. But the bullets—where had she put them? Beside the candles she kept for power outages, she thought. When she returned to the front door, the rifle tucked under her right arm, the box of shells in her left hand, Harmony was backing her truck across the street, where she parked it athwart the neighbors' driveway. She left the driver's-side door open.

"You should lock it up," Sarah whispered as they reentered the house. "The thieves might steal it."

"I installed the Club." Harmony took the rifle, which she proceeded to load. "Keep watch until I finish," she cautioned. "If they try to saw through the Club, I'll shoot at them. Otherwise, they'll think that the truck stalled, and I went to get help."

"Oh, excellent," Sarah agreed, peeking out the window. "The front door's opening," she reported. Harmony pushed the last bullet into the chamber and closed the rifle.

"It's my neighbor!" Sarah exclaimed. "I was sure he wasn't at home. Do you think he knows about the trucks in his backyard? Maybe he's coming here for help."

Sarah moved to answer the persistent doorbell with Harmony behind her, the rifle concealed in the folds of her long, full skirt.

"There's a truck blocking my driveway," Mr. Barrajas told Sarah, sounding irate. "The past few days it's been parked in your driveway, Professor Tolland. Why—"

"It's mine," said Harmony, giving him her most charming smile. "I stalled it and came back to call AAA."

"You stalled it in my driveway?" the man asked angrily.

Embarrassed, Sarah said, "I'll have to admit that I thought your house was being robbed, Mr. Barrajas. Are you aware that there are two trucks in your backyard?"

"They're my trucks. Now, I want that pickup moved."

"I *am* sorry." Sarah was growing increasingly nervous. The police would arrive any minute, making her mistake that much more embarrassing.

"I'll try again to get it started," said Harmony, and headed across the street.

"Why is she carrying a rifle?" asked the neighbor.

"Because I told her your house was being robbed. We were afraid the robbers might steal her truck, too."

The stream of Spanish that at this point began issuing from the neighbor's mouth sounded suspiciously like cursing to Sarah, although she didn't speak the language. Harmony had the hood of her truck up and was industriously poking around inside. "Does she know anything about motors?" Mr. Barrajas asked.

"I have no idea," Sarah replied. "Perhaps you should help her. Do *you* know anything about motors?"

"I pay people to work on my cars," was Barrajas's only comment. He started to cross the street but stopped as two police cars turned the corner and headed for his house. "You called the police?" He had turned to Sarah, his face showing the flush of rage in the light of an ornate Victorian street lamp.

"Certainly. I'm the block captain. It's my duty—"

"Well, tell them it was a mistake," he ordered.

"Yes, I suppose I should." Embarrassed and contrite, Sarah started across the street, but the police—four of them—were already circling the Barrajas house.

"Excuse me," Sarah called, but too late, for they had disappeared from sight. Mr. Barrajas looked surprisingly upset. "Well, it's nothing to worry about," she told him. "Your drivers can just point out—my goodness. What was that sound?" Barrajas began to move slowly away from her.

Suddenly Harmony was whirling from the truck and pointing the gun at Sarah's neighbor. "Stay right where you are," she called. More cracks and pops issued from the rear of the Barrajas house, along with several shouts.

"Harmony, what are you doing?" Sarah cried.

"Those were shots," said Harmony, "and as soon as he heard them, he started to leave."

Sarah looked from her neighbor to her guest, feeling somewhat confused. "Why would shots be fired? As I understand it from Elena, the police don't fire unless someone fires at them or is at least armed and threaten—" She cut herself off and glanced at Mr. Barrajas.

"Exactly," said Harmony, crossing the street with the rifle still trained on Sarah's neighbor.

"Well, surely you don't think Mr. Barrajas—I mean—well, if shots were fired, maybe we should all take shelter in my house. I'm sure it's just a misunderstanding, but—"

At this moment Elena came flying out the front door, nine-millimeter in hand. "Get down," she cried. "That was gunfire." Then she spotted Harmony with the rifle trained on a dark man in a business suit. "Mother, did you shoot that rifle? What's going on?" She eyed the deserted police cars nosed into the curb across the street, and her mother's truck blocking a driveway. "Were you holding a demonstration here, Mom?"

A Westside patrol officer hurried around the side of the house, gun out, heading for his car. "Ladies," he called when he saw them, "go back in the house. And put those guns away. You might hurt yourselves."

"I'm the person who called you," Sarah informed him.

"Yeah? Well, you'll probably get a medal. We found what looks like a shitload of cocaine back there."

"Nonsense," said Barrajas. "That's sugar. Didn't you see the bags?"

"Sure, but it's not sugar inside. Who are you?"

Harmony poked Barrajas with the rifle. "He owns the house, so it's undoubtedly his cocaine."

"In that case, keep the rifle on him, lady, while I call for backup."

"My ex son-in-law is a narcotics officer," Harmony put in.

"Mom . . ." Elena protested weakly.

"Frank Jarvis. Maybe you should call him," Harmony continued, ignoring her daughter. "You," she said, poking Barrajas again. "Put your hands behind your head." Barrajas gave Harmony a menacing look, which didn't seem to faze her.

"No wonder you didn't want to join the Neighborhood Crime Watch," Sarah said indignantly. "And I mistook your reluctance for some masculine prejudice against women."

38

Friday, November 1, 2:05 A.M.

Elena was astonished at the magnitude of the events Sarah had unwittingly set in motion. When the four Westside patrol officers circled the house, they found three men loading bags marked CREOLE COUNTRY PURE CANE SUGAR into the two trucks. On being told to put their hands up, two complied, but one, thinking himself unnoticed because he was on the far side of the second truck, pulled a gun and shot from cover, wounding an officer on the north side of the yard. The gunman was in turn shot by one of two officers circling the house from the south.

The two remaining truck loaders dove for cover after the first shot. The downed officer dragged himself behind a bush. Then a burst of gunfire erupted from the house, the work of a fourth man who had abandoned a cart loaded with sugar. Since he had an automatic weapon, the police retreated.

A fifth man, apparently in the living room, who had watched as Barrajas made his trip across the street to demand removal of the pickup in his driveway, tried to escape through a side door and was captured by officers at the southeast corner of the house. The uninjured officer on the north side circled, slipped in the front door and disarmed the man with the automatic weapon, leaving two of Barrajas's visitors armed and uninjured in the backyard. They could hear the patrolmen who had pinned them down behind their trucks calling for reinforcements, and gave themselves up.

This story Elena pieced together from reports to the sergeant, who arrived with six men a few minutes later. Narcotics officers, Frank among them, drove up five minutes after that, followed by ambulances, EMS medics who tended to the wounded, and the first members of the press, called to the scene by Harmony. Barrajas and his remaining men were handcuffed and forced to sit cross-legged on the decorative rockwork across the street. Elena went into the house, once matters were well in hand, to cover her nightgown with a coat. When she returned, Sarah and Harmony were talking to the press while the narcs examined the contents of the alleged sugar bags and searched the house.

"When the police department turns on capable officers at the first sign of political pressure," Harmony was saying, "citizens have to protect themselves."

"Could you explain that, ma'am," requested a reporter from Channel Seven, holding a microphone in her face.

Harmony flipped her long black hair, smiled charmingly, and blasted Armando Gaitan for suspending her daughter.

"And you were the person who noticed the drug dealers in action?" a reporter asked Sarah.

"Actually, I thought it was a robbery in progress," Sarah confessed. "I'm captain of our Neighborhood Crime Watch, which is, as you can see, extremely effective. Of course, I had no idea that Mr. Barrajas was a criminal. I simply thought him ill-mannered, as well as contemptuous of citizen involvement in local policing." She shot a superior glance at Barrajas.

Elena wished Sarah would shut up. Even in handcuffs, Barrajas looked dangerous. Frank stopped and commiserated with her about the suspension, offering support.

"Thanks," Elena mumbled. She didn't want to be in

Frank's debt. It hadn't been that friendly a divorce, although they hadn't been at each other's throats in some time.

"Sergeant," called the TV reporter, spotting Artie Potts leaving the front door of the Barrajas house, "could you tell us the value of the narcotics found here?"

"I'll bet the chief is sorry now that he's got Harmony on his tail," Frank added. "You wouldn't believe what a ruckus the protesters created at Five Points this afternoon."

"Oh, I'd believe it," Elena muttered. "I remember the protest she organized for Lance Potemkin last year. Did you find much stuff in the house?"

"Oh, yeah," Frank replied. "Sarah and Harmony put us onto something a lot bigger than they ever imagined."

"At least fourteen million street value in cocaine," Sergeant Potts said, answering the reporter.

"And the neighbor, Barrajas," Frank continued, "DEA's been lookin' into a Miguel Barrajas in Juarez."

"This one, I think, is Jaime."

Frank nodded. "His brother. We got us an important stash house here."

The sergeant was saying the same thing to the reporter. "We've got a narcotics dog in there now, and he's hurling himself against the walls."

"Wayne Quarles built that house," Elena noted, "and I've been wondering whether he was laundering drug money."

"We're lookin' into that ourselves," said Frank, surprised at the connection his ex-wife had just made.

Elena didn't mention that she'd suggested the investigation to Glen Patkin. "Any good information yet?" she asked.

Frank hesitated.

"There are stash houses all over town," Artie Potts was now telling the reporter. "But we didn't even have this one under surveillance. These two ladies have done the war on drugs a big favor."

Harmony and Sarah beamed. The handcuffed prisoners muttered imprecations among themselves.

Elena turned to Frank. "Sorry for asking," she said.

"Since I'm suspended, giving me information's like giving it to the enemy."

"Hey." Frank smiled. "I don't feel that way. It's just—well, the investigation's in the early stages. Money launderin's not easy to track."

She nodded.

"Hey, Jarvis." Elena turned toward the sergeant. "Not you, ma'am," said Potts, who still seemed unaware of Elena's connection to Frank. "Say, you're the woman who was suspended, right? I sure hate to see politics interfering with police work."

"Can I quote you?" asked Paul Resendez, who had just joined the crowd.

"Not if you ever want another interview," snarled Potts. "A cop can't fart but the press wants to quote him."

Resendez laughed. "We're not that hard up for news, Artie."

Potts scowled at him and waved Frank back into the house. "Got walls to knock down."

"So what's been happening?" Resendez asked Elena. "I obviously missed most of the fun."

She gave him a rundown.

"You want to make a statement about your suspension?"

"No," she replied.

"Guess I should ask your mother."

"Well, if you print everything she has to say, you'll have to drop tomorrow's advertising."

"In that case, maybe I'll go eyeball the prisoners. See if I recognize anyone." Resendez drifted off, and Elena followed. The men turned their faces away from her, but she got good enough looks to remember if she ever saw them again. She figured three-quarters of her available memory was used to store the faces and rap sheets of all the criminals she came into contact with.

"It might be nothing," Resendez murmured to her, "but since you came to grief, more or less, over Wayne Quarles, you might like to know that I think I recognized one of those guys. Potts says he's the one who tried to sneak out the side."

"And he's connected with Quarles?"

"Maybe. Seems to me I saw his picture in Nate's file, a story in *Diario* about the groundbreaking for that Mexican country-club deal. Remember? I looked Quarles up for you?"

Elena stared at Resendez. Barrajas lived in a Quarles house, and one of the man's compadres in the drug trade might be an investor in a Quarles real-estate venture. Maybe the case was beginning to fall into place, after all.

"Let me look at the picture again," said Resendez. "I'll call you tomorrow."

Elena gave him her new cell-phone number. "If it turns out you're right, I'll definitely owe you one."

"Terrific," he replied. "When you get reinstated and break the case, you'll give me an exclusive, right?"

"Right. *If* I get reinstated and break the case."

"If he wants that murder solved, Gaitan better reinstate you."

Elena thought so, too. Investigating without police powers put limitations on her, not the least of which was her own inability to adjust to her new status. She caught Frank before he left and asked him if he knew of any connection between this group of drug traffickers and Los Reyes Diablos.

"We didn't know squat about these people," he replied. "Only one of them was even a gleam in the DEA's eye. Sorry, babe. But the size of the stash makes it look like we should have known about them." He turned when he saw that Harmony and Sarah were returning to the house. "Hey, Harmony, we owe you one. You, too, Professor."

Everyone owed everyone one, Elena thought. She hoped that Barrajas and company weren't thinking in terms of "owing one" to the women who had, however inadvertently, brought them down.

39

••

Friday, November 1, 8:30 A.M.

Having been up half the night dealing with the drug bust, Elena felt tired and grumpy as she drove her truck downtown to the insurance company. It didn't help her mood that, being suspended, she couldn't join in questioning the men who had been arrested. There were things about Wayne Quarles that she wanted to learn. In the meantime she had to listen to an interview with the candidate on a local radio talk show.

"It has come to my attention that a major drug arrest was made last night," Quarles said, "not because of any intelligence gathered by the police, but because a female professor, who organized a Neighborhood Crime Watch, noticed suspicious activity going on across the street from her house. She and her house guest delayed the criminals until the police arrived fifteen minutes later. Now, I ask you? What kind of police force do we have when two women must do the work of professional law enforcement? I suppose I shouldn't be surprised that no arrest has been made in the murder of my beloved wife, nothing done beyond exacerbating the grief of me and my family with intrusive and unwarranted questions."

"Interestingly enough," said the host, "I believe the house guest of the professor you mentioned is the mother of the

Crimes Against Persons detective you got suspended, Mr. Quarles. And in fact, the detective, acting purely as a citizen because of her suspension, assisted in the arrest."

"I—er—hadn't heard that," Quarles stammered, no doubt sorry he'd ever brought the subject up. "And I didn't have anyone suspended. I may have thought Detective Jarvis's questions misguided, but I did not ask for her suspension, nor do I see why she is considered Hispanic. Neither her name nor her appearance would indicate . . ."

"Bad idea, Quarles," Elena said aloud. "What makes you think we all look alike or even have Spanish-sounding names?" Quarles got off the unfortunate subject and went on to discuss his budget proposals, all of which, he said, would allow the city council to lower taxes if he were elected.

"That'll be the day," muttered Elena, whose house taxes were more than the payment on her mortgage. She snapped the radio off, determined to vote for Mayor Nellie. Then her cell phone rang, and she clicked on.

"Victorio Amantodaro Cano. He's listed in the picture caption as an investor in the Quarles country-club deal in Juarez, which means he probably lost a bundle. And he's the same guy we saw carted off by cops last night."

"Resendez?" She felt a surge of elation. "Thank you. You just became my favorite reporter."

"I thought I already was."

Once at her desk in Personnel, she fended off some poor dork who wanted to make a claim of sexual harassment against his female boss and called Glen Patkin to ask that whoever was questioning last night's arrestees find out what connections the drug dealers had with Wayne Quarles, beyond the fact that they were arrested in a Quarles-built stash house. "They can use the Cano-Quarles connection as a lever," she added, passing on the information she had received from Resendez. Then she asked for an investigation of Madelaine Rocca, Quarles's mistress.

"You're doing pretty good for a woman who's been

suspended," Patkin observed. "Maybe we should have lunch again and exchange information."

Elena laughed. "You just want to eat well on my company credit card."

"Wrong," said Patkin. "I just want to convince you that it would be fun to date someone in I.A."

"Maybe next week," Elena told him. Her beeper had just sounded; it was the chief's number. "Gotta go," she said, and returned the call of Armando Gaitan, who had decided he'd made a mistake when he discouraged her from talking Harmony out of organizing demonstrations.

"Much as I admire your mother," he said, "I never expected she'd make me a target of the Hispanic Women's Council. Maybe you could—"

"It's a little late now," Elena interrupted regretfully. "Mother's in full swing at this point."

"So I gather. I heard her on TV last night at the drug bust." Gaitan sighed. "With both Quarles and your mother attacking us, the department is beginning to look bad."

"Well, you could unsuspend me . . ." Elena suggested.

"No, I want you to talk to a Captain de la Garza of the Federal Judicial Police in Juarez. See what you can find out about those men who were arrested last night. Concentrate on Jaime Barrajas and Victorio Cano."

"You know about Cano?"

"He was described to me as a chief, not an Indian."

"He's an investor in one of Quarles's projects."

"Ah." Gaitan was silent for a moment. "All the more reason to see what you can find out about him. With your insurance-company credentials, De la Garza might tell you more than he'd tell an official police representative."

Elena couldn't imagine why and said so.

"Mexican men like blondes, which I'm told you are now. Also he won't feel threatened by a woman with no official standing. And Texas Life has Mexican connections. If Freer arranges the interview, the captain might be cooperative."

Elena sighed. "I'll try."

"Good, and see what you can do about your mother. We're beginning to look like the bad guys."

"I hold out more hope for a favorable response from the Mexican cop than I do from Mom."

"A beautiful woman, your mother." Gaitan sighed ruefully.

"My dad thinks so," said Elena, just to remind the chief that Harmony wasn't available for serious flirtation, dates, or anything else; she was a married lady.

The Mexican Judicial Police evidently did like blondes, because Captain de la Garza actually kissed the hand that extended him the Texas Life & Casualty business card. Elena hated to tell the man anything about her investigation since his branch of law enforcement had been the object of so much bad press. Newspapers gave the impression that the Federal Judicial Police were more likely to be involved with the drug cartels than with trying to break them up.

"I'm investigating the murder of a Mrs. Hope Quarles in Los Santos," she explained. "We hold a very large policy on her life, with her husband as beneficiary." They were speaking in Spanish, and the captain complimented Elena on the excellence of hers. Elena smiled modestly and mentioned that her father was Hispanic and a sheriff in New Mexico.

"Ah, one of our lost colonies," Captain de la Garza mused sadly. "As is Texas."

"Indeed," Elena agreed. "My ancestors were once citizens of Mexico, and before that of Spain."

"As were mine," said the captain. "But how can I help you, most beautiful Señorita Carr?"

"Well, I am investigating the beneficiary, Mr. Quarles, who built a large country-club complex here in Juarez."

"I know of it."

"I was hoping you could tell me if Mr. Quarles has any criminal connections in Mexico."

"Have you reason to think he has?"

"A man who was arrested for possession and transportation of cocaine, one . . ." She consulted her notes. "One Señor Victorio Amantodaro Cano was pointed out to me as an investor in the country-club venture. Also the house where the narcotics were stored, which is owned by Señor Jaime Barrajas, was built by Señor Quarles."

"Well, Señorita Carr, this Jaime Barrajas, I do not know of him. Perhaps he is a citizen of your country."

"I believe he is, or at least a legal resident."

"But Victorio Amantodaro Cano is known to me, and I have never heard anything but that he is a respectable and legitimate businessman. Perhaps his presence in the house had nothing to do with the cocaine discovered there."

Elena doubted that. "So you do not think that Señor Cano is involved in the drug trade?"

"I would be very surprised if he were. Perhaps your police should reconsider connecting him with this case. Relations between our nations are touchy enough without respectable Mexican businessmen being falsely accused."

"Quite true," said Elena, thinking that the chances of Cano being innocent of involvement with all that cocaine were about as great as tortillas being banned in Mexico as harmful to the health. "However, you understand that I can act in no official capacity, except insofar as my own company is concerned. Certainly I can have no influence with the police. Do you personally know of any connection between Señors Quarles, Cano, and Barrajas?"

"Not personally, no. As I said, I do not know Señor Barrajas or anything about him. If Señor Quarles and Señor Cano have business relations, I daresay they are of the most legitimate nature. The country-club project, which unfortunately has yet to realize its true potential, was one of great promise for our city when it was conceived. I doubt that a man of Señor Quarles's wealth and reputation would have criminal connections."

Elena thanked the captain for his time, refused an invitation to lunch, and drove back across the border through horrendous traffic on the bridge. Winter inversion layers were already upon the city, and so many idling automobiles and trucks waiting to clear customs caused a choking smog. Her interview with the captain had been interesting if only because he claimed that a known drug dealer was a respectable businessman. Elena knew her reasoning was questionable but believed, nonetheless, that the captain's testimonial made Quarles and Cano doubly suspect. Especially if the Federal Judicial Police were as tight with the drug cartels as a friend in the DEA claimed.

She stopped for lunch at a drive-in and, listening to the radio as she ate, again heard Wayne Quarles being interviewed. This time he was complaining because the narcs and the DEA were tearing apart the house across the street from Sarah and tapping on walls and investigating closets in other houses he had built, much to the distress of home owners who had bought the houses.

"If someone used one of my houses for illegal purposes, it is certainly not my fault," said Quarles. "The police are seeking to derail both my campaign and my business."

After the interview the reporter said that the narcs were tearing out the very walls of the house on Westmoreland but wouldn't say what they were finding.

Elena reflected that if Quarles hadn't killed his wife, her death was certainly causing him more than personal grief. If he had killed her, of course, he deserved whatever he got. She had just dumped the fast-food wrappers into a trash container when her pager beeped. She glanced at the number, Sarah's at the university, and called on her cellular phone. "It's Elena? What's up?"

"There are men from federal and local law-enforcement agencies tapping on my walls. Is that legal?"

"I guess they have a blanket warrant for any house built by Quarles. Did they show you a warrant?"

"Yes, but I was so upset, I hardly read it, and I had to teach a class, so I couldn't even stay."

"Is Mom there?"

"Yes, she agreed to keep her eye on them."

Elena laughed. "In that case, I'd say your house is safe, and the cops are being harangued at every turn. We both know how she feels about the LSPD at this point."

"You seem remarkably cheerful for a woman who's been suspended," Sarah snapped. "Harmony says you'll be miserable if you have to keep working for an insurance company."

"It pays well," Elena retorted defensively. She'd have to be careful, be more morose.

"Since when did you care so much about money?"

Good point, Elena thought. But she didn't say so.

40

Friday, November 1, 2:00 P.M.

Twenty minutes in her office with the door closed, thinking over the evidence she'd gathered, did not make Elena any surer that Wayne Quarles had paid for his wife's murder, but she did feel a stronger conviction that he had been laundering money for a drug cartel, undoubtedly the one the police had stumbled on last night with Sarah's help.

When she got back from Juarez, she had returned a call from Frank, who said again that he wished there were something he could do to get her reinstated—she couldn't help but reflect on how much more supportive he was now than he'd been when they were married—and added that Narcotics had not found any more Quarles-built stash houses. The Barrajas house, however, had so many storage places between walls and behind closets that it could not have been modified after being built except at great expense, involving many workmen. However, none of the neighbors had observed workmen at the house over extended periods of time.

So, she reasoned, Barrajas, Cano, and company had provided Quarles with financing, in return for which he built them a stash house in a neighborhood where no one would expect to find one. That meant that Quarles had had the connections he'd have needed to contract for his wife's killing. Also he was dealing with people, to whom he probably owed money, who wouldn't hesitate to kill Hope if they thought her death would enable him to repay his debts. Nonetheless, Elena knew that she needed to establish a connection between the car thief in the alley and the cartel, or between the cartel and some other person who interrupted the attempted arrest of the car thief by shooting Monica Ibarra and Hope Quarles.

So what was the next move? It should help to put more pressure on Quarles and, through him, on the cartel. The narcs were doing what they could. She had only one contact in the DEA, but she had a better connection in the FBI. Maybe Perry Melon could help, or put her in touch with an agent who could. Her colleagues wouldn't be happy if she involved the feds, but what the heck! She was officially suspended.

Making up her mind, she called Patkin and asked him to fax her pictures and information on the men who had been arrested last night on Westmoreland. Patkin dithered, saying that sort of thing shouldn't go out of the department, or into the hands of unauthorized persons.

"I'm not unauthorized," she snapped.

Patkin suggested that they meet for dinner. She put him off. Finally he agreed, and the material began coming in on the fax machine just outside her office. She made copies and called Perry Melon, with whom she had worked a bomb case earlier in the year. She'd even dated him, until he discovered that she was also dating an Alcohol, Tobacco, and Firearms agent. At that point they both gave her up in the name of brotherhood among bomb guys. Obviously, it hadn't been true love.

"Listen," Melon said when she identified herself, "why don't you apply to become an FBI agent? I'll be glad to sponsor you. I should have called as soon as you got suspended. What a rotten deal. Do you need any money? Don't hesitate—"

Elena laughed. "I landed on my feet, Perry. I'm investigating the same case for the insurance company that holds a policy on Hope Quarles's life, and I've got some information the FBI might be interested in. You guys do money laundering, don't you?"

"Do money laundering?" He sounded horrified.

Elena grinned. "Investigate it."

"Oh. Sure. Not me personally, but Ken Parr's an expert."

"Great. So get in touch with him. We can set up an appointment, and I'll give you what I have."

"Let me put you on hold."

Did he have to get permission from his superiors to talk to a suspended local cop? she wondered. Evidently not. Perry was back in less than a minute telling her to come straight over to the federal building.

"You're not Elena Jarvis," said Melon when she entered his office. Then he looked again. "Are you?" She grinned. He grinned back and gave her a hug, obviously arousing the disapproval of his colleague for so doing. Perry was redheaded and freckled. Parr was dark and short, with a receding hairline and prominent glasses on a long nose. He looked like an accountant, and Elena wondered if he'd think her deductions fanciful. She had no substantive evidence, just gossip and speculation.

"So, Detective?" Parr took out a pen and notebook. Elena handed him the mug shots faxed from Patkin's office and a printout of the information they had on the six men who had been arrested, which was minimal at this point.

"I'm hoping you'll have something more on them," she confessed. Then she talked about the financial problems of the Quarles-built Trujillo Sports Complex with its dummy-corporation financing. She passed on what Freer had uncovered; again not much. She told them about the country-club venture in Mexico, its minimal success, and the mystery investor, Cano. She added that Cano had been described as a legitimate businessman by Captain de la Garza of the Mexican Federal Judicial Police. "But Cano was picked up in the cocaine bust last night in a Quarles-built stash house on Westmoreland Drive," she concluded.

"Our counterparts in Mexico are rarely without brotherly ties to the cartels," Parr commented dryly.

Elena nodded. "Does this stuff sound like it's worth investigating?" she asked.

A smile lit his saturnine face. "I'll want to play with it a bit, but it sounds like something for which we may need a federal grand-jury investigation."

Elena smiled back. "Terrific. It couldn't happen to a more deserving fellow than Wayne Quarles."

"Do you have something against the man?" Parr asked, frowning. "If this is some personal vendetta . . ."

"More a professional vendetta," Elena replied, opting for partial frankness. "I was investigating him after the murder of his wife. He's a candidate for mayor and managed to get me suspended."

"Ah." Rubbing a finger down the side of his long nose, Parr gave her connection to Quarles some thought, then said, "The Bureau is not influenced by local politics or politicians. However, we won't be investigating the murder, you understand. Murder is a local matter."

"I don't have a problem with that," said Elena. "*I'd* like to be the one to get him for the murder."

"That seems unlikely as long as you are under suspension. I doubt that in real life, no matter what you may have read in private-eye novels, that many insurance investigators solve murders."

"Who has time to read novels?" Elena asked.

When the page came through from the hospital, Elena called immediately and got Monica Ibarra's doctor. "She came out of it late this morning, and she wants to see you," he said.

"Let me get back to you."

"I can't guarantee—"

"Within a few minutes," Elena promised, and rang off, calling Patkin immediately to explain the situation. "We need to know anything she can tell us, and I'm the one she wants to talk to."

"I can't make that decision," said Patkin. "I'll get back to you."

"The doctor said to hurry."

"Jesus, is she dying?"

"I don't know. Look, I'll start driving over. Call me on the cell phone." Twenty minutes later, as she pulled into the hospital lot, Patkin called. "The chief says go ahead," he told her, "but visit her as a friend, not as a cop."

"Oh, right. Like she's in any condition to hear complicated explanations." Elena entered the hospital and hurried to the ICU, where Monica stared at her blankly.

"It's me," Elena whispered. "In disguise."

Monica giggled and reached out for her hand. "I remember," she said. "When I woke up, I remembered more about what happened."

"Good." Elena squeezed the thin hand, hoping Monica had indeed remembered more. She looked a little less fragile than she had before the last operation. Maybe she was going to make it. At least she was out of the coma; that had to be a good sign.

"You asked whose idea her joining C.O.P. was. Her husband thought of it because it would show support for the police."

Monica had already told her that. Several times. Didn't she remember?

"Eddie told me her husband and his friends are blaming me for Hope's death."

Eddie ought to keep his mouth shut, Elena thought. Monica didn't need to be reminded of problems she was in no condition to deal with.

"Well, her death wasn't my fault. She must have died after I was hit, and I sure didn't shoot her. And that Quarles—he's not ruining my career, or yours either."

Monica's hoarse voice strengthened with indignation. Maybe Eddie Diaz had known what he was doing, after all.

"I wouldn't die now no matter what. And I'm trusting you to find out who killed Hope. For both of us."

"Don't worry," said Elena. "I will. For both of us."

Monica smiled. "So her getting killed, it was her husband's fault and the killer's fault, not ours. She was real clear that it was his idea. She thought she'd just be a liability to me. Mrs. Q was a super lady," Monica concluded wistfully. "Didn't know anything about the streets or the job, but she was a nice woman."

"She say anything else about him? Her husband?"

"You think he had something to do with what happened?"

"Maybe."

"The guy stealing the car was definitely a gangbanger—baggy white pants held up by a rope, shaved head, black T-shirt."

Nothing new there.

"Let's see. He had crowned-devil tattoos."

Elena knew that. "Remember anything about his face?"

"I only saw it for a minute. Mrs. Q spotted him drilling the lock. I told her to stay back and move behind the Dumpster if he showed a weapon. Then I called for backup and started down the alley. I was very careful where I stepped. Didn't want to alert him. Wish she'd been quieter. I heard her feet scrape on the cement. I suppose she was moving behind the Dumpster. Just as I got to the car thief, he turned, almost like he knew I was there, like . . ." She paused a minute, thinking. "I heard a whistle about that time. You think someone alerted him? There had to be someone else. The car thief couldn't have shot me."

"Did he have a weapon?"

"I never saw one. He turned and dropped to the pavement. I had my gun out, but I was shot as he went down. I pulled the trigger, too, but I was keeling over myself, and no way could I have hit Mrs. Q. I never saw her again after I left her at the alley entrance."

Monica's voice had been hoarse throughout this recital. Now she started to cough. Elena quickly picked up the water glass from the table and held the bent straw to the young officer's lips. Monica sipped, lay back, and breathed shallowly. "I'm going to make it," she assured Elena.

"Absolutely," Elena agreed. "You look a lot better."

Monica nodded. "You asked about his face. Medium-dark skin, shaved head, stubbled chin, heavy eyebrows, eyes a little slanted, not much. The thing I remember most is his nose."

Elena nodded, listening closely, taking notes.

"He had this funny nose. On the left side, my left, the nostril was bigger, a lot bigger. It looked weird."

And that was all Ibarra remembered. But it was more than they'd had before. When Elena left the ICU, Leo was waiting for her. "I got word she had something to tell you," he explained. "Anything important?"

Elena repeated everything Monica had said, emphasizing the nostril, and Leo nodded, taking notes. He promised to run the description through every data bank and by every detective he could find. "Maybe we can get an ID," he said hopefully.

"Wouldn't that be a break?" They parted company, and Elena thought about that weird nostril as she drove home to dress for her symphony date with Sam Parsley, who had been embarrassed into taking her out to dinner by her mother.

Harmony herself would be attending a midnight prayer vigil sponsored by the Council of Hispanic Women in front of police headquarters—candles, mournful Hispanic songs, Hail Marys, complete with a priest. Elena had protested, but on the whole she thought the experience would be good for the chief, remind him of the woman's point of view. He mostly thought of women in terms of flirtation. He'd have a hard time flirting with Harmony if he appeared at the vigil. Elena's mother was not susceptible to charm in persons she perceived as the enemy.

A weird nose. There was something teasing her memory, but she couldn't quite call it up. No matter. If it was significant, it would come to her.

41

Friday, November 1, 9:35 P.M.

"Of course!" Elena exclaimed.

"What?" Sam Parsley turned to her. The Los Santos Symphony was girding itself to deliver a triumphant passage in a Brahms symphony as Elena realized that she had been napping, her head against the fuzzy tweed of Sam Parsley's comfortable shoulder, and that she had come awake with an exclamation. Around her people were saying, "Shhhhh."

Elena sighed. She seemed unable to get through an evening of classical music without embarrassing herself. But the moment of enlightenment that had come to her in her sleep was important. It concerned that nostril described by Monica Ibarra. In her dream she had been at Sarah's and observed men entering the Barrajas house across the street. One of them had an enlarged nostril, but he appeared in the dream as a body with a mug shot on its neck.

Did that mean that one of the mug shots she had carried to the FBI, photos she'd merely glanced at, showed a man with such a nostril? Why hadn't she noticed it the night the men were arrested at the Barrajas house? She had studied those faces, as she always did with criminals. Imagining herself back on Westmoreland, coat over her nightgown, the air cold on her face, cops, reporters, and neighbors swarming around, she deliberately called up each face. And there was the nostril, just a quick glimpse before the man turned his head away. Unless she was imposing Monica's description on a face that didn't actually have that characteristic.

"Go back to sleep," Sam whispered. "Classical music provides wonderful naps."

"Shhhh," their fellow concertgoers demanded.

Sam patted her hand, and Elena turned her head to smile at him, taking in his bushy hair, warm eyes, and rumpled clothes, all of which added up to a very comforting presence. But still she wouldn't be able to sleep again, not during this concert. Accordingly, she fidgeted through three more movements of the symphony, plus the clapping and the mandatory standing ovation that Los Santoans always gave performances. Elena thought the practice was motivated half by respect for the arts and half in preparation to dash to the underground parking garage to get home in time for Jay Leno on TV.

"I guess you didn't like Brahms," Sam said as they drifted down the steps with the crowd.

"Sure I did," Elena protested.

One eyebrow shot up in disbelief. "You slept through the first movement and squirmed through the next three."

"Actually," she admitted, "I didn't much notice the Brahms because I suddenly realized who shot Hope Quarles."

"Really?" Sam looked fascinated. "It came to you in your sleep?"

For a moment Elena thought he was being sarcastic, but Sam's expression indicated genuine interest. "I guess. When Monica described the man's nose to me, I knew I should be making some connection. Then I had this weird dream, and I woke up knowing."

Sam nodded. "The mind does amazing things in sleep. Think about a problem before you go to bed—or in your case before you go to the symphony—and you'll often wake up with a solution. What was the dream?"

Elena frowned. "It didn't have anything to do with the

mountain lion or our post-traumatic stress sessions." Sam continued to look expectant. "Are you about to psychoanalyze me?" she asked.

"Why not?" Sam answered reasonably. "I'm offering a free dream interpretation. Are you going to turn it down?"

"I already know what the dream meant. I saw these men walking into a stash house across the street from Sarah's. They all had mug shots for heads because they're in the drug trade. The one photo head I got a look at belonged to the man Monica described. He was also among the mug shots from the arrests last night, and I finally remembered where I'd seen that nostril. At least I hope so." When Sam looked surprised at her mention of a nostril, Elena laughed. "I don't have a nose fetish, Sam. This perp has one oversized nostril."

By then they had arrived at Sam's car. "But what if he's bonded out?" she said as she slid into the front seat, Sam holding the door for her. "And I'm suspended. I can't call to ask." Sam walked around to the driver's side. "Frank," said Elena. "First, I'll get the mug shot from my office. Then I'll go to see Frank."

"Frank, your ex-husband?"

"Right. He could find out if the man's still in jail. And he offered help when I saw him at the stash-house bust. Not that I want to be indebted to Frank," she added, rethinking her plan.

"You're on bad terms with your ex-husband?" Sam asked in that neutral, therapist tone.

"Used to be, but he was nice during the mountain-lion incident. Offered me his apartment, without him in it."

"Maybe he wants to reconcile," Sam suggested.

"If I thought so, I couldn't call him."

"In that case, we'll both visit him. He can hardly take it as an invitation if you arrive with another man."

"You're not another man; you're my therapist."

"Does he know that?"

"You're right, but I could call Frank. I don't actually have to go to his place."

"You're afraid to?" Sam asked.

"Of course not."

"Then you should go. You should show him the mug shot of the man you think killed Hope Quarles."

"You're just curious to meet my ex," Elena said, but she agreed. They went first to the bank building that housed Texas Life, talking themselves past the security guard with some difficulty. Elena hated not being able to use her badge. In this instance, she fed the guard a line about needing to pick up papers she had to read over the weekend. Sam looked at her askance, but she said defensively, "It's partially true. I have to show the photo to Frank tonight, and tomorrow I'll be working the case."

"Of course," Sam agreed dryly.

She collected the photos and looked up Frank's address.

"Shouldn't you call him first?" Sam asked.

"And give him the opportunity to play some stupid practical joke on me? I don't think so."

"He must be an unusual man," Sam remarked as they drove away.

"That was his car on the street," said Elena as she leaned on the bell. Frank's apartment was in an old building in the Central District—black cement with white stone lintels. The exterior was kind of neat, in Elena's opinion. The hallway, however, with its ragged-edged, footworn carpets, was not. She rang the bell again and at last heard the dead bolt being turned, but the door was opened by a young woman with uncombed blond hair. She wore only a T-shirt, probably Frank's.

"I need to speak to Frank Jarvis," said Elena.

"Who are you?" the blonde asked.

"Elena Jarvis."

"He's *married*?" Frank's guest cried indignantly.

"The hell I am," said Frank, appearing bare-chested,

zipping up a pair of jeans. "You picked a hell of a time to make your first visit here, Elena." Then remembering his companion, he said, "This is Crissie. Crissie, Elena."

"Sam, Crissie and Frank. Crissie and Frank, Sam." Elena waved casually to the various parties and walked into the apartment. "Come on in, Sam."

"Yeah, Sam," said Frank. "Whoever the hell you are, don't stand on ceremony. Come on in."

"Why's she got the same name as you?" Crissie demanded, trailing them into a living room that held a small TV, a black, lint-collecting sofa, and a leather recliner decorated with cigarette burns.

"She never changed it after we got divorced. How come you're here?" He'd turned to Elena.

"You offered your help." She took the mug shot from her purse. "I want you to take a look at this photo, then call the jail and see if the guy's bonded out."

Frank took the photo. "One of the yo-yos we arrested last night?"

"And, I think, the man who shot Hope Quarles."

Frank grunted and sat down at the end of his black sofa, lifting a phone from the floor. He had no tables. Glasses, ashtrays, and a fake Navajo rug also rested on the worn parquet. Frank identified himself and asked if Osbaldo Salazar was still a guest of the county. "He's under lock and key," Frank told Elena.

"Can you get them to call you if it looks like he's going to bond out?"

Frank made the arrangements. "You two want a drink or something?" he asked once he'd hung up.

Crissie said, "Gee, Frank, we were right in the middle of—"

"Mood's kind of gone down the toilet," Frank interrupted, looking embarrassed.

Elena suppressed a smile. She didn't care that Frank had a girl, but on the other hand, it didn't bother her that she'd interrupted a romantic moment. "You two just go on with what you were doing. Sam and I have to get home."

"You're living together?" Frank asked. He looked taken aback.

"I'm her therapist," said Sam.

Traitor, Elena thought, but said, "We've been to the symphony." She didn't want Frank to think she had no social life.

"Treatment for the mountain-lion business, huh? What's he trying to do? Bore you into normality?"

"Symphonies aren't so bad," Elena said loyally.

"But your description of the therapy has some merit," Sam put in. "A successful treatment for post-traumatic stress is forcing the subject to relive the trauma so many times that boredom sets in." He smiled at Frank as if he were a bright student who'd just given a particularly intelligent answer. "Very perceptive of you, Detective."

Of course, Elena knew that Frank had been talking about the boredom quotient of symphonies. Then beeping distracted them all. Frank, Elena, and Sam all reached for their pagers. Crissie said, "Oh, for Pete's sake."

"Mine," said Elena. "Can I use the phone?"

She didn't recognize the number, but she got Leo, who said, "Someone just tried to kill Monica Ibarra."

"Oh God. What happened?"

"Guy in a mask and scrubs went into her ICU unit with a syringe. She woke up and screamed and rolled off the bed. Diaz, her fiancé, had come off shift and was walking into the waiting room. He heard her and ran into the ICU. The guy with the syringe tried to get away. Diaz was pulling a gun when the guy winged him, so Diaz shot and killed him. No ID on the shooter. The stuff in the syringe is being analyzed. Some old guy in the ICU freaked out and had a heart attack and died. Ibarra is coughing blood, and she's asking for you."

"I'm on my way," said Elena. "Is she going to be O.K.?"

"Don't know."

"You're setting up guards on the ICU?"

"The place has cops coming out the windows."

"Why now?" Elena murmured. "If they wanted to kill her, why wait till now?"

"Beats me," Leo answered.

"The only difference is that she was finally able to give me a better description of the car thief, and I didn't tell anyone but you." She bit her thumbnail, thinking desperately. Had there been anyone eavesdropping in the ICU? Elena pictured the unit as it had been when she talked to Monica. Patients, mostly unconscious. One nurse down the far end. No one close enough to hear Monica talking about that nostril—Elena would have sworn to that. When she'd described the conversation to Leo in the waiting room, they were alone. She'd told Frank she knew who had killed Hope Quarles, but the attempt on Monica's life was occurring while she was talking to Frank. "Did you tell anyone, Leo?" she asked.

"Only my computer," he replied dryly.

"Sure? Think!"

"No, Elena. I was off shift by the time I got back to headquarters. Hell, I didn't even mention it to Concepcion when I got home," he said sharply. "I figured to start asking questions tomorrow."

"Is Monica in any shape to look at mug shots?"

"Doubt it," said Leo.

Elena groaned. Monica had been so determined that afternoon. But the case could self-destruct if she died. And that's what the killers wanted, of course. But how had they, whoever they were, found out about Monica's resurrected memory? Or had they simply gone after her because she'd finally emerged from the coma?

"This seems like more proof that we've got an information leak somewhere," Elena concluded, trying to remember if she'd told anyone beside Leo about the conversation with Monica. She hadn't. Only Frank.

"Well, it's not me," he snapped. "And we're the only two who knew what she said this afternoon."

"Even so, if we've got a leak somehow, we'd better find it fast."

"I thought you were suspended," Frank began when she'd hung up. "How come your partner's passing on information?"

"I guess because Ibarra trusts me. She thinks we're in the same boat. Screwed by Quarles and getting no support from the department. Someone tried to kill her tonight. He's dead, but there's no ID on him."

"I'll go over to the hospital with you. Maybe I'll recognize the shooter. If he's a dealer. He could be."

"What about me?" asked Crissie.

"Why don't you take a nap till I get back? Or Dr. Sam here can keep you company."

"As charming a prospect as that is," said Sam, "I find this case quite fascinating. I think I'd rather go to the hospital. Besides which, I'm providing Elena transportation."

"I can drive her," Frank offered quickly.

"No doubt, but I live closer to her present residence, so it would be more convenient for me to take her home after her visit to the hospital."

"I don't care who drives," Elena told them. "I just want to get over there."

42

••

Saturday, November 2, 8:45 A.M.

Elena called I.A. as soon as she awoke in the morning, but Glen Patkin was out of the office until Monday, and of course, they weren't about to give her a home number. She could call Leo, but she didn't want to get him in trouble. He'd taken a risk last night calling her about Monica, and for nothing. The trip to the hospital had been a washout because the doctors wouldn't allow anyone to see Monica. Eddie Diaz, arm bandaged, pale with worry, asked what would have happened if he hadn't arrived in time to hear her scream. Elena hadn't even gotten a look at the attacker. His body had been taken to the morgue. Diaz described him, and Frank went off to the morgue to look, but Elena didn't know how that had turned out. So she'd call Frank and ask.

"Jesus," he said. "You do interrupt at the worst times."

"Sorry," said Elena. "Crissie still there?"

"Yeah, an' not too happy. Lucky I don't have a phone in the bedroom."

"Did you ID the attacker?"

"Nah. I'm going in later this morning to look at mug shots. Just in case."

"I want to show my set to Monica, see if she recognizes Osbaldo Salazar, the nostril man. Can you get me in?"

"That's askin' a lot, Ellie."

"She doesn't trust anyone but me." Ellie? She'd hated that nickname! "Monica thinks everyone, including the department, is out to get both of us."

"Well, babe, I don't want to get my ass kicked over this, so how about I go over there and ask her if she wants to see you? Then I'll call you when she says yes."

"Great. I'll give you my cell-phone number and—"

"How come you get a cell phone an' I don't?"

"For God's sake, Frank, we're not in competition. We never were, no matter what your testosterone kept telling you when we were married."

"If we're goin' to get into old beefs, I'm not helpin' you."

Elena sighed. Her last remark had been ill conceived under the circumstances. "Texas Life gave it to me."

That seemed to mollify Frank. He said, "O.K. Give me the number."

Elena did so. "When are you leaving for the hospital? I'll head for their cafeteria, and you can call me there."

"Oh, real cool, Elena. No one will ever guess I'm bringin' you into the investigation if you do that. Anyway, I can't get over there for at least an hour."

"It's only twenty minutes to the hospital."

"I got other things to do first."

Elena was tempted to say sex had never taken him that long when they were married, but she restrained herself. Without Patkin, Frank was her connection, unless she called the chief himself, but he wasn't listed in the phone book either. Maybe she could use the time to talk her mother out of any further demonstrations or recruiting any other groups to protest the abominable suspension of Detective Elena Jarvis. Next Harmony would be calling in the Union of Brujas, if there was one, to put a hex on Chief Gaitan.

Her mother and Sarah were at the breakfast table when she went downstairs.

"You must have had quite an evening with Dr. Parsley." Harmony beamed at Elena. "You were out *very* late."

Elena reflected wryly that most mothers wouldn't be

delighted to think their daughters were starting an affair on a first date. But maybe having grown up in Chimayo had given her old-fashioned ideas about the expectations of mothers other than Harmony. "It was very interesting," she said. "After the symphony, we called on Frank—"

"Frank Jarvis?" Harmony looked astonished. "You've hardly spoken to the poor man since the divorce."

"He's found himself a nice blonde named Crissie. Then we all went to visit a friend at the hospital."

Harmony looked bemused. "Young people are so unromantic these days. Your father and I used to go dancing at the weekly *bailes* when we were courting."

"I had a strange evening," Sarah interjected. "Some man called me around eleven, wouldn't identify himself, said, 'Mind your own business, bitch,' and hung up."

Elena turned to her, frowning. "Did you recognize his voice?"

"Of course not. I don't associate with people who use the term 'bitch,' certainly not when addressing me."

"Did he sound threatening?"

"I can't say since I have no idea what he was talking about and he hung up immediately."

"Perhaps it was a student," Harmony suggested. "Have you given out any poor grades lately?"

"Dozens," said Sarah, "I'm a professor. I can hardly cease to give grades. I came to the conclusion that the call was a wrong number—"

Elena hoped that was the case, but the fact was that Sarah had, however inadvertently, recently brought down a drug ring.

"—or made by an inarticulate lunatic."

"Sarah, why don't you phone the department and report the call," Elena suggested.

"Why in the world would I do that?"

"In case it's related to your drug bust."

"Nonsense. The criminals are in jail, and I'm not disposed to put my safety into the hands of the local police.

They did, after all, allow my house to be robbed without arresting the burglars or recovering my possessions; then they suspended you for no good reason; and finally they were woefully late responding to my call night before last. If it weren't for your mother and myself, the criminals would certainly have escaped with all the drugs."

"True," said Harmony. "I think I'll point that out at today's demonstration."

"Oh, Mom, can't you quit that?" Elena protested. "It's not helping me, and I'm sure it's making Chief Gaitan mad."

"Injustice must be opposed. Since the senior citizens couldn't participate in the night prayer vigil, they've decided to have a knit-in at headquarters today."

"A *what*?"

"Now, don't be sarcastic, Elena. The ladies thought it up themselves. They'll all knit squares, white and black, and then we'll spell out 'Justice for Jarvis' with the squares in front of the building. We expect to get good TV coverage. The weekend assignment editors at several stations assured me they'd love to photograph the event. Evidently local news on the weekends tends to be slow."

"Well, watching a bunch of elderly knitters sounds about as slow as it gets," Elena muttered. Should she try to warn Gaitan what was coming? Oh, the hell with it, she decided. Since he hadn't made provisions for keeping her connected during the weekend, he'd have to be surprised when he turned on his TV, or when someone at headquarters called him with the news. A *knit-in*? When Harmony got into the act, you could be sure the unusual was about to happen.

Elena retreated to her room to wait for Frank's call while her mother went off to organize the knit-in and Sarah, from her downstairs office, began to call neighbors for a Sunday party to celebrate the spectacular first success of her Neighborhood Crime Watch program. The affair was to feature a covered-dish dinner, press coverage, and the auctioning of a painting donated by Paul Zifkovitz, the proceeds of which would go to buy two walkie-talkies and one bulletproof vest for the group. Sarah was rather miffed when Elena begged off helping on the grounds that she could no longer be the group's police liaison. "Call Krausling," she advised.

While she waited she thought about the leaks. For earlier information that Quarles and company had come up with, anyone could be the source, but only Elena and Leo knew what Monica had said yesterday, and Leo claimed he'd only told his computer, meaning he'd put it in a report. So what if someone was accessing the detectives' reports on the computer? Elena had no idea what security was like in the police system, but she did know someone who could tell her: Her buddy Maggie Daguerre, who had solved a computer crime that occurred at H.H.U. last Christmas. Maggie was still living with Christian Erlingson, the chairman of the university's psychology department. Accordingly, Elena looked his number up and called. Erlingson answered.

"Elena Jarvis?" he asked. "Aren't you the suspended detective?"

Before she could reply, Maggie came on the line and said, "What's up? You need a loan? A recommendation?"

"Some computer expertise," Elena replied.

Maggie groaned. "Every time you say that to me, I end up having to do some crapola file search."

Elena laughed. "You love it, Maggie." And she went on to tell her friend what she wanted to know—who had pulled up Leo's reports on the Quarles case. Particularly who might have accessed yesterday's report. "Can you do that?"

Maggie grumbled.

"Someone tried to kill Monica Ibarra last night because they had information only Leo and I knew, and the only place they could have gotten it from is—"

"All *right*!" Maggie exclaimed, and took down Elena's cell-phone number. "I'll get back to you."

"When?"

"When I find out."

"Hurry."

"I thought your were suspended."

"I'm sort of working pro bono."

"And now I am, too. We're both nuts."

Frank called at eleven to report that Monica Ibarra wasn't seeing anyone but doctors and he hadn't been able to get any hard information on her condition. However, he said he was chatting up an ICU nurse as a possible source.

"Is she blond?" Elena asked.

"What do you care?" he retorted. "Oh, and I'm hearing funny rumors about federal grand juries. Maybe you should turn on your radio. There are about six of our guys over here speculating on how the feds got hold of information on Quarles. Your name has been mentioned."

Elena felt a chill of excitement. Had Perry and his money-laundering expert, Parr, actually convinced a federal attorney to bring Quarles before a grand jury? If so, she didn't care what the department was saying about her. As soon as Frank got off the line, she turned on a news program and stretched out on her bed to listen. After stories about a ballet folklórico arriving in town from Mexico City, the robbery of a convenience store on Lee Trevino Drive, a man arrested for breaking the leg of his girlfriend's two-year-old with a tire iron, a nasty head-on car collision on Trans Mountain Road with three serious injuries, a knit-in by senior citizens at police headquarters in support of a suspended policewoman, and a barbecue being held to support the candidacy of Mayor Nellie Medrano-Caldicott, the announcer repeated the lead story: rumors were circulating in the federal courthouse that the name of Wayne Quarles, candidate for mayor, had been added to a list of people to be investigated by a federal grand jury whose term started Monday.

"All *right*!" Elena cried.

"Federal Prosecutor Gregorio Martinez refused requests for interviews," the announcer stated. "Candidate Quarles is unavailable for comment as well."

Elena was glad she had gone over to see Perry Melon.

Even if nothing came of the federal investigation, it would put pressure on Quarles. Whether or not he had paid to have his wife killed, the man was surely guilty of something. That house across the street, for instance—he had to have known about all those secret storage spaces that were being built in. We'll get him for something, she assured herself.

43

Saturday, November 2, 1:30 P.M.

"I shouldn't let you in at all," said the doctor. "We're talking lung transplant. There's a woman dying of head injuries from a car crash last night who looks like she might be a match if the next of kin give permission, and we've got a surgeon from Phoenix standing by."

"Monica's agreed?" Elena asked.

"She jumped at the idea. For some reason, she wants to go on being a policewoman."

Elena groaned. "Is she putting herself at risk?"

"She's already at risk," said the doctor. "The second operation didn't help, and after the attempt on her life last night—well, that was a real setback." He let them in—Elena, Frank, and Leo—with admonitions not to stay more than a few minutes and not to upset his patient.

"A lung transplant?" Frank looked horrified.

"Shhh," Elena whispered, and then they were standing around the bed in ICU with the folder of mug shots.

Monica looked at the six pictures of the men from the drug bust on Westmoreland and four more pulled at random from the files. Then she pointed to Osbaldo de la Cerda Salazar. "That's him," she whispered.

"You sure?" Elena asked.

"Never forget—his face."

An I.D. & R. tech was called in to videotape the identification, and Monica whispered, "Guess you're expecting me to die."

"No way," said Elena, "but we'll need it for the indictment, and you won't be out of here by then." What a liar I am, she thought. Monica looked terrible. Her fall out of bed last night had been a disaster—Elena could see that—even if Monica's scream had saved her life. The unidentified, now dead, assassin, disguised as a hospital worker, had been about to inject strychnine into her IV

"Just find the SOB," Monica whispered.

"Salazar's in jail. We're goin' over now to sweat him," said Frank.

"Your job is to get well," Leo told her gently. "We'll clear your name."

"I want Elena to question him," Ibarra whispered.

Elena's ex frowned. "Well, she's—"

"Suspended. I know."

"You better stop talking," said Frank. "The doc said—"

"She's got—the most—at stake—besides me."

"O.K.," Leo soothed.

"Promise," Monica insisted.

Leo sighed. "Promise."

And Leo kept that promise, despite stiff opposition at headquarters. Only when Elena insisted that the chief be called did the problem sort itself out. Reluctantly, the lieutenant in charge called Gaitan, expecting the chief to refuse. Instead, Gaitan said Elena could sit in as long as she wore her disguise and was introduced at the jail as a narcotics officer. "Borrow an ID for her," he told the lieutenant, "and don't mention this to anyone." Elena went home to retrieve her wig and don another of Sarah's outfits. On her way back, she got a call from Maggie, who said a civilian employee in I.D. & R. named Rose Maya had accessed Leo's report yesterday at four forty-five.

"You're a genius, Maggie," Elena exclaimed triumphantly. "Can you find out if she made any calls after that? And to what numbers?"

"You think she'd be that dumb?"

"It's worth a shot."

"I'll see."

Elena passed the information on at headquarters to Leo, who stormed back to Crimes Against Persons and enlisted Harry Mosconi, one of the detectives on weekend duty, to find out whatever he could about Rose Maya, particularly telephone-company information on numbers she called from her home phone.

Then, because the garage was blocked, the three left headquarters by the front door, threading their way through the crowd of the elderly ladies, who were knitting industriously. Harmony was surprised to see Elena and whispered, "Do Leo and Frank know who you are?"

"Shhhh," said Elena, and Harmony nodded with an air of complicity. Frank and Leo hustled the disguised Elena away before the press could get a good look at her. They drove her truck to the jail, all three jammed in the front seat.

"On advice of my lawyer, I'm not sayin' nothin'," Osbaldo Salazar announced.

"O.K.," Elena agreed, staring with interest at his gaping left nostril. "You keep your mouth shut and listen."

"Stop starin' at my nose. It ain't polite."

"I can't help it," said Elena. "That nostril is what's going to send you to death row."

He put his hand over his nose. "It ain't against the law to have a nose some blond narc don't like."

"It's against the law to shoot a cop, and she identified you by the nose."

"I didn't shoot no cop."

"So you shot Hope Quarles, and your friend shot Officer Ibarra. Either way it's a capital crime, and you're facing the big needle at Huntsville."

"I didn't do nothin'."

"Car theft's a felony. You killed a woman during the commission of a felony. That's capital murder. Killing a cop is capital murder."

"I ain't heard the cop is dead."

"She's dying, and she identified you as the car thief and her assailant. Deathbed statements carry a lot of weight in court. We got her on videotape pointing to your picture and saying, 'That's him.'"

"I didn't steal no car."

"The lock was drilled. If she hadn't showed up, you'd have stolen the car."

"An' I didn't assail no one. You ain't got nothin' on me. My lawyer's gonna git me bail."

Elena turned to the lawyer. "You already tried for bail, didn't you? No one from that drug bust got out."

"No one's *made* bail yet," said Ryan Morrissey. "You don't have to say anything else, Salazar. Keep your mouth shut."

"But I didn't do nothin'."

"You weren't moving millions of dollars in coke out of that house on Westmoreland?" Frank asked. "You were caught red-handed, man."

"I thought it was sugar. Them bags said sugar."

"Doesn't matter anyway," said Elena. "Capital murder is the charge."

"The cop don't know what she's talkin' about. She's so bad off, how's she gonna tell one guy from another?"

"Your nose." Elena went back to staring. Osbaldo Salazar shielded the telltale feature with his hand.

"I wanna go back to my cell," he said. "Don' I got the right to go back to my cell?" he asked his lawyer.

"Who do you think the jury's going to believe? The dying testimony of a policewoman or the word of a known drug dealer who shot Hope Masterson Quarles?" Elena asked.

"I heard *she* shot the lady. The cop."

"Where'd you hear that?"

"Newspaper."

"She says she didn't. She says she was shot before she ever saw Mrs. Quarles again. And the jury's going to believe her. You think responsible jurors are going to believe you when they've got the word of a top-notch policewoman, especially one who's dead?"

"She ain't dead!" Salazar insisted nervously. "How's she tellin' you this stuff if she's dead?"

"She's dying. Dying statements carry extra weight," Frank reiterated. "And someone tried to kill her last night. That looks real bad. Like your drug friends are trying to protect you by killing the witness. That constitutes retaliation and attempted capital murder."

Salazar paled. "She didn't see me kill nobody, 'cause I didn't kill nobody."

"You saying someone else did the two killings, and you just witnessed them?" asked Leo. "You trying to cop a plea?"

"My client has nothing more to say," said Morrissey.

"Sounds like your lawyer has interests other than yours, Osbaldo," Elena observed. "Maybe he's gonna let you face the needle to protect someone more important."

"My client has already said he wishes to return to his cell," said Morrissey.

"Sure. You think about it, Osbaldo, when you're sitting on that stainless-steel john upstairs. Think about the capital-murder charge you're facing, think about who your lawyer's really representing."

"Who are you, anyway?" Morrissey asked Elena. "I thought I knew everyone in Narcotics."

"I'm new," Elena told him, "and good. I got the ID on Osbaldo here, and we all have an interest in this case—Narcotics, Crimes Against Persons. Even the feds are getting in on the act. If Quarles is in bed with a drug cartel, you'd better let him know he's next."

"I don't represent Mr. Quarles," the lawyer said stiffly.

"Well, maybe he'll be calling. You are, after all, the preferred attorney among scumbags in the drug trade."

"Every man deserves the best defense he can afford."

"And Wayne Quarles suddenly has a lot of money. I imagine he can afford the best, if that's you."

Elena couldn't think of the last time she'd enjoyed an interrogation so much. And she expected Salazar to break. He was already sweating. Tonight he'd dream of being strapped to that gurney at Huntsville. He'd dream of the needle sliding into his arm. He'd dream of dying.

As she drove home, the news broadcast she listened to was particularly interesting. Rumors about Quarles and the federal grand jury were repeated. Who had leaked that gem? she wondered. The FBI or the federal prosecutor's office? According to the reporter, the federal prosecutor still refused to comment. Quarles, when interviewed after a monster rally at the county coliseum, said the rumor was meant to derail his campaign; he deplored such dirty political tactics. He said his wife, were she alive, would be disappointed in Nellie Medrano-Caldicott. But he sounded shaken nonetheless. Elena congratulated herself on her decision to go to the FBI; it had been a smart move.

Mayor Nellie, interviewed at city hall, said she hadn't heard the rumor, didn't know anything about the grand jury, whose proceedings were supposed to be secret, and remarked that she'd hate to win an election because her opponent had been slandered. Still, Elena doubted that the mayor would refuse to accept a victory on those grounds.

The announcer went on to report that police were moving closer to solving the murder of Hope Masterson Quarles, that they had a suspect in custody, not the policewoman whom rumors had blamed for the shooting. He reported the attempt on the life of Monica Ibarra the night before and said television newscasts would show a picture of the dead assassin. The police were hoping for a citizen identification.

Lastly, the announcer covered the knit-in at police headquarters in support of suspended detective Elena Jarvis. "Senior citizens haven't forgotten that Jarvis caught the serial killer of five elderly men, previously thought to have been slain in burglaries," the newscaster said. "The detective's suspension is raising eyebrows all over town, and more demonstrations are anticipated. Chief Gaitan was not available for comment."

Elena grinned. The chief knew better than to say anything, given the fact that her mother would be the person who'd respond to his words. Harmony made a formidable opponent, especially for a man who was half in love with her.

44

Sunday, November 3, 2:30 A.M.

Elena tumbled out of bed to the stutter of automatic weapons. But how could that be? A drive-by in Sussex Hills? She must have been dreaming. Then she remembered the stash house across the street and stopped reaching toward the lamp. Instead, she reached up and opened the drawer where she kept her Glock. The renewed rattle of gunfire and the tinkle of breaking glass caused her to hurry. "Sarah! Mom! Can you hear me?" she called.

"What's happening?" Sarah called back.

"Stay down. Don't turn on any lights." Gun in hand, Elena inched cautiously toward the hall. The shooters must be in front of the house. And one Glock against automatic weapons was not good odds. She heard another burst hit the house. The barrage was followed by a single shot. Who the hell had fired that? Then she heard the squeal of tires.

"I think I got one," Harmony called. The voice came from the guest bathroom in front of the house.

Elena groaned. "For God's sake, Mom. Stay down."

"I don't understand what's happening," Sarah yelled.

"Hush up, both of you. We need to listen. In case someone's in the house?" Elena padded down the hall.

"Where are the police?" Sarah again.

"I'm the police," Elena muttered.

"You're suspended," Harmony reminded her.

"Shhhh!"

All was silent. Elena strained her ears for any little sound that might indicate an intruder. You'd think the alarm system would have been triggered. It evidently wasn't keyed for random gunfire. She reached the head of the stairs and peered over, studying the foyer with its dim night-light. Rising cautiously, both hands steadying the nine-millimeter, heart in her throat, she took the stairs, one step at a time, hating her exposed position. From the landing to the first floor, there was no place to hide. The silence continued. No one shot at her.

Elena began checking downstairs and had reached Sarah's study when she heard the sound of a speeding car. She hit the floor, and not a second too soon. Bullets sprayed over her head, damaging books and paintings. Again a single shot rang out. Damn! Her mother was shooting, which meant that she was exposing herself. One more burst of gunfire and the noise of the motor receded, leaving the sounds of broken objects falling from shelves. But no voices. Elena's heart went cold.

"Mom?" she called. Nothing.

"Mom?" Elena was crouched behind Sarah's journal-reading chair, the room a shambles. There was no sound at all, nothing to indicate that Harmony was alive. Tears began to gather in Elena's eyes at the thought of her beautiful, nutty, wonderful mother, dead. Or wounded. "Oh, Mom," she whispered.

"Here." A hushed voice in her ear galvanized already brutalized nerves into action, and Elena leaped up, gun raised.

"For heaven's sake, Elena, are you going to shoot me?"

Elena lowered the gun, her hands shaking. The voice, somewhat strained and strange, was her mother's. "Oh, my God, Mom. You scared me."

"But you called, so I came down," Harmony said calmly.

"I was just—I was afraid you'd been—"

"Shot? Well, I probably couldn't have answered, in that case. Do you think we can turn the lights on now?"

"No," said Elena, and called out to Sarah.

"I'm dialing 911," Sarah called back. "That was gunfire, wasn't it?"

Elena succumbed to nervous laughter. Here was Sarah, organizing a Crime Watch, buying guns, raising money for bulletproof vests and walkie-talkies, and she had to ask if the damage done to her house was the result of gunfire. "Tell them we were sprayed by automatic weapons," Elena answered.

"Are you laughing?" asked Harmony, aghast.

"No, Mom, I'm having a nervous breakdown."

"Oh, you poor child." Harmony put her arms around her daughter. "You're a very brave girl to come down here all by yourself. And you're a good policewoman. Don't let anyone tell you different. Is that what you were doing at headquarters this afternoon, being harassed by Internal Affairs?"

Elena sniffed.

"Well, you don't have to tell me. I suppose the police are very secretive about such things. And you're not having a nervous breakdown, dear. You're just understandably upset." All during this piece of motherly reassurance, which Elena accepted while she continued to tremble, Harmony had been patting Elena's cheek and hair with the hand that didn't hold the rifle. The rifle, unfortunately, was digging into Elena's back throughout her mother's kind embrace.

"Everyone O.K. in there?" called a male voice from outside. Harmony and Elena both gripped their weapons.

Sarah called from upstairs, probably through a broken window, "Hello there, Mr. Lee. Was your house shot at, too?"

"Shot at?" The neighbor two doors down sounded horrified. "No, was yours?"

"I believe so. I've called the police. Give me a moment, and I'll be down." Sarah descended the stairs almost immediately, carrying her Gunsmith, Inc., handgun by the barrel and wearing a navy-blue robe with white piping, hair neatly combed. From the bulge in her pocket, Elena assumed that she'd remembered to bring bullets.

Sirens were approaching as Sarah opened her front door, with its line of bullet holes ruining the tasteful trefoil carving. "I certainly hope my home owner's insurance covers military attack," she murmured to Elena.

Now that the shooters had evidently pulled out, Elena had time to wonder who they had been. The conclusion she came to was that Sarah and her house guests had all been targeted by the drug cartel, whose operations they had interrupted the other night. Was it a warning, none too subtle, not to testify against any of those who'd been arrested, an attempt to stop any further obstruction of the drug trade by Neighborhood Watch programs, or just plain old vengeance? What a mess! And it had begun so innocently. With Sarah trying to stop what she assumed to be a burglary of Jaime Barrajas's house.

People with coats thrown over their nightclothes began to emerge from the homes up and down the block, first hesitantly, then indignantly. The Westside patrol arrived, trying to discount the story of two barrages of automatic-weapons fire. After they'd seen the damage and collected slugs, they stopped arguing.

When the first question was asked about the attackers, there was silence. Then Harmony replied, "They were driving an 'eighty-six Chrysler four-door sedan, black with red detailing along the sides. I believe there were three men in the car, one of whom I certainly shot."

The officers gaped at her. "If you don't mind my asking, ma'am," said a patrolman who had introduced himself as Officer Charles Perlmutter, "how did you happen to recognize the car? Do you know the owner?"

"Tía Josefina's nephew on her mother's side owns one, which he bought with his winnings from an Indian casino."

"I see. A family feud. What's his address?" asked the officer, prepared to write down information on the nephew.

"He lives in Trampas, New Mexico, and his car is light blue," said Harmony. "But our family does not shoot at each other. As for the color and detailing on the criminal's car, I saw it as the Chrysler came under those globe lights next door." She turned to the owner of the ornate fixture and said, "I just love your lights. So Dickensian."

The owner obviously didn't know whether to be offended or complimented. Officer Perlmutter wrote down Harmony's description, but it evidently galled him to do so.

"Why don't you put it on the radio before the car crosses a bridge into Mexico?" Harmony suggested.

"Did it have Frontera plates?" he responded.

"I didn't see the plates, but isn't that where criminals go when the Los Santos police are chasing them?"

Perlmutter's partner called in the vehicle description. More police cars pulled up. Unmarked cars joined the traffic jam in front of Sarah's house. Harmony offered to make coffee for everyone. The neighbor with the Dickensian lights sidled up to her and admired her long black hair, earning himself a lovely smile.

He's a goner, Elena thought, until a woman who was apparently the man's wife grabbed his arm and dragged him into their house. At that juncture a TV news van arrived, and Harmony all but embraced its occupants. Frank pulled up and headed for Elena, asking whether she thought the shooting was connected to the stash house.

"Or the Quarles case or both," she said, low-voiced. "Maybe it was the Diablo Kings."

"Kind of out of their territory," he replied. "Nice nightgown." Frank eyed her with some of the fire that had burned between them early in their marriage.

"I didn't have time to get a robe," Elena muttered, embarrassed. She was wearing, over her underpants, a long T-shirt that had once belonged to Frank. Damn! She didn't want him getting ideas.

"This is a disgrace," Harmony was saying to the press. "I had to shoot at those bandits myself because my daughter's been suspended. The chief's action has put us in harm's way."

"For God's sake, someone tell her we've already been offered protection," said Elena, looking from Frank to Vince de la Rosa, who, under orders from his captain, had told her the house and its occupants would be provided with twenty-four-hour surveillance until the shooters were caught. "Frank, lend me your jacket. I'm not showing myself on TV in a thigh-length T-shirt."

"Sure." He took the garment off. "But it's not long enough to cover your thighs, which are too nice to cover anyway."

"Oh, shut up." She took the jacket and tied it around her waist. She looked pretty weird, but now at least she was covered to the knee.

"If my daughter hadn't been suspended by the political toadies at police headquarters, she could have defended us." Harmony was in her element in front of the TV cameras.

"Mom," Elena whispered, pulling at the sleeve of her mother's loose robe. "Knock it off."

45

Sunday, November 3, 9:00 A.M.

By Sunday morning five of the six people who had been found staring at the bodies in the alley were brought in to view a lineup. The sixth, the hit-and-run victim, was still in a hospital. One witness picked out Osbaldo Salazar as a man he had seen climbing into a blue car a half block from the scene of the crime.

While the lineup was being organized, Maggie had reported that no calls out had been made on Rose Maya's I.D. & R. phone. However, Mosconi reported to Leo that a frequent call from Rose's home, including one at five-thirty on Friday, was to Reymundo Carrascas, who had an address in El Segundo Barrio and several narcotics arrests. "That's definitely worth pursuing," said Leo, and telephoned the captain who headed I.D. & R. to report that one of his people was associating with criminals and accessing files she had no need to see.

With Salazar back in the interrogation room, Elena, still disguised as a narc, said casually, "Now, we've got someone who saw you leaving the scene, not to mention Ibarra, who's identified you as the guy right where it happened."

Salazar was sweating, the armpits of his orange jail togs dark with perspiration. "I want a new lawyer."

"Sure," said Leo. "Who do you want?"

Salazar's face screwed itself up into lines of anxiety and confusion. "I ain't got the money for a good lawyer."

"They never paid you for the hit?" Frank asked.

Salazar stared at him accusingly. "I ain't fallin' for that."

"If you don't have any money, how come you could afford Ryan Morrissey?" Leo asked.

"I got friends. But they ain't payin' for no two lawyers."

Leo nodded. "Especially an attorney who might advise you to rat them out."

"I din' say that." The sweat dripped down the man's face, running into the neckline of his shirt.

"You want a public defender?" Elena asked.

"They ain't no good," said Salazar. "Are they?"

"You ever heard of Alope Randall? Maybe I could get her," said Elena, who knew the labor lawyer from another case. Since Alope had offered to defend her pro bono on the suspension, Elena wanted to return the favor by providing a paying client—in this case the county.

"I heard of her, but she don't do no criminal stuff, does she? Ain't she lawyer to them garment-worker women?"

"Alope handled the case when a garment worker was accused of murder," said Elena. "Just kept hanging in there till we had to let the woman go. If you're thinking of a plea bargain, she could handle that."

Could she get Alope to take the case? The county would pay her fee, which was more than most of her clients did. Randall ran the Border Legal Clinic—pro bono clients. She lived on an inheritance from her father and her share of tribal profits she inherited from her mother, who had been a Mescalero Apache.

"I'll take her," Salazar decided.

"Hey, I gotta talk her into it," said Elena.

"Well, I ain't sayin' no more till I got a new mouthpiece."

By noon Ryan Morrissey had come to see his client and been turned away. Sheriff's deputies reported that he was furious when Salazar refused his visit. Also by noon Alope Randall had taken the case and spent an hour closeted with Salazar. When she came out, she said to Elena, who hadn't revealed her identity and whom Alope hadn't recognized, "Nice dirtbag you people handed me. I better get paid promptly by the county. My clinic needs security bars. Damn gangbangers broke in and stole our computers, even my chair and desk."

Elena remembered that splintery furniture and marveled that anyone would bother to steal it. "Is Salazar ready to deal?"

"You got an Assistant D.A. handy who can make a deal?"

"Depends on what you're asking for. A hired hit is capital murder. So is murder in the commission of a felony and murder of a cop."

"Ibarra's dead? Damn. I represented a cousin of hers who got stiffed on her wages when that place on Magoffin closed down."

"Not dead. But she could still die. She had to have a lung transplant."

"Well, if my client had anything to do with a murder . . ."

"We've got witnesses."

"Nobody saw him shooting."

"Come on, Ms. Randall."

"If my client decides to cooperate, he's going to need protection, and you'll have to guarantee not to ask for the death penalty."

"I'll get an A.D.A. over here," said Elena, elated. It was coming together. If Salazar rolled over, they'd find out what really happened. Maybe. No guarantee he wouldn't lie. But if he gave them names, there'd be others to arrest and question. One way or another, they'd sort out the truth.

"My client's scared. You understand what I'm saying?"

"Sure. His employers are more dangerous than we are."

"If I were you, I'd get the D.A. himself in on this," Randall advised. "You got a high-profile case here, Detectives. I don't want some underling making promises, then having the D.A. back off or the feds take over and dump the plea."

Elena nodded and left with Leo to make the calls that would start the plea-bargaining process. It looked like Salazar just wanted to stay alive, even if he had to do his living at Huntsville.

46

••

Sunday, November 3, 2:30 P.M.

At the meeting were Salazar and Alope Randall, Leo and Lieutenant Beltran of C.A.P., Frank and Lieutenant Costas of Narcotics, Elena as a fake narc, and the district attorney, to whom Elena had to be introduced under her new name.

The agreement pounded out between Alope Randall and the D.A. was that Salazar would cop to first-degree murder with no recommendation for the death penalty, that while in the county jail he would be segregated and protected from the general population, then put in a federal penitentiary under protective custody after his conviction. In return he would tell them what had happened in the alley and reveal the identity of the person or persons behind it. Both Salazar and Randall promised that the information would be worth the deal made to get it. With the agreement ironed out and a tape recorder running, Salazar began to talk.

"I ain't no big shot in the organization, *comprende*? Jus' do what I'm told. An' I din' shoot the cop. Din' know there was gonna be no cop there. They tell me, this Quarles woman—we had a picture—would be comin' by in a cop T-shirt. She'll see me drillin' the car lock. When she comes in to look, Eduardo, he'll shoot her."

"Eduardo who?" asked the D.A.

"Rocha. Eduardo Rocha. *Madre de Dios,* I never thought

I'd be rattin' on Eduardo, but then I wouldna gone along if I'd knowed what was goin' down."

"Where does he live?" asked Elena.

"El Segundo Barrio. House looks like shit on the outside, but it's a real nice place. Better'n mine."

"Address?" Elena asked.

He gave it. "But if he's smart, he's long gone. That ain't gonna queer my deal, is it?"

Lieutenant Costas murmured to Frank, who stepped out of the room.

"So what happened in the alley? Who shot Officer Ibarra?" the D.A. prompted.

"Eduardo. He's supposed to whistle when the lady comes into the alley. He does, but when I turn around, here's this real cop with her gun out, an' Eduardo, he's at the end of the alley with his hand over this Quarles lady's mouth, the one we're supposed to hit. I 'bout shit my pants when I seen the cop. I drop down so the cop don' shoot me, an' Eduardo, he shoots the cop, an' she shoots. Her bullet don' go nowhere 'cause she's hit, but *Madre de Dios,* I think we're screwed for sure. Someone's gonna hear the shot, 'cause the cop don' got no silencer on her gun like Eduardo does."

"Were you carrying?" Leo asked.

"Yeah, but I wasn' supposed to shoot no one. I'm just along for insurance. A decoy to get her inna alley. Like how come a lady like her's out playin' cop, anyway?"

"So Ibarra's down. Who shot Quarles?" the D.A. asked.

Salazar shivered and looked toward Alope Randall.

"You want the deal, you talk," she said, face hard.

He gulped. "Eduardo's draggin' her inna the alley, an' he says, 'Get the cop's gun.' I don' wanna. I say, '*Porqúe,* Eduardo? I don' need no gun. I got one.' 'Get the gun,' he says. 'It's gonna look like the cop shot the woman.' The woman, she's wigglin', an' Rocha whispers in her ear, an' she stops. He tells her she keeps it up, he's gonna rape her; she goes along, she don' git killed, jus' shot. I din' know what he said till later. I'm thinkin', if the cop gets blamed, me an' Eduardo, we're inna clear. So I pick up her gun. It's layin' in some trash beside her. Then Eduardo says, 'Shoot this one with the gun,' an' I say, 'I ain't bein' paid to shoot no one,' an' he says, 'You wan' me to tell the boss, you didn' do what he said?' and I say, 'He din' say nothin' about me shootin' no one,' an' Eduardo says, 'O.K., *estúpido,* you hold her an' I'll shoot her,' an' I'm thinkin' the bullet could go through her an' hit me, an' I'm thinkin' if Eduardo tells the boss I din' do what I was told, there'll be a hit out on me by tomorrow, so I . . ."

He paused again, looking toward his lawyer, who nodded. "So Eduardo points at the middle of the *O* on her cop T-shirt, an' I shoot her. Then Eduardo drops her an' takes the gun outta my hand an' wipes it off an' puts it in the cop's hand, an' we take off. That's it. I din' mean to kill no one. Eduardo tricked me. No one said I was gonna have to—"

"Who paid you?" asked the D.A.

Salazar's face twisted with fear.

"It's part of the deal," Alope Randall reminded him, "and they're going to protect you."

"Yeah." He didn't sound hopeful about the efficacy of the protection. "Miguel Barrajas," he said, shivering, his knuckles white where his clenched fists rested on the table.

"Why?" asked the D.A.

"I tole you I ain't no big shot. How'd I know?"

"But Barrajas is the head of the drug cartel?" the narcotics lieutenant asked.

Salazar nodded, short, hard breaths flaring the outsized nostril along with the normal one. "He's the big boss. He don' live here. He jus' comes over."

"And Jaime Barrajas?" Frank asked. He had just returned to the room and had fish to fry besides the murder.

"Miguel's brother. He handles distribution this side a' the river."

"Where does Rocha fit into the trade?" Frank asked.

"He works for Jaime, packagin' the coke, recruitin' the drivers, like that. If someone's gonna get whacked, Eduardo, he usually does it if it ain't in Mexico. Miguel's got guys in Juarez for Mexico hits."

"Where do Los Reyes Diablos fit in?" Elena asked.

Salazar grinned. "I put them tattoos on with ink." He pushed up his sleeves to display his arms, now bare of crowned devils. "My idea," he said proudly. "Eduardo, he says, 'Beautiful, man,' when I say I'm gonna draw on the gang stuff so everyone'll think some kids done it."

"The woman you killed was Hope Quarles," said Elena. "Why would Miguel Barrajas want her dead?"

"He don' tell me why he wants stuff. Don' tell me nothin'."

"Was anything said about her husband, Wayne Quarles?" From the corner of her eye, she could see the D.A. frowning.

Salazar scratched his head. "I run out of cigarettes." He had been smoking steadily. The air was thick with his smoke and that of the two narcs. Frank tossed him a pack, and Salazar lit up. "I heard his name once. Quarles. He owed Miguel money. Tha's what I heard. It ain't healthy to owe Miguel Barrajas money. You know? Maybe Miguel had Quarles's old lady whacked to let him know he better pay back the *dinero* or take a hit himself. He done that in Juarez—Miguel. Killed a whole family—babies an' all, 'cause the papa, he hijacked a truck of marijuana Miguel had comin' from the interior."

Elena supposed the death of Hope Quarles could have been a warning, or Barrajas's way of making sure that Quarles had the money to repay his debts. If so, the department had nothing to connect Quarles to the murder. Maybe there *was* nothing, but he was dirty otherwise—money laundering, consorting with drug dealers.

What she couldn't figure was why they'd set up the hit so that it involved a policewoman. Salazar didn't know, unless he was lying about his surprise at seeing Monica there. Maybe Barrajas thought it was somehow funny to implicate a police officer in a hit he'd commissioned.

But Elena wondered whether the scenario didn't have something to do with the election. Fermin Gil and, to a lesser extent, Quarles were making political hay out of the killing. Had Barrajas done it that way to scare Quarles as well as give him a campaign issue? Did he hope to control the mayor once Quarles assumed office? What drug lord wouldn't want to own the mayor of a border city on his distribution route?

"What do you know about Fermin Gil?" she asked Salazar.

"I already told you everythin' I know," said Salazar. "Do I get my own guard now?"

"Isolation," said the D.A. "That's the safest place until you testify and we can stow you in a federal prison."

As the group left the interrogation room, various discussions started up, Elena with Frank, the D.A. with Beltran and Costas. Beltran caught up with Elena at the gun lockers. "How come the feds are investigating Wayne Quarles? Did you sic them on him?" he demanded.

Elena gave him a look of wide-eyed innocence. "I'm a narc now. I'd need my new lieutenant's permission to go to the feds."

Beltran frowned. "Don't be a smart-ass with me. You've got a motive for going after Quarles. Before you start any vendettas, you better keep in mind that Salazar didn't implicate Wayne Quarles."

"If he owes them money, they've got their hooks into him," she replied somberly.

"That doesn't tie him to his wife's murder."

"True," she agreed. "Do we know yet if it was Rose Maya who leaked the ballistics on the gun that killed Hope Quarles?"

"I.A.'s looking into it," said Beltran.

She'd call Glen Patkin. "Who's going after Rocha?"

"Narcotics has already checked out the house. He's not there, so they're setting up surveillance."

"And Jaime Barrajas?" she asked.

"He's not talking to anyone but his attorney. I don't think we'll be getting his brother's whereabouts from him, even if we could go after Miguel in Mexico."

"Yeah. Well . . ." Just then her pager went off, so she headed for her truck and cell phone, calling over her shoulder, "If Rocha comes back, I'd like to help take him."

"We'll see, *niña,*" said Beltran.

Damn, she hated being called that. She answered the page and got Chief Gaitan. "Do you know that your mother has both the senior citizens and the Hispanic women outside headquarters holding what they're calling 'Fiesta Elena'?" he demanded. "Can't you talk to the woman?"

"Not without telling her the truth," said Elena. "You could unsuspend me, and she'd probably go home. She just came down to purify my house—"

"I won't even ask what that means," the chief grumbled.

"—which she's done, but now she thinks she needs to protect her daughter from political harassment."

Gaitan sighed gustily. "I'm the one who needs protection. They've got a mariachi band out there, they're making speeches about what a male chauvinist pig I am, your mother's selling pecan pies to raise money to sue us, and the most popular activity is the dart throw. The Hispanic women are taking fifty cents a dart from anyone who wants to spear a picture of *me*."

"Oh Lord," Elena groaned. "Look, I'm sorry, but—"

"Did you get anything from Salazar?"

"He gave us Ibarra's shooter, admitted to shooting Hope Quarles himself, and implicated a drug lord named Miguel Barrajas."

"But he didn't give us Quarles?"

"Nope. So I guess I'm still suspended."

"At least Texas Life is paying you well, and when you're reinstated, you'll get back pay."

"I will?" I'm going to be rich! Elena thought.

As she started her truck, there was a knock on her window. She looked up to see Alope Randall peering in at her. Reluctantly, Elena rolled the glass down. "Ms. Randall?" she said politely.

"Detective Jarvis?" Alope responded sarcastically. "What the hell's going on?"

What to say? Elena felt a little panicky. "I'm undercover. I hope you won't—"

Randall laughed. "No skin off my nose. I'm just glad to know the bastards realized they couldn't suspend you."

47

Monday, November 4, 3:05 A.M.

The police contingent all wore black clothes and bulletproof vests, but it was the S.W.A.T. team, in helmets and full body armor, who would actually go in. Two men had returned to Eduardo Rocha's house after midnight, one helped by the other. Elena got the call around two when the surveillance team, in consultation with headquarters, decided that it wasn't worth risking the loss of Rocha by waiting to see who else turned up at his house. They gave him two hours after the lights went out, then began the approach.

Elena and Leo were crouched behind a junked car across the street from Rocha's crumbling adobe. That place looked worse than her house had looked when she and Frank first bought it, yet Salazar had said it was nice inside. Of course, who could tell what a drug dealer would consider nice? Sarah had thought Jaime Barrajas's expensive furnishings tasteless.

Frank, who had joined the S.W.A.T. team sometime during the last six months, was going in with the others, but on the dark street she couldn't even tell which one he was. Elena shivered inside her black jacket because the temperature must have dropped forty degrees from the balmy high of seventy-two that had greeted her when she left the jail.

She heard a dog bark, then stop abruptly. Had some cop slugged the animal? Leo touched her arm and pointed. The shadows of the S.W.A.T. team flitted through the darkness toward the house. She hoped the place wasn't booby-trapped.

Then there were shouts of "Police" and splintering crashes as the doors were kicked in front and back. Gunfire. She tensed. Elena didn't love Frank anymore, but she didn't wish him ill. Two more shots, and they began to come out, three people dragged struggling from the house by the black-garbed team.

Three was one more inhabitant than the team had anticipated, but that shouldn't be any surprise. However, if one of the three wasn't Rocha, they were screwed. He'd hear that his house had been stormed and never come back.

"Got a wounded guy here. Bullet's still in him," called the team leader. "Radio EMS."

"Shit. Let him bleed," said a short, stocky cop.

"He's not bleeding. Someone shot him before we got here," said the leader.

Elena and Leo came forward. "Is it Rocha?" she asked, interested. "The one who's wounded?"

Frank shoved a hand into the man's pocket.

"Like what you feel, pig?" snarled the prisoner.

Frank shone a light on the driver's license in the wallet he had retrieved. "Rocha," he confirmed.

"How'd you get shot?" Elena asked, studying the man, who would be another addition to the rogues' gallery she carried in her head. Rocha had a low forehead, wide cheekbones, and a broad, bulgy nose. An ugly guy.

"I don't answer no questions from bitch cops," he replied, giving her a lewd once-over.

Frank cracked him on the elbow with the flashlight, then said, "Oops. Sorry about that."

"Tell it to my lawyer," was the hot reply.

"If the bullet's still in him, be sure the doctor saves it," said Elena. "My mom says she winged one of the drive-bys who shot up the house."

Frank laughed. "If it matches, we'll just give him to Harmony and that *bruja* she hangs out with."

Elena was surprised to see Rocha turn pale in the light of the torch. Well, well, she thought. Our drug-dealing murderer is afraid of witches.

"You ain't giving me to nobody," said Rocha. "My lawyer, he have me out by ten in the morning."

"No bail on this one, Rocha," said Leo. "You're headed for death row, ratted out by your compadres."

"I don' fall for no pig lies." Rocha sneered.

"Spill your guts, maybe you'll get life instead of the needle, but we know you were paid to kill Mrs. Quarles, even if you didn't have the *cojones* to do it yourself."

"Who told you this lie?" demanded Rocha.

"Don't matter," said one of the team members. "You're dead meat, man."

Elena was staring at Eduardo Rocha, remembering how scared she'd been when she thought her mother had been killed by gunfire. "Tell 'em to forget the local anesthetic when they dig out that bullet," she suggested.

"Puta!" he snarled.

Frank hit him again with the flashlight.

"Knock it off," said his lieutenant. Rocha was loaded into an ambulance and sent off with three men guarding him. His two companions were delivered to Central Command for questioning, and the rest of the cops returned to the house to execute a search warrant.

Elena went home. Maybe she could get another two hours of sleep before the investigation began again. That is, if they let her in on questioning Rocha. She was getting sick of being a fake suspendee. Even if it did pay well.

48

••

Monday, November 4, 9:30 A.M.

After the arrest of Eduardo Rocha, Elena had collapsed into bed toward morning, forgetting to set her alarm. She was dragged from sleep by a call from Milton Freer, her pseudo-boss at Texas Life. "It's nine-thirty, and you're not in your office, Ms. Carr," he said reproachfully. "We do expect a full day's work from you. You're being well paid to—"

"You got a big portion of last night," Elena grumbled. "We arrested a second man for the murder of Hope Quarles."

"Her husband?" Freer asked eagerly.

"No," she admitted, "and no one's connected him to the killing yet, but he seems to have—well—business connections to the man who ordered his wife's death."

Freer sighed and let Elena go back to bed. She wondered again if she'd be allowed to participate in the interrogation of Rocha, decided they'd call if her request was approved, and dropped back to sleep. At eleven Glen Patkin called. "Were you asleep?" he asked. "At this hour?"

"I was out late."

"Yeah, it's all over town. Quarles is complaining about police deception, about the chief saying you were suspended, then allowing you to go on S.W.A.T. operations. He says the whole investigation of his wife's killing is a cover-up and the department is trying to wreck his campaign by casting suspicion on him with the feds, and investigating him and his family, and refusing to tell him anything about rumored arrests in the case."

"How does he know I was there last night? Granted, I wasn't in disguise, but there were no media people around, and I don't see how Rose Maya could have sent them word. I didn't file a report, and surely by now she's been barred from the department computer system. By the way, has she been questioned?"

"Funny you should ask." He laughed. "She denied the whole thing yesterday. Said she didn't know what we were talking about, and maybe someone using her computer accessed Weizell's reports. She claims the guy she's been calling, Reymundo Carrascas, is her cousin and couldn't care less about police business. He's become a solid citizen since his early brushes with the law and doesn't even want to hear the police mentioned."

"You believe her?" asked Elena.

"Not for a minute. One of the guys you arrested last night at Rocha's house was—guess who?—Reymundo Carrascas. He gave a false name, but when he was printed, the Automated Fingerprint Identification System threw up his real name, plus a few more aliases. So her cousin who isn't interested in the Quarles murder, according to her, is up to his neck in it.

"We pulled her in again this morning, and she cried all over my office and said how was she to know why Cousin Rey was interested in the case? He's a good guy and pays for her mother's blood-pressure medicine, which costs a fortune, so of course she chats with him, et cetera, et cetera. We'll charge her. Whether the D.A. can get a conviction or even wants to try—that's another matter."

"I hope she goes to jail," said Elena. "Indirectly, she's responsible for the attempt at the hospital on Monica's life. But I don't see how she could have known that I was at the

Rocha bust last night. And if she knew, who would she tell? Her cousin was in custody."

"True," Patkin agreed. "Maybe one of the guys we arrested recognized you and got the word out."

Frustrated, Elena said, "Anyone asked Quarles where he got his information?"

"Resendez from the *Times* did, and Quarles claims he does have a friend or two in the department, but we can't find one. You didn't call him up to crow, did you? I know you're looking to nail Quarles, although from what I've heard, no one's given him up."

"You're a bastard, you know that, Patkin?"

"Just doing my job. If you tell me you're not his source, I'll take it under advisement."

"Thanks a bunch. Must be awful to suspect your own," she muttered.

"Well, if you understand that, maybe you'd like to go out sometime—movies, a club, a—"

"Did it ever occur to anyone that Quarles knows about my being there last night because Rocha's lawyer told him? I presume Rocha has talked to a lawyer."

"Right after he came out of the anesthetic. But as far as I know, you haven't tied Quarles to Rocha. Or have you?"

"No," she admitted. "But if he *is* connected to Rocha, that would explain how he knew I was there last night."

"How?"

"Because Rocha's lawyer would have told him," she explained patiently, "which ties Quarles to the drug cartel and the murder of Hope Quarles."

"Come on, Jarvis, that's circular reasoning. Quarles knows about you because he's part of the cartel, and he's part of the cartel because he knows about you?"

"Yeah," she said, dispirited. She didn't have a thing on Quarles. He might even be an innocent dupe in the money-laundering thing, with no idea what kind of people his investors were. In which case, she'd screwed up his life for no reason. She felt a moment's unease, then assured herself that such thinking was crazy. Quarles was guilty of something. Adultery if nothing else.

"Anyway," Patkin was saying, "Gaitan says you better not show up at the jail to see Rocha—who's about to be transferred from Thomason—not with all the stink about a suspended cop hanging out with the good guys."

"Oh, great!" Her anger at Quarles and Gil rushed back. "I'll tell you, Patkin, it really infuriates me that Quarles, who's almost certainly dirty, even if I'm not sure how, is still calling the shots where I'm concerned."

"You're not missing anything. The only thing Rocha said when they questioned him was that he has an alibi for the morning Hope Quarles was killed. Unfortunately, the alibi checks out."

"What about the bullet in him? What about the weapon used to shoot Ibarra? Maybe it's in his house. And who's the alibi witness? He's probably lying. Unless Salazar lied . . ." She sure hoped not. Salazar had been their only real break so far. "If Osbaldo lied, then, by God, we ought to put him in with the general jail population. Tell him we're going to do that. Tell him the deal is off and he's back to a capital-murder charge. See what he says."

"I'll pass on your suggestions," Patkin said dryly. "As for the twenty-two slug that hit Ibarra, they're tearing Rocha's house apart. We're waiting on ballistics for the slug in Rocha. And they're grilling the two guys who were arrested with him. O.K.?"

"O.K.," she muttered.

"So go back to sleep. I'll call when I hear something. Oh, and the chief says tell your mother if she shows up at headquarters again, he's going to go outside and give her a big kiss. He says every time he sees her, he's overcome with lust."

"He didn't say that," Elena protested.

Patkin laughed. "Yeah, as a matter of fact, he did. I'd even think he meant it if I hadn't heard people laughing in the background."

When Patkin hung up, Elena lay back and pictured the chief kissing Harmony . . . with full press coverage. She could believe he was overcome with lust. Harmony affected men that way. Well, she would warn her mother. Threaten to send the newspaper pictures to the sheriff.

Having made that decision, she thought about the case and gritted her teeth in frustration. Why the hell hadn't she worn the wig last night? She hated to be cut out of the loop when she should be trying to nail Rocha. Sighing, knowing she wouldn't be able to go back to sleep, she asked herself, What next? Drive over to the insurance company? Wait by the phone for news? Hunt up her mother and threaten her with scandal? Getting dressed would be a good first move. She glanced across the room at the itchy blond wig and groaned. If she'd worn it last night, Wayne Quarles wouldn't be complaining about police deceit this morning.

When Elena arrived downstairs, it was lunchtime, and much to her relief, Harmony was in the kitchen rather than over at headquarters being kissed by the chief for the delectation of the media. Harmony and Concepcion Weizell were seated in the breakfast nook, eating what looked like chicken tacos and drinking coffee as they chatted. The windows showed blue skies and sunshine stretching out to the next mountain range and beyond.

Concepcion rose and threw her arms around Elena. "You and Sarah are better than fairy godmothers," she exclaimed.

"We are?" Elena stared at her partner's wife. "Who's taking care of the quintuplets?"

"Bless you, the family-dynamics class sends students every day, and the babies love them. At least now that the students are getting used to child care, the babies love them." Concepcion giggled. "One changes a diaper while the other takes notes. They're doing a project on how new and inexperienced parents feel in the early months after the birth of a child. You wouldn't believe it, but some of those kids have never held a baby. One of the boys threw up when he had to change a poopy diaper."

"Wonderful," Elena commented. "Did you make him clean up the vomit?"

"Of course I did. I'm the boss. And I get to go out every day now that I have the students trained." Concepcion beamed. "I'm a new woman. I haven't burst into tears in a week. And I owe it all to you and Sarah. If you hadn't brought her along to baby-sit, and she hadn't gotten the Fongs to baby-sit, and the Fongs hadn't insisted on the students doing it so they wouldn't have to again . . ."

Elena grinned. "I'm glad it worked out."

"And now the house."

"They're getting you a house? This fast?" Elena laughed. "You've got to hand it to H.H.U. They know how to spend money."

"Oh, it's a bargain," said Concepcion. "They're buying it from the department, which will get it from the drug raid."

"What drug raid?" Elena asked suspiciously.

"The one you and Sarah and your mother led."

"They're buying you the stash house across the street?" Elena couldn't believe it and wondered how Sarah would feel about living near five children. She might prefer drug dealers. On the other hand, when they got a little older she might arm the kids with bulletproof vests, walkie-talkies, and Mace and send them out on patrol.

"I really think you should reconsider, Concepcion," said Harmony, who had prepared Elena a plate of tacos and poured her a cup of coffee. "That house sends off terrible vibes, a truly vicious aura."

"So we'll get your *curandera* to fix it," said Concepcion.

"And the neighborhood is dangerous. We were shot at several nights ago," Harmony added.

"The drug dealers are being rounded up," said Concepcion, "and it's a beautiful house! I can't believe I'm going to live there."

"There's hardly one interior wall intact," continued Harmony, who had evidently inspected the place with the ecstatic Concepcion.

"The university can put in walls." Concepcion hugged herself in delight. "Six bedrooms! And a swimming pool!"

"Children drown in pools," said Harmony.

"Not when each child has a family-dynamics student watching every move they make," retorted Concepcion, beginning to look resentful.

Elena broke into the dialogue before it escalated by telling her mother about Chief Gaitan's threat.

"Just let him try it." Harmony laughed. "I'll knock his socks off."

"How?" asked Elena, alarmed.

"With a love potion from Marialita that will keep the man in lust and pining for the rest of his life," Harmony replied smugly. "Suspend my daughter? Threaten me? I'll fix him."

"Now, Mom," Elena protested. That hadn't worked out very well. She should have known her mother wasn't one to back away from a threat. Poor Chief Gaitan. On the other hand, maybe she should be thinking, poor Elena.

"Fortunately, since you're already suspended, I can retaliate without hurting your career."

"That's what you think," Elena murmured. Obviously, her mother hadn't heard about her participation in the raid last night and the unfortunate response from the enemy.

"What was that?" her mother asked.

"Nothing." She was still under strict orders not to admit that her suspension was a fake. Quarles was already making trouble. The department didn't need any more. If only they could get something solid on him. If he turned out to be a victim instead of a bad guy, she was going to feel remorse, and it wouldn't help her career either. The chief might decide not to reinstate her, and for reasons other than her mother's kooky demonstrations.

49

••

Tuesday, November 5, 9:00 A.M.

Elena dropped into her chair at Texas Life, hating the way things were happening without her. At one yesterday afternoon, as she was leaving for her "job," an officer picked up Sarah's rifle, the one Harmony claimed to have used to wing a drive-by shooter. Rocha's lawyer was pushing for bail and being stonewalled while the department tried to break his alibi or get something else on him. By four they had it. The rifling on the bullet taken from Rocha's arm matched the rifling on Sarah's rifle. They got a warrant charging him with the drive-by, which Texas law no longer deemed simple reckless conduct which was only a class-A misdemeanor. The drive-by warrant delayed his bail hearing.

Then the DPS lab matched the rifling on slugs dug out of Sarah's walls and furniture to an automatic rifle found in Rocha's house, ran the fingerprints on the weapon, and matched those to Rocha's alibi witness, who had a previous arrest, but no conviction, for possession with intention to distribute. The alibi witness was picked up and both men charged: aggravated assault with a deadly weapon.

To sweeten the pot, retaliation was added to the warrant on the grounds that the men had been attempting to intimidate or eliminate witnesses who would testify in the cocaine trial of Jaime Barrajas, Victorio Cano, and company. Retaliation made the charge a first-degree felony, life, or five to ninety-nine years, and a big fat fine.

Elena was elated. Even if Rocha was never convicted of Hope Quarles's murder, he was in big trouble. Of course, Harmony would have to go before a grand jury to explain why she'd shot Rocha, but the D.A.'s office had assured her that she'd be no-billed.

Patkin had told Elena at nine Monday night that Rocha had been moved from the hospital to the jail infirmary and put under heavy guard. Sheriff's deputies reported that he was a lot less cocky than he had been before his alibi got himself arrested. But the officers at Rocha's house still hadn't found the .22 that put a bullet in Ibarra's lung.

Ibarra, whom Elena visited Monday night, had been sitting up, looking a little better. "I've got a new lung," she said, very happy to hear about the arrests that exonerated her in Hope Quarles's death. At eleven that night the witness from the alley who had recognized Salazar made a photo identification of Rocha as the man accompanying Salazar, climbing into the blue car a half block from the murder scene. So they were closing in on Rocha, but that didn't mean he'd talk even if he was charged with the Quarles murder. Elena went to bed Monday night and had trouble sleeping. Now she was having trouble sitting still at her insurance-company desk.

Freer called her to his office, and she passed on what information she had. "What good does that do us?" he complained. "Unless Wayne Quarles conspired in his wife's death, we're out three million dollars. And what are you doing, Detective—I mean Ms. Carr?"

"Waiting," Elena replied curtly. She went back to her office and fidgeted. She read her case notebook. She thought the whole investigation through. But the important stuff was happening elsewhere. Without her. Because of Quarles.

At ten-ten Leo called. "The chief says to put on your blond wig and get over to the jail. We've got the SOB."

Elena felt an adrenaline surge. "How? What—"

"The twenty-two. He didn't get rid of it, after all. Your ex found it taped under the seat of this falling-down outhouse in the backyard. The guy's got plumbing, for God's sake. You'd think he'd have the outhouse removed. Instead he uses it to stash stuff. They also found two kilos of coke and another gun they think might have been used in a killing two years ago—the guy shot execution-style in the motel on Alameda. Remember that one? DPS is doing ballistics on that hit right now. And Rocha's lawyer's on the way, so get your buns over here, babe. We're finally on a roll."

"I can't believe you said that," she retorted.

"That we're on a roll?" Leo asked innocently.

"Calling me babe, referring to my posterior. I'm going to report you to the sexual-harassment police."

Leo laughed. "You can't; you're suspended."

Elena looked at Rocha's ugly face and realized that he didn't even recognize her in the blond wig and prim business suit, again borrowed from Sarah. Nor did his lawyer tumble to the deception. She was introduced as Detective Peralta from Narcotics. The same group that had listened to Osbaldo Salazar's confession now gathered to confront Rocha and his expensive lawyer—Lieutenants Beltran and Costas, Frank, Leo, Elena, and the D.A.

"I demand that my client be released," said the lawyer. "We're prepared to put up bail on the aggravated-assault charge, and he has a verifiable alibi for the time of the murder. Just because the witness has been arrested doesn't negate my client's right to bail."

Eduardo Rocha nodded. "I need decent docs, not some jailhouse nurse. You're lookin' at a lawsuit for—"

"You're goin' down, Rocha," said Frank, relishing the words. "The only lawsuit you'll be filin' is one of those death-row appeals."

"I didn't do nothin'; you ain't got nothin'."

"You don't have to say a word, Eduardo," the lawyer advised him.

"We got the gun, man," said Frank.

"Don' know what you're talkin' about," the prisoner replied.

"The one taped under the seat in your shit house? You don't remember that one? The twenty-two? That was supposed to make it look like a gang killin' after Salazar thought up the idea of inkin' on the gang tattoos?"

"Salazar who?" Rocha tried to look cool.

"Osbaldo de la Cerda Salazar," said Frank. "Big name for a little mutt like him. You gonna tell us you don't know Osbaldo? We found his prints in your house, Rocha. You oughta get a cleanin' woman. You oughta throw away the guns you kill with. We found another one. Smith an' Wesson. Remember that? Ballistics is seein' right now what crime it matches up to."

"If someone stowed guns in my backyard, it ain't nothin' to do with me."

"So how come your prints are on 'em? You're careless, man."

Elena could tell that Frank was really enjoying himself. Interrogating a prisoner, he was nasty and intimidating. She could remember him trying that stuff on her at the end of the marriage, but it had made her madder, not less determined to dump him.

"You got nothin' on me." Rocha sounded less certain.

"You shot a cop, man. She's over there at Thomason dyin'."

No reports on Monica's condition were currently being given to the press, nor were any media people allowed to visit. Consequently, Rocha could have no idea that, having received the new lung, she had been taken from intensive care and stashed in a well-guarded room under another name.

"We got the gun with your prints, we got a witness that

puts you in the area just after the killin's, so your alibi is for shit, man, an' we got Osbaldo—"

"You listenin' to that dope? He's got fuck all for brains. What kinda witness you think he's gonna make?"

"I have to agree with Mr. Rocha," said the lawyer. "Salazar is trying to save his own neck."

"He *has* saved his own neck," said the D.A., speaking up for the first time. "He's given us everything we need, not just Mr. Rocha but the Barrajas brothers as well."

"He's lyin' . . . Salazar." Rocha spoke nervously, sweat beading on his low, bunched forehead.

"We're satisfied with his story. He passed a lie-detector test," said the D.A.

"You know as well as I that those aren't admissible in court." Rocha's lawyer glared at him.

"True, but the test reassures us that Mr. Salazar is telling the truth. Would Mr. Rocha like to take a test since he's disputing his partner's veracity?"

"He ain't no partner of mine," snapped Rocha. "He's a fuckin' rat turd."

His lawyer gave him a quelling look, then returned to the district attorney. "My client will take no tests and answer no questions."

"Then we're through here," the D.A. concluded. "We have both testimony and evidence to send your client to Huntsville, and be assured, I will ask for, and get, the death penalty." He turned to Eduardo Rocha. "You have nothing to bargain with, sir. Salazar has used up all the chips."

"You're dead," Frank added. "Get that through your thick head. Salazar may be dumb, but he knew enough to save his own butt, which leaves you with nothin'. If we'd already sewed you into a body bag, you couldn't be deader."

"I got nothin' to say," Rocha snarled.

"True," said the D.A., rising to leave. "There's nothing you *can* say. I'd advise you to plead guilty and throw yourself on the mercy of the court. That's the only option you have left, but I doubt even that will save your life."

Disappointed, Elena left the room with the others. That was it. All kinds of people were going down, but Wayne Quarles wasn't one of them—unless the federal grand jury indicted him for some white-collar crime. Damn. She'd been wrong. Quarles might be a scumbag, but he evidently hadn't commissioned his wife's murder. His bankers had apparently done that for him. And Miguel Barrajas was still free in Mexico. If Quarles was elected mayor—well, it didn't bear thinking on. "I'm going out to vote," she said to Leo.

She had a hard time of it because the picture on her driver's license didn't match her wig. The election clerk, a new volunteer, refused to give her a ballot. The precinct judge had to be called; Elena had to remove the wig. Then the clerk, angry at being overruled, said, "Why are you wearing that wig, anyway?"

Elena replied, "Blondes have more fun," but she wasn't having more fun, even when she cast her vote for Mayor Nellie. What a mess if Quarles won. She was shoving her ballot into the metal box when her pager went off. Probably Freer calling to ask for an update. As soon as he found out that Quarles wasn't involved in the murder, Elena would lose her temporary position at Texas Life.

And if Quarles was elected, he might insist that she not be reinstated. She'd fight it, of course. The union and the civil-service code ought to stymie him, but she'd never become a sergeant. She could make a perfect score on the test, but in the end, promotion was up to the brass, and the brass answered to the mayor and the city council. She was tempted to ignore the page, but the habit of responsibility sent her to a phone booth in the grade school where she voted.

"Come on back to the jail," said Leo. "Rocha and his lawyer want to talk."

"What about? He hasn't got anything to put on the table."

"He seems to think he has."

Elena sighed. "It's probably bullshit."

"Don't you wanna be there in case it isn't?"

50

Tuesday, November 5, 2:05 P.M.

"I got somethin' you want," said Rocha, "but I ain't riskin' my life by tellin' you without you meet my terms."

"What life?" Leo muttered.

"You lied about the cop. She ain't dyin'. If she was gonna die, she'da done it by now, an' it'd be in the fuckin' newspaper on the front page." He sneered and added, "Don' know why I fell for that crapola story."

Since Monica had been sitting up in bed, looking cheerful, and breathing through her new lung Monday night, Elena couldn't really contradict him, and no one else seemed to want to.

"So no murder charge. O.K.?" Rocha looked smug. "I didn' shoot the Quarles woman. Baldo did. I'll plead to assault an'—"

"No," said the D.A. "The charge is capital murder. You're as culpable in Hope Quarles's death as Salazar, and you're going down for it."

"Come on, we're bargainin' here. You ain't playin' the game," Rocha complained. "I ain't givin' you nothin' if you're gonna fry me anyway."

"You've got nothing to give," said Beltran. "You're wasting our time."

"He does have something," the lawyer insisted. "And he

is risking his life to give it to you. If you're going to demand the death penalty anyway—"

"What's he got?" Lieutenant Costas asked suspiciously.

"Something big," said the lawyer.

Elena was staring at the two of them. Was it Quarles? Was Rocha going to give them Quarles, who might be the next mayor? "You're going to have to let the district attorney be the judge of whether it's important enough," she said quietly. The men all turned to her in surprise, for she'd said nothing throughout the interrogation of Rocha.

The D.A. narrowed his eyes. "The assault plea is out. I might agree not to ask for the death penalty, but—"

"That's all I get?" cried Rocha.

"You held her while Salazar shot her. You told him to do it," said Elena. "You're guiltier than he is if we're splitting hairs."

"That's shit. I din' shoot her. That's what counts."

"No, it doesn't," Elena disagreed calmly. "It doesn't count at all. A good woman's dead because you were willing to kill her for money, or whatever you got. You're a hired gun, and you're never going to spend another day out of prison. Whether or not you die or get life and protection from your bosses depends on whether you really have anything to tell the district attorney."

Rocha looked taken aback. His lawyer studied Elena. "You're the detective who was suspended, aren't you?"

"Does it matter?"

"I suppose not." He turned to his client. "Well?" he asked. "Do you want to go to court or plead?"

"What kinda deal is that they're offerin'? I gotta spend the rest of my life in some rat-hole Texas prison?"

"You chose death for Hope Quarles. Now you can choose it for yourself," said Elena. "Officer Ibarra, for one, will be glad to see you get the needle. It's more humane than you deserve."

"That's what you want, too, isn't it, *madre de putas*?"

"Watch your mouth," the D.A. warned.

"To see my butt on death row?" Rocha stared malevolently at Elena. "Well, I ain't goin'. 'Cause I got somethin' that will blow your asses off, all you upright citizens. You screw me on the deal after I tell you, Mr. D.A., me an' my lawyer go to the press. You'll never get elected to nothin' as long as you live. Got that?"

"The deal is life without parole but no death penalty if what you've got is worth it," said the D.A.

"Quarles," said Rocha triumphantly.

Elena had to bite her lip to keep from grinning. "Which Quarles?" she asked.

"Whaddaya mean, which? Her ol' man. He's the one had her killed. He owed my bosses, so they set it up. So they'd get paid, an' so they'd get themselves a mayor. Ain't that gonna be somethin'? He gets elected, an' then he gets arrested. You got the guts to arrest the new mayor, Mr. D.A.?"

"Tell us why Mr. Quarles would want his wife dead," said the D.A.

"For the money, man. She had it; he couldn't get at it. So he got financin' from my bosses, an' then he screwed it up. They're tryin' for clean money an' profits, an' he's losin' their stake. It don' work that way, not with the Barrajas brothers."

"Jaime was in on it, too?" Elena asked, referring to Sarah's neighbor.

"Havin' her killed? Oh, yeah. It was Jaime's idea we do it while she was with a cop. Give Quarles a boost in the polls, screw up you pigs. Worked pretty good."

"Not really," the D.A. put in dryly. "You have any proof that Quarles was involved?"

"You think you're gonna cover this up, huh? He give me a picture of her so I wouldn't hit the wrong woman. Signed 'To Wayne, with love, Hope.' It's at my sister's house. A little insurance. That good enough for you? An' he showed me this appointment book a' hers with the patrol date. She had this map she drew showin' where she walks with the cops. Jaime made a copy of it while Quarles was talkin' to Miguel. Go look in their house for her appointment book. Quarles says he's gotta get it back home before she misses it, an' why don't we hit her when she's in the police garage across from Central Command. That's where them police volunteers park. Or maybe car-jack her on the way home. Quarles says this."

"When and where did this meeting take place?" asked Leo.

Rocha grinned. "Three days before we killed her. Inna Bassett Buildin'. In his lawyer's office."

"Fermin Gil was there?" Elena asked.

"Yeah. He laughs when we got the deal set an' says to Quarles, 'Now you can marry your little hot-pants campaign girl,' an' Quarles says, 'I hope I can do better than that.'"

They had Gil, too! Elena felt elation washing over her. But Quarles—that slimy, hypocritical bastard, with all his talk about how he'd always longed for his wife's approval, how he'd never marry again because she'd been such a wonderful woman. Elena ground her teeth to think that she'd half believed him at one point.

"You still not sure I'm tellin' the truth?" Rocha asked the D.A. "This janitor saw us leave the office. Dark-skinned guy, about five-two, red birthmark on his left cheek. Ask him." Rocha grinned. "Maybe he'll remember me. He'll sure remember Quarles, 'cause Quarles called him by name. Said, 'Sorry to hold you up, Nido.'"

"We'll have to check this out," said Beltran.

"No problema," said Rocha. "First time I ever told a cop the truth. So we got a deal?"

"If your story checks out," the D.A. agreed.

"Try questionin' Gil first. He'll roll over on Quarles so fast you won't have time to fart. I can tell a guy who'll rat—like Baldo. Never did trust that dumb shit."

"Takes one to know one," Elena murmured, and they fanned out over the city to check the story of Eduardo Rocha. Leo talked his way into the Quarles house by the simple expedient of asking Wendy Pickentide to see her mother's appointment calendar. In it he found the C.O.P. notation and the map. Leo gave Wendy a receipt and took the book to the car, where Elena waited.

They found the picture of Hope Quarles in the possession of Rocha's sister. She lived two blocks away from his house in an apartment with tattered bedsheets hung at the windows instead of draperies and a large-screen TV. The sister balked at giving them anything until Leo remarked that it was O.K. with him, but the picture would make the difference between her brother living and dying. "I guess he was lying about you having it," Leo said. They turned to leave, and the sister chased them out the door waving the photo, which said, *To Wayne, with love, Hope.*

"This is one arrest it's going to be a pleasure to make," said Elena.

Frank and another narc tracked down the janitor and showed him pictures of Quarles, Gil, the two Barrajas brothers, and Rocha, along with ten mug shots of people unconnected with the case. The janitor identified four of five conspirators, but not Miguel Barrajas, saying one man had had a hat on and kept his face turned away. Nido told them what a nice man Señor Quarles was. Always gave him a big tip at Christmas. And Quarles didn't even have an office in the building, just came there to see his lawyer, who never gave a workingman a dime. Señor Gil had nothing but contempt for the poor.

It was seven-thirty by the time the warrants were issued, and even then the judge was reluctant, afraid he'd be accused of playing politics. "The election is over," Elena pointed out. "The polls closed fifteen minutes ago." She had been informally reinstated by the chief at six-fifteen. The judge read statements from the investigating officers and signed. "It'll be a hell of a thing if he wins," the judge muttered.

Eight uniforms went to Quarles campaign headquarters with Leo, Elena, and Frank, but Elena had the pleasure of making the actual arrest, and she took special delight because, without her blond wig, Quarles recognized her and frowned. "I thought you were—" Then he changed his mind and said expansively, "This is too important a day for old grudges. Somebody bring the detective a cup of coffee. We won't switch to champagne for at least two hours."

The coffee was provided, but Elena handed hers to someone in the crowd that had gathered to celebrate. "Wayne Quarles, I'm arresting you for the murder of your wife, Hope Masterson Quarles."

"Get this woman out of here," snarled Fermin Gil, who had arrived at Quarles's side in time to hear Elena.

She turned to Quarles's lawyer. "Fermin Gil, we have a warrant for your arrest as well."

"This is outrageous!" Gil was red with anger. Quarles looked as if someone had sucker-punched him. "What charge?" Gil demanded.

"Conspiracy to commit murder," Elena replied. Patrol officers were already behind the two, handcuffing them as Elena read them their rights.

Through the crowded room, whispers spread beyond the circle of arresting officers to the outer corners in a shock wave of disbelief as word passed among Quarles's once optimistic supporters. The polls had shown their candidate to be in a dead heat with the incumbent that morning. Now the election was lost before the ballots were counted.

Epilogue

Tuesday, November 5, 9:25 P.M.

What a pleasure it had been to take Wayne Quarles and Fermin Gil through the booking procedure. Quarles had kept saying they'd made a mistake; he'd never do anything to hurt his dear Hope. Once Elena heard him whisper to Gil, "You got me into this. They were your connections."

"Shut up," Gil snapped.

After that they were both silent. Free to go, Elena drove her pickup to the hospital, where she made reluctant cops let her in and reluctant nurses wake Monica up.

"Her husband?" Monica looked astounded.

"That's right," said Elena. "And we got every one of them except Miguel Barrajas. He's in Mexico, but maybe we can extradite him."

Monica smiled tearfully. "Sorry about this. I'm not as tough as I used to be." She sighed. "I wonder what happens to me now. When I get out of the hospital. You think they'll let me stay a cop?" She wiped her eyes with a Kleenex. "I had such plans. You know? I was gonna get married, have a baby, be a sergeant. What now?" she asked sadly.

Elena bit her lip. What could she say? Monica's body could reject the new lung. "You'll be getting married for sure," Elena said encouragingly. "Eddie's been here every minute he was off shift. A baby? I don't know, but I don't see why not. Have you asked the doctor?"

"'Fraid to," Monica admitted. "I guess the big question is the department. I wanted to be a detective, like you."

"I don't know." Elena scratched her head absentmindedly, then jerked her nails away. Even without the damn wig, her head itched. Well, Harmony would probably know what to do, especially if it could be done with herbs. "I guess you wait. You could come out of this as good as new, you know. The first step is to keep them from putting you on disability, and I'll do everything I can to help. Then—well, maybe you could—"

"Be someone who visits public schools?" Monica asked wearily.

"How about one of those guys who does criminal trends for the commands?"

"A desk jockey," said Monica.

"Monica, by this time next year, you could be back on the street. And if not, they ought to let you stay. They owe you. But maybe you won't want to stay under those circumstances."

Monica turned her head away to stare at her darkened window. "I want to stay. Under any circumstances."

"Then we'll work on that," Elena told her, and leaned over to give the young officer a hug. "I'll be back. O.K.?"

Monica returned the hug. "And thanks. You cleared my name."

"It was a departmental effort, believe me," Elena replied.

When she arrived at Sarah's, Elena found Sam Parsley, her psychologist and friend, sitting by the front door, reading a psychiatric journal by flashlight. "Sam? How come you're here? I didn't miss a session, did I?"

"I've come to take you out to celebrate," he replied, marking his place and clicking off his light.

"Celebrate what?" she replied abstractedly. Her mind was still on Monica and the young officer's iffy future.

"Your reinstatement. And the arrest of the killers. Aren't you feeling celebratory?"

Elena looked into Sam's warm eyes and smiled. "Why, yes. I guess I should be celebrating." Her spirits rose, and she allowed Sam to lead her to his car, where he had to push aside student papers and journal articles to make room for her. "Where are we going?" she asked.

"It's a surprise," he replied. And it was. Not a pleasant one either, for twenty minutes later they pulled up in front of Elena's own adobe house, which was shining with interior lights, the street lined with cars, music and conversation spilling out the open front door.

"Sam," she said reproachfully, "I thought this was a celebration, not therapy." She understood that reoccupying her house was the last step in her recovery from post-traumatic stress, but the thought of taking that step, of entering that house, made her shudder. Sam couldn't stuff enough people in there to convince her that there wouldn't be a mountain lion under the dining-room table, snarling, waiting to jump her, and a gnawed, bloodied corpse in the bedroom that looked, if you could take it for anything but a predator's victim, like Michael Futrell, whom she had loved then. But not now.

"You can't chicken out of this," said Sam. "They're all waiting for you."

"All who?" she muttered.

"Your neighbors, your friends, your colleagues. Even the chief is here."

"Oh Lord. Is my mother here, too?"

"Of course."

"Hurry up." Elena grabbed Sam's hand, sprinting for the house with the thought that she had to prevent Harmony from giving the chief that love potion she had threatened to obtain. What if it killed him? Or really worked, so that he couldn't concentrate on the department because of infatuation with Harmony?

She burst through the open front door into the entry hall,

only to be stopped by a huge cheer coming from her living room, where she noticed dozens of people, a strange TV, and two kegs of beer. Her coffee table overflowed with chips and dips in mismatched bowls. Bags of pretzels had been stored in her round corner fireplace.

"She's going to win," yelled Frank.

"I told you that," snapped Gloria Ledesma, the crankiest of Elena's elderly neighbors.

"Mayor Nellie's winning?" Elena asked the person next to her, who happened to be Sarah.

"They just announced the results of the public-school election. The children voted for her," said Sarah. "How does it feel to be home?"

With that question Elena realized that she was actually inside her house, and she'd forgotten about what happened here last spring. She glanced uneasily toward the dining room, but all she saw were more people, no mountain lions. "O.K.," she said hesitantly.

"Ah, here's the guest of honor," boomed Chief Gaitan, coming from the kitchen with Harmony on his arm. Elena eyed them nervously. Gaitan didn't look as if he were about to keel over from love-potion overdose or make a sexual attack on Harmony. And Harmony didn't have a wicked twinkle in her eye.

"Welcome home, dear," she said, and hugged Elena.

Behind Harmony came Marialita, the *curandera*. "I put a keep-out spell on your house," she announced. "No evil speerits or dangerous animals can pass your doors."

"Great," said Elena, listening in her mind for the bad memories. Nothing yet. No flashbacks. She hadn't even jumped when that cheer went up.

"Let me take this opportunity to officially, publicly, and personally welcome you back to the department, Detective Jarvis," Chief Gaitan began. "And for the information of her friends and family, she was never really suspended. She was undercover, pursuing her own hunches about the Quarles murder, which turned out to be right on target."

More cheering, more hugs from colleagues, some of whom she'd never have allowed the opportunity under any other circumstance, more hugs from friends and neighbors.

"You might have told me, Armando," Harmony complained. "I can keep a secret."

"Well, I could certainly have saved myself a lot of public outrage if I had," said Gaitan.

"Exactly, and what am I going to do with the Elena Jarvis Defense Fund? We made fourteen hundred dollars selling my pecan pies and the darts to throw at your picture."

"Give it to Monica Ibarra," Elena suggested somberly. "For her dowry." She turned to the chief. "I hope the department isn't going to put her on disability."

The chief's face darkened. "We have fitness qualifications."

"She was injured in the line of duty."

"Disability pay is—"

"She wants to stay a cop. Even with a transplanted lung, there are jobs she could do, given time, maybe any of them. And she's smart, and hardworking, and loyal, and—"

Gaitan threw up his hands. "We'll find something for her."

"Something good," Elena persisted.

"Stollinger," Gaitan shouted. The captain—Elena hadn't even known he was in attendance—wandered into the room with a beer in hand. "I'm delegating you to find a suitable job for Officer Monica Ibarra, something to show our appreciation for what she's been through," Gaitan told him.

"O.K." Stollinger looked taken aback. "On my turf?"

"Yes." Gaitan looked toward Elena. "That way you can keep your eye on her."

"Thanks, Chief." Elena beamed at him. Harmony rose on tiptoe and kissed his cheek, bringing a flush to his handsome face. "Mom," Elena whispered.

"Oh, don't be such a prude," Harmony retorted, laughing.

The party roared on, Elena talking to well-wishers, discussing the case with other cops, but avoiding the back of the house until Sam slipped up beside her and murmured, "Been in the bedroom yet?" She shook her head. "Want me to go with you?" he offered.

For a minute she stared bleakly out into her yard, then turned to Sam. "I guess it's something I need to do by myself. Is it full of people?"

"No, I told your mother to shut that door."

Elena nodded and set her paper cup down on the hearth. "Well, no use putting it off." She worked her way among the guests, heading for the back of the house.

Her lieutenant stopped her briefly to say, "Don't you think it's time you took the sergeant's exam?"

She felt a little rush of surprise and pleasure. Hearing that from Beltran meant he thought she was ready for command. Was she?

A minute later she had her hand on the doorknob of the room where she'd found Mark Futrell's body. Her bedroom. The door, once kicked in because the murderer had fixed it to lock her in with the big cat, had been repaired. Sarah had seen to that. When Elena entered, the blood was gone from the floors and walls, from the bedspread that her mother had woven back in Chimayo. But most important, the ghosts were gone.

She heard another cheer go up from the front of the house. Mayor Nellie had won. The voters of Los Santos had had more sense than to elect Wayne Quarles, even without knowing that their police department suspected him of a murder that he had, in fact, commissioned.

Elena walked over and sat down on her bed, smiling. She could sleep in her own house tonight. She was O.K. And maybe she would take that sergeant's exam. Maybe she'd start studying tomorrow.